U0165632

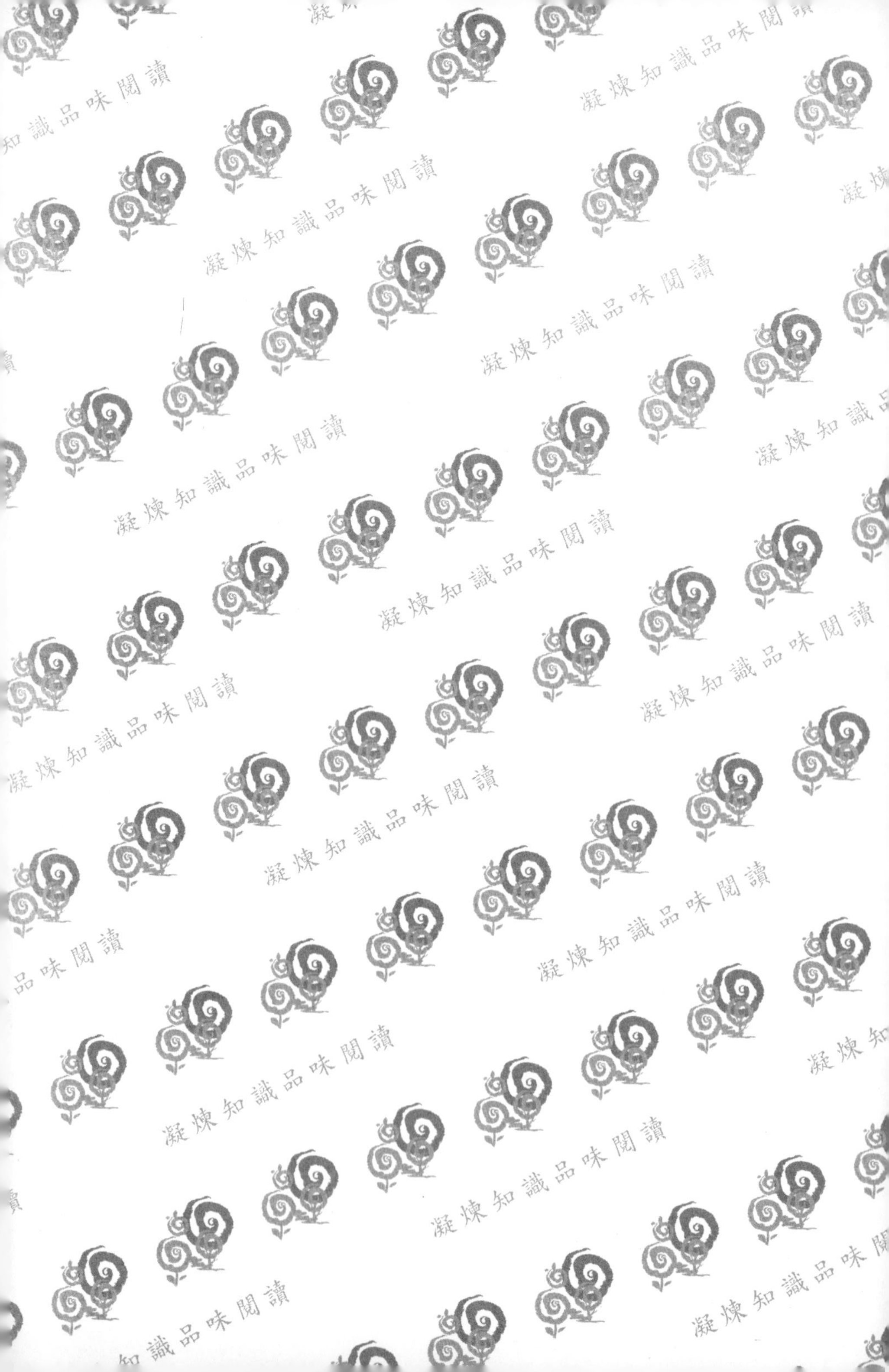
凝煉知識品味閱讀

國際華語學習辭典
Learner's
Mandarin
Chinese
Dictionary
for Beginner Level
您好

Foreword

The Learner's Mandarin Chinese Dictionary (LMCD) is a practical reference work designed to meet the requirements of those who need a beginning dictionary in learning Mandarin Chinese. It will be useful for starters, false starters and re-starters as well.

The LMCD, first of the kind in Taiwan, is highly original in comparison with its counterparts published elsewhere in the world. Following the latest trend of the pedagogical lexicography, the focus of concern is on beginners' level, on sentence organisation and on bilingual dimension. From this perspective, the main features of the LMCD can be summarized as follows.

(1) **Core vovabulary**

The core vocabulary you find in the LMCD comprises a set of commonly-used words, statistically speaking and a set of situational-relevant words, functionally speaking, keeping a balance between knowledge needs and communication needs of the users.

(2) **Definition**

The definition contains one and only equivalent, word or expression, in English, which will be explicitly contextualized in the sentence-example that follows. This one-to-one correspondance in fact functions as a quick finder of the meaning involved. Different equivalents for a given word are marked with letters (a, b, c).

(3) **Part-of-Speech**

The part of speech is always given with a terminology familiar to the English-speaking users and different parts of speech are marked with numbers (1, 2, 3). The designation of the part of speech is largely based on careful and objective observations conducted within the framework of the sentence-example.

(4) **Example-sentence**

At least one example-sentence is given for every entries, written in plain Chinese. From this perspective, the LMCD is in nature a sentence dictionary.

(5) **Short sentence**

All the example-sentences are deliberately short in length, e.g 12 Chinese character-space, which allow you to grasp, to memorize temporarily the whole structure of the sentence without any movement from your eyeballs.

(6) **Self-containedness**

All the example-sentences are lexically self-contained, that means that we include only words which appear in the text of the Dictionary in our example-sentences.

(7) **Openness**

The situations involved in our example-sentences are by no means limited to the life on campus, but go far beyond, meeting the needs of those with self-taught options.

(8) **Culture-specific items**

We are keen on including items specific to the Chinese culture of Taiwan, in our text as well as in our example-sentences, enhancing the interest of foreign students in the growth of our society.

(9) **Parallel translation**

We practise parallel approach between the Chinese example and the English translation, in that the item chosen in Chinese text and its equivalent appeared in English text are in bold type, facilitating the mutual reading of both text.

(10) **Inclusion of variants**

The last but not the least merit of the Dictionary is its inclusion of variants from other Chinese communities in the neighborhood of Taiwan and Mainland China, e.g. Hong Kong, Singapore and Malaysia, which enrich the very content of the Dictionary.

We hope you enjoy using the Learners' Mandarin Chinese Dictionary at home, in the office or wherever you may be!

Learner's Mandarin Chinese Dictionary — for Beginner Level

How to use the Dictionary

This Dictionary includes 2,378 words and has 6,156 sample Chinese and English sentences. Also provided are 10 appendixes that are useful for Chinese learners.

1. Objective

The objective of this dictionary is to assist Chinese learners of beginning level in mastering the basic vocabulary that is necessary in daily situations. These situations include personal information, residences, occupations, leisure and entertainment, transport and travel, social interactions, body and medical treatment, education and learning, shopping, food and cooking, banking and postal affairs, and safety.

Based on the approach to learning Chinese, the content adopts the sentence-based approach in conveying the word meanings with Chinese and English sample sentences, English definitions, and remarks on the parts of speech.

2. Functions

The functions of this dictionary including:

(1) To serve as references for non-native Chinese learners.

(2) To serve as references for setting up and designing of teaching Chinese as a second language courses.

(3) To serve as references for compilation of Chinese teaching materials, and research and development of educational software.

(4) To serve as the basis of and references for constructing Chinese test items.

(5) To serve as references for teachers of Chinese in preparing their lessons.

3. Notes on usage

(1) **Order of headwords**

a. This dictionary contains entries that mostly base on words as units, including single characters and words with multiple characters. All headwords are listed in the order of Hanyu pinyin.

b. If the same word has different sound and meaning, it will be listed as separate headwords, such as【長】change and【長】zhǎng in the following example:

Entry in Chinese	Hanyu pinyin	Zhuyin	English translation of the entry	Parts of speech	Chinese sample sentence	English sample sentence
長	change	ㄔㄤˊ	be long	Vs	這根繩子不夠長。	The rope is not quite long enough.
長	zhǎng	ㄓㄤˇ	to grow	V	蔬菜長得很好。	The vegetables are growing well.

c. If the same word belongs to different parts of speech, there will be separate entry for each, for example,【跟】has separate entries according to its different parts of speech as in【跟1】【跟2】【跟3】as shown below:

Entry in Chinese	Hanyu pinyin	Zhuyin	English translation of the entry	Parts of speech	Chinese sample sentence	English sample sentence
跟1	gēn	ㄍㄣ	and	Conj	我跟她是同事。	She and I are colleagues.
					他跟你一起做吧。	He and you do it together.
					我跟我太太都是美國人。	Both my wife and I are Americans.
跟2	gēn	ㄍㄣ	with	Prep	跟我走吧。	Come with me.
					我要跟你談談。	I want to have a word with you.
跟3	gēn	ㄍㄣ	to follow	V	貓跟著我進廚房。	The cat followed me into the kitchen.
					他們在跟著我們嗎？	Are they following us?
					跟著我，我會告訴你怎麼走。	Follow me and I'll show you the way.

d. If the different senses of a word belong to the same part of speech but each has different meaning, or the corresponding English content are different, there will be separate entry for each. As a noun,【部分】has two separate entries of【部分a】and【部分b】, as shown below:

Entry in Chinese	Hanyu pinyin	Zhuyin	English translation of the entry	Parts of speech	Chinese sample sentence	English sample sentence
部分a	bùfen	ㄅㄨˋ ˙ㄈㄣ	part	N	我只完成計畫的第一部分。	I've only finished the first part of the plan.
部分b	bùfen	ㄅㄨˋ ˙ㄈㄣ	some of	N	這裡住的人，有部分是外國人。	Some of the people living here are foreigners.

(2) **Content of entries**

Each entries in this dictionary include a symbol for the core entry, the entry in Chinese, pinyin, the English translation, its part of speech, a Chinese sample sentence, a corresponding English sample sentence, and a regional corresponding word. A brief introduction and example are listed below:

a. Symbol for the core meaning: Entries of core meaning are marked with a star（★）

b. The entry in Chinese: the entries in the main part of this dictionary are printed in Traditional Chinese characters.

c. Pinyin: this dictionary uses Hanyu Pinyin and Zhuyin.

d. English translation: every entry in this dictionary has its English translation.

e. Part of speech: every entry in this dictionary is marked with its lexical category. The method of annotation will be illustrated in the next part.

f. Sample Chinese sentence: every entry in this dictionary provides a sample Chinese sentence that demonstrates its usage.

g. English translation of the sample sentence: every Chinese sample sentence of the entries in this dictionary comes with a corresponding English sample sentence.

h. Regional corresponding word: the entries in this dictionary are current usage common in Taiwan; it also provides corresponding words as used in Mainland China, Hong Kong and Macau, Singapore and Malaysia for reference. The symbols for corresponding words are: Mainland China (CN), Hong Kong (HK), Singapore (SG), Malaysia (MY).

Symbol for core meaning	Entry in Chinese	Hanyu Pinyin	Zhuyin	English translation of the entry	Part of speech	Chinese sample sentence	English sample sentence	Correspond-ing word
★	出a	chū	ㄔㄨ	to be out	V	過了橋，我們就出了城了。	We are out of the town once we cross the bridge.	
★	出b	chū	ㄔㄨ	to exit	V	請從右門進，從左門出。	Please enter by the right door and exist through the left door.	
	出發	chūfā	ㄔㄨ ㄈㄚ	take one's departure	Vp	你該出發了。	It's time that you take your departure.	
	出口	chūkǒu	ㄔㄨ ㄎㄡˇ	exit	N	我在電影院的出口等你。	I'm waiting for you at the exit of the cinema.	
	出生	chūshēng	ㄔㄨ ㄕㄥ	be born	Vp	Jane是五十年代後期出生的。	Jane was born in the late fifties.	

(3) **Annotation of parts of speech**

The principles of annotation for the parts of speech in this dictionary follow that made known in the paper "Pedagogical Grammar for Modern Chinese Lexical Categories" (Shou-hsin Teng, 2010) in classifying each word into different parts of speech. There are eight different categories: Noun, Verb, Adverb, Conjunction, Preparation, Measure, Particle and Determiner (as shown in Table 1). We also added the State Verb as Adjective into the categeries.

Table 1: The parts of speech in Modern Chinese

Parts of Speech	Symbol	Sample words
名詞（Noun）	N	水、書餐廳、上、裡、六
動詞（Verb）	V	吃、看、知道、覺得、溫暖
形容詞（Adjective / State Verb）	Adj/Vs	溫暖、冷、熱鬧、害羞
副詞（Adverb）	Adv	就、才、非常、一定、很
連詞（Conjunction）	Conj	跟、可是、雖然、所以
介詞（Preparation）	Prep	在、到、從、關於、對
量詞（Measure）	M	個、本、隻、公斤、場、次
助詞（Particle）	Ptc	了、啊、吧、嗎、呢、喔
定詞（Determiner）	Det	這、那、每、某

Table 2: Overall table of the parts of speech symbols

Symbol	Parts of speech	Sample words
N	Noun 名詞	水、書、年、餐廳
V	Action Verb 動作動詞	吃、看、拿、研究

Symbol	Parts of speech	Sample words
Adj/Vs	Adjective / State Verb 形容詞（狀態動詞）	溫暖、冷、熱鬧、害羞
Vp	Process Verb 變化動詞	破、死、畢業、生病
Vaux	Auxiliary Verb 助動詞	能、會、可以、要
Vi	Action Verb, Intransitive 動作動詞，不及物	站、回、繼續、服務
Vst	State Verb, Transitive 狀態動詞，及物	知道、覺得、考慮、相信
Vpt	Process Verb, Transitive 變化動詞，及物	融化、打敗、贏
Vs-attr	State Verb, Attributive 唯定狀態動詞	國際、外籍、中等、急性
Vs-pred	State Verb, Predicative 唯謂狀態動詞	差不多、不錯、多、夠
V-sep	Verb, Separable 可離合動作動詞	上課、開會、休假、睡覺
Vs-sep	State Verb, Separable 可離合狀態動詞	關心、擔心、抱歉、通風
Vp-sep	Process Verb, Separable 可離合變化動詞	畢業、消炎、失火、受傷
Adv	Adverb 副詞	就、才、非常、難道
Conj	Conjunction 連詞	跟、可是、雖然、所以
Prep	Preparation 介詞	在、到、從、關於
M	Measure 量詞	個、本、隻、公斤
Ptc	Particle 助詞	了、啊、吧、嗎
Det	Determiner 定詞	這、那、每、某

★ 啊[a] ā
ㄚ

Ptc exclamation marker, showing admiration

- 啊，下雪了。
Oh, it's snowing.

★ 啊[b] ā
ㄚ

Ptc asking for repetition

- 啊，你說什麼？
Eh, what did you say?

★ 啊[c] ā
ㄚ

Ptc showing puzzled surprise

- 啊，他早上就走了。
What, he left in the morning?

★ 啊[d] ā
ㄚ

Ptc showing realization

- 啊，原來是你！
Ah, so it's you!

★ 矮[a] ǎi
ㄞˇ

Vs. /Adj short (of stature)

- 司機是一個矮胖的男人。
The driver is a short fat man.

★ 矮[b] ǎi
ㄞˇ

Vs. /Adj be short (of stature)

- 我很矮，但我弟弟很高。
I'm quite short but my brother is very tall.

★ 矮[c] ǎi
ㄞˇ

Vs. /Adj low

- Chris跳過矮牆。
Chris jumped over the low wall.

★ 矮[d] ǎi
ㄞˇ

Vs. /Adj be low

- 對他來說，桌子太矮了。
The table is too low for him.

★ 愛[a] ài
ㄞˋ

Ptc to love

- Ian十分愛她。
Ian loves her dearly.
- 你說你愛我，是眞的嗎？
Are you serious when you said

you loved me?

★ **愛** [b] ài ㄞˋ

Vst to love

- 我非常愛我的奶奶。
  I love my grandma so much.
- 我愛我的丈夫和孩子。
  I love my husband and children.

★ **愛** [c] ài ㄞˋ

Vst to like to

- 我愛聽音樂。
  I like to hear music.

★ **愛** [d] ài ㄞˋ

Vst to enjoy

- 我愛參加聚會。跟人聊天。
  I enjoy going to parties and talking to people.

★ **愛** [e] ài ㄞˋ

Vst be apt to

- Mary特別愛笑。
  Mary is particularly apt to laugh.

★ **愛** [f] ài ㄞˋ

Vst to tend to

- 他愛遲到。
  He tends to be late.

安排 ānpái ㄢ ㄆㄞˊ

V to arrange

- 他們正在安排下次的會議。
  They are arranging for the next meeting.

安靜 [a] ānjìng ㄢ ㄐㄧㄥˋ

Vs. /Adj quiet

- 病人需要安靜。
  The patients need quiet.

安靜 [b] ānjìng ㄢ ㄐㄧㄥˋ

Vs. /Adj be quiet

- 孩子們很安靜。
  The children are quiet.

安全 [1] ānquán ㄢ ㄑㄩㄢˊ

Vs. /Adj safety

- 安全第一。
  Safety first.

安全 [2] ānquán ㄢ ㄑㄩㄢˊ

N be safe

• 這兒夜間外出安全嗎？
Is it safe to go out at night here?

安全帶 ānquándài ㄢ ㄑㄩㄢˊ ㄉㄞˋ

N seat belt

• 請繫安全帶。
Please put on your seat belt.

安全帽 ānquánmào ㄢ ㄑㄩㄢˊ ㄇㄠˋ

N helmet

• 騎機車必須戴安全帽。
Wearing a helmet while driving a motocycle is a must.

★ 按[a] àn ㄢˋ

V to press

• 如果是，按一；如果不是，按二。
If yes, press one; if not, press two.

★ 按[b] àn ㄢˋ

V to push

• 按這裡就可以關上洗衣機。
You can stop the washing machine by pushing here.

★ 按[c] àn ㄢˋ

V to ring

• 我按了好幾次門鈴。
I rang several times the doorbell.

★ 按照 ànzhào ㄢˋ ㄓㄠˋ

Prep according to

• 按照他說的去做，沒錯。
Act according to what he said and you can't go wrong.

B

★ **八** bā ㄅㄚ

N eight

- 還有八個座位。
  There are eight seats left.
- 中國人喜歡數字八。
  Chinese people like the number eight.

芭樂 bālè ㄅㄚ ㄌㄜˋ

N guava

SG MY 番石榴

- 芭樂對消化很好。
  Guava is good for digest.

巴士 bāshì ㄅㄚ ㄕˋ

N transliteration for 'bus'

CN 公交車

- 巴士上有許多人。
  There were a lot of people on the bus.

★ **把**[1] bǎ ㄅㄚˇ

M a handful of

- 她送給我一把臺灣茶葉。
  She gave me a handful of Taiwan tea.

★ **把**[2a] bǎ ㄅㄚˇ

Prep preposition, used to place the object of an action in preverbal position, implying result

- 請把門關上。
  Please close the door.
- Mike把冰箱修好了。
  Mike has fixed the refrigerator.
- 她很快就把房間打掃乾淨了。
  She cleaned up her room in no time.

★ **把**[2b] bǎ ㄅㄚˇ

Prep preposition, used to place the object of an action, implying location

- 你把錢花到哪兒去了？
  Where did you spend the money?
- 請你把行李放在那兒。
  Please put your baggage over there.
- 我可以把車停在這兒嗎？

May I park my car here?

★ **把** [2c] bǎ ㄅㄚˇ

Prep preposition, used to place the object of an action, implying beneficiary

- 你把錢給我。
  You give me that money.
- 我還沒有把這封信寄給他呢！
  I still haven't sent this letter to him!
- 請你幫我把這些東西帶給她。
  Please take these things to her for me.

爸爸 bàba ㄅㄚˋ ˙ㄅㄚ

N dad

- 那是你爸爸嗎？
  Is that your dad?

吧 [1a] ba ˙ㄅㄚ

Ptc modal particle, indicating request

- 晚上我們一起吃飯吧？
  Shall we have dinner this evening?

吧 [1b] ba ˙ㄅㄚ

Ptc modal particle, indicating consent

- 你想買，那你就去買吧！
  If you want to buy it, go and buy it then.

吧 [2] ba ˙ㄅㄚ

Ptc interrogative marker, indicating supposition

- 你很忙吧？
  You're very busy, aren't you?
- 我想這些東西很貴吧？
  They are very expensive, I presume?

★ **白** [a] bái ㄅㄞˊ

Vs. /Adj white

- Jane穿著一件白T恤。
  Jane is wearing a white T shirt.
- 媽媽給了我一片白巧克力。
  Mom gave me a piece of white chocolate.

★ **白** [b] bái ㄅㄞˊ

Vs. /Adj blank

- 這只是一張白紙。
  This is only a blank sheet of paper.

白板 báibǎn ㄅㄞˊ ㄅㄢˇ

N whiteboard

- 老師叫我把答案寫在白板上。
  The teacher asked me to write the answer on the whiteboard.

白飯 báifàn ㄅㄞˊ ㄈㄢˋ

N plain rice

- 再來一碗白飯。
  Another bowl of plain rice, please.

白酒[a] báijiǔ ㄅㄞˊ ㄐㄧㄡˇ

N culture-specific item for Chinese hard liquor

- 我不喝白酒，只喝啤酒。
  I don't drink hard liquor. I only drink beer.

白酒[b] báijiǔ ㄅㄞˊ ㄐㄧㄡˇ

N white wine

- 吃魚最好喝白酒。
  White wines go well with fish.

★白天[a] báitiān ㄅㄞˊ ㄊㄧㄢ

N daytime

- 臺北白天的溫度是攝氏20度。
  Daytime temperature is 20℃ in Taipei.

★白天[b] báitiān ㄅㄞˊ ㄊㄧㄢ

N by day

- 他晚上工作，白天睡覺。
  He works by night and sleeps by day.

★白天[c] báitiān ㄅㄞˊ ㄊㄧㄢ

N during the day

- 你白天都做些什麼？
  What do you do during the day?

百 bǎi ㄅㄞˇ

N hundred

- 這裡有一百個人。
  There are one hundred people here.
- 這本書有好幾百頁。
  This book has many hundreds of pages.
- 這條褲子花了我八百元。
  This pair of trousers costs me NT$800.

拜 bài ㄅㄞˋ

V to worship

- 拜祖先是中國人的習慣。
  It's a custom for Chinese to worship their ancestors.

拜拜 bāibāi ㄅㄞ ㄅㄞ

interjection transliteration for 'bye bye'

- 拜拜，各位！我們明天見。
  Bye-bye, everyone! I'll see you tomorrow!

拜年 bàinián ㄅㄞˋ ㄋㄧㄢˊ

V-sep to pay a New Year call

- 中國人過年的時候會互相拜年。
  Chinese people are used to pay to each other a New Year call.

班[1] bān ㄅㄢ

M measure word for service in public transportation

- 我們只好坐下一班火車。
  We had to take the next train.
- 我坐上了最後一班公車。
  I caught the last bus of the day.
- 飛高雄的飛機每天有五班。
  There are five flights to Kaohsiung every day.

★ 班[2a] bān ㄅㄢ

N class (schooling)

- 三年級有兩個班。
  There are two classes in grade three.

★ 班[2b] bān ㄅㄢ

N grade

- 大學的時候，她比我低一班。
  She was my junior by one grade at university.

★ 搬[a] bān ㄅㄢ

V to change from one place to another

- 鋼琴很重，要三個人搬。
  It took three men to move the heavy piano.
- 要搬那桌子並不容易。
  It was not easy to move that table.

★ 搬[b] bān ㄅㄢ

V to move to a different place

- 下星期我們搬辦公室。

We're moving offices next week.

搬家 bānjiā ㄅㄢ ㄐㄧㄚ

V-sep to move one's house

- Mary一年搬了三次家。
  Mary has moved three times in one year.
- 我的房子太小，所以決定搬家。
  My house is too small, so I've decided to move.

班機 bānjī ㄅㄢ ㄐㄧ

N air service

- 兩個城市之間有班機來往。
  There's a regular air service between the two cities.

★ **半** [1a] bàn ㄅㄢˋ

N bound word, used to indicate clock time: half

- 現在是一點半。
  It is half past one.

★ **半** [1b] bàn ㄅㄢˋ

N bound word, used to indicate half of something

- 我走了一個半小時。
  I walked for one and a half hours.

半 [2] bàn ㄅㄢˋ

Det determiner, followed by an unit word

- 半個小時不夠。
  Half an hour is not enough.
- 他寫了不到半頁就停下來了。
  He had scarcely written half a page before he stopped.

拌 bàn ㄅㄢˋ

V to dress

- 你拌沙拉，我來煎魚。
  You dress a salad, and I'll fry fish.

★ **辦** [a] bàn ㄅㄢˋ

V to deal with

- 這件事有點難辦。
  This matter is quite hard to deal with.

★ **辦** [b] bàn ㄅㄢˋ

V to do with

- 這件事我該怎麼辦？

What shall I do with this matter?

★ **辦** [c] bàn ㄅㄢˋ

V to act

- 他說得對，我們就這樣辦吧。
  What he said is right, we'll act upon it.

辦法 [a] bànfǎ ㄅㄢˋ ㄈㄚˇ

N idea

- 我有更好的辦法。
  I got a better idea.

辦法 [b] bànfǎ ㄅㄢˋ ㄈㄚˇ

N means

- 我們得想個辦法把工作完成。
  We must get the job done by some means or other.

辦法 [c] bànfǎ ㄅㄢˋ ㄈㄚˇ

N way of doing something

- 我想不出任何辦法。
  I do not see any way to do it.

辦公室 bàngōngshì ㄅㄢˋ ㄍㄨㄥ ㄕˋ

N office

- 她正在辦公室打電腦。
  She's using the computer in the office.

★ **幫** [1a] bāng ㄅㄤ

V to help

- 我該怎麼幫你呢？
  How can I help you?
- 我能幫幫你嗎？
  Can I help you?

★ **幫** [1b] bāng ㄅㄤ

V to help someone to do something

- 我幫你提行李吧。
  Let me help with your luggage.
- 你幫我搬這張桌子，好嗎？
  Could you help me move the table?

幫 [2] bāng ㄅㄤ

Prep preposition, used as a request

- 來幫我接一下電話。
  Answer the phone for me, would you?

★ **幫忙** bāngmáng ㄅㄤ ㄇㄤˊ

V-sep to help

• 我能幫上什麼忙嗎？
Is there any way that I can help?

★ 棒 bàng ㄅㄤˋ

Vs. /Adj great (spoken)

• 我買了新車。
—喔，好棒！
I've got a new car. --- Oh, great!

棒球 bàngqiú ㄅㄤˋ ㄑㄧㄡˊ

N baseball

• Ted正在投棒球。
Ted is throwing a baseball.

★ 包 1a bāo ㄅㄠ

M unit word for parcel

• 這包信件重兩公斤。
The parcel of mails weighs 2 kilo.

★ 包 1b bāo ㄅㄠ

M unit word for packet

• Ian每天抽一包香菸。
Ian consumes a packet of cigarettes every day.

★ 包 1c bāo ㄅㄠ

M unit word for pack

• 她給了我一包口香糖。
She gave me a pack of gum.

★ 包 2a bāo ㄅㄠ

V to wrap

• 每個蘋果都用紙包著。
Each apple was wrapped in paper.

★ 包 2b bāo ㄅㄠ

V to package up

• 我包了一些衣服寄給我妹妹。
I packaged up some clothes to send to my sister.

包裹 bāoguǒ ㄅㄠ ㄍㄨㄛˇ

N parcel

• 郵差上午送來一個包裹。
The postman brought a parcel this morning.

★ 包括 a bāokuò ㄅㄠ ㄎㄨㄛˋ

V to include

• 你一共花了八百塊，包括飲料。
Your total expenses, including the drinks, are NT$800.

★ 包括[b] bāokuò ㄅㄠ ㄎㄨㄛˋ

V be inclusive

- 租金什麼都包括了。
  The rent is all inclusive.

★ 包括[c] bāokuò ㄅㄠ ㄎㄨㄛˋ

V to incorporate

- 計劃書已經包括了你的建議。
  The proposal has incorporated your suggestions.

包子 bāozi ㄅㄠ ˙ㄗ

N culture-specific item, for Chinese bun (stuffed and steamed)

- 我想我午飯就吃豬肉包子吧。
  I think I'll have pork buns for lunch.

保單 bǎodān ㄅㄠˇ ㄉㄢ

N policy

- 看清楚保單內容，東西丟了不擔心。
  Check your policy; you don't have to worry in case of loss.

保費 bǎofèi ㄅㄠˇ ㄈㄟˋ

N insurance premium

- 今年我的保費漲了。
  My insurance premium has been increased this year.

保管 bǎoguǎn ㄅㄠˇ ㄍㄨㄢˇ

V to keep something for someone

- 請你保管一下我的腳踏車。
  Would you keep my bicycle for me for a while?

保姆 bǎomǔ ㄅㄠˇ ㄇㄨˇ

N nanny

- 他們找了個保姆看孩子。
  They have a nanny to look after their children.

★ 保險 bǎoxiǎn ㄅㄠˇ ㄒㄧㄢˇ

N Insurance

- 你買的保險夠不夠？
  Have you got adequate insurance?

保重 bǎozhòng ㄅㄠˇ ㄓㄨㄥˋ

V take good care of (health)

- 請多多保重身體。
  Please take very good care of your health.

爆 bào ㄅㄠˋ

V to burst

- 汽車輪胎突然爆了。
  The tire on the car suddenly burst.

報到[a] bàodào ㄅㄠˋ ㄉㄠˋ

Vi to report

- 到了以後請立刻報到。
  Please report immediately on arrival.

報到[b] bàodào ㄅㄠˋ ㄉㄠˋ

Vi to report for duty

- 你星期一上午必須報到。
  You should report for duty on Monday morning.

報告[1] bàogào ㄅㄠˋ ㄍㄠˋ

N report

- 我明天要交這份報告。
  I have to submit the report tomorrow.

報告[2] bàogào ㄅㄠˋ ㄍㄠˋ

V to report

- 一個學生報告了研究結果。
  The outcome of the research was reported by a student.

報警[a] bàojǐng ㄅㄠˋ ㄐㄧㄥˇ

Vi to call the police

- 快！快報警！
  Quick! Call the police!

報警[b] bàojǐng ㄅㄠˋ ㄐㄧㄥˇ

Vi to report to the police

- 車子丟了，你報警了嗎？
  Have you reported the car theft to the police?

報名 bàomíng ㄅㄠˋ ㄇㄧㄥˊ

V to sign up to do something

- 她們都報名學跳舞了。
  They have all signed up to learn dancing.

抱歉 bàoqiàn ㄅㄠˋ ㄑㄧㄢˋ

discourse marker I'm sorry

- 抱歉，讓你久等了。
  Sorry to keep you waiting.
- 抱歉，這裡沒有人叫Chris。
  I'm sorry but there's no one here called Chris.

A B C D E F G H J K L M N O P Q R S T W X Y Z X-

爆炸 bàozhà
ㄅㄠˋ ㄓㄚˋ

V to explode

- 汽車爆炸了，但沒有人受傷。
  The car exploded but nobody was injured.

報紙 bàozhǐ
ㄅㄠˋ ㄓˇ

N newspaper

- 我能看看你的報紙嗎？
  Can I have a read of your newspaper?

★杯[a] bēi
ㄅㄟ

M unit word for cup

- Amy給我倒了一杯咖啡。
  Amy poured out a cup of coffee for me.

★杯[b] bēi
ㄅㄟ

M unit word for glass

- 你要一杯酒還是半杯？
  Do you want a full glass of wine or half a glass?

★杯子[a] bēizi
ㄅㄟ ˙ㄗ

N cup

- 桌子上的杯子是空的。
  The cup on the table is empty.

★杯子[b] bēizi
ㄅㄟ ˙ㄗ

N glass

- 我的生日禮物是這個杯子。
  I got this cup for my birthday.

★北 běi
ㄅㄟˇ

N north

- 往北開，你就會看見加油站。
  Drive north and you'll find the gas station.

★北部 běibù
ㄅㄟˇ ㄅㄨˋ

N northern part

- 城市的北部有幾所大學。
  Several universities are located at the northern part of the city.

★北方[a] běifāng
ㄅㄟˇ ㄈㄤ

N the north

- 風是從北方吹來的。
  The wind is blowing from the north.

★北方[b] běifāng
ㄅㄟˇ ㄈㄤ

N in the north

- 我聽說北方正在下雪。
  I heard that it's snowing in the north.
- 北方生活費用比南方高。
  It is more expensive to live in the north than in the south.

背 bèi ㄅㄟˋ

N back of body

- 我的背又痛了。
  My back's been troubling me again.

★被[a] bèi ㄅㄟˋ

Prep passive marker, rendered by "by"

- 帽子被風吹跑了。
  The cap was blown off by the wind.
- 那本書被Kevin拿走了。
  The book has been taken away by Kevin.

★被[b] bèi ㄅㄟˋ

Prep passive marker, not shown in English

- Martin先生被選爲部門主任。
  Mr. Martin was elected the director of the department.

被子 bèizi ㄅㄟˋ ˙ㄗ

N quilt

- 我給我的小孩買了一床被子。
  I bought a quilt for my child.

★本來 běnlái ㄅㄣˇ ㄌㄞˊ

Adv originally

- 我們的店本來很小。
  Our store was originally quite small.
- 我們本來計劃只住幾天的。
  We originally planned to stay for just a few days.
- 我本來想去，可是後來沒去。
  Originally I wanted to go, but in the end I didn't go.

鼻塞 bísāi ㄅㄧˊ ㄙㄞ

Vs. /Adj be stuffed-up

CN 音：bísè

- 我鼻塞，也許感冒了。
  I'm stuffed-up. I'm afraid I've caught a cold.

鼻水 bíshuǐ ㄅㄧˊ ㄕㄨㄟˇ

N snot

- 天氣太冷，我開始流鼻水了。
  It's getting too cold, and I have a snotty nose.

鼻涕 bítì ㄅㄧˊ ㄊㄧˋ

N mucus

- 把你的鼻涕擦乾淨。
  Clean up mucus in your nose.

★ 鼻子 bízi ㄅㄧˊ ˙ㄗ

N nose

- Bill的鼻子很大。
  Bill has a big nose.
- 她的鼻子跟她媽媽的很像。
  She's got her mother's nose.

★ 比[1] bǐ ㄅㄧˇ

V to compare

- 這沒法比。
  It's out of comparison.

★ 比[2a] bǐ ㄅㄧˇ

Prep than, used with a comparative form

- 我做飯比她好。
  I cook better than she does.
- 他們來得比我們早。
  They came earlier than us.
- Sarah比她姐姐漂亮。
  Sarah was prettier than her sister.

★ 比[2b] bǐ ㄅㄧˇ

Prep than, used with a comparative pattern "more… than"

- 法文比中文難學嗎？
  Is French more difficult than Chinese?

★ 筆 bǐ ㄅㄧˇ

N pen

- 你可以把筆借給我嗎？
  Could you lend me your pen?

筆記 bǐjì ㄅㄧˇ ㄐㄧˋ

N notes

- 我把我的筆記帶來了。
  I've got my notes with me.

★ 比較[1] bǐjiào ㄅㄧˇ ㄐㄧㄠˋ

V to compare

- 把這幅畫跟那幅比較一下。

Try to compare this picture with that one.

• John和Mary在比較他們的成績。
John and Mary are comparing their scores.

★ **比較** 2a bǐjiào ㄅㄧˇ ㄐㄧㄠˋ

Adv relatively

• 他們的辦公室還是比較新。
Their office is relatively new.

★ **比較** 2b bǐjiào ㄅㄧˇ ㄐㄧㄠˋ

Adv comparatively

• 這篇文章寫得比較好。
This paper is comparatively well written.

比賽 1a bǐsài ㄅㄧˇ ㄙㄞˋ

N match

• 他們輸掉了跟英國隊的比賽。
They lost their match with England.

比賽 1b bǐsài ㄅㄧˇ ㄙㄞˋ

N contest

• 我姐姐參加了跳舞比賽。
My sister entered a dancing contest.

比賽 2 bǐsài ㄅㄧˇ ㄙㄞˋ

Vi to compete in a game

• 我們來比賽跑一百公尺。
Let's compete in 100-metres.

★ **必須** bìxū ㄅㄧˋ ㄒㄩ

Vaux must

• 必須向大家講清楚。
It must be made clear to all.

• 你必須跟我去看醫生。
You must go and see the doctor with me.

• 你必須在中午以前準備好。
You must get everything ready before noon.

畢業 bìyè ㄅㄧˋ ㄧㄝˋ

Vp-sep to graduate

• 我畢業了！
I graduated!

• 她是英語系畢業的。
She graduated in English from university.

★ **邊** a biān ㄅㄧㄢ

N side

- Mary坐在床邊。
  Mary sat on the side of the bed.

★ 邊[b] biān
ㄅㄧㄢ

N margin

- 桌布有彩色的邊。
  The table cloth has a coloured margin.

★ 遍 biàn
ㄅㄧㄢˋ

M time, used to express frequency.

- 請再說一遍。
  Please say it again.
- 這封信我已經看了好幾遍了。
  I've read over this letter several times.

★ 變[a] biàn
ㄅㄧㄢˋ

Vp to change

- 語言總是在變。
  Language is subject to change.
- 市區電話費不變。
  The charge for local calls will not change.
- 我的計畫沒有變，我還是想去。
  There is no change in my plans. I still want to go.

★ 變[b] biàn
ㄅㄧㄢˋ

Vp to shift

- 颱風的方向變了。
  The path of the typhoon has shifted.

便利 biànlì
ㄅㄧㄢˋ ㄌㄧˋ

Vs. /Adj convenient

- 住在學校附近便利得很。
  Living near the campus is very convenient.

標準[1] biāozhǔn
ㄅㄧㄠ ㄓㄨㄣˇ

N criteria

- 你買汽車的時候，標準是什麼？
  What are your criteria when you're buying a car?

標準[2] biāozhǔn
ㄅㄧㄠ ㄓㄨㄣˇ

Vs. /Adj correctly

- Chris中文說得很標準。
  Chris speaks Chinese quite correctly.

★ 表 biǎo
ㄅㄧㄠˇ

N form

• 你能幫我塡表嗎?
Can you help me to fill the form.

表哥 biǎogē ㄅㄧㄠˇ ㄍㄜ

N cousin; elder male cousin.

◇ Note that the prefix「表」is used to indicate all children of uncles and aunts, and the correct interpretation in age and sex depend on context.

• 我表哥過去住在英國北部。
My cousin used to live in the north of England.

表姐 biǎojiě ㄅㄧㄠˇ ㄐㄧㄝˇ

N cousin; elder female cousin

• 我表姊去年生了個女孩。
My cousin had a baby girl last year.

表妹 biǎomèi ㄅㄧㄠˇ ㄇㄟˋ

N cousin; younger female cousin

• 她和她的表妹相當親密。
She is very close to her cousin.

表弟 biǎodì ㄅㄧㄠˇ ㄉㄧˋ

N cousin; younger male cousin

• 我和我表弟在同一個班。
My cousin and I are in the same class.

表演[1] biǎoyǎn ㄅㄧㄠˇ ㄧㄢˇ

N performance

• 他們的表演不太成功。
Their performance is disappointing.

表演[2] biǎoyǎn ㄅㄧㄠˇ ㄧㄢˇ

V to give a performance

• 請你用中文表演一個節目。
Would you give a performance in Chinese?

★別 bié ㄅㄧㄝˊ

Adv not to do something, used in imperative

• 別急！
No hurry!

• 別走了，在這裡住兩天吧！
Don't leave. Stay here for a couple of days.

• 別生氣，我下次不會這樣做了。
Don't get angry. I won't do

that again.

★別的[a] biéde
ㄅㄧㄝˊ ˙ㄉㄜ

Det other

- 當然還有別的辦法。
  Of course, there are other ways of doing this.

★別的[b] biéde
ㄅㄧㄝˊ ˙ㄉㄜ

Det another

- 我們再玩別的遊戲吧！
  Let's play another game.

★別的[c] biéde
ㄅㄧㄝˊ ˙ㄉㄜ

Det some others

- 我不喜歡這個，給我看些別的。
  I don't like this one. Show me some others.

賓館 bīnguǎn
ㄅㄧㄣ ㄍㄨㄢˇ

N hotel

SG MY 酒店（大型豪華的），旅店／旅館（一般較小的）。

HK 特指男女幽會的時鐘酒店。

- 這家賓館不提供牙膏。
  This hotel does not provide toothpaste.

冰[1] bīn
ㄅㄧㄥ

N ice

- 這裡的冰很厚，可以在上面走。
  The ice here is thick enough for walking on it.

冰[2] bīn
ㄅㄧㄥ

Vs. /Adj to freeze up

- 把魚放進冰箱裡冰起來。
  Put the fish into the refrigerator and freeze it up.

冰糖 bīngtáng
ㄅㄧㄥ ㄊㄤˊ

N crystal sugar

- 她喜歡喝熱咖啡加冰糖。
  She likes to drink hot coffee with crystal sugar.

冰箱 bīngxiāng
ㄅㄧㄥ ㄒㄧㄤ

N refrigerator

SG MY 「冰櫥」或「雪櫃」

- 你們的冰箱該換了。
  You have to change your refrigerator.

餅 bǐng
ㄅㄧㄥˇ

N flat bread

• 餅是中國北方常見的食物。
Flatbread is the common food in northern China.

病 1a bìng ㄅㄧㄥˋ

N illness

• 現在的老人有各種病。
There is a lot of illness among the elderly people just now.

• Bill得了重病，幾個星期後死了。
Bill contracted a serious illness and died a few weeks later.

病 1b bìng ㄅㄧㄥˋ

N disease

• 她的病治好了。
She is cured of her disease.

病 2a bìng ㄅㄧㄥˋ

Vs. /Adj to become ill

• John感冒了，病了三天。
John has been ill with a cold for three days.

病 2b bìng ㄅㄧㄥˋ

Vs. /Adj to be sick

• 我不能上班，因爲我病了。
I can't go to work because I'm sick.

病假 bìngjià ㄅㄧㄥˋ ㄐㄧㄚˋ

N sick leave

• 她昨天請病假。
She asked a sick leave yesterday.

病人 bìngrén ㄅㄧㄥˋ ㄖㄣˊ

N patient

• 醫生說病人已經完全好了。
The doctor reported the patient fully recovered.

★ 薄 bó ㄅㄛˊ

Vs. /Adj thin

• 這種紙很薄。
This paper is very thin.

• 這房子的牆太薄。
The walls of the house are too thin.

• 別在冰上走，冰還太薄。
Don't walk on the ice yet. It's still too thin.

伯父 bófù
ㄅㄛˊ ㄈㄨˋ

N uncle; father's elder brother

- 我伯父很喜歡小孩。
  My uncle likes kids.

博士 bóshì
ㄅㄛˊ ㄕˋ

N a Ph D degree holder

- 我們的總經理是經濟學博士。
  Our general manager is a doctor of economy.

博物館 bówùguǎn
ㄅㄛˊ ㄨˋ ㄍㄨㄢˇ

N museum

- 明天去參觀科學博物館。
  Let's visit the science museum tomorrow.

脖子 bózi
ㄅㄛˊ ˙ㄗ

N neck

SG MY 頸項。HK 頸、頸部

- Mike的脖子受了傷。
  Mike hurt his neck.

播 bò
ㄅㄛˋ

V to broadcast

SG MY 「做」（口語），如：現在在做什麼戲？= 現在在播什麼節目？

- 電視上正在播球賽。
  Television is now broadcasting the ball game.

★ 不必 búbì
ㄅㄨˊ ㄅㄧˋ

Adv do not have to

- 你不必這麼做。
  You don't have to do so.

★ 不錯 1a búcuò
ㄅㄨˊ ㄘㄨㄛˋ

Vs-pred be good

- 聽起來不錯。
  It sounds good to me.

★ 不錯 1b búcuò
ㄅㄨˊ ㄘㄨㄛˋ

Vs-pred be quite nice

- 她人不錯。
  She is quite nice.

★ 不錯 1c búcuò
ㄅㄨˊ ㄘㄨㄛˋ

Vs-pred lovely

- 我認爲這個想法不錯。
  I think it's a lovely idea.

不錯 2a búcuò
ㄅㄨˊ ㄘㄨㄛˋ

discourse marker yes

- 不錯，Ann是昨天來的。
  Yes, Ann did come yesterday.

A B C D E F G H J K L M N O P Q R S T W X Y Z X-

不錯[2b] búcuò ㄅㄨˊ ㄘㄨㄛˋ

discourse marker that's right

• 不錯，我說的就是這種鞋子。
That's right. I was referring to this kind of shoes.

★不但//而且

bú dàn //ér qiě
ㄅㄨˊ ㄉㄢˋ//ㄦˊ ㄑㄧㄝˇ

Conj not only, but

• 我不但聽到過，而且看見過。
I not only heard about it, but actually saw it.

不但//也 bú dàn// yě ㄅㄨˊ ㄉㄢˋ//ㄧㄝˇ

Conj not only, but

• 不但我們需要幫助，他們也需要。
Not only we, but they also need help.

不二價 búèrjià ㄅㄨˊ ㄦˋ ㄐㄧㄚˋ

V-pred price

CN 一口價。HK 實價

• 這些衣服不二價。
These clothes are at a fixed price.

★不過[1a] búguò ㄅㄨˊ ㄍㄨㄛˋ

Adv not more than

• 這條裙子不過一千元。
This skirt costs no more than NT$1000.

★不過[1b] búguò ㄅㄨˊ ㄍㄨㄛˋ

Adv at most

• 我看Kevin不過三十歲。
I guess Kevin is at most 30 years old.

不過[2a] búguò ㄅㄨˊ ㄍㄨㄛˋ

Conj but

• 你可以去，不過早點回來。
You may go, but come back early.

不過[2b] búguò ㄅㄨˊ ㄍㄨㄛˋ

Conj however

• 天很冷，不過我還是想去游泳。
It's very cold. However, I'd still like to go swimming.

★不用[a] búyòng ㄅㄨˊ ㄩㄥˋ

Vaux no need

• 不用介紹了，我們認識。
There was no need for introductions because we know each other.

不用[b] búyòng ㄅㄨˊ ㄩㄥˋ

Vaux no need to

• 哪兒都有計程車，你不用擔心。
There are taxis everywhere, you don't need to worry.

• 我去機場送你吧！
－不用了，謝謝。
I'll see you off at the airport.
--- There's no need to, thank you.

不用[c] búyòng ㄅㄨˊ ㄩㄥˋ

Adv not have to

• Mary週末不用上班。
Mary doesn't have to work at weekends.

• 我自己去吧，你不用去。
I'll go by myself, you don't have to come.

補[a] bǔ ㄅㄨˇ

V to make up

• 老師上星期請假，明天要補課。
Tomorrow the teacher will make up the lessons he's missed while he was on leave last week.

補[b] bǔ ㄅㄨˇ

V to take extra lessons

• Sue上星期缺了不少課，所以要補課。
Since she missed a lot of school last week, Sue needed to take extra lessons.

補[c] bǔ ㄅㄨˇ

V to nourish (tonic)

• 喝點雞湯補一補吧！
You'd better nourish yourself on chicken soups.

補位 bǔwèi ㄅㄨˇ ㄨㄟˋ

N waiting list

• 我還在等候飛機補位。
I am still on the flight wait list.

補習 bǔxí ㄅㄨˇ ㄒㄧˊ

V-sep to take a make-up course

• Jane正在補習中文。
Jane's taking a make-up course of Chinese.

A B C D E F G H J K L M N O P Q R S T W X Y Z X-

補習班 bǔxíbān
ㄅㄨˇ ㄒㄧˊ ㄅㄢ

N after-class school

- 他星期天還要去補習班。
  He has to go to after-class school at Sunday.

★ 不 [1] bù
ㄅㄨˋ

reply tag not

- 她不會說中文。
  She can't speak Chinese.
- 他不關心這件事。
  He doesn't care about this matter.
- 我不是James，我是Chris。
  I'm not James. I'm Chris.

不 [2] bù
ㄅㄨˋ

reply tag no, used as a negative reply

- 你在學法文嗎？
  －不，我在學中文。
  Are you studying French? No, I'm studying Chinese.

★ 部 [a] bù
ㄅㄨˋ

M measure word for book

- 這部小說已經翻譯成中文了。
  The novel was translated into Chinese.

★ 部 [b] bù
ㄅㄨˋ

M measure word for film

- 那是一部很棒的電影。
  It's an excellent film.

★ 部 [c] bù
ㄅㄨˋ

M measure word for machine
SG MY HK 「架」

- 這部電視機壞了。
  The television isn't working properly.

★ 部分 [a] bùfen
ㄅㄨˋ ㄈㄣˋ

N part

- 我只完成計畫的第一部分。
  I've only finished the first part of the plan.

★ 部分 [b] bùfen
ㄅㄨˋ ㄈㄣˋ

N some of

- 這裡住的人，有部分是外國人。
  Some of the people living here are foreigners.

佈告欄 bùgàolán ㄅㄨˋ ㄍㄠˋ ㄌㄢˊ

N bulletin board

- 牆上有一塊大佈告欄。
  There's a big bulletin board on the wall.

★ 不管 bùguǎn ㄅㄨˋ ㄍㄨㄢˇ

Conj whether/or not

- 不管你喜歡不喜歡，你得離開。
  Whether you like it or not, you'll have to leave.

不管誰/都

bùguǎn shéi / dōu
ㄅㄨˋ ㄍㄨㄢˇ ㄕㄟˊ/ ㄉㄡ

Conj no matter who

- 不管誰都可以參加這個會議。
  It doesn't matter who is to attend the meeting.

★ 不久[a] bùjiǔ ㄅㄨˋ ㄐㄧㄡˇ

Adv soon

- 她不久就會回來。
  She'll be back soon.

★ 不久[b] bùjiǔ ㄅㄨˋ ㄐㄧㄡˇ

Adv a moment ago

- Steve剛走不久。
  Steve just left a moment ago.

不久以前

bùjiǔyǐqián
ㄅㄨˋ ㄐㄧㄡˇ ㄧˇ ㄑㄧㄢˊ

Adv lately

- 他不久以前從香港回來。
  He had lately returned from Taiwan.

部門 bùmén ㄅㄨˋ ㄇㄣˊ

N department

- 你在哪個部門上班？
  In which departments do you work?

★ 不然[a] bùrán ㄅㄨˋ ㄖㄢˊ

Conj or

- 穿上大衣，不然你會感冒的。
  Put on your coat, or you'll catch a cold.
- 快，不然我們會趕不上巴士。
  Hurry up, or we'll miss the bus.

A B C D E F G H J K L M N O P Q R S T W X Y Z X-

★ **不然** [b] bùrán ㄅㄨˋ ㄖㄢˊ

Conj otherwise

- 你現在得走了，不然你會遲到。
  You'll have to go now, otherwise you'll be late.

★ **不少** bùshǎo ㄅㄨˋ ㄕㄠˇ

Vs. /Adj a lot of

- 我在臺灣有不少朋友。
  I have a lot of friends in Taiwan.
- 昨天不少人參加了會議。
  A lot of people attended the meeting yesterday.
- 我生日的時候收到不少禮物。
  I got a lot of presents for my birthday.

★ **不同** [a] bùtóng ㄅㄨˋ ㄊㄨㄥˊ

Vs. /Adj to differ from

- A和B在設計上不同。
  A differs from B in design.

★ **不同** [b] bùtóng ㄅㄨˋ ㄊㄨㄥˊ

Vs. /Adj be different

- 人和人不同，不能比較。
  People are different and cannot be compared.

部位 bùwèi ㄅㄨˋ ㄨㄟˋ

N body part

- 我感覺身體的各個部位都不舒服。
  I feel bad in every parts of my body.

★ **不小心** bùxiǎoxīn ㄅㄨˋ ㄒㄧㄠˇ ㄒㄧㄣ

Adv mindlessly

- 他不小心打破了杯子
  Mindlessly he broke the glass.

★ **不怎麼** [a] bùzěnme ㄅㄨˋ ㄗㄣˇ ˙ㄇㄜ

Adv not that

- 她今天不怎麼高興。
  She's not that happy today.

★ **不怎麼** [b] bùzěnme ㄅㄨˋ ㄗㄣˇ ˙ㄇㄜ

Adv not particularly

- 我不怎麼喜歡他。
  I don't particularly like him.

★ 擦 cā ㄘㄚ

V to wipe

- 別用袖子擦鼻子！
  Don't wipe your nose on your sleeve!
- Mary在自己的圍裙上擦手。
  Mary wiped her hands on her apron.

★ 才 cái ㄘㄞˊ

Adv don't... until

- 我今天才知道他不是中國人。
  I didn't know that he was not Chinese until today.
- 他解釋了我才明白怎麼回事。
  I don't understand what was going on until he explained it to me.

材料 cáiliào ㄘㄞˊ ㄌㄧㄠˋ

N ingredient

- 我要去買一些做蛋糕的材料。
  I have to buy ingredients for a cake.

裁判 cáipàn ㄘㄞˊ ㄆㄢˋ

N referee

SG 評判

- 裁判吹響了哨子，比賽結束。
  The referee whistled and the game was over.

菜[a] cài ㄘㄞˋ

N vegetable

- 醫生要他多吃菜，少吃肉。
  The doctor advices him to eat more vegetable and less meat.

菜[b] cài ㄘㄞˋ

N dish

- 今天的晚餐有三道菜。
  The dinner tonight consists of three dishes.

菜單 càidān ㄘㄞˋ ㄉㄢˋ

N menu

• 今天菜單上有什麼菜？
What's on the menu today?

★ 餐[1] cān ㄘㄢ

N bound word for meal

• 他今天只吃兩餐。
He has only two meals today.

★ 餐[2] cān ㄘㄢ

N bound word for meal

• 晚飯是我們一天中的主餐。
Dinner is the main meal of the day for us.

• 三百元包括三餐飯和飲料。
300 dollars include three meals with beverages.

餐廳 cāntīng ㄘㄢ ㄊㄧㄥ

N dining hall
SG MY 餐館

• 校園裡有三個餐廳。
There are three dining halls on campus.

★ 參加[a] cānjiā ㄘㄢ ㄐㄧㄚ

V to join

• 歡迎你參加我們的俱樂部。
You're welcome to join our club.

• 請你跟我們一起參加討論。
Please join us in the discussion.

★ 參加[b] cānjiā ㄘㄢ ㄐㄧㄚ

V to participate

• 每個人都可以參加選舉。
Everyone can participate in an election.

• 我們有興趣參加這個活動。
We're interested in participating in this event.

艙 cāng ㄘㄤ

N cabin

• 艙裡面沒有人。
There was no one in the cabin.

蒼蠅 cāngyíng ㄘㄤ ㄧㄥˊ

N fly (small flying insect)

• 蒼蠅眞討厭！
What a nuisance the flies are!

操場 cāochǎng ㄘㄠ ㄔㄤˇ

A B C D E F G H J K L M N O P Q R S T W X Y Z X-

N playground

- 孩子們在操場上跑來跑去。
  The children were running in the playground.

草地 cǎodì ㄘㄠˇ ㄉㄧˋ

N the grass

- 不許在草地上走。
  You're not supposed to walk on the grass.

草莓 cǎoméi ㄘㄠˇ ㄇㄟˊ

N strawberry

- 這些草莓很新鮮。
  These strawberries are very fresh.

廁所 cèsuǒ ㄘㄜˋ ㄙㄨㄛˇ

N restroom

- 商場每層都有一間廁所。
  There is a restroom on each floor of the arcade.

叉子 chāzi ㄔㄚ ˙ㄗ

N fork

- 我需要一把叉子吃點心。
  I need a fork for the dessert.

★ 層 [a] céng ㄘㄥˊ

M layer

- 這結婚蛋糕有三層。
  The wedding cake has three layers.
- 電視機上有一層塵土。
  There's a layer of dust on the TV set.

★ 層 [b] céng ㄘㄥˊ

M level

- 這棟大樓一共有四十五層。
  The building has 54 levels.

★ 插 chā ㄔㄚ

V to insert

- Mary試著把鑰匙插進鎖裡。
  Mary tried to insert the key into the lock.

★ 差 [a] chā ㄔㄚ

Vs. /Adj be short

- 我們差幾把椅子。
  We're a couple of chairs short.

★ 差 [b] chā ㄔㄚ

Vs. /Adj be short

- John那裡還差大約一百元。
  John's still about 100 dollars short.

★ 差不多 1a chàbùduō
ㄔㄚˋ ㄅㄨˋ ㄉㄨㄛ

Vs-pred all right (= satisfactory)

- 飯菜怎麼樣？
  —差不多。
  What's the food like? --- It's all right.

★ 差不多 1b chàbùduō
ㄔㄚˋ ㄅㄨˋ ㄉㄨㄛ

Vs-pred more or less

- 我們年齡差不多。
  We are more or less the same age.

★ 差不多 2 chàbùduō
ㄔㄚˋ ㄅㄨˋ ㄉㄨㄛ

Adv more or less

- 兩篇文章說的內容都差不多。
  The two articles say more or less the same thing.

★ 查 chá
ㄔㄚˊ

V to check

- Amy正在查哪家旅館有空房間。
  Amy's checking which hotels have vacancies.

茶 chá
ㄔㄚˊ

N tea

- 我給她倒了一杯茶。
  I've poured her a cup of tea.

茶壺 cháhú
ㄔㄚˊ ㄏㄨˊ

N teapot

- 那是一個很不錯的茶壺。
  That's a nice teapot.

茶葉 cháyè
ㄔㄚˊ ㄧㄝˋ

N tea (leaves)

- 茶葉要泡一會兒，味道才會出來。
  Let the tea steep a little while, and the flavour will come out.

★ 長 cháng
ㄔㄤˊ

Vs. /Adj be long

- 這根繩子不夠長。
  The rope is not quite long enough.

★ 常常 chángcháng
ㄔㄤˊ ㄔㄤˊ

Adv often

- Mary常常在週末工作。
  Mary often works at the weekend.
- 晚飯後他常常帶著狗散步。
  He often takes his dog for a walk after dinner.

腸胃 chángwèi ㄔㄤˊ ㄨㄟˋ

N stomach

- 我的腸胃很不舒服。
  I have trouble with my stomach.

★ 場[a] chǎng ㄔㄤˇ

M measure word for game

- 打一場網球，怎麼樣？
  What about having a game of tennis?

場[b] chǎng ㄔㄤˇ

M measure word for movie

- 這家電影院一天放五場電影。
  This cinema has five movie shows a day.

★ 唱 chàng ㄔㄤˋ

V to sing

- 我不會唱那首歌。
  I don't know how to sing that song.
- Mary在音樂會上唱得不錯。
  Mary was singing well at the concert.

產假 chǎnjià ㄔㄢˇ ㄐㄧㄚˋ

N maternity leave

- 婦女應有三個月的帶薪產假。
  Women should have a three-month paid maternity leave.

超過 chāoguò ㄔㄠ ㄍㄨㄛˋ

V to exceed

- 價格可能超過十萬台幣。
  The price could exceed one hundred thousand TW dollars.

超級 chāojí ㄔㄠ ㄐㄧˊ

Vs-attr super

- 我家附近有一個很大的超級市場。
  There is a very big supermarket.

超級市場

chāojíshìchǎng
ㄔㄠ ㄐㄧˊ ㄕˋ ㄔㄤˇ

N supermarket

- 我在附近的超級市場買東西。
  I go shopping at a nearby supermarket.

超速 chāosù
ㄔㄠ ㄙㄨˋ

Vp-sep speeding

- 警察發現他超速。
  The police caught him speeding.

超重 chāozhòng
ㄔㄠ ㄓㄨㄥˋ

Vp-sep be overweight

- 醫生說我超重五公斤。
  I'm overweight by 5 kilo according to the doctor.

潮濕 cháoshī
ㄔㄠˊ ㄕ

Vs. /Adj humid

- 香港夏天又熱又潮濕。
  Hong Kong is very hot and humid in the summer.

吵[1a] chǎo
ㄔㄠˇ

V to argue

- 你們別吵了，行不行？
  Can't you stop arguing with each other?

吵[1b] chǎo
ㄔㄠˇ

V to quarrel

- 他們夫婦倆又吵了。
  The couple quarreled again.

吵[2] chǎo
ㄔㄠˇ

Vs. /Adj be noisy

- 房間朝著大街，太吵了。
  The room faces a main street. It's too noisy.

炒 chǎo
ㄔㄠˇ

V to stir-fry

- 雞肉炒一分鐘，然後放蔬菜。
  Stir-fry the chicken for one minute, then add the vegetables.

炒飯 chǎofàn
ㄔㄠˇ ㄈㄢˋ

N fried rice

- 我要一份炒飯。
  May I have a helping of fried rice?

程度 chéngdù
ㄔㄥˊ ㄉㄨˋ

N degree

- John在某種程度上是對的。
  John was right to some degree.

★ 車 chē
ㄔㄜ

N car; vehicle

- 你有車嗎？
  Do you have a car?
- 我的車壞了。
  My car has broken down.

襯衫 chènshān
ㄔㄣˋ ㄕㄢ

N shirt

MY 白衣

HK 恤衫

- 我上班要穿襯衫打領帶。
  I have to wear a shirt and tie to work.

稱 chèng
ㄔㄥˋ

V to weigh

- 他稱了一些番茄給我。
  He weighed some tomatoes and gave them to me.

成功 chénggōng
ㄔㄥˊ ㄍㄨㄥ

Vs. /Adj successful

- 手術很成功。
  The operation was successful.

成績 chéngjī
ㄔㄥˊ ㄐㄧ

N grade

CN chéng jì

- 她努力學習，得到了好成績。
  She worked hard and got good grades.

成績單 chéngjīdān
ㄔㄥˊ ㄐㄧ ㄉㄢ

N report card

- 讓我看看你的成績單。
  Let me have a look at your report card.

成人 chéngrén
ㄔㄥˊ ㄖㄣˊ

N adult

- 門票成人五十元，兒童免費。
  Admission fee: 50 dollars for adults, free of charge for children.

城市 chéngshì
ㄔㄥˊ ㄕˋ

N city

- 城市中心是商業區。
  The city centre is a business district.

程式 chéngshì ㄔㄥˊ ㄕˋ

N program for computer

- Alex很會寫電腦程式。
  Alex's very good at writing computer program.

★吃 chī ㄔ

V to eat

- 她吃了我的蛋糕。
  She ate my cake.
- 我們晚飯吃餃子吧！
  Let's eat Chinese dumplings for dinner.

尺[1] chǐ ㄔˇ

N ruler

- Mary用尺量桌子的長度。
  Mary used a ruler to measure the length of the table.

尺[2] chǐ ㄔˇ

M Chinese unit of length, equal to 1/3 metre

- 我要的是一尺左右。
  What I want is one chi or so.

尺寸 chǐcùn ㄔˇ ㄘㄨㄣˋ

N size

- 你知道你自己衣服的尺寸嗎？
  Do you know your clothing size?

沖 chōng ㄔㄨㄥ

V brew

- 他太太給我們沖了一壺茶。
  His wife brewed a pot of tea for us.

★重 chóng ㄔㄨㄥˊ

Adv (to do something) again

- 我打算全部重寫這篇文章。
  I intended to write the essay all over again.

寵物 chǒngwù ㄔㄨㄥˇ ㄨˋ

N pet

- 他們養了一隻小狗當寵物。
  They keep a puppy as a pet.

★ **抽** chōu ㄔㄡ

V to draw out from (among)

- Mary從盒子裡抽出一張紙巾。
  Mary drew a tissue from the box.
- Steve從書堆下面抽出一封信。
  Steve drew a letter from underneath the books.

醜 chǒu ㄔㄡˇ

Vs. /Adj be ugly

- 現在我感到自己眞的又胖又醜。
  I feel really fat and ugly at the moment.

臭 [a] chòu ㄔㄡˋ

Vs. /Adj to smell badly

- 他的腳很臭。
  His foot smells badly.

臭 [b] chòu ㄔㄡˋ

Vs. /Adj to stink

- 那條魚臭了。
  That fish stinks.

★ **出** [a] chū ㄔㄨ

V to be out

- 過了橋，我們就出城了。
  We are out of the town once we cross the bridge.

★ **出** [b] chū ㄔㄨ

V to exit

- 請從右門進，從左門出。
  Please enter by the right door and exist through the left door.

出發 chūfā ㄔㄨ ㄈㄚ

Vp take one's departure

- 你該出發了。
  It's time that you take your departure.

出口 chūkǒu ㄔㄨ ㄎㄡˇ

N exit

- 我在電影院的出口等你。
  I'm waiting for you at the exit of the cinema.

出生 chūshēng ㄔㄨ ㄕㄥ

Vp be born

- Jane是五十年代後期出生的。

Jane was born in the late fifties.

出院 chūyuàn ㄔㄨ ㄩㄢˋ

Vp-sep leave hospital

- 病人是自願出院的。
  The patient left hospital of his own accord.

出租 chūzū ㄔㄨ ㄗㄨ

V to hire out

- 他們按日出租汽車。
  They hire out their cars by the day.

★ 初 chū ㄔㄨ

Vs-attr bound word, indicating first in order

- 他們是初次見面。
  They met each other for the first time.

齣 chū ㄔㄨ

M measure for play in a theatre

- 週末劇院將上演一齣新戲。
  There will be a new play in the theatre this weekend.

初級 chūjí ㄔㄨ ㄐㄧˊ

Vs-attr elementary

- Sue正在學習初級德文。
  Sue's taking an elementary course in German.

廚房 chúfáng ㄔㄨˊ ㄈㄤˊ

N kitchen

- Mary在廚房做午飯。
  Mary was in the kitchen preparing lunch.

廚具 chújù ㄔㄨˊ ㄐㄩˋ

N kitchenware

- 廚具部在三樓。
  The kitchenware department is on Level 3.

★ 除了 chúle ㄔㄨˊ ˙ㄌㄜ

Prep except for

- 我們家除了我，都去過日本。
  Everyone in my family has been to Japan, except for me.
- 桌上除了幾本書，沒有別的。
  There is nothing else on the table except some books.

處方 chǔfāng
ㄔㄨˇ ㄈㄤ

N prescription

SG 配方

MY 藥方

- 他拿著醫生開的處方到藥房買藥。
  He went into a chemist's to get the prescription filled.

★處理 chǔlǐ
ㄔㄨˇ ㄌㄧˇ

V to deal with

- 碰到問題應該馬上處理。
  You should deal with problems as they arise.

★穿[a] chuān
ㄔㄨㄢ

V to pass through

- 我穿過廣場到了旅館。
  I passed through the square to the hotel.
- 這根線能穿過那根針嗎？
  Can this thread pass through the hole of that needle?

★穿[b] chuān
ㄔㄨㄢ

V to wear (clothes)

- 我穿40號的鞋。
  I wear size 40 shoes.
- John經常穿黑上衣。
  John usually wears a black coat.

船 chuán
ㄔㄨㄢˊ

N ship

- 我登上了一艘晚上出發的船。
  I boarded a ship that was sailing in the evening.

傳真 chuánzhēn
ㄔㄨㄢˊ ㄓㄣ

V to fax

- 旅館名單我會傳真給你。
  I'll fax you the list of hotels.

窗户 chuānghù
ㄔㄨㄤ ㄏㄨˋ

N window

SG MY 「窗口」

HK 「窗門」

- 好像有人在窗戶外面。
  It would seem that there's someone outside the window.

窗口 chuāngkǒu
ㄔㄨㄤ ㄎㄡˇ

N window (for ticket)

- 請到第七號窗口買票。
  Please buy your ticket at Window no 7.

窗子 chuāngzi ㄔㄨㄤ ˙ㄗ

N window

- 風太大了，請把窗子關上。
  It's too windy. Could you shut the window, please?

★床 chuáng ㄔㄨㄤˊ

N bed

- 我換了床就睡不好覺。
  I can't sleep well in a strange bed.
- 房間很小，只有一張床。
  It was a small room, with only a bed.

闖 chuǎng ㄔㄨㄤˇ

V break into

- 我們開會的時候，他突然闖進了會議室。
  He suddenly broke into the conference room while we were having a meeting.

★吹 chuī ㄔㄨㄟ

V to blow

- 今天吹東風。
  The wind blows from the east today.
- John吹了兩三聲喇叭。
  John blows two or three notes on his trumpet.

春季 chūnjì ㄔㄨㄣ ㄐㄧˋ

N spring (season)

- 春季班下星期一開始上課。
  Spring courses will start next Monday.

★春天 chūntiān ㄔㄨㄣ ㄊㄧㄢ

N spring

- 春天這地方都是遊客。
  In the spring the place is crowded with tourists.

詞典 cídiǎn ㄘˊ ㄉㄧㄢˇ

N dictionary

- 有不懂的詞，可以查詞典。
  Consult a dictionary for words you don't know.

詞彙 cíhuì ㄘˊ ㄏㄨㄟˋ

N vocabulary

- 我的華語詞彙相當少。
  My vocabulary of Chinese is awfully poor.

辭職 cízhí
ㄘˊ ㄓˊ

V-sep to quit one's job

- Mike正在考慮辭職。
  Mike's thinking about quitting his job.

★次 cì
ㄘˋ

N times

- 我第二次去才找到他。
  I found him when I went the second time.
- 這藥每天三次，每次兩片。
  Take two pills each time and three times a day.

蔥 cōng
ㄘㄨㄥ

N green onion

- 這道菜要加點蔥。
  You'd better add some green onions to this dish.

★從 cóng
ㄘㄨㄥˊ

Prep from

- Mary從英國來。
  Mary came from England.
- John從車站走回家。
  John walked home from the station.

★從來 cónglái
ㄘㄨㄥˊ ㄌㄞˊ

Adv ever (used with negative)

- 我覺得我從來沒有到過這裡。
  I don't think I've ever been here before.
- 我的父母幾乎從來不看電視。
  My parents hardly ever watch TV.

★從前 cóngqián
ㄘㄨㄥˊ ㄑㄧㄢˊ

N once upon a time

- 從前，大門是可以不上鎖的。
  Once upon a time you used to be able to leave your front door unlocked.

粗 cū
ㄘㄨ

Vs. /Adj be thick

- 這根繩子太粗了，要一根細的。
  This rope is too thick. We need a thin one.

醋 cù
ㄘㄨˋ

N vinegar

- 她愛吃酸的，什麼東西都

放醋。
She's fond of sour flavors, and adds vinegar to whatever she eats.

脆 cuì ㄘㄨㄟˋ

Vs. /Adj be crisp

- 這些蘋果又脆又新鮮。
These apples were crisp and fresh.

存 cún ㄘㄨㄣˊ

V to deposit

- Anne一有錢就存銀行裡。
As soon as she gets some money, Anne deposits it in the bank.

存款[1] cúnkuǎn ㄘㄨㄣˊ ㄎㄨㄢˇ

N savings

- 他靠銀行存款生活。
He lives on bank savings.

存款[2] cúnkuǎn ㄘㄨㄣˊ ㄎㄨㄢˇ

V-sep to make deposit

- 我想在儲蓄帳戶裡存款。
I'd like to make a deposit into my savings account.

存摺 cúnzhé ㄘㄨㄣˊ ㄓㄜˊ

N passbook

MY 銀行簿子

- 我會把這筆錢存入你的存摺。
I'll make an entry in your passbook.

★錯 cuò ㄘㄨㄛˋ

Vp wrong

- 這個答案是錯的。
The answer is wrong.

★錯誤 cuòwù ㄘㄨㄛˋ ㄨˋ

N mistake

- 這是學華語的人常犯的錯誤。
It's a common mistake among learners of Chinese.

D

搭 dā ㄉㄚ

V to take (public transport)

- 你上學搭什麼公車？
  What bus do you take to school?
- 我們搭頭班火車到臺北。
  We took the first train to Taipei.

打[1] dǎ ㄉㄚˇ

N a dozen

- 他的雞蛋賣五十元一打。
  His chicken eggs sell for 50 dollars a dozen.

★打[2] dǎ ㄉㄚˇ

V to hit

- 我不小心打到他的手。
  I accidentally hit him on hand.

打敗 dǎbài ㄉㄚˇ ㄅㄞˋ

Vpt to defeat

- 他們二比一打敗我們。
  They defeated us two-one.

打工 dǎgōng ㄉㄚˇ ㄍㄨㄥ

V-sep to do a part-time job

SG 臨時

- 我下課後還要去打工。
  I have to do a part-time job after classes.

打擾 dǎrǎo ㄉㄚˇ ㄖㄠˇ

V to bother

- 他常常問問題來打擾我。
  He always bothers me with questions.

打折 dǎzhé ㄉㄚˇ ㄓㄜˊ

V-sep to give a discount

- 如果你多買，我會給你打折。
  I'll give you a discount if you buy more.

★大 dà ㄉㄚˋ

Vs. /Adj big

- 他們在賺大錢。
  They were earning big money.
- 你現在是個大孩子了。

You're a big boy now.

★ 大便[a] dàbiàn ㄉㄚˋ ㄅㄧㄢˋ

N feces

- 地上有狗大便。
There are some dog feces on the ground.

大便[b] dàbiàn ㄉㄚˋ ㄅㄧㄢˋ

Vi to have a shit

- 我要去大便。
I need to have a shit.

★ 大概[a] dàgài ㄉㄚˋ ㄍㄞˋ

Adv approximately

- 到那裡大概需要半個小時。
It will take approximately half an hour to get there.

★ 大概[b] dàgài ㄉㄚˋ ㄍㄞˋ

Adv roughly

- 這裡大概有一百人。
There were roughly 100 people there.

大號 dàhào ㄉㄚˋ ㄏㄠˋ

N large (size)

- 這種裙子有小號、中號和大號。
The skirt comes in small, medium and large.

★ 大家 dàjiā ㄉㄚˋ ㄐㄧㄚ

N everyone

- 大家都準備好了嗎？
Is everyone ready to go?
- 他報告結束時感謝大家。
He concluded the report by thanking everyone.

大樓 dàlóu ㄉㄚˋ ㄌㄡˊ

N building

- 那棟大樓有三十層高。
That building has thirty floors.

大門 dàmén ㄉㄚˋ ㄇㄣˊ

N main gate

- 他打開大門，走到街上。
He opened the main gate and came to the street.

大名 dàmíng ㄉㄚˋ ㄇㄧㄥˊ

N culture-specific item, a very polite form of request when asking your hearer's name

CN 學名

• 請問您的大名是？
May I ask your name, please?

大聲 dàshēng ㄉㄚˋ ㄕㄥ

Vs. /Adj loud

• 他們在食堂裡大聲交談。
They talked loud in the canteen.

大腿 dàtuǐ ㄉㄚˋ ㄊㄨㄟˇ

N thigh

• 我的大腿很痠。
My thighs were aching.

大小 dàxiǎo ㄉㄚˋ ㄒㄧㄠˇ

N size

• 這些帽子的大小都一樣。
These hats are all of a size.

大學 dàxué ㄉㄚˋ ㄒㄩㄝˊ

N college

• 這所大學的語言教學很不錯。
The college has a good name for languages.

大學生 dàxuéshēng ㄉㄚˋ ㄒㄩㄝˊ ㄕㄥ

N undergraduate

• Mary給大學生講中國文學。
Mary lectures to undergraduates on Chinese literature.

★ 大洋洲 Dàyángzhōu ㄉㄚˋ ㄧㄤˊ ㄓㄡ

N Oceania

• 大洋洲包括太平洋許多島國。
The Oceania includes lots of island-countries of the Pacific Ocean.

★ 帶[a] dài ㄉㄞˋ

V to bring

• 我能帶孩子來嗎？
Can I bring my children with me?

• 沒必要帶這麼多衣服。
It's unnecessary to bring so many clothes.

★ 帶[b] dài ㄉㄞˋ

V to take care of

• 我不在的時候，我的孩子由Anne帶。
Anne took care of my children while I was away.

★ 戴[a] dài ㄉㄞˋ

V to wear (glasses)

- John戴著眼鏡看書。
  John wore glasses for reading.

★ **戴** [b] dài ㄉㄞˋ

V to wear (gloves)

- Mary開車時都戴著手套。
  She wears a pair of gloves when she drives.

★ **戴** [c] dài ㄉㄞˋ

V to wear (hat)

- 太陽很大，你還是戴頂帽子吧！
  You'd better wear a hat in the hot sunlight.

★ **戴** [d] dài ㄉㄞˋ

V to wear (watch)

- Ben戴著一支新的手錶。
  Ben wears a new watch.

大夫 dàifū ㄉㄞˋ ㄈㄨ

N doctor, polite form of address, usually used with the surname of the person you speak/refer to

- 林大夫對病人很有耐心。
  Doctor Lin was very patient with the patients.

★ **袋子** dàizi ㄉㄞˋ ˙ㄗ

N bag

- 袋子底下有番茄。
  There are some tomatoes at the bottom of the bag.
- 我幫你拿幾個袋子吧！
  Let me relieve you of some of your bags.

★ **單** dān ㄉㄢ

Vs-attr single

- Ruth來自單親家庭。
  Ruth comes from a single-parent family.

單人 dānrén ㄉㄢ ㄖㄣˊ

Vs-attr single

- 有帶洗手間的單人房嗎？
  Do you have a single room with bath?

單身 dānshēn ㄉㄢ ㄕㄣ

Vs. /Adj single

- Eva三十歲了，還是單身。
  Eva is 30 years old and still single.

單行道 dānxíngdào ㄉㄢ ㄒㄧㄥˊ ㄉㄠˋ

N one-way street

MY 單向道

- 這是單行道，你不能往回開。
  This is one-way street. You can't turn back.

★ 擔心[1] dānxīn ㄉㄢ ㄒㄧㄣ

Vs-sep be anxious

- 我很擔心會失去工作。
  I'm anxious about losing my job.
- 我們在擔心他們的安全。
  We were anxious about their safety.

擔心[2] dānxīn ㄉㄢ ㄒㄧㄣ

V to worry

- 你不知道我多擔心啊！
  You have no idea how worried I was!
- 她沒來電話，我有點擔心。
  It worried me a bit that she didn't phone.

★ 單子[a] dānzi ㄉㄢ ˙ㄗ

N form

- 麻煩你幫我填這個單子？
  Could you help me to fill in this form?

★ 單子[b] dānzi ㄉㄢ ˙ㄗ

N list

- 把牙膏加進購物單子裡吧！
  Can you add toothpaste to the shopping list?

★ 淡 dàn ㄉㄢˋ

Vs. /Adj be bland (in flavor)

- 這道菜的味道淡了一點。
  The dish is rather bland.

蛋 dàn ㄉㄢˋ

N egg

- 一天吃一顆蛋剛剛好。
  One egg for each day is just enough.

蛋白 dànbái ㄉㄢˋ ㄅㄞˊ

N egg white

- 小孩愛吃蛋白，不愛吃蛋黃。
  Children prefer egg white to yolk.

蛋白質 dànbáizhí ㄉㄢˋ ㄅㄞˊ ㄓˊ

N protein

- 多吃蛋白質，身體會更健康。
  Eat more protein to build you up.

蛋餅 dànbǐng ㄉㄢˋ ㄅㄧㄥˇ

N omelet

- 我早餐喜歡吃蛋餅。
  I like to eat omelet for breakfast.

蛋黃 dànhuáng ㄉㄢˋ ㄏㄨㄤˊ

N yolk

- 把蛋黃打一打，再加牛奶。
  Beat up the yolk and add the milk.

淡季 dànjì ㄉㄢˋ ㄐㄧˋ

N slack season

- 對許多旅館來說，冬天是淡季。
  Winter is the slack season for many hotels.

★但是[a] dànshì ㄉㄢˋ ㄕˋ

Conj but

- 我想學，但是我沒有時間。
  I'd like to learn, but I haven't got the time.

★但是[b] dànshì ㄉㄢˋ ㄕˋ

Conj however

- 我告訴她了，但是她不聽。
  I told her. However, she didn't listen.

★當 dāng ㄉㄤ

V to serve as

- 有時候他在餐廳當服務員。
  Sometimes he served as waiter at a restaurant.

當地 dāngdì ㄉㄤ ㄉㄧˋ

N locality

- 我在當地買了一棟房子。
  I bought a house in the locality.

★當然[1] dāngrán ㄉㄤ ㄖㄢˊ

Adv certainly

- 我當然不會讓他在這裡過夜。
  I'm certainly not going to let him stay overnight.

當然 [2] dāngrán ㄉㄤ ㄖㄢˊ

Reply tag Of course

- 可以教我中文嗎？
  —當然！
  Could you please teach me Chinese? --- Of course!

★ 擋 dǎng ㄉㄤˇ

V to block

- 那輛車擋住出口了。
  The car blocked the exit.

檔案 dǎngàn ㄉㄤˇ ㄢˋ

N file

- 我把他的檔案放回抽屜裡了。
  I put his file back in the drawer.

當 dàng ㄉㄤˋ

V to flunk

- 他上學期被當了三科。
  He flunked three courses last semester.

刀 dāo ㄉㄠ

N knife

- 我需要一把刀來切牛排。
  I need a knife to cut the steak.

刀子 dāozi ㄉㄠ ˙ㄗ

N knife

- Mary用刀子把瓜切成塊。
  Mary used a knife to cut the melon into sections.

★ 倒 dǎo ㄉㄠˇ

Vi to topple over

- 那面牆快倒了。
  That wall is soon going to topple over.
- 暴風雨中，有三棵樹倒了。
  Three trees toppled over in the storm.

★ 到 [1a] dào ㄉㄠˋ

V to arrive

- 你什麼時候到的？
  When did you arrive?

★ 到 [1b] dào ㄉㄠˋ

V to arrive (plus destination)

- 飛機幾點到臺北？
  What time does the plane arrive in Taipei?

★ 到[2] dào
ㄉㄠˋ

Prep to

- 到工業區的路程需要三小時。
  The journey to the industrial area takes three hours.

倒 dào
ㄉㄠˋ

V to pour

- 請給我的杯裡倒些水。
  Please pour some water into my glass.
- Kate在咖啡裡倒了些牛奶。
  Kate poured milk into her coffee.

★ 道 dào
ㄉㄠˋ

M measure word for course of meal

- 那天我們點了五道菜。
  We ordered a five-course meal that day.

到達 dàodá
ㄉㄠˋ ㄉㄚˊ

Vi to arrive

- 火車整點到達。
  The train arrived on time.

★ 地 di
˙ㄉㄧ

Ptc suffix, used to form adverbs, as -ly in English

- 她高興地笑了。
  She smiled happily.

★ 的[a] de
˙ㄉㄜ

Ptc focus particle, showing emphasis

- 我學文學的。
  I studied literature.
- 他去年開始學中文的。
  He started to learn Chinese last year.

★ 的[b] de
˙ㄉㄜ

Ptc particle used for nominalization

- 開車的哪裡去了？
  Where's the driver?
- 裙子，我喜歡黃色的。
  As for skirt, I prefer the yellow one.

★ 的[c] de
˙ㄉㄜ

Ptc possessive marker

- 這是Matt的帽子。
  This is Matt's hat.

★ 得[a] dé
ㄉㄜˊ

V to get

- Ann華語考試得了個甲。
  Ann got a grade A in Chinese.
- 我的胃病就是這麼得的。
  That was how I got my stomach trouble.

★得[b] dé
ㄉㄜˊ

V to obtain

- 他賣房子得了一大筆錢。
  He obtained a large sum of money by selling houses.

★得 de
˙ㄉㄜ

Ptc complement marker, showing degree. Usually omitted in English translation

- Mary唱得很好。
  Mary sings very well.
- John唸得很流利。
  John reads fluently.
- 地板髒得不得了。
  The floor is extremely dirty.

★得[a] děi
ㄉㄟˇ

Vaux to have to

- 我得在三點之前到。
  I have to arrive by three.

★得[b] děi
ㄉㄟˇ

Vaux must

- 她說我們得等一會兒。
  She said we must wait a little while.
- 汽車得讓行人先走。
  Cars must yield to pedestrains.

★燈[a] dēng
ㄉㄥ

N lamp

- 桌子上的燈太亮了。
  The lamp on the table is too bright.

★燈[b] dēng
ㄉㄥ

N light

- 開開燈，好嗎？
  Could you switch the light on, please?
- 這個房間的燈壞了。
  The light in this room is out of order.

登記 dēngjì
ㄉㄥ ㄐㄧˋ

V to register

- 他們是上星期五登記結婚的。
  They registered for marriage last Friday.

★ 等[1] děng
ㄉㄥˇ

V to wait

- 我們需要等很長時間嗎？
  Shall we have long to wait?
- 在附近等我，我很快就回來。
  Wait around for me. I'll be back soon.

★ 等[2a] děng
ㄉㄥˇ

Ptc used for enumeration

- 我去了英國、法國、德國等國家。
  I visited the UK, France, Germany and other countries.

★ 等[2b] děng
ㄉㄥˇ

Ptc used for enumeration, followed by figure

- 我訪問了英、法、德等三個國家。
  I toured three countries: the UK, France and Germany.

★ 等等 děngděng
ㄉㄥˇ ㄉㄥˇ

Ptc etcetera

- 他了解我的生活、工作，等等。
  He knew all about my life, my job, etc.
- 成員多數是經理、律師，等等。
  The members are mostly managers, lawyers, etc.

★ 低 dī
ㄉㄧ

Vs. /Adj be low

- 天花板太低。
  The ceiling is too low.
- 我的數學分數很低。
  My mark in math was very low.

滴[1] dī
ㄉㄧ

M measure for drop of liquid

- 我感覺到有幾滴雨落在頭上。
  I felt a few drops of rain on my head.

滴[2] dī
ㄉㄧ

V to drip

- 雨水從雨傘滴在她的肩膀上。
  Water dripped from the umbrella onto her shoulder.

★ 底 dǐ
ㄉㄧˇ

N bottom

- 這個鍋的底漏了。
  The bottom of the pot leaks.
- 玻璃杯的底是濕的。
  The bottom of the glass is wet.

底下 dǐxià
ㄉㄧˇ ㄒㄧㄚˋ

Adv underneath

- 我的筆在桌子底下。
  My pen goes underneath the table.

底薪 dǐxīn
ㄉㄧˇ ㄒㄧㄣ

N base pay

MY 「基薪」

- 我的工資是底薪加獎金。
  My salary consisted of base pay and bonus.

★ 第 dì
ㄉㄧˋ

Det ordinal prefix, as the suffix -th in English

- 百米比賽中他得到第五名。
  He finished fifth in the 100 metres.

地板 dìbǎn
ㄉㄧˋ ㄅㄢˇ

N floor

- 我看見她在廚房擦地板。
  I found her in the kitchen, scrubbing the floor.

★ 地方 dìfāng
ㄉㄧˋ ㄈㄤ

N place

CN dìfang

- 這就是事故發生的地方。
  This is the place where the accident happened.
- 你好像對這個地方很熟悉。
  You seem to be familiar with this place.

地面 dìmiàn
ㄉㄧˋ ㄇㄧㄢˋ

N ground

- 地面太濕，沒法坐。
  The ground is too wet to sit.

地球 dìqiú
ㄉㄧˋ ㄑㄧㄡˊ

N earth

- 救救我們的地球。
  Save our earth.

地勢 dìshì
ㄉㄧˋ ㄕˋ

N terrain

- 那裡地勢不平，走路小心。
  Take care when you walk on

that terrain, which is rather uneven.

地鐵 dìtiě
ㄉㄧˋ ㄊㄧㄝˇ

N subway

- 地鐵很方便。
The subway is very convenient.

地位 dìwèi
ㄉㄧˋ ㄨㄟˋ

N position

- 婦女的社會地位提高了。
The position of women in society has been improved.

地震 dìzhèn
ㄉㄧˋ ㄓㄣˋ

N earthquake

- 昨天南部地區發生了地震。
An earthquake struck southern region yesterday.

地址 dìzhǐ
ㄉㄧˋ ㄓˇ

N address

- 你搬家的話，把地址寄給我。
Send me an address if you move.

★ 弟弟 dìdi
ㄉㄧˋ ˙ㄉㄧ

N younger brother

- 我得送我弟弟上學。
I have to take my little brother to school.
- Jane一直很想有個弟弟。
Jane had always longed for a brother.

★ 店 diàn
ㄉㄧㄢˋ

N shop

- 前面有一家小店。
There is a small shop ahead.
- 我把雨傘忘在那家書店裡了。
I left my umbrella in that bookshop.

電費 diànfèi
ㄉㄧㄢˋ ㄈㄟˋ

N electricity bill

- 電費你付了嗎？
Have you paid the electricity bill?

★ 電[a] diàn
ㄉㄧㄢˋ

N electricity

- 房租不包括水費、電費。
Fees for water and electricity are not included in the rent.

★ 電[b] diàn ㄉㄧㄢˋ

N power

- 我們已經三天沒有電了。
  We have been out of power for three days.

★ 點[1] diǎn ㄉㄧㄢˇ

V to order (meal)

- 我自己點了咖啡，給她點了茶。
  I ordered myself coffee, and tea for her.
- 他給我們每人點了一份牛排。
  He ordered a beef steak for each of us.

★ 點[2a] diǎn ㄉㄧㄢˇ

N dot

- 你這個字寫錯了，少了一點。
  This character you wrote is incorrect-a dot is missing.

★ 點[2b] diǎn ㄉㄧㄢˇ

N point

- 薪水增長了百分之三點七。
  The salary increased by three point seven percent.

★ 點[3] diǎn ㄉㄧㄢˇ

M measure for o'clock

- 上午十點供應茶和餅乾。
  Tea and biscuits will be provided at 10 o'clock in the morning.

電池 diànchí ㄉㄧㄢˋ ㄔˊ

N battery

- 電池沒電了。
  The battery has run down.

★ 電話[a] diànhuà ㄉㄧㄢˋ ㄏㄨㄚˋ

N call

- Gary給你打過電話。
  There was a call from Gary for you.

★ 電話[b] diànhuà ㄉㄧㄢˋ ㄏㄨㄚˋ

N telephone

- 我可以用一下你的電話嗎？
  May I use your telephone?

★ 電腦 diànnǎo ㄉㄧㄢˋ ㄋㄠˇ

N computer

CN 計算機

- 眞不幸，我的電腦壞了。
Unfortunately my computer was down.
- 我會用電腦打漢字。
I can type Chinese characters on a computer.

電暖器

diànnuǎnqì
ㄉㄧㄢˋ ㄋㄨㄢˇ ㄑㄧˋ

N heater

- 你關掉電暖器了嗎？
Did you turn the heater off?

電器 diànqì ㄉㄧㄢˋ ㄑㄧˋ

N appliance

- 一停電，廚房的電器都沒法用。
None of the kitchen appliances worked when the power went out.

電視 diànshì ㄉㄧㄢˋ ㄕˋ

N television

- 今晚電視演什麼？
What's on television tonight?

電視機 diànshìjī ㄉㄧㄢˋ ㄕˋ ㄐㄧ

N TV set

- 那台電視機很不錯。
That is a nice TV set.

電視台 diànshìtái ㄉㄧㄢˋ ㄕˋ ㄊㄞˊ

N station

- 球賽由哪個電視台直播？
Which station will televise live the game?

電台 diàntái ㄉㄧㄢˋ ㄊㄞˊ

N radio

- 通知已經在電台上公佈。
The announcement was broadcast on radio.

電梯 diàntī ㄉㄧㄢˋ ㄊㄧ

N lift

- 我們乘電梯到了第二十層。
We took the lift to the 20thfloot.

電影 diànyǐng ㄉㄧㄢˋ ㄧㄥˇ

N film
SG MY 戲

- 你最近看過什麼好的電影嗎？
Have you seen any good films recently?

電影院 diànyǐngyuàn
ㄉㄧㄢˋ ㄧㄥˇ ㄩㄢˋ

N cinema

SG MY 戲院

- 那電影正在當地的電影院上映。
  That film is on at the local cinema.

電子 diànzǐ
ㄉㄧㄢˋ ㄗˇ

N electronic

- 他在大學主修電子工程。
  He major in electronic engineer.

電子郵件
diànzǐyóujiàn
ㄉㄧㄢˋ ㄗˇ ㄧㄡˊ ㄐㄧㄢˋ

N e-mail

- 你有消息就發電子郵件給我。
  Send me an e-mail when you have any news.

碟 dié
ㄉㄧㄝˊ

M measure for dish

- Ann給我一碟水果。
  Ann gives me a dish of fruit.

頂樓 dǐnglóu
ㄉㄧㄥˇ ㄌㄡˊ

N top floor

- 頂樓的房間都是空的。
  Rooms at the top floor are vacant.

訂[1] dìng
ㄉㄧㄥˋ

V to order

- 我向那家書店訂了二十本書。
  I've ordered 20 books from that bookshop.

訂[2] dìng
ㄉㄧㄥˋ

V to book

- 我訂了下個月二十日的機票。
  I've booked an air-ticket for the 20th of next month.

釘 dìng
ㄉㄧㄥˋ

V to staple

- 我把名單全釘起來。
  I stapled all the lists together.

訂金 d ìngjīn
ㄉㄧㄥˋ ㄐㄧㄣ

N deposit

- 買這輛車我得付多少訂金？

How much do I have to pay as deposit on the car?

★ 丟 diū ㄉㄧㄡ

V to lose

SG 丟失

- 他丟了那封信。
He lost the letter.

★ 東部 dōngbù ㄉㄨㄥ ㄅㄨˋ

N eastern part

- 東部地勢比較高。
The eastern relief is relatively higher.

★ 東方 dōngfāng ㄉㄨㄥ ㄈㄤ

N The East

- 這種音樂來自東方。
This kind of music originated in the East.

冬季 dōngjì ㄉㄨㄥ ㄐㄧˋ

N winter

- 我喜歡冬季運動，如滑雪。
I love winter sports, such as skiing.

★ 冬天 dōngtiān ㄉㄨㄥ ㄊㄧㄢ

N winter

- 這裡冬天一般會下雪。
It usually snows here in the winter.

★ 東西[a] dōngxi ㄉㄨㄥ ˙ㄒㄧ

N stuff

- 那是什麼東西？
What kind of stuff is that?

★ 東西[b] dōngxi ㄉㄨㄥ ˙ㄒㄧ

N things

- 我沒有看過這種東西。
I've never seen such a thing.

★ 東亞 Dōngyǎ ㄉㄨㄥ ㄧㄚˇ

N East Asia

- 我一直很想到東亞國家旅遊。
I longed to visit East-Asian countries.

★ 懂 dǒng ㄉㄨㄥˇ

Vst to understand

- 我不懂你說什麼？
I don't understand what you are driving at.
- 他希望能多懂點華語。
He wishes he understood Chi-

nese better.

★**動** dòng ㄉㄨㄥˋ

V to move

- 火車開始動了。
  The train began to move.
- 別動我的東西。
  Don't move my things.

★**棟** dòng ㄉㄨㄥˋ

M measure for buildings

MY 座

- 那棟房子去年就被拆掉了。
  The house was pulled down last year.

★**動作**[a] dòngzuò ㄉㄨㄥˋ ㄗㄨㄛˋ

N action

- 打網球得注意手腕動作。
  You should pay attention to your wrist action when playing tennis.

★**動作**[b] dòngzuò ㄉㄨㄥˋ ㄗㄨㄛˋ

N movement

- John用手做了一個向上的動作。
  John made an upward movement with his hand.

★**都** dōu ㄉㄡ

Adv all

- 他們都走了。
  They have all gone.
- 這些答案都對。
  These answers are all right.

豆漿 dòujiāng ㄉㄡˋ ㄐㄧㄤ

N soy milk

SG MY 豆奶

- 我喜歡喝咖啡，但更喜歡喝豆漿。
  I prefer soy milk to coffee.

都市 dūshì ㄉㄨ ㄕˋ

N city

- 在都市生活很便利。
  Living in the city is very convenient.

★**讀** dú ㄉㄨˊ

V to read

- 請跟我讀。
  Please read after me.
- 他讀信的時候顯得很高興。
  His spirits rose as he read the

letter.

讀書 dúshū ㄉㄨˊ ㄕㄨ

V-sep to read book

- 你在讀什麼書？
  What book are you reading?

度 dù ㄉㄨˋ

N degree

- 今天很冷，只有攝氏八度。
  It's very cold today. It's only 8℃.

肚子 dùzi ㄉㄨˋ ˙ㄗ

N stomach

- 我肚子痛。
  My stomach hurts.

★短 duǎn ㄉㄨㄢˇ

Vs. /Adj be short (in length)

- 我女兒留著短頭髮。
  My daughter has short hair.
- 這條街很短，只有十幾棟房子。
  This is a short street, with only a dozen of houses.

短期 duǎnqí ㄉㄨㄢˇ ㄑㄧˊ

N short, only used before noun

- Max上中文短期課程。
  Max's attending a short course on Chinese.

★段 duàn ㄉㄨㄢˋ

M section of

- 這一段路不平，開車小心。
  This section of the road is quite rough, be careful when driving.

★堆 duī ㄉㄨㄟ

M pile of

- 房間裡有一堆髒衣服。
  There is a pile of dirty laundry in the room.

隊 duì ㄉㄨㄟˋ

N team

- 你想不想參加棒球隊？
  Would you like to join the baseball team?

★對[1] duì ㄉㄨㄟˋ

Vs. /Adj be correct

• 你處理的方式是對的。
Your approach is correct.

★ 對[2] duì ㄉㄨㄟˋ

M pair of

• Mary戴著一對漂亮的耳環。
Mary was wearing a pair of beautiful earrings.

★ 對[3a] duì ㄉㄨㄟˋ

Prep for

• 吸菸對你的健康不好。
Smoking is not good for your health.

★ 對[3b] duì ㄉㄨㄟˋ

Prep to

• Kate一直對我很好。
Kate is always nice to me.

• 你對她說了些什麼？
What did you say to her?

★ 對面 duìmiàn ㄉㄨㄟˋ ㄇㄧㄢˋ

N opposite side

• John正坐在我的對面。
John sat directly opposite me.

★ 蹲 dūn ㄉㄨㄣ

Vi to squat

• 這個動作是要先蹲下去，再站起來。
The movement requires squatting down before getting up.

燉 dùn ㄉㄨㄣˋ

V to stew

• 丈夫給妻子燉了一隻雞。
The husband stewed a chicken for his wife.

★ 多[1] duō ㄉㄨㄛ

Vs. /Adj a lot

• 會說中文的人很多。
A lot of people can speak Chinese.

★ 多[2] duō ㄉㄨㄛ

Adv more

• 你感冒了，要多喝水。
You've got a cold, so drink more water.

★ 多少 duōshǎo ㄉㄨㄛ ㄕㄠˇ

N how many

MY 幾多

- 你需要多少？
  How many do you need?

★ 多數 duōshù ㄉㄨㄛ ㄕㄨˋ

N most of

- 班上多數都喜歡運動。
  Most of students in class like sport.

噁心[1] ěxīn ㄜˇ ㄒㄧㄣ

Vs-sep feel like vomiting

- 我的胃不舒服，一直覺得噁心想吐。
  I feel bad in my stomach, and I feel like vomiting.

噁心[2] ěxīn ㄜˇ ㄒㄧㄣ

Vs. /Adj disgusting

- 這部電影看起來很噁心。
  The film is just disgusting.

★ 二 èr ㄦˋ

N two

- 你得坐二路公車。
  You should take bus number two.

兒子 érzi ㄦˊ ˙ㄗ

N son

- 他們有一個兒子和一個女兒。
  They have a son and a daughter.

★ 而且[a] érqiě ㄦˊ ㄑㄧㄝˇ

Conj and also

- 她很會唱歌，而且還會彈鋼琴。
  She sings beautifully, and also plays piano.

★ 而且[b] érqiě ㄦˊ ㄑㄧㄝˇ

Conj moreover

- 房租合理，而且地點很好。
  The rent is reasonable and, moreover, the location is perfect.

★ 耳朵 ěrduō ㄦˇ ˙ㄉㄨㄛ

N ear

- John有一對大耳朵。
  John has big ears.

耳塞 ěrsāi ㄦˇ ㄙㄞ

N earplug

- 如果這裡太吵，你可以戴耳塞睡覺。
  If it's too noisy here, you can

sleep with your earplugs on.

二手 èrshǒu ㄦˋ ㄕㄡˇ

Vs-attr second-hand

- 買二手汽車可能有風險。
Buying a second-hand car can be a risky business.

發燒 fāshāo ㄈㄚ ㄕㄠ

V-sep to run a fever

- 我好像有點發燒。
  I feel as if I'm running a fever.

發生[a] fāshēng ㄈㄚ ㄕㄥ

Vp to happen

- 發生了什麼事？
  What happened?

發生[b] fāshēng ㄈㄚ ㄕㄥ

Vp to take place

- 臺灣發生了許多變化。
  Lots of changes have taken place in Taiwan.

★發現[1] fāxiàn ㄈㄚ ㄒㄧㄢˋ

N discovery

- 這是一項重要的發現。
  This is an important discovery.

★發現[2a] fāxiàn ㄈㄚ ㄒㄧㄢˋ

V to discover

- 她發現了一個新方法。
  She discovered a new method.
- 我在抽屜裡發現了一封信。
  I discovered a letter in the drawer.

發現[2b] fāxiàn ㄈㄚ ㄒㄧㄢˋ

V to find out

- 我們發現他有了女朋友。
  We found out that he had a girlfriend.
- 我發現他們去年已經結婚。
  I found out that they had been married last year.

發炎 fāyán ㄈㄚ ㄧㄢˊ

V-sep to have inflammation

- 我喉嚨有點發炎。
  I have a slight inflammation in my throat.

發展[1] fāzhǎn ㄈㄚ ㄓㄢˇ

N growth

- 這個城市的發展非常快。
  The city's growth has been

very fast.

發展[2] fāzhǎn
ㄈㄚ ㄓㄢˇ

V to develop

- 她的小店發展成爲一家超級市場。
  Her little store has been developed into a supermarket.

罰 fá
ㄈㄚˊ

V to punish

- 誰在這裡抽菸都要罰。
  Anyone caught smoking here will be punished.

罰單 fádān
ㄈㄚˊ ㄉㄢ

N ticket

- 他由於亂停車，收到了罰單。
  He got a ticket for illegal parking.

法律 fǎlǜ
ㄈㄚˇ ㄌㄩˋ

N law

- 我們必須按法律辦事。
  We must act as the law requires.

法學院 fǎxuéyuàn
ㄈㄚˇ ㄒㄩㄝˊ ㄩㄢˋ

N law school

- 他打算到法學院讀書。
  He intended to go to the Law School.

翻 fān
ㄈㄢ

V to flip over

- 把鍋裡的雞蛋翻一下。
  Flip the egg over in the pan.

翻譯[1] fānyì
ㄈㄢ ㄧˋ

N translation

- 他們一星期作一次華語翻譯。
  They do one Mandarin translation a week.

翻譯[2a] fānyì
ㄈㄢ ㄧˋ

V to interpret

- 他們不會說華語，我得翻譯。
  They don't speak Mandarin, so I have to interpret.

翻譯[2b] fānyì
ㄈㄢ ㄧˋ

V to translate

- 她翻譯過很多書。
  She has translated many books.

番茄 fānqié ㄈㄢ ㄑㄧㄝˊ

N tomato

- 這菜裡的番茄太多了。
  There's too much tomato in this dish.

反對 fǎnduì ㄈㄢˇ ㄉㄨㄟˋ

Vst be in opposition to

- John反對我的計畫。
  John was in opposition to my plan.

★飯[a] fàn ㄈㄢˋ

N cooked rice

- 他一連吃了兩碗飯。
  He ate two bowls of rice in a breath.

飯[b] fàn ㄈㄢˋ

N meal

- 她每頓飯都在家裡吃。
  She eats all her meal at home.

飯[c] fàn ㄈㄢˋ

N food

- 小孩在發燒，不想吃飯。
  The child has a fever and he's been off his food.

飯店[a] fàndiàn ㄈㄢˋ ㄉㄧㄢˋ

N restaurant

SG MY 餐館、餐廳

- 這家飯店專做日本菜。
  This restaurant specializes in Japanese cuisine.

飯店[b] fàndiàn ㄈㄢˋ ㄉㄧㄢˋ

N hotel

SG MY 旅店、酒店、旅館

- 請你幫我訂飯店。
  Please make room reservation for me at the hotel.

飯廳 fàntīng ㄈㄢˋ ㄊㄧㄥ

N dining room

- 旅館的飯廳在二樓。
  The dining room of the hotel is on the second floor.

範圍 fànwéi ㄈㄢˋ ㄨㄟˊ

N range

- 我看書的範圍很廣。
  My reading is of a very wide range.

★方便 fāngbiàn ㄈㄤ ㄅㄧㄢˋ

Vs. /Adj convenient

A B C D E F G H J K L M N O P Q R S T W X Y Z X-

- 三點鐘你方便嗎？
  Is three o'clock convenient for you?
- 住在城裡買東西方便。
  With city living, shopping is convenient.
- 搭捷運快，方便而且便宜。
  Traveling by MRT is fast, convenient and cheap.

方法 fāngfǎ ㄈㄤ ㄈㄚˇ

N method

- 我會用不同的方法再試一次。
  I'll try again using a different method.

方面 fāngmiàn ㄈㄤ ㄇㄧㄢˋ

N aspect

- 他在這方面十分好。
  He's really good in this aspect.

★方向 fāngxiàng ㄈㄤ ㄒㄧㄤˋ

N direction

- 你的方向錯了。
  You're in the wrong direction.
- 我們往哪個方向走呢？
  In which direction are we going?
- John看見我便改變了方向。
  On seeing me, John changed direction.

防 fáng ㄈㄤˊ

V be on guard against

- 你得防著他。
  You must be a bit on guard against him.

房東 fángdōng ㄈㄤˊ ㄉㄨㄥ

N landlord

SG 房主

- 他的房東把租金增加了一倍。
  His landlord doubled the rent.

★房間 fángjiān ㄈㄤˊ ㄐㄧㄢ

N room

- 我的房子有五個房間。
  My house has five rooms.
- 我們在七樓，七〇二房間。
  We're on the seventh floor, room 702.
- 這間房間不大，但是很舒服。
  The room is not big, but it's very comfortable.

★

房客 fángkè ㄈㄤˊ ㄎㄜˋ

N tenant

- 檯燈是上一個房客留下來的。
  The table lamp was left by the previous tenant.

房屋 fángwū ㄈㄤˊ ㄨ

N house

- 你喜歡什麼類型的房屋？
  What type of house do you like?

★

房子 fángzi ㄈㄤˊ ˙ㄗ

N house

- Mary進了房子。
  Mary went into the house.
- 他們有錢就買房子。
  They will buy a house once they have the money.
- 這是我們新買的房子。
  This is our newly bought house.

房租 fángzū ㄈㄤˊ ㄗㄨ

N rent

- 請按時付房租。
  Please pay your rent on time.

★

放[a] fàng ㄈㄤˋ

V to release (place)

- 小鳥從籠子放了出來。
  The bird was accidentally released from its cage.

放[b] fàng ㄈㄤˋ

V to place

- 我把牛奶放進冰箱裡。
  I placed the milk in the refrigerator.
- Bob把信放在我面前。
  Bob placed the letter in front of me.
- 她給自己倒了杯茶放在桌上。
  She poured herself a cup of tea and placed it on the table.

放[c] fàng ㄈㄤˋ

V to put

- 菜裡少放點鹽。
  Don’t put too much salt in the dish.
- 你把報紙放在哪裡了？
  Where did you put the newspaper?
- 請在我的可樂裡放些冰塊。

Could you put some ice cubes in my coke?

非 fēi ㄈㄟ

Vs-attr negative prefix, as non- in English

- 非工作人員不能進入辦公室。
  No access for non-employees to the office.

★ 非常 fēicháng ㄈㄟ ㄔㄤˊ

Adv extraordinarily

- 她幹得非常好。
  She did extraordinarily well.
- 我們非常幸運。
  We were extraordinarily lucky.
- 他唱歌的時候聲音非常大。
  He has an extraordinarily loud voice when singing.

★ 非洲 Fēizhōu ㄈㄟ ㄓㄡ

N Africa

- 非洲很大。
  Africa is very big.

飛機 fēijī ㄈㄟ ㄐㄧ

N plane

- 飛機在上午十點起飛。
  The plane is to take off at 10 a.m.

肥 féi ㄈㄟˊ

Vs. /Adj fat

- 這塊肉眞肥。
  This piece of meat has a lot of fat in it.

肥皂 féizào ㄈㄟˊ ㄗㄠˋ

N soap

- 請給我一塊新的肥皂。
  Please give me a new cake of soap.

肺 fèi ㄈㄟˋ

N lungs

- 他長年抽菸，肺受到了損害。
  His lungs were damaged by years of smoking.

費 fèi ㄈㄟˋ

N bound word, for fee

- 我還沒繳註冊費。
  I haven't paid the registration fee yet.

費用[a] fèiyòng ㄈㄟˋ ㄩㄥˋ

N cost

- 臺北的生活費用比較高。
  The cost of living is comparatively high in Taipei.

費用[b] fèiyòng ㄈㄟˋ ㄩㄥˋ

N expenses

- 這筆費用由我們負擔。
  We'll bear the expenses.

分[1] fēn ㄈㄣ

M minute

- 現在是九點十分。
  It's now ten minutes past nine.

分[2] fēn ㄈㄣ

V to divide

- 這本書分成五部分。
  The book is divided into five sections.
- 把全班人分成三個小組。
  Divide the class into three groups.
- 你們打算怎樣分這筆錢？
  How would you like to divide the money?

分店 fēndiàn ㄈㄣ ㄉㄧㄢˋ

N branch

- 這家超級市場在全臺灣都有分店。
  The supermarket has branches all over Taiwan.

分公司 fēngōngsī ㄈㄣ ㄍㄨㄥ ㄙ

N branch company

- 我們在臺南有分公司。
  We have branch company in Tainan.

分機 fēnjī ㄈㄣ ㄐㄧ

N extension

- 你打702分機就能找到我。
  You can get me on extension 702.

★分鐘 fēnzhōng ㄈㄣ ㄓㄨㄥ

N minute

- 幾分鐘後，她回來了。
  She returned a few minutes later.
- 我上班路上要花二十分鐘。
  It takes me 20 minutes to get to work.

A B C D E F G H J K L M N O P Q R S T W X Y Z X-

- 五分鐘不是一段很長的時間。
  Five minutes is not a long time.

分租 fēnzū ㄈㄣ ㄗㄨ

V to share

SG 轉租

- 我和同學分租一層公寓。
  My classmate and I are sharing an apartment.

粉 fěn ㄈㄣˇ

N bound word for powder

- 回家路上記得買點肥皂粉。
  Remember to get some soap powder on your way home.

粉筆 fěnbǐ ㄈㄣˇ ㄅㄧˇ

N chalk

- 我可以要一支粉筆嗎？
  May I have a piece of chalk?

★ 份[a] fèn ㄈㄣˋ

M measure word for document

- 你訂哪一份報紙看？
  What newspaper do you subscribe to?
- 我已經給他們送去一份報告。
  I've sent out a report to them.

份[b] fèn ㄈㄣˋ

M measure word for job

- 我會得到那份工作的。
  I'm going to get that job.
- 她幹這份工作有五年了。
  She's been in the job for five years.

★ 風 fēng ㄈㄥ

N wind

- 風小了。
  The wind is falling.
- 風開始越來越大。
  The wind is beginning to pick up.
- 風把我的帽子吹跑了。
  The wind blew my hat away.

風景 fēngjǐng ㄈㄥ ㄐㄧㄥˇ

N scenery

- 山的風景很好看。
  Mountain scenery is beautiful.

鳳梨 fènglí ㄈㄥˋ ㄌㄧˊ

N pineapple

CN 菠蘿

SG MY 黃梨

• 我們吃新鮮鳳梨當點心。
For dessert, we ate fresh pineapple.

佛 fó ㄈㄛˊ

N Buddha

• 公園裡有一座佛像。
There's a statue representing Buddha in the park.

佛教 fójiào ㄈㄛˊ ㄐㄧㄠˋ

N Buddhism

• 西方國家也信佛教的。
Buddhism is also practiced in Western countries.

敷 fū ㄈㄨ

V to apply

• 護士在他傷口上敷藥。
The nurse applied some remedy to his wound.

★ 扶 fú ㄈㄨˊ

V to hold

• 扶著我，我忽然頭暈。
Hold me, I suddenly feel dizzy.

• 請你幫我扶一下腳踏車。
Could you hold my bicycle for a minute, please?

• 扶好，你呀，火車要開動了。
Hold tight, you! The train is going to start.

★ 幅 fú ㄈㄨˊ

M measure word for paintings

• 她送給我兩幅中國畫。
She gave me two Chinese paintings.

福利 fúlì ㄈㄨˊ ㄌㄧˋ

N welfare

• 政府應多關心人民的福利。
The government should care more about the welfare of the people.

福利社 fúlìshè ㄈㄨˊ ㄌㄧˋ ㄕㄜˋ

N school grocery

SG MY 食堂。HK 小賣部

• 你能到學校福利社幫我買些紙嗎？
Could you stop at the school grocery and pick up some sheets of paper for me?

★ 付 fù ㄈㄨˋ

V to pay

- 這頓午飯誰付錢？
  Who will make payment for lunch?
- 買票的錢我已經付了。
  I've paid for the tickets.
- 你付計程車的錢好嗎？
  Would you mind paying the taxi driver?

副 1a fù ㄈㄨˋ

prefix [rank] assistant

- 生意忙，他就雇一位副經理。
  When the shop is busy, he employs an assistant manager.

副 1b fù ㄈㄨˋ

prefix [rank] deputy

- 他妻子是學校的副校長。
  His wife is the deputy head of the school.

副 1c fù ㄈㄨˋ

prefix [rank] vice

- 她丈夫是醫院的副院長。
  Her husband is a vice-director of the hospital.

副 2a fù ㄈㄨˋ

M measure word for appearance of human being

- Mary那副模樣像她母親。
  Mary has her mother's looks.

副 2b fù ㄈㄨˋ

M measure word for glasses

- Jane戴了一副新眼鏡。
  Jane wore a new pair of sunglasses.

腹部 fùbù ㄈㄨˋ ㄅㄨˋ

N stomach

- 他緊緊按著腹部，因爲很痛。
  He clasped his stomach because it hurt so much.

★ 附近 a fùjìn ㄈㄨˋ ㄐㄧㄣˋ

N nearby

- 你住在附近嗎？
  Do you live nearby?
- 車就停在附近。
  The car is parked nearby.
- 附近有沒有郵局？
  Is there a post office nearby?

附近[b] fùjìn ㄈㄨˋ ㄐㄧㄣˋ

N (in the) neighborhood

- 這附近有好的飯館嗎？
  Are there any good restaurants in the neighborhood?
- 臺北附近的房子相當貴。
  Houses in the neighborhood of Taipei are rather expensive.

★父母 fùmǔ ㄈㄨˋ ㄇㄨˇ

N parents

- 代我向你的父母問好。
  Remember me to your parents.
- 她還跟父母住在一起。
  She's still living with her parents.
- 我父母結婚四十年了。
  My parents have been married for 40 years.

★父親 fùqīn ㄈㄨˋ ㄑㄧㄣ

N father

- 我出生的時候，我父親三十歲。
  My father was 30 years old when I was born.
- 我父親生日，我給他買了領帶。
  I bought my father a tie for his birthday.

★服務[1] fúwù ㄈㄨˊ ㄨˋ

N service

- 我們這裡沒有這種服務。
  We don't offer such service here.
- 我對你們的服務很不滿意。
  I'm very dissatisfied with your service.

★服務[2] fúwù ㄈㄨˊ ㄨˋ

V to serve

- Ron在銀行服務了十年。
  Ron served in the bank for 10 years.
- 我能為大家服務，感到很高興。
  I'm happy to be able to serve you all.

服務生 fúwùshēng ㄈㄨˊ ㄨˋ ㄕㄥ

N waiter

- 那服務生馬上送上我們點的菜。
  The waiter brought our orders at once.

A B C D E F G H J K L M N O P Q R S T W X Y Z X-

副修 fùxiū ㄈㄨˋ ㄒㄧㄡ

V minor

CN 輔修

- Ida主修經濟學，副修華語。
  Ida majored in economy and minored in Mandarin.

複印 fùyìn ㄈㄨˋ ㄧㄣˋ

V to photocopy

- 把支票給我，我要複印一下。
  Give me the check and I'll get it photocopied.

副作用 fùzuòyòng ㄈㄨˋ ㄗㄨㄛˋ ㄩㄥˋ

N side effects

- 這藥對心臟有些副作用。
  The remedy could produce some side effects on the heart.

G

★ **該** gāi ㄍㄞ

Vaux should

- 我該走了。
  I should be leaving.
- 她不該來。
  She should't have come.
- 這時候他們該到臺北了。
  By now they should have reached Taipei.

★ **改** gǎi ㄍㄞˇ

V to correct

- 發現有錯你可以改。
  You can correct any mistakes you may find.
- 她坐著改學生的作業。
  She sat correcting the students' homework.

改善 gǎishàn ㄍㄞˇ ㄕㄢˋ

V to improve

- 她努力改善我們的工作條件。
  She's always trying to improve our working conditions.

蓋 gài ㄍㄞˋ

V to cover

- 蓋上鍋子，燉兩個小時。
  Cover the casserole and stew it for two hours.

蓋子 gàizi ㄍㄞˋ ˙ㄗ

N lid

- 注意蓋上蓋子。
  Make sure the lid is on.

★ **乾** gān ㄍㄢ

Vs. /Adj dry

- 洗的衣服乾了嗎？
  Is the washing dry yet?.
- 等雨傘乾了再收起來。
  Make sure the umbrella is dry-before folding it.
- 頭髮乾了，你才好出去。
  Make sure your hair is dry before you go out.

★ **乾脆** [a] gāncuì ㄍㄢ ㄘㄨㄟˋ

Adv decisive

- Ben辦事很乾脆。

Ben is very decisive in whatever he does.

乾脆[b] gāncuì
ㄍㄢ ㄘㄨㄟˋ

Adv simply

- 他乾脆不承認有這回事。
  He simply denied that such a thing had ever happened.

乾季 gānjì
ㄍㄢ ㄐㄧˋ

N dry season

CN 旱季

- 這個地區開始進入乾季。
  The region began to enter the dry season.

★ 乾淨 gānjìng
ㄍㄢ ㄐㄧㄥˋ

Vs. /Adj clean

CN gānjing

- 臺北街道很乾淨。
  The streets are quite clean in Taipei.
- 這玻璃杯乾淨嗎？
  Is this glass clean?

乾燥 gānzào
ㄍㄢ ㄗㄠˋ

Vs. /Adj be dry

- 北方氣候乾燥。
  The climate of the north is dry.

★ 趕[a] gǎn
ㄍㄢˇ

V to rush

- 我趕在週末之前寫好報告。
  I rushed to finish the report before the weekend.

趕[b] gǎn
ㄍㄢˇ

V to catch up

- 我還有一些工作要趕著做。
  I have some work to catch up on.

趕[c] gǎn
ㄍㄢˇ

V to hurry

- Kate急忙趕回家。
  Kate hurried home.

★ 感覺[1a] gǎnjué
ㄍㄢˇ ㄐㄩㄝˊ

N feeling

- 這僅僅是我個人的感覺。
  That's only my own feeling.
- 我的感覺是我們應該拒絕。
  My feeling is that we should say no.

感覺[1b] gǎnjué
ㄍㄢˇ ㄐㄩㄝˊ

N emotion

- 我對王小姐很有感覺。
  I tend to get emotional with Miss Wang.

★感覺[2] gǎnjué
ㄍㄢˇ ㄐㄩㄝˊ

V to feel

- 你感覺怎麼樣？
  How do you feel?
- 我感覺不舒服。
  I don't feel well.
- 你感覺好些了，我很高興。
  I'm glad you're feeling better.

趕快[a] gǎnkuài
ㄍㄢˇ ㄎㄨㄞˋ

Adv in a hurry

- 他趕快到學校。
  He was in a hurry to go to the school.

趕快[b] gǎnkuài
ㄍㄢˇ ㄎㄨㄞˋ

Adv hurry up

- 時間不多了，我們趕快做。
  Let's hurry up and do it, as time is running out.

感冒 gǎnmào
ㄍㄢˇ ㄇㄠˋ

V-sep to catch cold

- 她感冒好幾天了。
  It has been several days since she caught cold.

★感謝[a] gǎnxiè
ㄍㄢˇ ㄒㄧㄝˋ

V to feel grateful

- 我們非常感謝他們的幫忙。
  We're very grateful of their help.

感謝[b] gǎnxiè
ㄍㄢˇ ㄒㄧㄝˋ

V to appreciate

- 感謝他對我的關心。
  I appreciate his concern for me.

★剛 gāng
ㄍㄤ

Adv just

- 我剛吃完午飯。
  I have just eaten lunch.

★剛才 gāngcái
ㄍㄤ ㄘㄞˊ

Adv just now

- 火車剛才進了站。
  The train entered the station just now.

- 我剛才看見了他們。
  I saw them just now.
- 醫生剛才給我檢查了身體。
  The doctor gave me a medical check just now.

★剛剛[a] gānggāng ㄍㄤ ㄍㄤ

Adv just

- 小孩剛剛睡了。
  The child has just fallen asleep.
- Steve剛剛離開這裡。
  Steve has just left here.

剛剛[b] gānggāng ㄍㄤ ㄍㄤ

Adv a minute ago

- Mary剛剛在這裡。
  Mary was here a minute ago.

鋼琴 gāngqín ㄍㄤ ㄑㄧㄣˊ

N piano

- 我們準備買一架新鋼琴。
  We're buying a new piano.

★高 gāo ㄍㄠ

Vs. /Adj tall

- 他比我高。
  He's taller than me.
- 你跟你父親一樣高。
  You're as tall as your father.
- 這孩子九十公分高。
  This child is 90 cm tall.

高級 gāojí ㄍㄠ ㄐㄧˊ

Vs-attr first-class

- 這家旅館眞高級。
  This hotel is really first-class.

高鐵 gāotiě ㄍㄠ ㄊㄧㄝˇ

N high speed rail

CN 「動車」、「高鐵」

- 我搭高鐵回臺北。
  I returned to Taipei by high speed rail.

★高興 gāoxìng ㄍㄠ ㄒㄧㄥˋ

Vs. /Adj happy

- 我眞爲你高興。
  I'm so happy for you.
- 我很高興來到這裡。
  I'm very happy to be here.
- 他被派到臺灣，高興得很。
  He was extremely happy about being sent to Taiwan.

★告訴 gàosù ㄍㄠˋ ㄙㄨˋ

V to tell

CN gàosu

- 告訴他們別等了。
  Tell them not to wait.
- 也許你應該告訴她。
  Maybe you should tell her.
- 他告訴你姓名了嗎？
  Did he tell you his name?

★ 歌 gē ㄍㄜ

N song

- 請給我們唱一首歌吧。
  Sing us a song, please.
- 你知道那首歌的歌詞嗎？
  Do you know the words to that song?

★ 哥哥 gēge ㄍㄜ ˙ㄍㄜ

N elder brother

- Mary有一個哥哥。
  Mary has an elder brother.

隔壁 gébì ㄍㄜˊ ㄅㄧˋ

N next door

- 我家在這家商店的隔壁。
  We live next door to the shop.

★ 各 gè ㄍㄜˋ

Det each

- 隊裡的各個成員必須下午到。
  Each member of the team must arrive this afternoon.

★ 個 ge ˙ㄍㄜ

M general classifier

- 街上沒幾個人。
  There are few people in the street.
- 替我想一個辦法。
  Think of an idea for me.
- 離這裡只有兩個小時的車程。
  It’s only two hours’ drive from here.

個人 gèrén ㄍㄜˋ ㄖㄣˊ

N personal

- 這件事是我個人的事情。
  This matter is my personal affair.

★ 各位 gèwèi ㄍㄜˋ ㄨㄟˋ

N everyone

- 各位請注意。
  Attentions please, everyone.
- 各位都準備好了，我就開始。
  If everyone is ready, I’ll begin.

A B C D E F G H J K L M N O P Q R S T W X Y Z X-

個性 gèxìng ㄍㄜˋ ㄒㄧㄥˋ

N personality

- 她丈夫個性很強。
  Her husband has a strong personality.

★ 給[1] gěi ㄍㄟˇ

V to give

- 請給我一枝筆。
  Please give me a pen.
- 你可以給我打九折嗎？
  Could you give me a 10% discount?

★ 給[2a] gěi ㄍㄟˇ

Prep to

- 老師留給學生很多作業。
  The teacher assigned a lot of homework to the students.

給[2b] gěi ㄍㄟˇ

Prep for

- 她給我們當翻譯。
  She serves as an interpreter for us.
- Ann給孩子們唱了一首歌。
  Ann sang a song for the children.

★ 跟[1] gēn ㄍㄣ

Conj and

- 我跟她是同事。
  She and I are colleagues.
- 他跟你一起做吧。
  He and you do it together.
- 我跟我太太都是美國人。
  Both my wife and I are Americans.

★ 跟[2] gēn ㄍㄣ

Prep with

- 跟我走吧。
  Come with me.
- 我要跟你談談。
  I want to have a word with you.

★ 跟[3] gēn ㄍㄣ

V to follow

- 貓跟著我進廚房。
  The cat followed me into the kitchen.
- 他們在跟著我們嗎？
  Are they following us?
- 跟著我，我會告訴你怎麼走。
  Follow me and I'll show you the way.

羹 gēng ㄍㄥ

N a kind of thick soup

- 請給我點一個牛肉羹。
  Please order for me a beef thick soup.

★ 更 gèng ㄍㄥˋ

Adv even

- 天更黑了。
  It's getting even darker.
- 這裡晚上更安靜。
  It's even quieter at night.
- 我高，我妹妹更高。
  I'm tall, but my younger sister is even taller.

公佈 gōngbù ㄍㄨㄥ ㄅㄨˋ

V to announce

- 最新的數字將在明天公佈。
  The latest figures will be announced tomorrow.

公車 gōngchē ㄍㄨㄥ ㄔㄜ

N local bus

CN 公交車在大陸指屬於公家的車，政府給官員們配備的車。

SG MY 巴士

- 她搭公車去學校。
  She took the bus to the school.

★ 公尺 gōngchǐ ㄍㄨㄥ ㄔˇ

N meter

CN MY 米

- 小孩才一公尺高。
  The child is just 1 meter tall.
- 出口在前面一百公尺。
  The exit is 100 meters ahead.

★ 公分 gōngfēn ㄍㄨㄥ ㄈㄣ

N centimeter

CN MY 厘米

- 小蟲有兩公分長。
  The insect is two centimeters long.

公關 gōngguān ㄍㄨㄥ ㄍㄨㄢ

N public relations

- 對做生意的人來說，公關很重要。
  Public relations are crucial for businessmen.

★ 公斤 gōngjīn ㄍㄨㄥ ㄐㄧㄣ

N kilogram

- 這個箱子重十公斤。
  The box weighs 10 kilos.

★ 公克 gōngkè ㄍㄨㄥ ㄎㄜˋ

N gram

CN 克

- 這道菜要準備500公克的麵粉。
  500 grams of flour are needed for this dish.

公立 gōnglì ㄍㄨㄥ ㄌㄧˋ

Vs-attr public

- 他在公立醫院當醫生。
  He's a doctor in public hospital.

★ 公里 gōnglǐ ㄍㄨㄥ ㄌㄧˇ

N kilometer

- 離臺北大約一百公里。
  It's about 100 km from Taipei.

公路 gōnglù ㄍㄨㄥ ㄌㄨˋ

N road

- 房子離公路有一段距離。
  The house stands back from the road.

公司 gōngsī ㄍㄨㄥ ㄙ

N company

- 你在哪家公司上班？
  Which company do you work for?

公務員 gōngwùyuán ㄍㄨㄥ ㄨˋ ㄩㄢˊ

N government employee

- 他打算畢業後當公務員。
  He wants to be a government employee after he graduated.

公演 gōngyǎn ㄍㄨㄥ ㄧㄢˇ

Vi to give a performance in public

- 我們正在準備系上的畢業公演。
  Our department is preparing to give a performance in public on graduation day.

公寓 gōngyù ㄍㄨㄥ ㄩˋ

N apartment

- 她住在學校附近的公寓。
  She lives in an apartment close to the campus.

公園 gōngyuán ㄍㄨㄥ ㄩㄢˊ

N park

- 我把孩子們帶到公園去了。
  I took the kids to the park.

工廠 gōngchǎng ㄍㄨㄥ ㄔㄤˇ

N factory

- 他在這裡擁有幾家家具工廠。
He owned several furniture factories here.

工讀生 gōngdúshēng ㄍㄨㄥ ㄉㄨˊ ㄕㄥ

N part-time student

CN 實習生

- 這家公司在徵工讀生。
The company is recruiting part-time students.

工具 gōngjù ㄍㄨㄥ ㄐㄩˋ

N tool

- 我在車後放一套工具。
I keep a set of tools in the back of my car.

工人 gōngrén ㄍㄨㄥ ㄖㄣˊ

N worker

- 工廠僱用了七百個工人。
The plant employed 700 workers.

工作[1] gōngzuò ㄍㄨㄥ ㄗㄨㄛˋ

N job

- 你喜歡自己的工作嗎？
Do you enjoy your job?

工作[2] gōngzuò ㄍㄨㄥ ㄗㄨㄛˋ

V to work

- 你一天工作幾小時？
How many hours do you work a day?

功課 gōngkè ㄍㄨㄥ ㄎㄜˋ

N school assignment

- 他總是覺得功課難做。
He always finds school assignment hard.

恭喜 gōngxǐ ㄍㄨㄥ ㄒㄧˇ

V congratulation

- 恭喜你得了一等獎。
Congratulations on your first prize.

狗 gǒu ㄍㄡˇ

N dog

- 我養了一條狗。
I keep a dog.

夠[1] gòu ㄍㄡˋ

Vs-pred adequate

- 如果要翻譯，他的中文能力還不夠。
His abilities in Chinese aren't

adequate to do translation works yet.

- 她買的保險不夠。
She wasn't adequately insured.

夠[2] gòu ㄍㄡˋ

complement sufficiently

- 人人都吃夠了。
Everybody ate sufficiently.

姑姑 gūgū ㄍㄨ ㄍㄨ

N aunt (father's sisters)

- 我姑姑的興趣是種花。
My aunt was interested in growing flowers.

骨頭 gútou ㄍㄨˊ ˙ㄊㄡ

N bone

CN gǔtou

- 狗喜歡吃骨頭。
All dogs love bones.

古代 gǔdài ㄍㄨˇ ㄉㄞˋ

N ancient time

- Grace對中國古代音樂有興趣。
Grace's interested in Chinese music of ancient time.

古蹟 gǔjī ㄍㄨˇ ㄐㄧ

N antiquities

CN gǔjì

- 我們參觀了幾處古蹟。
We've visited several of the antiquities.

顧客 gùkè ㄍㄨˋ ㄎㄜˋ

N customer

- 對我們來說，顧客第一。
For us, our customers come first.

故事 gùshì ㄍㄨˋ ㄕˋ

N story

- 我母親很會編故事。
My mother is good at making up stories.

★掛 guà ㄍㄨㄚˋ

V to hang up

- 把你的外套掛在衣櫥裡。
Hang your jacket up in the closet.

掛號 guàhào ㄍㄨㄚˋ ㄏㄠˋ

V-sep be registered

- 這封信應該掛號。

This letter should be registered.

掛號信 guàhàoxìn ㄍㄨㄚˋ ㄏㄠˋ ㄒㄧㄣˋ

N registered letter

- 我剛收到公司的一封掛號信。
  I just got a registered letter from my company.

★怪 guài ㄍㄨㄞˋ

Vs. /Adj strange

- 他的華語發音很怪。
  His pronunciation of Mandarin is very strange.

★關 guān ㄍㄨㄢ

V to close

- 請關門。
  Please close the door.

關節 guānjié ㄍㄨㄢ ㄐㄧㄝˊ

N joint

- 我全身關節都痛。
  I ache all over at every joint.

關係[a] guānxì ㄍㄨㄢ ㄒㄧˋ

N relation

- 這兩件事沒有關係。
  These two matters bear no relation to each other.

關係[b] guānxì ㄍㄨㄢ ㄒㄧˋ

N relationship

- 我和同事關係很好。
  I have quite a good relationship with my colleagues.

★關心 guānxīn ㄍㄨㄢ ㄒㄧㄣ

Vs-sep be concerned with

- 他們對這些事並不關心。
  They don't concern themselves with such things.

★關於[a] guānyú ㄍㄨㄢ ㄩˊ

Prep about

- 她的書是關於鄉村生活的。
  Her books are about village life.
- 我們談了許多關於孩子的事。
  We talked plenty about our kids.

關於[b] guānyú ㄍㄨㄢ ㄩˊ

Prep with regard to

• 關於下星期的會，我知道的很少。
I know little with regard to the meeting next week.

館 guǎn ㄍㄨㄢˇ

N bound word, institution of public interest

• 我星期日要參觀科學館。
I have to visit the Science Museum on Sunday.

管理[1] guǎnlǐ ㄍㄨㄢˇ ㄌㄧˇ

N management

• 公司的失敗是由於管理不好。
The company's failure was due to bad management.

管理[2] guǎnlǐ ㄍㄨㄢˇ ㄌㄧˇ

V to supervise

• 他管理一千多名員工。
He supervises a staff of more than 1000.

管理費 guǎnlǐfèi ㄍㄨㄢˇ ㄌㄧˇ ㄈㄟˋ

N management fee
CN 物業費

• 她住的地方不需要繳管理費。
The place she lives is exempt from management fee.

管理員 guǎnlǐyuán ㄍㄨㄢˇ ㄌㄧˇ ㄩㄢˊ

N keeper

• 你可以向宿舍管理員借拖把。
You can ask the housekeeper for a mop.

冠軍 guànjūn ㄍㄨㄢˋ ㄐㄩㄣ

N champion

• Ted當時是網球冠軍。
Ted was tennis champion at that time.

光 guāng ㄍㄨㄤ

N light

• 別擋我的光。
Don't stand in my light.

光臨 guānglín ㄍㄨㄤ ㄌㄧㄣˊ

N polite form for requesting someone's presence

• 我們期待你的光臨。
We're looking forward to seeing you on that occasion.

光線 guāngxiàn ㄍㄨㄤ ㄒㄧㄢˋ

N light

• 這房間光線很差。
The light in this room is poor.

廣播 guǎngbò ㄍㄨㄤˇ ㄅㄛˋ

Vi to broadcast

• 這條新聞將在晚上八點廣播。
This information will be broadcast at 8 p.m.

逛 guàng ㄍㄨㄤˋ

V to stroll

• 一起去逛夜市吧？
How about a stroll down the night market?

逛街 guàngjiē ㄍㄨㄤˋ ㄐㄧㄝ

V-sep to stroll around the streets
MY 走街

• 我假日喜歡去逛街。
I enjoy strolling along on holiday.

貴 guì ㄍㄨㄟˋ

Vs-attr expensive

• 太貴了，我買不起。
It's too expensive, I can't afford it.

★ 跪 guì ㄍㄨㄟˋ

V to kneel down

• 她跪下擦地。
She knelt down and began to mop the floor.

櫃 guì ㄍㄨㄟˋ

N bound word for cabinet
MY 櫥

• 她有一個很大的鞋櫃。
She has a very big shoe cabinet.

貴賓 guìbīn ㄍㄨㄟˋ ㄅㄧㄣ

N guest of honour

• 他是晚會上的貴賓。
He was guest of honour at the evening party.

規定¹ guīdìng ㄍㄨㄟ ㄉㄧㄥˋ

N stipulation

• 按照規定，計畫要在一年內完成。
According to the stipulation, the project should be finished in a year.

規定² guīdìng ㄍㄨㄟ ㄉㄧㄥˋ

V to stipulate

- 學校規定學生必須在九月前註冊。
  The school stipulates that students must be registered before September.

櫃檯 guìtái ㄍㄨㄟˋ ㄊㄞˊ

N counter

- 請你到九號櫃檯付錢。
  Could you pay at the counter no. 9, please?

★櫃子 guìzi ㄍㄨㄟˋ ˙ㄗ

N cabinet

- 我把文件都存放在櫃子裡。
  I keep all my papers in the cabinet.

鍋 guō ㄍㄨㄛ

N pan

- 她往鍋裡打了一個雞蛋。
  She cracked an egg into the pan.

鍋貼 guōtiē ㄍㄨㄛ ㄊㄧㄝ

N fried dumpling

- 午餐吃鍋貼，好嗎？
  Shall we have fried dumplings for lunch?

鍋子 guōzi ㄍㄨㄛ ˙ㄗ

N pots and pans

CN 鍋

- 廚房裡有各種鍋子。
  There are all sort of pots and pans in the kitchen.

國[a] guó ㄍㄨㄛˊ

N bound word for country

- 中國和美國都是世界上的大國。
  China, as well as USA are two big countries in the world.

國[b] guó ㄍㄨㄛˊ

N bound word for nation

- 這條新聞會向全國廣播。
  The statement will be broadcasted to the nation.

國際 guójì ㄍㄨㄛˊ ㄐㄧˋ

Vs-attr international

- 英文是國際語言。
  English is an international language.

國家 guójiā ㄍㄨㄛˊ ㄐㄧㄚ

N country

• 你來自哪個國家？
What country do you come from?

國立 guólì ㄍㄨㄛˊ ㄌㄧˋ

Vs-attr national

• 我畢業於國立大學。
I graduated from a national university.

國語 guóyǔ ㄍㄨㄛˊ ㄩˇ

N national language, term used specially in Taiwan, equal to Mandarin Chinese in general

CN 普通話

SG 華語

• 我在臺北買了一本國語辭典。
I bought a dictionary of Mandarin Chinese in Taipei.

果汁 guǒzhī ㄍㄨㄛˇ ㄓ

N fruit juice

• 六盒果汁應該夠了。
Six cartons of fruit juice should suffice.

★過 guò ㄍㄨㄛˋ

Ptc aspect marker (experiencer)

• 你去過法國嗎？
Have you been to France?

• Jane以前當過秘書。
Jane was once a secretary.

• Nick從來沒生過病。
Nick has never been ill.

★過 guò ㄍㄨㄛˋ

V to pass

• 我天天從你家門口過。
I pass by your home every day.

過敏 guòmǐn ㄍㄨㄛˋ ㄇㄧㄣˇ

Vp-sep allergic

• 我對花過敏。
I'm allergic to flowers.

H

★ 還 hái
ㄏㄞˊ

Adv still

- 你還在這裡嗎？
Are you still here?
- 我還得去三次。
I still have to go three more times.
- 我還要吃這個藥嗎？
Do I still need to take this medicine?

海報 hǎibào
ㄏㄞˇ ㄅㄠˋ

N poster

- 我看到了一張音樂會的海報。
I noticed a poster advertising a concert.

海邊 hǎibiān
ㄏㄞˇ ㄅㄧㄢ

N by the sea

- 我們在海邊度週末。
We spent our week-end by the sea.

★ 還是 háishì
ㄏㄞˊ ㄕˋ

Adv still

- 今天還是她當我們的翻譯。
She's still our interpreter today.
- 如果能安排，我還是希望你來。
If arrangements could be made, I still hope you will come.

還有[a] háiyǒu
ㄏㄞˊ ㄧㄡˇ

Conj and also

- John有兩個兄弟，還有一個姊姊。
John has two brothers, and also a sister.

還有[b] háiyǒu
ㄏㄞˊ ㄧㄡˇ

Conj as well as

- 他會說中文、英文，還有德文。
He can speak Chinese, English, as well as German.

★ 孩子 háizi
ㄏㄞˊ ˙ㄗ

N child

- 這孩子學東西很快。
  This child is quick to learn.

children

- 孩子長大就要獨立。
  When children grow up, they need to be independent.

害羞 hàixiū
ㄏㄞˋ ㄒㄧㄡ

Vs. /Adj shy

- 他太害羞了，不敢邀請她跳舞。
  He was too shy to ask her to dance with him.

寒冷 hánlěng
ㄏㄢˊ ㄌㄥˇ

Vs. /Adj frigid

- 一月份天氣很寒冷。
  The weather in January is quite frigid.

寒流 hánliú
ㄏㄢˊ ㄌㄧㄡˊ

N cold current

- 寒流來了，小心著涼。
  Here comes the cold current. Mind you don't catch a cold.

汗 hàn
ㄏㄢˋ

N sweat

- John滿臉是汗。
  John's face was running with sweat.

漢字 hànzì
ㄏㄢˋ ㄗˋ

N Chinese character

SG MY 華文字、中文字

- 信封上寫的是漢字。
  The envelope was written in Chinese characters.

行[a] háng
ㄏㄤˊ

N trade

- 你做哪一行都必須有耐心。
  Patience is required for all trade you are in.

行[b] háng
ㄏㄤˊ

N line

- 他們排成了三行。
  They fall into three lines.

航空 hángkōng
ㄏㄤˊ ㄎㄨㄥ

N airline

- 你搭哪家航空？
  Which airline do you fly?

航空信 hángkōngxìn
ㄏㄤˊ ㄎㄨㄥ ㄒㄧㄣˋ

N airmail

- 你寄的航空信明天就會到。
  The airmail sent by you will arrive tomorrow.

★ 好[a] hǎo ㄏㄠˇ

Vs. /Adj good

- 我們是好朋友。
  We're good friends.
- 教華語是個好職業。
  Teaching Mandarin is a good occupation.
- 你聽到那好消息了嗎？
  Have you heard the good news?

好[b] hǎo ㄏㄠˇ

Vs. /Adj so as to

- 戴上眼鏡吧，好看得更清楚。
  Put your glasses on, so as to read more clearly.

好[c] hǎo ㄏㄠˇ

Vs. /Adj easy

- 華語好學嗎？
  Is Mandarin easy to learn?
- 這個問題好解決。
  The problem can be easily solved.
- 這本書可不好買。
  This book is not easily available.

★ 好吃 hǎochī ㄏㄠˇ ㄔ

Vs. /Adj delicious

- 那咖哩雞好吃極了。
  That's a delicious chicken curry.

★ 好看 hǎokàn ㄏㄠˇ ㄎㄢˋ

Vs. /Adj good-looking

- 這個便宜，而且好看。
  This one is cheap and also good-looking.

★ 好聽 hǎotīng ㄏㄠˇ ㄊㄧㄥ

Vs. /Adj pleasant (to the ears)

- 這首歌好聽。
  This is a very pleasant song.

好玩 hǎowán ㄏㄠˇ ㄨㄢˊ

Vs. /Adj fun

CN hǎo wánr

- 去海灘一定好玩。
  A trip to the beach would be fun.

好像[a] hǎoxiàng
ㄏㄠˇ ㄒㄧㄤˋ

Adv seemingly

- 他好像沒注意到天在下雨。
  He was seemingly oblivious to the rain.

好像[b] hǎoxiàng
ㄏㄠˇ ㄒㄧㄤˋ

Adv apparently

- 你好像沒聽懂上課內容。
  You apparently did not understand the instructions.

★號碼 hàomǎ
ㄏㄠˋ ㄇㄚˇ

N number

- 你的座位號碼是多少？
  What's your seat number?

★喝 hē
ㄏㄜ

V to drink

- 我不常喝茶。
  I don't drink often.
- Sam吃飯的時候喝了些酒。
  Sam drank some wine with dinner.
- 你一天應當儘量喝一公升水。
  You should try to drink a liter of water a day.

★河 hé
ㄏㄜˊ

N river

- 這條河太寬，我游不過去。
  The river is too broad, I can't swim across it.

★和 hàn
ㄏㄢˋ

Conj and

- 我和她都在學華語。
  She and I are both learning Mandarin.

合約 héyuē
ㄏㄜˊ ㄩㄝ

N contract

CN SG MY 合同

- 租房子要注意合約內容。
  Pay attention to the terms of the contract when renting a house.

合租 hézū
ㄏㄜˊ ㄗㄨ

V to share

- Ron跟他們合租一個套房。
  Ron shares an apartment with them.

★ **黑** hēi ㄏㄟ

Vs. /Adj black

- 他養了一隻黑狗。
  He keeps a black dog.
- 我買了一雙黑鞋子。
  I bought a pair of black shoes.
- 那些照片是黑白的。
  Those photos are black and white.

黑板 hēibǎn ㄏㄟ ㄅㄢˇ

N blackboard

- 請在黑板上寫下你的答案。
  Please write down your answers on the blackboard.

★ **很** hěn ㄏㄣˇ

Adv very

- 這裡很少下雪。
  It doesn't snow very often.

★ **紅** hóng ㄏㄨㄥˊ

Vs. /Adj red

- 顏色是紅的。
  The colour is red.

紅茶 hóngchá ㄏㄨㄥˊ ㄔㄚˊ

N black tea

- 中國人喝紅茶，不加糖和牛奶。
  The Chinese don't put sugar or milk in their black tea.

紅酒 hóngjiǔ ㄏㄨㄥˊ ㄐㄧㄡˇ

N red wine

- 我睡前習慣喝一杯紅酒。
  I'm used to drinking a glass of red wine before going to bed.

紅燒 hóngshāo ㄏㄨㄥˊ ㄕㄠ

V to braise in soy sauce

- 我們做紅燒魚吧。
  Let's braise the fish in soy sauce.

猴子 hóuzi ㄏㄡˊ ˙ㄗ

N monkey

- 在動物園裡看猴子很有趣。
  It is fun to watch the monkeys at the zoo.

喉嚨 hóulóng ㄏㄡˊ ㄌㄨㄥˊ

N throat

CN hóu long

- 一根魚骨頭卡在他喉嚨

裡。
A fish bone was stuck in his throat.

★ 厚 hòu ㄏㄡˋ

Vs. /Adj thick

- 這本書又厚又重。
  The book is both thick and heavy.
- 這塊木板十公分厚。
  This plank is 10 cm thick.

★ 後 hòu ㄏㄡˋ

N behind

- 他跑在前，我們緊跟在後。
  He was in the lead and we followed close behind.

★ 後來 hòulái ㄏㄡˋ ㄌㄞˊ

Adv later

- 後來，她找到一份教師的工作。
  Later, she got a job as a teacher.

★ 後面 hòumiàn ㄏㄡˋ ㄇㄧㄢˋ

N back

CN hòumian

- Mary在後面。
  Mary is in the back.
- 後面還有座位。
  There are vacant seats at the back.
- 請在支票後面簽字。
  Please sign on the back of the check.

★ 後年 hòunián ㄏㄡˋ ㄋㄧㄢˊ

N the year after next

- 她今年三歲，後年就五歲了。
  She's 3 this year, and she'll be 5 the year after next.

★ 後天 hòutiān ㄏㄡˋ ㄊㄧㄢ

N the day after tomorrow

- 我們後天見。
  I'll see you the day after tomorrow.

後頭[a] hòutou ㄏㄡˋ ˙ㄊㄡ

N behind

- 我排在她的後頭。
  I stood behind her in line.

後頭[b] hòutou ㄏㄡˋ ˙ㄊㄡ

N back

• 我們坐在公車的後頭。
We sat in the back of the bus.

候補 hòubǔ ㄏㄡˋ ㄅㄨˇ

Vi standby

• 我們可以讓你後補。
We can put you on standby.

呼吸 hūxī ㄏㄨ ㄒㄧ

V to breathe

• 這裡太悶了，我幾乎沒法呼吸。
It's so airless in here, I can hardly breathe.

壺 1 hú ㄏㄨˊ

M pitcher of

• 她給我們泡了一壺茶。
She made a pitcher of tea for us.

壺 2 hú ㄏㄨˊ

N kettle

• 壺裡還有水嗎？
Is there any water left in the kettle?

湖 hú ㄏㄨˊ

N lake

• 他們在湖上划船。
They're boating on the lake.

護士 hùshì ㄏㄨˋ ㄕˋ

N nurse

• Kate是醫院兒童病房的護士。
Kate works as a nurse in the children's ward at the hospital.

護照 hùzhào ㄏㄨˋ ㄓㄠˋ

N passport

• 護照要隨時帶在身上。
A passport should be carried with you at all times.

戶頭 hùtóu ㄏㄨˋ ㄊㄡˊ

N bank account

SG MY 戶口

• 我在當地銀行開了個戶頭。
I've opened a bank account with a local bank.

★ 花 huā ㄏㄨㄚ

N flower

• 花開了。
The flower has blossomed.

• Ann戴著一朵花。
Ann is wearing a flower.

華氏 huáshì ㄏㄨㄚˊ ㄕˋ

N fahrenheit

• 這是攝氏還是華氏溫度？
Is it the temperature in Celsius or in Fahrenheit?

畫[1] huà ㄏㄨㄚˋ

N drawing

• 在比賽中他的畫得了第一名。
His drawing won first place in the contest.

畫[2] huà ㄏㄨㄚˋ

V to paint

• 門上畫了一棵綠樹。
A green tree was painted on the door.

話 huà ㄏㄨㄚˋ

N word

• 這種話你不能說。
You can't say such word.

• 我想跟你講句話。
I want to have a word with you.

★壞[a] huài ㄏㄨㄞˋ

Vp bad

• 我剛拔了一顆壞牙。
I've just had a bad tooth out.

• 壞事可以變成好事。
Bad things can be turned to good things.

• 多數人不喜歡壞消息。
Most people don't like bad news.

壞[b] huài ㄏㄨㄞˋ

Vp evil

• 這些都是壞主意！
All these are evil thoughts!

歡迎 huānyíng ㄏㄨㄢ ㄧㄥˊ

V welcome

• 我們都歡迎你來。
We all welcome you to come.

還 huán ㄏㄨㄢˊ

V to return

• 我得還你那本書。
I must return that book to you.

環境 huánjìng ㄏㄨㄢˊ ㄐㄧㄥˋ

N environment

- 我們有一個很好的學習環境。
We have an excellent learning environment.

★換 huàn ㄏㄨㄢˋ

V to exchange

- 她到銀行換美元去了。
She went to the bank to exchange US dollars.
- 我想換件尺寸較小的襯衫。
I'd like to exchange this shirt for a smaller one.

★黃 huáng ㄏㄨㄤˊ

Vs. /Adj yellow

- 那足球隊員剛領了一張黃牌。
That footballer just got a yellow card.

★回 huí ㄏㄨㄟˊ

Vi to return (place)

- 你什麼時候回國？
When are you returning to your native country?

回教 huíjiào ㄏㄨㄟˊ ㄐㄧㄠˋ

N Islam

- 我信回教。
I believe in Islam.

回收 huíshōu ㄏㄨㄟˊ ㄕㄡ

V recycle

- 我們回收罐、瓶子和紙張。
We recycle cans, bottles and paper.

會[a] huì ㄏㄨㄟˋ

Vaux be able to

- 我一直想學會講華語。
I've always wanted to be able to speak Chinese.

會[b] huì ㄏㄨㄟˋ

Vaux can

- 你會游泳，是吧？
You can swim, can't you?

匯 huì ㄏㄨㄟˋ

V to remit

- 他給女兒匯了五千美元。
He remitted $5000 USD to his daughter.

燴飯 huìfàn ㄏㄨㄟˋ ㄈㄢˋ

N stewed rice

- 我媽媽做的牛肉燴飯很好吃。
  My Mum's beef stewed rice is really delicious.

會話 huìhuà ㄏㄨㄟˋ ㄏㄨㄚˋ

N conversation

- 他們教華語不注重會話。
  They teach Chinese but do not emphasize conversation.

匯率 huìlǜ ㄏㄨㄟˋ ㄌㄩˋ

N exchange rate

SG 交換率

- 那裡你可以得到較高的匯率。
  You can get a more favourable exchange rate there.

葷 hūn ㄏㄨㄣ

N meat dish

- 她信佛，不吃葷。
  She's a believer in Buddhism, and avoids meat dishes.

婚假 hūnjià ㄏㄨㄣ ㄐㄧㄚˋ

N wedding leave

- 公司同意她請婚假。
  The company has granted her a wedding leave.

婚禮 hūnlǐ ㄏㄨㄣ ㄌㄧˇ

N wedding

- 她的婚禮是在星期天。
  Her wedding is on Sunday.

活 huó ㄏㄨㄛˊ

Vs. /Adj live

- 她從市場買回一隻活雞。
  She brought home a live chicken from the market.

活動 huódòng ㄏㄨㄛˊ ㄉㄨㄥˋ

N activity

- 今天學校裡有許多活動。
  There has been a lot of activity in the school today.

活潑 huópō ㄏㄨㄛˊ ㄆㄛ

Vs. /Adj lively

- 這孩子真活潑。
  The child is very lively.

★ 火 huǒ ㄏㄨㄛˇ

N fire

- 房子著火了。
The house is on fire.
- 狗怕火。
Dogs are afraid of fire.

火車 huǒchē ㄏㄨㄛˇ ㄔㄜ

N train

- 這列火車開往臺北。
The train is bound for Taipei.

火鍋 huǒguō ㄏㄨㄛˇ ㄍㄨㄛ

N hot pot

- 我們冬天最喜歡吃的是火鍋。
Our favourite winter dish is hot pot.

火災 huǒzāi ㄏㄨㄛˇ ㄗㄞ

N fire

- 小心火災。
Beware of fire.

或 huò ㄏㄨㄛˋ

Conj or

- 我明天或後天會來。
I'll come tomorrow or the day after tomorrow.

★ 或是 huòshì ㄏㄨㄛˋ ㄕˋ

Conj or, used in an interrogative

- 你想要藍色、黃色或是紅色的？
What do you want, blue, yellow or red?

貨 huò ㄏㄨㄛˋ

N goods

- 我訂了一批貨。
I contracted for a batch of goods.

J

機 jī ㄐㄧ

N bound word for machine

- 洗衣機正在大減價。
  Washing-machines are on sale.

機車 jīchē ㄐㄧ ㄔㄜ

N scooter

CN SG 摩托車

- 騎機車上班很方便。
  It's very convenient to go to work by scooter.

★機會 jīhuì ㄐㄧ ㄏㄨㄟˋ

N opportunity

CN jīhui

- 她沒給我說話的機會。
  She didn't give me an opportunity to speak.
- 這個機會太好了，可別錯過。
  It was too good an opportunity to miss.

機票 jīpiào ㄐㄧ ㄆㄧㄠˋ

N flight ticket

- 請確定你帶了護照和機票。
  Check that you have your passport and fight ticket with you.

機械 jīxiè ㄐㄧ ㄒㄧㄝˋ

N machine

- 他對機械很有興趣。
  He is very interested in machine.

雞 jī ㄐㄧ

N chicken

- 這隻雞看起來比那隻肥。
  This chicken looks fatter than that one.

雞排 jīpái ㄐㄧ ㄆㄞˊ

N fried chicken breast

- 雞排好吃，但是不要吃得太多。
  Fried chicken breast is delicious, but don't eat them too much.

雞肉 jīròu ㄐㄧ ㄖㄡˋ

N chicken (meat)

- 我愛吃白肉，像雞肉。
  I love white meat, such as chicken.

肌肉 jīròu ㄐㄧ ㄖㄡˋ

N muscle

- Ted有強壯的肌肉。
  Ted has big muscles.

基督教 jīdūjiào ㄐㄧ ㄉㄨ ㄐㄧㄠˋ

N Christianity

- 這是個關於基督教的宗教班。
  This is a religion class on Christianity.

積極 jījí ㄐㄧ ㄐㄧˊ

Vs. /Adj be motivated

- 他們工作努力，十分積極。
  They are hardworking and highly motivated.

★ 急 jí ㄐㄧˊ

Vs. /Adj hasty

- 我們別急，坐一會兒。
  Let's not be hasty --- sit down for a moment.

急性 jíxìng ㄐㄧˊ ㄒㄧㄥˋ

Vs-attr acute

- Bob得了急性肝炎。
  Bob has an acute attack of hepatitis.

急診 jízhěn ㄐㄧˊ ㄓㄣˇ

N emergency treatment

- Ken受了傷，被送去醫院急診。
  Ken was injured and was sent to hospital for emergency treatment.

★ 極了 jíle ㄐㄧˊ ˙ㄌㄜ

Adv extremely, used with Vs

- 這兩天我忙極了。
  I'm extremely busy these days.
- 他第一次當父親，高興極了。
  Becoming a father for the first time, he was extremely delighted.

吉他 jítā ㄐㄧˊ ㄊㄚ

N guitar

- Jane很會彈吉他。
  Jane plays the guitar very well.

★幾 jǐ ㄐㄧˇ

N how many

- 你能在這裡住幾天？
  How many days can you stay here?
- 你們每星期去那裡幾次？
  How many times do you go there every week?

★記 jì ㄐㄧˋ

V to record

- 我記下他的電話號碼。
  I've recorded his phone number.

寄 jì ㄐㄧˋ

V to post

- 我要寄這封信去香港。
  I want to post this letter to Hong Kong.

繫 jì ㄐㄧˋ

V to tie

- 她在禮物上繫了一條紅絲帶。
  She tied a red ribbon around the present.

★計畫 jìhuà ㄐㄧˋ ㄏㄨㄚˋ

N plan

- 我們同意他們的計畫。
  We advocate their plans.

★計劃 jìhuà ㄐㄧˋ ㄏㄨㄚˋ

V to plan

- 我們計劃週末去臺南。
  We plan to go to Tainan at the weekend.

計畫書 jìhuàshū ㄐㄧˋ ㄏㄨㄚˋ ㄕㄨ

N proposal

- 他正在學習用中文寫計劃書。
  He's learning how to write proposals in Chinese.

計程車 jìchéngchē ㄐㄧˋ ㄔㄥˊ ㄔㄜ

N taxi

CN 出租車

SG MY 的士、德士

- 你最好還是叫一輛計程車。
  You'd better catch a taxi.

計算機[a] jìsuànjī ㄐㄧˋ ㄙㄨㄢˋ ㄐㄧ

N computer

SG MY 電腦

- 這條信息已經存入計算機。
  The information is stored on computer.

計算機[b] jìsuànjī
ㄐㄧˋ ㄙㄨㄢˋ ㄐㄧ

N calculator

- 考試時可以帶小計算機。
  Small calculators are allowed in the exam.

記得[a] jìde
ㄐㄧˋ ˙ㄉㄜ

Vst to remember

- 離開辦公室前記得關燈。
  Remember to turn off the lights before you leave the office.
- 記得當初怎麼跟你講的？
  Remember what I told you, eh?

記得[b] jìde
ㄐㄧˋ ˙ㄉㄜ

Vst to know by heart

- 我記得他的電話號碼了。
  I succeeded in knowing his phone number by heart.

季軍 jìjūn
ㄐㄧˋ ㄐㄩㄣ

N third place

- 他得到中文演講比賽的季軍。
  He finished third in the speech contest in Chinese.

技術 jìshù
ㄐㄧˋ ㄕㄨˋ

N technique

- 公司在開發一項新技術。
  The company is developing a new technique.

繼續 jìxù
ㄐㄧˋ ㄒㄩˋ

Vi to continue

- Mary生了孩子以後，還繼續工作。
  Mary continued to work after she had her baby.

加[a] jiā
ㄐㄧㄚ

V to add

- 如果湯太濃，加水。
  If the soup is too thick, add water.
- 她在湯裡加了些鹽和胡椒。
  She added a little salt and pepper to the soup.

加[b] jiā
ㄐㄧㄚ

V to include

- 我們加上他共五個人。
  We are five, including him.

加油站 jiāyóuzhàn ㄐㄧㄚ ㄧㄡˊ ㄓㄢˋ

N petrol station

MY 油站

- 我的車在加油站加油。
  I refilled my car at the petrol station.

★ 

家 1a jiā ㄐㄧㄚ

M measure word for restaurant

- 這家旅館接受信用卡。
  This restaurant takes credit card.

家 1b jiā ㄐㄧㄚ

M measure word for shops

- 她曾經給一家公司當會計。
  She worked as an accountant for a firm.

★ 家 2a jiā ㄐㄧㄚ

N home

- 我到家時收到一封信。
  An envelope was waiting for me when I got home.
- 我女兒搬回我們的家住。
  My daughter moved back to our home.

家 2b jiā ㄐㄧㄚ

N family

- 你家有多少人？
  How many of you are there in the family?
- 她家仍然保留著那裡的房子。
  Her family still has its house over there.

家教 jiājiào ㄐㄧㄚ ㄐㄧㄠˋ

N tutor

SG 補習老師。MY 補習

- 我想請一個中文家教。
  I'd like to hire a tutor for Chinese lessons.

家具 jiājù ㄐㄧㄚ ㄐㄩˋ

N furniture

- 我喜歡老家具，不喜歡新家具。
  I prefer old furniture to new stuff.

家人 jiārén ㄐㄧㄚ ㄖㄣˊ

N family member

- 我們家人個個都長得很

高。
My family members are all very tall.

家庭 jiātíng ㄐㄧㄚ ㄊㄧㄥˊ

N family

- 我整個家庭都支持我。
  My whole family is right behind me.

夾克 jiákè ㄐㄧㄚˊ ㄎㄜˋ

N jacket
CN jiākè。MY 冷衣、寒衣。

- 鑰匙在我的夾克口袋裡。
  The keys are in my jacket pocket.

★假 jiǎ ㄐㄧㄚˇ

Vs-attr fake

- 這是一張假身分證。
  This is a fake identity card.

★架[1a] jià ㄐㄧㄚˋ

M measure word for airplane

- 一架飛機正在桃園機場降落。
  An airplane is landing at TY airport.

架[1b] jià ㄐㄧㄚˋ

M measure word for piano

- 靠牆有一架鋼琴。
  A piano stood against the wall.

架[2] jià ㄐㄧㄚˋ

N rack

- 架上有許多好看的杯子。
  There are lots of pretty cups on the rack.

架子 jiàzi ㄐㄧㄚˋ ˙ㄗ

N shelf

- 把這些杯子放在架子上。
  Put the cups on the shelf.

★價錢 jiàqián ㄐㄧㄚˋ ㄑㄧㄢˊ

N price

- 這價錢多少？
  What's the price of this?

駕照 jiàzhào ㄐㄧㄚˋ ㄓㄠˋ

N driver's license

- 考駕照怎麼考？
  What is the procedure for getting a driver's license?

間 jiān ㄐㄧㄢ

M measure word for house

• 他在臺南有三間房子。
He owns three houses Tainan.

煎 jiān ㄐㄧㄢ

V to fry

• Mary在煎晚飯吃的魚。
She's frying fish for dinner.

肩 jiān ㄐㄧㄢ

N bound word for shoulder

• 他把手放在我肩上。
He puts his hand on my shoulder.

肩膀 jiānbǎng ㄐㄧㄢ ㄅㄤˇ

N shoulder

• 我左肩膀痛。
My left shoulder hurts.

★剪 jiǎn ㄐㄧㄢˇ

V to cut (with scissors)

• Anne剪下報紙上的文章。
Anne had cut out the article of the newspaper.

★減 jiǎn ㄐㄧㄢˇ

V to decrease

• 病人減到九個人。
The number of patients decreased to 9.

減少[a] jiǎnshǎo ㄐㄧㄢˇ ㄕㄠˇ

V to reduce

• 我的體重減少了幾公斤。
I reduced my weight by a couple of kilograms.

減少[b] jiǎnshǎo ㄐㄧㄢˇ ㄕㄠˇ

V to decrease

• 老師說遲到的人減少了。
Teachers reported that the number of late-comers decreased.

檢查[a] jiǎnchá ㄐㄧㄢˇ ㄔㄚˊ

V to check

• 檢查一下護照準備好了嗎？
Let us just check whether we get all our passports ready.

檢查[b] jiǎnchá ㄐㄧㄢˇ ㄔㄚˊ

V to examine

• 他仔細地檢查了簽名。
He examined the signature closely.

★簡單 jiǎndān ㄐㄧㄢˇ ㄉㄢ

Vs. /Adj simple

- 我的問題很簡單。
  My question is simple.

剪刀 jiǎndāo ㄐㄧㄢˇ ㄉㄠ

N scissors

- 桌子上有把剪刀。
  There's a pair of scissors on the table.

★件 [a] jiàn ㄐㄧㄢˋ

M measure word for clothes

- 她上星期買了三件衣服。
  She bought three pieces of clothing last week.

件 [b] jiàn ㄐㄧㄢˋ

M measure word for things

- 今天下午我有兩件事情要做。
  I have two things to do this afternoon.

★見 [a] jiàn ㄐㄧㄢˋ

V to meet

- 我們好像在哪裡見過。
  Apparently we've met somewhere before.
- 我希望你見見我的丈夫。
  I'd like you to meet my husband.

見 [b] jiàn ㄐㄧㄢˋ

V to see

- 見到你很高興。
  It's a pleasure to see you.
- 我從來沒見過這種鳥。
  I've never seen a bird like that before.

健保 jiànbǎo ㄐㄧㄢˋ ㄅㄠˇ

N health insurance

CN 醫保

- 我有健保，看醫生不用花太多錢。
  I'm covered by health insurance, so I don't have to pay much in medical treatment.

健康 [1] jiànkāng ㄐㄧㄢˋ ㄎㄤ

N health

- 健康是最重要的。
  Health is the most important thing to be considered.

健康 [2] jiànkāng ㄐㄧㄢˋ ㄎㄤ

Vs. /Adj healthy

- 我真的老了，但我還很健

康。
I'm old, to be sure, but I'm healthy.

健行 jiànxíng ㄐㄧㄢˋ ㄒㄧㄥˊ

[Vi] to jog

- 今天天氣很好，適合出門健行。
  The weather today is lovely, suitable to go jogging outdoors.

薑 jiāng ㄐㄧㄤ

[N] ginger

- 這些菜裡有一點薑。
  There's a little ginger in these dishes.

★**將來** jiānglái ㄐㄧㄤ ㄌㄞˊ

[N] future

- 將來怎樣現在還不清楚。
  We don't know what the future would be.

講[a] jiǎng ㄐㄧㄤˇ

[V] to talk

- 老師講得太快，我聽不懂。
  The teacher was talking so fast I could not understand him.

講[b] jiǎng ㄐㄧㄤˇ

[V] to say

- 她和你講了什麼？
  What dis she say to you?

講師 jiǎngshī ㄐㄧㄤˇ ㄕ

[N] lecturer

- 她是歷史系的講師。
  She's a lecturer in the Department of History.

獎金 jiǎngjīn ㄐㄧㄤˇ ㄐㄧㄣ

[N] prize money

- 他得了一百萬元獎金。
  He won a million in prize money.

獎學金 jiǎngxuéjīn ㄐㄧㄤˇ ㄒㄩㄝˊ ㄐㄧㄣ

[N] scholarship

- Mike 申請大學的獎學金。
  Mike applied a scholarship to the university.

醬 jiàng ㄐㄧㄤˋ

[N] sauce

- 他吃任何東西都不加醬。
  He never add sauce to anything he eat.

醬油 jiàngyóu ㄐㄧㄤˋ ㄧㄡˊ

N soy sauce

- 我吃水餃喜歡加醬油。
  I love boiled dumplings with soy sauce.

降[a] jiàng ㄐㄧㄤˋ

V to descend

- 今天的氣溫降了三度。
  The temperature today has descended by three degrees.

降[b] jiàng ㄐㄧㄤˋ

V to go down

- 電梯從三樓降下。
  The lift is going down from Level 3.

降落 jiàngluò ㄐㄧㄤˋ ㄌㄨㄛˋ

Vi to land

- 飛機安全降落。
  The plane landed safely.

★交 jiāo ㄐㄧㄠ

V to turn in

- 每個人都要交一份報告。
  Everyone has to turn a report in.

交換 jiāohuàn ㄐㄧㄠ ㄏㄨㄢˋ

V to exchange

- 主人和客人交換了禮物。
  The host and the guest exchanged gifts.

交通 jiāotōng ㄐㄧㄠ ㄊㄨㄥ

N traffic

- 那條路上交通很繁忙。
  There's heavy traffic on that road.

郊區 jiāoqū ㄐㄧㄠ ㄑㄩ

N suburbs

- 他在市區工作而家住在郊區。
  He works in the city and lives in the suburbs.

★教 jiāo ㄐㄧㄠ

V to teach

- 我教孩子畫畫。
  I teach children drawing.
- 我有空教他華語。
  I teach him Mandarin in my free time.

教書 jiāoshū ㄐㄧㄠ ㄕㄨ

V-sep to teach

• Mary在那所學校教書。
Mary teaches at that school.

焦 jiāo ㄐㄧㄠ

Vs. /Adj be burned

• 肉焦了，沒法吃。
The meat was burned, and uneatable.

膠帶 jiāodài ㄐㄧㄠ ㄉㄞˋ

N adhesive tape

MY 膠布

• Ben用膠帶把海報貼在牆上。
Ben tried to fix the posters to the wall with adhesive tape.

嚼 jiáo ㄐㄧㄠˊ

V to chew

• 吃東西要慢慢嚼。
You should chew your food carefully.

★腳 jiǎo ㄐㄧㄠˇ

N foot (body part)

• 他左腳受了傷。
His left foot is injured.

• 我踩了你的腳了吧？
Did I step on your foot?

繳[a] jiǎo ㄐㄧㄠˇ

V to pay

• 我已經繳了這學期的學費。
I've already paid the tuition fee for this semester.

繳[b] jiǎo ㄐㄧㄠˇ

V to hand over

• 請把考卷繳上來。
Please hand over the answer sheets.

攪 jiǎo ㄐㄧㄠˇ

V to stir

• 她用湯匙攪了攪咖啡。
She stirred he coffee with a spoon.

繳費 jiǎofèi ㄐㄧㄠˇ ㄈㄟˋ

V make payment

• 你可以在任何一家銀行繳費。
You can make payment in any bank.

腳跟 jiǎogēn ㄐㄧㄠˇ ㄍㄣ

N heel

- 穿上新鞋，我的腳跟就痛。
  My heels hurt when I put on my new shoes.

腳踝 jiǎohuái ㄐㄧㄠˇ ㄏㄨㄞˊ

N ankle

- 襪子可以保護腳踝。
  Socks can protect your ankles.

腳踏車 jiǎotàchē ㄐㄧㄠˇ ㄊㄚˋ ㄔㄜ

N bicycle

CN 自行車

SG MY 腳車

- Bill買了一台新的腳踏車。
  Bill has bought a new bicycle.

腳趾 jiǎozhǐ ㄐㄧㄠˇ ㄓˇ

N toe

- 我的腳趾比他的長一點。
  My toes are a bit longer than his.

餃子 jiǎozi ㄐㄧㄠˇ ˙ㄗ

N dumpling

- 你會包餃子嗎？
  Do you know how to make Chinese dumplings?

叫 1a jiào ㄐㄧㄠˋ

V to yell

- 這孩子一生氣就大叫。
  The child yells when he got angry.

叫 1b jiào ㄐㄧㄠˋ

V to make (causative)

- 他的話真叫我生氣。
  What he said made me angry.

★叫 2a jiào ㄐㄧㄠˋ

Vst to go by the name of

- 我們這條狗叫Bobby。
  Our dog goes by the name of Bobby.

叫 2b jiào ㄐㄧㄠˋ

Vst be named

- 我認得好幾個叫Lee的人。
  I know several people named Lee.

教練 jiàoliàn ㄐㄧㄠˋ ㄌㄧㄢˋ

N coach

- 教練看上去要換人了。
  It looks as though the coach is going to make a substitution.

教師 jiàoshī ㄐㄧㄠˋ ㄕ

N teacher

- 她丈夫是一個體育教師。
  Her husband is a PE teacher.

教室 jiàoshì ㄐㄧㄠˋ ㄕˋ

N classroom

SG MY 課室

- 我們的教室在七樓。
  Our classroom is on the seventh floor.

教授 jiàoshòu ㄐㄧㄠˋ ㄕㄡˋ

N professor

- 系裡有十位講師和三位教授。
  The department has ten lecturers and three professors.

教堂 jiàotáng ㄐㄧㄠˋ ㄊㄤˊ

N church

- 我們不想去教堂時遲到。
  We didn't want to be late for church.

教育 jiàoyù ㄐㄧㄠˋ ㄩˋ

N education

- 臺灣非常重視教育。
  Taiwan places great importance on education.

★ 接 jiē ㄐㄧㄝ

V to pick up

- 下班後我會開車接她。
  I'll drive over to pick her up after work.

節 jié ㄐㄧㄝˊ

M measure word for period (school)

- Mary今天有三節中文課。
  Mary has three periods of Chinese today.

節目 jiémù ㄐㄧㄝˊ ㄇㄨˋ

N program

- 昨天的電視節目好極了。
  The TV program yesterday was wonderful!

結婚 jiéhūn ㄐㄧㄝˊ ㄏㄨㄣ

V-sep to marry

- Jane三十歲跟他結婚。
  Jane, 30, is married to him.

結業 jiéyè ㄐㄧㄝˊ ㄧㄝˋ

Vp-sep to complete a course

- 大部分學生在七月結業。
  The majority of students would complete their courses in July.

捷運 jiéyùn ㄐㄧㄝˊ ㄩㄣˋ

N Mass Rapid Transit (term used in Taiwan)

CN 地鐵、輕軌

- 坐捷運五分鐘就可以到學校。
  It takes just five minutes to go to the school by traveling on MRT.

結帳 jiézhàng ㄐㄧㄝˊ ㄓㄤˋ

V-sep to have the bill

MY 收錢、埋單

- 請給我們結帳。
  Could we have the bill, please?

★姊姊 jiějie ㄐㄧㄝˇ ˙ㄐㄧㄝ

N elder sister

CN 姐姐寫作「姊」時讀作zǐ。

- 我有一個哥哥，沒有姊姊。
  I've an elder brother, and not an elder sister.

★姊妹 jiěmèi ㄐㄧㄝˇ ㄇㄟˋ

N sisters

CN zǐmèi。只有「姊妹」，沒有「姊姊」

- 她們是姊妹。
  They are sisters.

★借 jiè ㄐㄧㄝˋ

V to borrow

- 借東西要還。
  If you borrow something, you must return it.
- 我向他借了一千元。
  I borrowed one thousand dollars from him.
- 你從圖書館借書，必須簽名。
  You have to sign books out when you borrow them from the library.

介紹 jièshào ㄐㄧㄝˋ ㄕㄠˋ

V to present

- 請允許我介紹Carter先生。
  May I present Mr. Carter?

斤 jīn ㄐㄧㄣ

N one half kilo; catty

- 價錢每斤在50元到70元之間。
  The price for each half kilo ranges between 50-70 dollars.

今年 jīnnián ㄐㄧㄣ ㄋㄧㄢˊ

N this year

- 今年比往年熱。
  This year it's hotter than it was in the previous years.

今天 jīntiān ㄐㄧㄣ ㄊㄧㄢ

N today

- 今天是幾月幾日？
  What's the date today?

儘管 jǐnguǎn ㄐㄧㄣˇ ㄍㄨㄢˇ

Adv not to hesitate to (to be interpreted as adverbial use)

- 有疑問的話，請儘管跟我聯繫。
  Please do not hesitate to contact me if you have any queries.

緊張 jǐnzhāng ㄐㄧㄣˇ ㄓㄤ

Vs. /Adj nervous

- 我緊張得說不出話來。
  I was too nervous to speak
- 他老是緊張，考試總吃虧。
  He is so nervous that he always gets the worst of it in an exam.
- 要跟她一起工作，我眞緊張。
  I'm really nervous about having to work with her.

近[a] jìn ㄐㄧㄣˋ

Vs. /Adj near

- 我家離車站很近。
  My home is quite near to the station.

近[b] jìn ㄐㄧㄣˋ

Vs. /Adj close

- 兩人坐得很近。
  The two of them sat quite close together.
- 商店很近，不用開車去。
  The store is close by. There's no need to drive.

進 jìn ㄐㄧㄣˋ

Vi to enter

- 她沒敲門就進了房間。
  She entered the room without knocking.

進口 jìnkǒu ㄐㄧㄣˋ ㄎㄡˇ

V to import

- 這批貨物是從非洲進口的。

This batch of goods was imported from Africa.

★ **經過** jīngguò ㄐㄧㄥ ㄍㄨㄛˋ

Vi to pass

- 這公車經過時代廣場嗎？
  Does this bus pass Times Square?

經濟艙 jīngjìcāng ㄐㄧㄥ ㄐㄧˋ ㄘㄤ

N economy class

- 我總是坐經濟艙旅行。
  I always travel economy class.

經理 jīnglǐ ㄐㄧㄥ ㄌㄧˇ

N manager

- 我可沒有當經理的本事。
  I don't have the capability to be a manager.

★ **經驗** jīngyàn ㄐㄧㄥ ㄧㄢˋ

N experience

- 這個經驗對我很有價值。
  This experience is very valuable for me.
- John在這方面有些經驗。
  John has some experiences in this respect.

頸部 jǐngbù ㄐㄧㄥˇ ㄅㄨˋ

N neck

- 運動的時候避免頸部受傷。
  Mind you don't hurt your neck when playing sports.

警察 jǐngchá ㄐㄧㄥˇ ㄔㄚˊ

N police officer

- 車上有四個警察。
  Four police officers are in the car.

警車 jǐngchē ㄐㄧㄥˇ ㄔㄜ

N police car

- 警車停在那裡，不知道爲什麼。
  There're police cars stationed over there, and I don't know for what reasons.

鏡子 jìngzi ㄐㄧㄥˋ ˙ㄗ

N mirror

- 浴室裡有鏡子。
  There is a mirror in the bathroom.

★ **九** jiǔ ㄐㄧㄡˇ

N nine

- 最後一個數字是九。
  The last number is nine.

★ 久 jiǔ ㄐㄧㄡˇ

Vs. /Adj long

- 你在臺灣住了多久？
  How long have you been living in Taiwan?
- 你們會出去很久嗎？
  Will you be out for a long time?
- 時間太久了，我記不清了。
  It was too long ago, I can't remember it clearly.

酒 jiǔ ㄐㄧㄡˇ

N wine

- Joe在聚會上喝了幾杯酒。
  Joe drank several glasses of wine at the party.

酒店 jiǔdiàn ㄐㄧㄡˇ ㄉㄧㄢˋ

N hotel

- 這家酒店是幾星級的？
  How many stars has this hotel got?

酒精 jiǔjīng ㄐㄧㄡˇ ㄐㄧㄥ

N alcohol

- 我比別人對酒精更敏感。
  I'm more susceptible to alcohol than others.

★ 舊[a] jiù ㄐㄧㄡˋ

Vs. /Adj used

- 我有一輛舊車。
  I have a used car.

舊[b] jiù ㄐㄧㄡˋ

Vs. /Adj old

- 這支舊錶沒有什麼價值。
  This old watch doesn't have much value.
- 你爲什麼留著這些舊報紙？
  Why do you keep all these old newspapers?

救 jiù ㄐㄧㄡˋ

V to save

- 我的朋友來救我了。
  My friends came to save me.

救護車 jiùhùchē ㄐㄧㄡˋ ㄏㄨˋ ㄔㄜ

N ambulance

MY 救傷車

- 他被救護車送到醫院去。
  He was taken by ambulance to the hospital.

救命 jiùmìng ㄐㄧㄡˋ ㄇㄧㄥˋ

V-sep to save life

- 你救了我的命！
  You saved my life!

★就[a] jiù ㄐㄧㄡˋ

Adv then

- 不去就不去吧！
  If you don't want to go, then don't.

★就[b] jiù ㄐㄧㄡˋ

Adv as early as

- 他們昨天就離開了。
  They left as early as yesterday.
- 他1990年就當了教授了。
  He became professor as early as 1990.

★就是 jiùshì ㄐㄧㄡˋ ㄕˋ

Conj even if

- 就是下雨，我也要去。
  Even if it rains, I'll go.
- 就是他去，我也不去。
  I won't go even if he goes.
- 就是他請我去，我也不去。
  I won't go even if he asked me to.

★就算 jiùsuàn ㄐㄧㄡˋ ㄙㄨㄢˋ

Conj even if

- 就算下雨，我們也每天散步。
  Even if it's raining, we go for a walk every day.

舅舅 jiùjiu ㄐㄧㄡˋ ˙ㄐㄧㄡ

N uncle

- 這是我舅舅。
  This is my uncle.

橘子 júzi ㄐㄩˊ ˙ㄗ

N mandarin (fruit)

- 這橘子很甜，很好吃。
  This mandarin is sweet, and very delicious.

★舉 jǔ ㄐㄩˇ

V to lift up

- 這椅子太重，我舉不起來。

The chair is too heavy for me to lift up.

聚餐 jùcān
ㄐㄩˋ ㄘㄢ

V-sep to have a dinner party

- 這個星期天大家聚餐。
  Let's have a dinner party this Sunday.

聚會[1] jùhuì
ㄐㄩˋ ㄏㄨㄟˋ

N party

- 今晚你去參加聚會嗎？
  Are you going to the party tonight?

聚會[2] jùhuì
ㄐㄩˋ ㄏㄨㄟˋ

V-sep to party

- 週末聚會之後，我們都累極了。
  After a weekend's partying, we were very tired.

颶風 jùfēng
ㄐㄩˋ ㄈㄥ

N hurricane

- 新聞報導說，颶風快來了。
  They say on the news that the hurricane's coming.

★ 距離[1] jùlí
ㄐㄩˋ ㄌㄧˊ

N distance

- 請和前面的車子保持距離。
  Please keep your distance from the car in front of you.

★ 距離[2] jùlí
ㄐㄩˋ ㄌㄧˊ

Prep from

- 這裡距離那裡多遠？
  How far is it from here to there?

句型 jùxíng
ㄐㄩˋ ㄒㄧㄥˊ

N sentence pattern

- 今天老師教了新句型。
  The teacher teaches new sentence patterns today.

句子 jùzi
ㄐㄩˋ ˙ㄗ

N sentence

- 我不懂這個句子。
  I don't understand this sentence.

劇院 jùyuàn
ㄐㄩˋ ㄩㄢˋ

N theatre

- 劇院內外都擠滿人。
  The theatre is packed with people both inside and outside.

★ 覺得[a] juéde ㄐㄩㄝˊ ˙ㄉㄜ

Vst to feel

- 天氣太熱，她覺得快要暈倒了。
  The heat made her feel faint.

★ 覺得[b] juéde ㄐㄩㄝˊ ˙ㄉㄜ

Vst to think

- 我不覺得是那樣。
  I don't think that that's so.
- 你覺得這部電影怎麼樣？
  What do you think of the film?
- 我覺得這襯衫不大適合我穿。
  I don't think this shirt really suits me.

★ 決定[1a] juédìng ㄐㄩㄝˊ ㄉㄧㄥˋ

Vp to decide

- 他無法決定怎麼做。
  He can't decide what to do.
- 幫我決定買哪條裙子好。
  Help me decide which skirt to buy.
- 我已經決定今年不去日本。
  I've decided against going to Japan this year.

★ 決定[1b] juédìng ㄐㄩㄝˊ ㄉㄧㄥˋ

Vp to determine

- 我們的價格由市場來決定。
  Our prices are determined by the market.

★ 決定[2] juédìng ㄐㄩㄝˊ ㄉㄧㄥˋ

N decision

- 我希望你改變這個決定。
  I hope you will change this decision.

K

咖啡 kāfēi ㄎㄚ ㄈㄟ

N coffee

- 給我們來三杯咖啡吧。
  Can we have three coffees, please?

卡 kǎ ㄎㄚˇ

N card

- 用這張卡買東西可以打九折。
  You can get 10% off when using this card in shopping.

卡車 kǎchē ㄎㄚˇ ㄔㄜ

N truck

SG 貨車。

MY 羅里、貨車

- 卡車每星期來一次收回收物。
  The truck collects the recycling once a week.

卡片 kǎpiàn ㄎㄚˇ ㄆㄧㄢˋ

N card

- 你卡片上的號碼是多少？
  What are the numbers on your card?

卡通 kǎtōng ㄎㄚˇ ㄊㄨㄥ

N cartoon

- 我和我的小孩都喜歡看卡通。
  My kids and I love watching cartoon.

★開[a] kāi ㄎㄞ

V to open

- 所有的窗子都開著。
  All the windows were open.
- 我聽到門開了然後又關上。
  I heard a door open and then close.
- 別再開可樂了，我喝夠了。
  Don't open another Coke, I've had enough of it.

★開[b] kāi ㄎㄞ

V to turn on

- 誰開了電視？

Who's turned the television?

- 你覺得熱就開空調。
  Turn on the air-conditioner if you're hot.
- 由於房間太暗，我開了燈。
  I turned on the lights because the room was dark.

★開[c] kāi ㄎㄞ

V to hold (meeting)

- 今年的大會將在這裡開。
  This year's conference will be held here.

開[d] kāi ㄎㄞ

V to hold (party)

- 我們下星期開個慶祝會吧。
  Let's hold a celebration party next week.

開刀 kāidāo ㄎㄞ ㄉㄠ

V-sep to have an operation

- 她的背部開過刀。
  She had an operation on her back.

★開關 kāiguān ㄎㄞ ㄍㄨㄢ

N switch

- 這機器的開關壞了。
  The switch of this machine is out of order.
- 我找不著電燈的開關。
  I can't reach the light switch.

開會 kāihuì ㄎㄞ ㄏㄨㄟˋ

V-sep to have a meeting

- 每星期一上午我們開會。
  Every Monday morning we have a meeting.

開始[a] kāishǐ ㄎㄞ ㄕˇ

Vi to begin

- 電影什麼時候開始？
  What time does the film begin?
- 會議上午十點開始。
  The meeting begins at 10 am.
- 學生在第三年開始學法語。
  In the third year students begin the study of French.

開始[b] kāishǐ ㄎㄞ ㄕˇ

Vi to start

- 我們還沒有開始上課。
  We haven't started our lessons yet.

A B C D E F G H J K L M N O P Q R S T W X Y Z X-

開水 kāishuǐ
ㄎㄞ ㄕㄨㄟˇ

N boiled water

- 請把這些菜用冷開水沖一下。
  Please rinse the vegetables with cold boiled water.

開學 kāixué
ㄎㄞ ㄒㄩㄝˊ

Vp-sep to start (school)

- 學校很快就要開學了嗎？
  Does school start soon?

開演 kāiyǎn
ㄎㄞ ㄧㄢˇ

Vp to start (play)

- 我們到劇場時，戲已經開演了。
  The play had already started when we got to the theatre.

★ 看 1 kān
ㄎㄢ

V to watch over

- 保姆正在看著幾個小孩。
  The nanny was watching over the little kids.

看 2a kàn
ㄎㄢˋ

V to see

- 你從這裡看更清楚。
  You can see better from here.
- 最近他一直不來看我。
  He never comes to see me these days.

看 2b kàn
ㄎㄢˋ

V to look

- 仔細看，你會找到的。
  Look carefully, you can find it.
- 他不敢看著我的眼睛。
  He didn't dare to look me in the eye.

看 2c kàn
ㄎㄢˋ

V to watch

- 我說我們去看電影吧！
  I say we should watch a film.
- 我們爬上山頂看日出。
  We climbed to the top of the mountain to watch the sun come up.

★ 看 2d kàn
ㄎㄢˋ

V to read

- 我每天看報紙。
  I read newspaper every day.
- 我帶了一本書在火車上看。
  I took a book with me to read

on the train.

★ **看**[3] kàn ㄎㄢˋ

Vs. /Adj to depend on

- 這要看他忙不忙。
  That depends on whether he's busy or not.
- 明天去不去，完全得看天氣。
  Whether we'll go or not tomorrow wholly depends on the weather.

看病 kànbìng ㄎㄢˋ ㄅㄧㄥˋ

V-sep to see a doctor

- 我一直勸他去看病。
  I've been trying to convince him to see a doctor.

★ **考慮** kǎolǜ ㄎㄠˇ ㄌㄩˋ

Vst to consider

- 你說的辦法值得考慮。
  What you propose is worth considering.
- 我們還在考慮搬到哪裡去。
  We're still considering moving to.
- 我希望現在就考慮這個問題。
  I wish that the question be considered now.

考試[1] kǎoshì ㄎㄠˇ ㄕˋ

N exam

- 這次考試太難了。
  This exam was too difficult!

考試[2] kǎoshì ㄎㄠˇ ㄕˋ

V to take the exam

- 你們什麼時候考試？
  When will you take the exam?

考試卷 kǎoshìjuàn ㄎㄠˇ ㄕˋ ㄐㄩㄢˋ

N exam paper

- 請幫我發考試卷。
  Could you help me distribute the exam papers, please?

烤 kǎo ㄎㄠˇ

V to grill

- 她喜歡吃烤香腸，不太喜歡吃煎的。
  She likes to eat grilled sausages, rather than fried.

烤箱 kǎoxiāng ㄎㄠˇ ㄒㄧㄤ

N oven

- 我聞到了烤箱裡烤雞的味道。
I can smell the chicken roasting in the oven.

★靠 kào ㄎㄠˋ

V to lean against

- Ron把腳踏車靠在牆上。
Ron leant his bicycle against the wall.
- 他走累了，靠著樹休息。
He was tired from walking, leaning against the tree for a rest.

科[1] kē ㄎㄜ

N course (school)

- 我喜歡這兩科：數學和英文。
I enjoy these two courses: math and English.

科[2] kē ㄎㄜ

N [bound form] bound word for section (administration)

- 保險科在左邊。
The insurance section is on the left.

★棵 kē ㄎㄜ

M measure word for trees

- 我們種了三棵蘋果樹。
We planted three apple trees.

★顆[a] kē ㄎㄜ

M measure word for tooth

- 牙醫拔掉了我兩顆牙。
The dentist pulled two of my teeth.

顆[b] kē ㄎㄜ

M measure word for grain

- 我左眼裡面有一顆沙子。
There's a grain of sand in my left eye.

顆[c] kē ㄎㄜ

M for head (vegetable)

- 我們用了整顆生菜做沙拉。
We used a whole head of lettuce for the salad.

科技 kējì ㄎㄜ ㄐㄧˋ

N technology

- 現代科技使我們更容易交流。
Modern technology had made it easy for us to communicate.

科學 kēxué ㄎㄜ ㄒㄩㄝˊ

N science

- 現代科學發展迅速。
  Modern science has been developing very rapidly.

瞌睡 kēshuì ㄎㄜ ㄕㄨㄟˋ

N to doze off (note that in Chinese, the support verb da/打 must co-occur in the context to form a compound verb)

- 演講我聽了一半就打瞌睡。
  I dozed off in the middle of the speech.

咳 ké ㄎㄜˊ

V cough

- 你咳得太厲害，去看看醫生吧。
  You have a bad cough. Why not go to see a doctor?

咳嗽 késòu ㄎㄜˊ ㄙㄡˋ

Vi to cough

CN késou

- 我咳嗽了一個晚上。
  I coughed all night long.

★ 渴 kě ㄎㄜˇ

Vs. /Adj thirsty

- 我們又餓又渴。
  We were hungry and thirsty.
- 如果你渴就喝點東西。
  Have a drink if you're thirsty.

★ 可愛[a] kěài ㄎㄜˇ ㄞˋ

Vs. /Adj lovely

- 這小女孩眞可愛！
  What a lovely little girl!

可愛[b] kěài ㄎㄜˇ ㄞˋ

Vs. /Adj cute

- 她笑起來很可愛。
  She has a cute smile.

可可 kěkě ㄎㄜˇ ㄎㄜˇ

N cocoa

- 我給你沖一杯熱可可吧！
  Let me brew you a cup of hot cocoa.

★ 可憐[1] kělián ㄎㄜˇ ㄌㄧㄢˊ

Vs. /Adj pathetic

- 那小孩看上去眞可憐。
  The child looked so pathetic.

可憐[2] kělián
ㄎㄜˇ ㄌㄧㄢˊ

Vs. /Adj to take pity on

- 我用不著你可憐。
  I don't want your pity.

可能[1a] kěnéng
ㄎㄜˇ ㄋㄥˊ

Adv possibly

- 你明天到這裡來嗎？－可能吧！
  Will you be here tomorrow? --- Possibly.
- 他一個人不可能喝那麼多酒。
  He can't possibly have drunk all that on his own.

可能[1b] kěnéng
ㄎㄜˇ ㄋㄥˊ

Adv probably

- Mary可能在辦公室裡。
  Mary is probably in the office.
- 可能需要一個星期左右。
  It will probably take about a week.

可能[2] kěnéng
ㄎㄜˇ ㄋㄥˊ

N possibility

- 要他回來，沒有可能。
  There's no possibility asking him to come back.
- 有兩種可能，兩種都不好。
  There are two possibilities, and neither one is good.

可怕 kěpà
ㄎㄜˇ ㄆㄚˋ

Vs. /Adj frightening

- 這種病很可怕，還沒有藥治。
  This disease is frightening, as there's still no medicine for it.

★可是[a] kěshì
ㄎㄜˇ ㄕˋ

Conj but

- 房間不大，可是很安靜。
  The room is small but very quiet.
- 學華語有用，可是相當難。
  Learning Chinese is useful all right, but quite hard.
- 我很想去，可是我太忙了。
  I'd like to go but I'm too busy.

可是[b] kěshì
ㄎㄜˇ ㄕˋ

Conj however

- 他不想去，可是他必須

去。
He has no wish to go, however he should go.

★ 可惜 [1a] kěxí
ㄎㄜˇ ㄒㄧˊ

Vs. /Adj pity
CN kěxī

- 你不能來，眞是可惜。
What a pity that you couldn't come.

可惜 [1b] kěxí
ㄎㄜˇ ㄒㄧˊ

Vs. /Adj unfortunate

- 可惜她不會說華語。
It was unfortunate that she couldn't speak Chinese.
- 可惜你那麼快就要走。
It's unfortunate that you have to leave so soon.

★ 可惜 [2] kěxí
ㄎㄜˇ ㄒㄧˊ

Adv unfortunately
CN kěxī

- 可惜，我們來的時候你出去了。
Unfortunately, you were out when we arrived.

可以 [1a] kěyǐ
ㄎㄜˇ ㄧˇ

Vaux can

- 這房間可以住四個人。
This room can accommodate four people.
- 如果你願意，我可以教你跳舞。
I can teach you to dance if you like.

可以 [1b] kěyǐ
ㄎㄜˇ ㄧˇ

Vaux may

- 你可以走了。
You may go now.
- 問題可以這樣解決。
The problem may be solved in this way.

可以 [2a] kěyǐ
ㄎㄜˇ ㄧˇ

Vs. /Adj acceptable

- 買九點的票，也是可以的。
It's also acceptable that you purchase the nine o'clock tickets.

可以 [2b] kěyǐ
ㄎㄜˇ ㄧˇ

Vs. /Adj all right

- 吃得怎麼樣？
—可以。
What's the food like? --- It's

all right.

課 kè ㄎㄜˋ

N course

- 這學期我有四門課。
  I have four courses this semester.

課程 kèchéng ㄎㄜˋ ㄔㄥˊ

N course

- 完成這個課程，都會拿到證書。
  Upon completion of the course, everyone will receive a certificate.

客滿 kèmǎn ㄎㄜˋ ㄇㄢˇ

Vp to book up

- 旅館已經客滿。
  The hotel has been booked up.

客氣[a] kèqì ㄎㄜˋ ㄑㄧˋ

Vs. /Adj kind

- Mary是個客氣又友善的人。
  Mary is a kind and friendly person.

客氣[b] kèqì ㄎㄜˋ ㄑㄧˋ

Vs. /Adj polite

- 他們都很客氣，沒有提出反對。
  They were all too polite to object.

客人 kèrén ㄎㄜˋ ㄖㄣˊ

N guest

- 他們在門口歡迎客人。
  They welcomed their guests at the door.

客廳 kètīng ㄎㄜˋ ㄊㄧㄥ

N living room

- 我們的客廳有兩套沙發。
  Our living room has two sofas.

空地 kòngdì ㄎㄨㄥˋ ㄉㄧˋ

N empty lot

- 他們買下了河邊的一塊空地。
  They bought an empty lot near the river.

空間 kōngjiān ㄎㄨㄥ ㄐㄧㄢ

N space

- 我需要自己的空間。
  I need space to be myself.

空調 kōngtiáo ㄎㄨㄥ ㄊㄧㄠˊ

N air conditioner

- 空調壞了，所以教室裡很熱。
  The air conditioner got broken, so it's rather hot in the classroom.

口[1] kǒu ㄎㄡˇ

N mouth (in literary use)

- 感冒時常常是口、鼻先不舒服。
  When you catch a cold, you usually feel unwell with your mouth and your nose first.

口[2] kǒu ㄎㄡˇ

M measure word for people

- 他家有五口人。
  There are five people in his family.

口服 kǒufú ㄎㄡˇ ㄈㄨˊ

V be taken orally

- 這藥是口服的。
  The medicine is taken orally.

口味 kǒuwèi ㄎㄡˇ ㄨㄟˋ

N taste

- 我們的口味大致相同。
  We have roughly the same tastes.

口香糖 kǒuxiāngtáng ㄎㄡˇ ㄒㄧㄤ ㄊㄤˊ

N gum

MY 塑膠糖

HK 香口膠

- 有口香糖黏在我的鞋底上了。
  Some gum stuck to the bottom of my shoe.

口罩 kǒuzhào ㄎㄡˇ ㄓㄠˋ

N face mask

- 我冬天戴口罩來保暖。
  I wear face mask in winter to keep warm.

★哭 kū ㄎㄨ

V to cry

- 不要緊，別哭了。
  It's all right. Don't cry.
- 小孩哭著要媽媽。
  The child was crying for his mother.
- 她把臉轉了過去，哭了起來。
  She turned away and started to

cry.

★ 苦 kǔ ㄎㄨˇ

Vs. /Adj bitter

- 這生菜又老又苦。
  This lettuce is old and bitter.
- 這咖啡喝起來太苦了。
  The coffee tastes too bitter.

褲子 kùzi ㄎㄨˋ ˙ㄗ

N trousers

- 這條褲子短了一點。
  This pair of trousers is a bit too short.

★ 塊 1a kuài ㄎㄨㄞˋ

M measure word for small piece of objects

- 一塊巧克力夠了。
  Just a piece of chocolate.
- 你要來一塊口香糖嗎？
  Would you like a piece of chewing gum?

塊 1b kuài ㄎㄨㄞˋ

M measure word for meat

- 你要來一塊烤雞肉嗎？
  Would you like a piece of barbecued chicken?

塊 1c kuài ㄎㄨㄞˋ

M measure word for rock

- 我們坐在那塊大石頭上吧！
  Let's sit on that big rock.

塊 2 kuài ㄎㄨㄞˋ

N standard unit of money in China and some other countries (e.g. US, Canada, etc.), divided into 100 smaller units

- 一共是八十塊。
  The total is 80 dollar.

★ 快 a kuài ㄎㄨㄞˋ

Vs. /Adj fast

- 這汽車能開多快？
  How fast can the car go?
- 我們華語老師說話太快了。
  Our Chinese teacher talks too fast.

快 b kuài ㄎㄨㄞˋ

Vs. /Adj quick

- 小孩學東西快。
  The kid is quick at learning.
- 雞很快就能做好。
  Chicken can be quick to pre-

pare.

快遞 kuàidì ㄎㄨㄞˋ ㄉㄧˋ

N express

- 我們會用快遞寄出包裹。
  We'll send the package express.

★快樂 kuàilè ㄎㄨㄞˋ ㄌㄜˋ

Vs. /Adj happy

- 我們在這裡非常快樂。
  We've been very happy here.
- 孩子們在學校裡很快樂。
  The children seem very happy at school.

筷子 kuàizi ㄎㄨㄞˋ ˙ㄗ

N chopstick

- 請再來一雙筷子。
  Another pair of chopsticks, please.

睏 kùn ㄎㄨㄣˋ

Vs. /Adj sleepy

- 我睏得很。
  I'm terribly sleepy.

L

★ **辣** là ㄌㄚˋ

Vs. /Adj spicy

- 這湯眞辣！
  What a spicy soup that was!

拉麵 lāmiàn ㄌㄚ ㄇㄧㄢˋ

N la-mian (transliteration for hand-pull noodles)

- 我最喜歡吃牛肉拉麵。
  I enjoy very much beef la-mian.

★ **來** lái ㄌㄞˊ

Vp to come

- Mary要來這裡。
  Mary wants to come here.
- 你什麼時候來？
  When are you going to come?
- 她們說她們來不了。
  They said that they couldn’t come.

★ **來回** láihuí ㄌㄞˊ ㄏㄨㄟˊ

V to make a round trip

- 從台北到北京可以一天來回。
  On can make a round trip between Taipei and Beijing within one day.

來回票 láihuípiào ㄌㄞˊ ㄏㄨㄟˊ ㄆㄧㄠˋ

N return ticket

CN 往返票 / 雙程票

- 你要單程票還是來回票？
  Do you want a single or a return ticket?

★ **藍** lán ㄌㄢˊ

Vs. /Adj blue

- 我們這裡天天看到藍天。
  We can see the blue sky every day here.

爛 làn ㄌㄢˋ

Vs. /Adj rotten

- 這些蘋果都爛了。
  All these apples are rotten.

籃球 lánqiú ㄌㄢˊ ㄑㄧㄡˊ

N basketball (game)

- 我喜歡打籃球。
  I enjoy playing basketball.

勞保 láobǎo ㄌㄠˊ ㄅㄠˇ

N worker insurance

- 所有工作人員都參加了勞保。
  All the workers took out insurance against loss of working capability.

★ 老[1] lǎo ㄌㄠˇ

Vs. /Adj old

- 她父親很老。
  Her father is very old.
- Ted那麼老還工作。
  Ted is so old, yet he still works.
- 我希望老的時候還能游泳。
  I hope I'll still be able to swim when I get old.

★ 老[2] lǎo ㄌㄠˇ

Adv always (colloq)

- 這裡的天氣老在變。
  The weather here is always changing.
- 你老犯同樣的錯誤。
  You always make the same mistake.
- 她老說她要搬回老家去。
  She's always talking about moving to her hometown.

老闆[a] lǎobǎn ㄌㄠˇ ㄅㄢˇ

N boss(business owner)

- 我一直想自己當老闆。
  I've always wanted to be my own boss.

老闆[b] lǎobǎn ㄌㄠˇ ㄅㄢˇ

N boss(administration)

- 他是我的老闆。
  He is my boss.

★ 老人 lǎorén ㄌㄠˇ ㄖㄣˊ

N old person

- 許多老人獨自生活。
  A lot of old people live alone.

老師 lǎoshī ㄌㄠˇ ㄕ

N teacher

- 他是中文老師。
  He's a teacher of Chinese.

老鼠 lǎoshǔ ㄌㄠˇ ㄕㄨˇ

N mouse

- 那隻老鼠比小貓還大。

That mouse is bigger than a kitten.

垃圾 lèsè ㄌㄜˋ ㄙㄜˋ

N garbage

CN SG lāji

- 晚會過後，到處都是垃圾。
  After the meeting, there was garbage everywhere.

★ 了[1] le ˙ㄌㄜ

Ptc aspect marker indicating completion of action

- 雨停了。
  The rain has stopped.
- 早上他喝了三杯咖啡。
  In the morning he had three cups of coffee.
- 我昨天晚上看了一部華語電影。
  I saw a Chinese film last night.

★ 了[2] le ˙ㄌㄜ

Ptc sentence-final particle indicating change of situation

- 天黑了。
  It has become dark.
- 樹葉變黃了。
  Leaves have turned yellow.
- 我不再住在宿舍了。
  I no longer live in the dormitory.

★ 累 lèi ㄌㄟˋ

Vs. /Adj tired

- 我非常非常累。
  I'm very, very tired.
- 我累得都能睡三天。
  I'm so tired I could sleep for three days.
- 我們走了那麼多路，有點累。
  We were somewhat tired after our long walk.

★ 冷 lěng ㄌㄥˇ

Vs. /Adj cold

- 水太冷，不適合游泳。
  The water is too cold for swimming.
- 我在發抖，因爲我很冷。
  I'm shaking because I'm cold.
- 天氣從來沒有這麼冷過。
  It has never been so cold.

冷凍 lěngdòng ㄌㄥˇ ㄉㄨㄥˋ

V to freeze

- 我會把肉冷凍起來。

I'll freeze the meat.

冷靜 lěngjìng ㄌㄥˇ ㄐㄧㄥˋ

Vs. /Adj cool

- 遇事要保持冷靜。
  Keep your cool when in trouble.

冷氣 lěngqì ㄌㄥˇ ㄑㄧˋ

N air conditioning, term used in Taiwan

- 太熱了！我們開冷氣吧！
  It's too hot! Let's turn the air conditioning on.

冷氣機 lěngqìjī ㄌㄥˇ ㄑㄧˋ ㄐㄧ

N air conditioner, term used in Taiwan
CN 空調機

- 她想在夏天前買一台冷氣機。
  She wants to buy an air conditioner before summer.

梨 lí ㄌㄧˊ

N pear

- 我要一公斤梨。
  I'd like a kilo of pears, please.

★ 離 lí ㄌㄧˊ

Prep away from

- 車站離我們家十分鐘。
  The station is ten minutes away from our house.

離婚 líhūn ㄌㄧˊ ㄏㄨㄣ

V-sep to divorce

- 他們離了婚。
  They divorced each other.

★ 離開[a] líkāi ㄌㄧˊ ㄎㄞ

V to depart

- 我離開香港以前打了電話給他。
  I called him before departing Hong Kong.

離開[b] líkāi ㄌㄧˊ ㄎㄞ

V to leave

- 我會儘快離開。
  I'll leave as soon as I possibly can.
- 他的女朋友離開了他。
  His girlfriend left him.
- Kevin離開臺南去臺北。
  Kevin left Tainan for Taipei.

★ 裡 lǐ ㄌㄧˇ

N [bound form] bound word for the inside of a space

• 箱子裡有什麼？
What's inside the box?

裡面 lǐmiàn ㄌㄧˇ ㄇㄧㄢˋ

N inside

CN lǐ mian

• 關燈吧！裡面沒人。
Could you turn off the light? There's nobody inside.

裡頭 lǐtou ㄌㄧˇ ˙ㄊㄡ

N inside (used after a noun and can be simply rendered in English by the preposition 'in' in certain contexts)

• 學生們還在教室裡頭討論報告。
The students continued discussing the report with each other in the classroom.

禮拜 lǐbài ㄌㄧˇ ㄅㄞˋ

N week (term used in Taiwan)

• 你下個禮拜哪天有空？
Which day are you available next week?

禮拜天 lǐbàitiān ㄌㄧˇ ㄅㄞˋ ㄊㄧㄢ

N Sunday

• 因爲昨天放假，所以這個禮拜天要補課。
Yesterday was a holiday, so we have to make up the lessons this Sunday.

理髮 lǐfǎ ㄌㄧˇ ㄈㄚˇ

V-sep to get a hair cut

CN lǐ fà

• 我得理髮了。
I must get my hair cut.

理髮廳 lǐfǎtīng ㄌㄧˇ ㄈㄚˇ ㄊㄧㄥ

N barbershop/hairdresser's

CN SG MY měifàdiàn美髮店/理髮店

• 我通常在那家理髮廳理髮。
I usually have my hair cut in that barbershopat that hairdresser's.

禮貌 [1] lǐmào ㄌㄧˇ ㄇㄠˋ

Vs. /Adj be polite

• Jane對人總是很禮貌。
Jane is always polite to people.

禮貌 [2] lǐmào ㄌㄧˇ ㄇㄠˋ

N courtesy

• 到機場去接你是我們的禮貌。
To go to the airport to meet you is our courtesy.

禮物 lǐwù ㄌㄧˇ ㄨˋ

N present

- 這件小小的禮物，請你收下。
  Please accept this small present.

李子 lǐzi ㄌㄧˇ ˙ㄗ

N plum

- 李子可以做成酒。
  We can make wine from plums.

立刻 lìkè ㄌㄧˋ ㄎㄜˋ

Adv immediately

- 請等一下，我立刻就來。
  Wait a minute, please. I'll be with you immediately.

力氣 lìqì ㄌㄧˋ ㄑㄧˋ

N strength

- 搬動那個大箱子需要力氣。
  It takes strength to move that trunk.

例如[a] lìrú ㄌㄧˋ ㄖㄨˊ

Conj for example

- 他會幾種語言，例如：英語、法語。
  He can speak several languages, for example English and French.

例如[b] lìrú ㄌㄧˋ ㄖㄨˊ

Conj for instance

- 許多人要來，例如Joy和Sally。
  Lots of people want to come, for instance Joy and Sally.

歷史 lìshǐ ㄌㄧˋ ㄕˇ

V history

- 這個地區的歷史很有意思。
  The local history of the area is fascinating.

利用 lìyòng ㄌㄧˋ ㄩㄥˋ

V to make use of

- 你得利用每一個機會說華語。
  You should make use of every opportunity to speak Chinese.

連 lián ㄌㄧㄢˊ

Prep even

- 連Eva都去了。
  Even Eva went along too.
- 他連看都沒看。

He didn't even look.

- 她連上樓的力氣都沒有。
  She hasn't even the strength to walk upstairs.

聯絡 liánluò ㄌㄧㄢˊ ㄌㄨㄛˋ

V to contact

CN 聯繫

- 他聯絡我們辦了一個聚會。
  He contacted us and had a get-together.

聯誼 liányí ㄌㄧㄢˊ ㄧˊ

N group blind date

- 他們是在大學聯誼時認識的。
  They were acquainted with each other on a group blind date at the university.

蓮霧 liánwù ㄌㄧㄢˊ ㄨˋ

N wax fruit

MY 水蓊

- 蓮霧是我喜歡吃的臺灣水果。
  Wax fruit is my favourite fruit in Taiwan.

練習[1] liànxí ㄌㄧㄢˋ ㄒㄧˊ

V to practice

- 她在練習演講。
  She's practicing giving a speech.

練習[2] liànxí ㄌㄧㄢˋ ㄒㄧˊ

N exercise

- 練習十分簡單，幾乎誰都會做。
  The exercises are so simple that almost anyone can do them.

★量 liáng ㄌㄧㄤˊ

V to measure

- 護士量了小孩的身高。
  The nurse measured the child's height.
- 我量了房間的長和寬。
  I measured the length and width of the room.
- 你買窗簾以前量了窗子沒有？
  Did you measure the windows before buying the curtains?

涼拌 liángbàn ㄌㄧㄤˊ ㄅㄢˋ

V to dress cold food with sauce

- 黃瓜可以涼拌著吃。
  Cucumbers can be eaten cold with sauce.

涼麵 liángmiàn ㄌㄧㄤˊ ㄇㄧㄢˋ

N noodles served cold with sauce

- 天氣太熱，我只想吃涼麵當晚餐。
  The weather is so hot that I want nothing but noodles served cold with sauce for dinner.

涼爽 liángshuǎng ㄌㄧㄤˊ ㄕㄨㄤˇ

Vs. /Adj be cool and comfortable

- 今天天氣很涼爽。
  It's quite cool and comfortable today.

★ 兩[1] liǎng ㄌㄧㄤˇ

numeral two

- Matt多住了兩天。
  Matt stayed two more days.
- 我不能同時做兩件事。
  I can't do two things at once.
- 我不知道你會說兩種外語。
  I wasn't aware that you can speak two foreign languages.

★ 兩[2] liǎng ㄌㄧㄤˇ

M liang, a unit for measuring weight, equal to 31.25 grams. There are 16 liang in a jin.

- 我要送給他四兩茶葉當禮物。
  I'll make him a present of four liang of tea.

晾 liàng ㄌㄧㄤˋ

V to hang

- Mary把床單晾在曬衣繩上。
  Mary hung the sheets on the washing line.

★ 輛 liàng ㄌㄧㄤˋ

M measure word for vehicles

- 他們在追那輛計程車。
  They were running after the taxi.
- 他在存錢買一輛新的自行車。
  He's saving up for a new bicycle.

聊 liáo ㄌㄧㄠˊ

V to chat

- 我們聊了一會兒天氣。
  We chatted briefly about the weather.

聊天 liáotiān ㄌㄧㄠˊ ㄊㄧㄢ

V-sep to chat

- 我喜歡跟朋友在電話裡聊天。
  I like to chat to my friends on the phone.

了解[a] liǎojiě ㄌㄧㄠˇ ㄐㄧㄝˇ

Vst to get to know

- 當你了解她，就會知道她人很好。
  When you get to know her, you'll realize that she's a very nice person.

了解[b] liǎojiě ㄌㄧㄠˇ ㄐㄧㄝˇ

Vst to understand

- 我了解他的意思。
  I understand what he means.
- 多年來我們互相了解。
  We have understood each other for many years.

鄰居 línjū ㄌㄧㄣˊ ㄐㄩ

N neighbour

- 昨天搬來了一戶新鄰居。
  We've got a new neighbor yesterday.

零 líng ㄌㄧㄥˊ

N zero

- 如果不參加考試，老師會給零分。
  If you don't sit for the exam, the teacher would just give you a zero.

★ 凌晨 língchén ㄌㄧㄥˊ ㄔㄣˊ

N early hours of the morning

- 他星期天凌晨去世。
  He died in the early hours of Sunday morning.

領 lǐng ㄌㄧㄥˇ

V to pick up (goods)

- 我要到郵局去領包裹。
  I have to go to the post office to pick up my package.

★ 另外[a] lìngwài ㄌㄧㄥˋ ㄨㄞˋ

Adv besides

- 另外，我要你答應我一件事。
  Besides, I want you to promise me one thing.
- 我不想去，另外，我也沒錢去。
  I don't want to go, and besides I can't afford it.

另外[b] lìngwài
ㄌㄧㄥˋ ㄨㄞˋ

Adv in addition

- 另外，我們還要去參觀工廠。
  In addition, we'll visit a factory.
- 另外，請你打掃一下廚房地板。
  In addition, I'd like for you to sweep the kitchen floor.
- 他給了我票，另外還給了些錢。
  He gave me the ticket and some money in addition.

★ 流 liú
ㄌㄧㄡˊ

V to flow

- 水流得很急。
  The water is flowing very fast.
- 這條河向東流。
  The river flows in an easterly direction.
- 血從他手指的傷口流出來了。
  Blood flowed from the cut in his finger.

流感 liúgǎn
ㄌㄧㄡˊ ㄍㄢˇ

N flu

- 我得了流感，去不了。
  I couldn't go because I had flu.

★ 流行[a] liúxíng
ㄌㄧㄡˊ ㄒㄧㄥˊ

Vst fashionable

- 這種服裝開始流行。
  These clothes are becoming fashionable.

流行[b] liúxíng
ㄌㄧㄡˊ ㄒㄧㄥˊ

Vst popular

- 這首民歌在青年中很流行。
  This folk song is very popular among the young people.

★ 留[a] liú
ㄌㄧㄡˊ

Vi to leave behind

- 他去了臺灣，把孩子留給我。
  He departed for Taiwan, leaving the children behind with me.

留[b] liú
ㄌㄧㄡˊ

Vi to stay

- 你爲什麼不留他們吃飯？
  Why don't you ask them to stay for dinner?

留學 liúxué
ㄌㄧㄡˊ ㄒㄩㄝˊ

V-sep to study abroad

- 他們全都想留學。
  They all want to study abroad.

留言 liúyán ㄌㄧㄡˊ ㄧㄢˊ

V to leave a message

- 他不在，所以我留言給他秘書。
  He wasn't in, so I left a message to his secretary.

柳丁 liǔdīng ㄌㄧㄡˇ ㄉㄧㄥ

N orange (used in Taiwan)

CN 橙子

SG MY 橙

- 晚飯後還有柳丁吃。
  Oranges are served after dinner.

★ 六 liù ㄌㄧㄡˋ

numeral six

- 他休假六個星期。
  He had six week's leave.
- 她六點鐘剛過就到了。
  She arrived just after six o'clock.

龍 lóng ㄌㄨㄥˊ

N dragon

- 中國人喜歡在龍年生孩子。
  Chinese people like to have their baby in the Year of Dragon.

龍捲風 lóngjuǎnfēng ㄌㄨㄥˊ ㄐㄩㄢˇ ㄈㄥ

N tornado

- 亞洲國家比較少有龍捲風。
  Tornados seldom descend on Asian countries.

樓 lóu ㄌㄡˊ

N building

- 那座樓有二十三層。
  That building has 23 stories.

樓上 lóushàng ㄌㄡˊ ㄕㄤˋ

N upstairs

- 她的辦公室在樓上。
  Her office is upstairs.

樓梯 lóutī ㄌㄡˊ ㄊㄧ

N stairs

- 我們走上了四層樓梯。
  We walked up four flights of stairs.

樓下 lóuxià ㄌㄡˊ ㄒㄧㄚˋ

N downstairs

- 樓下有一輛車等著。
There's a car waiting downstairs.

漏 lòu ㄌㄡˋ

V to leak

- 屋頂漏得很厲害。
The roof leaks badly.

爐子 lúzi ㄌㄨˊ ˙ㄗ

N stove

- Mary在爐子上煮雞湯。
Mary prepares chicken soup on a stove.

滷 lǔ ㄌㄨˇ

V to stew in soy sauce

- 他很會滷排骨，大家都喜歡吃。
He's good at stewing spare ribs in soy sauce, that all of us appreciate.

路[a] lù ㄌㄨˋ

N road

- 一隻狗突然跑到路中間。
A dog suddenly ran into the middle of the road.
- 他們就住在這條路的前面。
They live just along the road.
- 這條路再往前一點就是超級市場。
You'll see the supermarket a bit further up the road.

路[b] lù ㄌㄨˋ

N route

- 他叫司機走到機場最快的路。
He asked the driver to take the quickest route to the airport.

路邊 lùbiān ㄌㄨˋ ㄅㄧㄢ

N roadside

- 我把車停在路邊。
I parked my car at the side of the road.

路口 lùkǒu ㄌㄨˋ ㄎㄡˇ

N junction

- 從七號路口進入高速公路。
Join the expressway at Junction 7.

錄取 lùqǔ ㄌㄨˋ ㄑㄩˇ

V to admit

• 她被國立臺灣大學錄取了。
She has been admitted to NTU.

論文 lùnwén
ㄌㄨㄣˋ ㄨㄣˊ

N thesis

• 我剛寫好我的論文。
I've just finished writing my thesis.

旅館 lǚguǎn
ㄌㄩˇ ㄍㄨㄢˇ

N hotel

• 你住在哪家旅館？
What hotel are you staying at?

旅客 lǚkè
ㄌㄩˇ ㄎㄜˋ

N traveler

• 警察檢查那個旅客的行李。
The police carried out a check on the luggage of that traveler.

旅途 lǚtú
ㄌㄩˇ ㄊㄨˊ

N travel

• 她把旅途看到的都寫下來。
She wrote down all she saw on her travels.

旅行 lǚxíng
ㄌㄩˇ ㄒㄧㄥˊ

V to take a trip

• 我計畫七月份去亞洲旅行。
I'm planning to take a trip to Asia in July.

旅遊 lǚyóu
ㄌㄩˇ ㄧㄡˊ

Vi to tour

• 我們夏天要到歐洲去旅遊。
We're touring Europe this summer.

★ 綠 lǜ
ㄌㄩˋ

Vs. /Adj green

• 我覺得她那條綠裙子很好看。
I find that her green skirt looks good.

綠茶 lǜchá
ㄌㄩˋ ㄔㄚˊ

N green tea

• 中國人愛喝綠茶。
The Chinese are fond of green tea.

M

★媽媽[a] māma ㄇㄚ ˙ㄇㄚ

N mom

- 媽媽，我可以到Mary家去嗎？
  Mom, can I go over to Mary's house?

媽媽[b] māma ㄇㄚ ˙ㄇㄚ

N mother

- 我媽媽說今晚我得待在家裡。
  My mother says that I have to stay home tonight.

麻[a] má ㄇㄚˊ

Vs. /Adj to feel numb

- 我感覺到舌頭越來越麻。
  I could feel my tongue growing numb.

麻[b] má ㄇㄚˊ

Vs. /Adj analgesic

- 她才站了三分鐘，腳就麻了。
  She started to suffer from analgesic after standing for 3 minutes.

★麻煩 máfán ㄇㄚˊ ㄈㄢˊ

Vs. /Adj troublesome

CN máfan

- 這樣做很麻煩。
  This procedure is very troublesome.
- 做這個工作太麻煩。
  It would be troublesome to do this work.
- 旅行最麻煩的是收拾行李箱。
  What's most troublesome about a trip is to pack and unpack the suitcase.

麻將 májiàng ㄇㄚˊ ㄐㄧㄤˋ

N mahjong

- 我一點也不會打麻將。
  I'm no good at mahjong.

馬 mǎ ㄇㄚˇ

N horse

- 我以前從未騎過馬。

I've never been ridden a horse before.

馬路 mǎlù
ㄇㄚˇ ㄌㄨˋ

N road

- 我看見Mike在馬路對面。
  I saw Mike on the other side of the road.

★馬上 [a] mǎshàng
ㄇㄚˇ ㄕㄤˋ

Adv immediately

- 我馬上決定離開。
  I decided to leave immediately.
- 我馬上聽出她的聲音。
  I immediately recognized her voice.
- 電話鈴響了，她馬上去接。
  The telephone rang, and she answered it immediately.

馬上 [b] mǎshàng
ㄇㄚˇ ㄕㄤˋ

Adv right away

- 我馬上就去。
  I'll go right away.
- 我建議我們馬上走。
  I suggest we set off right away.
- 我馬上打電話給他。
  I'll phone him right away.

馬桶 mǎtǒng
ㄇㄚˇ ㄊㄨㄥˇ

N toilet

- 用完後請沖馬桶。
  Flush the toilet after using it.

★嗎 ma
˙ㄇㄚ

Ptc sentence final particle, used to transform a statement into a question

- 你找我嗎？
  Are you looking for me?
- 你要說什麼嗎？
  Do you want to say something?
- 他是中國人嗎？
  Is he Chinese?

★嘛 ma
˙ㄇㄚ

Ptc sentence final particle, used for emphasizing

- 這是我的嘛！
  Obviously this is mine.
- 事實就是這樣嘛！
  That's just the way things are!
- 這樣做就是不對嘛！
  Of course it was acting improperly!

★買 mǎi
ㄇㄞˇ

V to buy

- 買一送一。
  Buy one get one free.
- 我的錢只夠買一罐可樂。
  I have barely enough money to buy a Coke.
- 這是我在臺灣買的第一本書。
  This is the first book I bought in Taiwan.

★ 賣 mài ㄇㄞˋ

V to sell

- 這幅畫賣多少錢？
  What does this painting sell for?
- Ida把自己的電腦賣給我。
  Ida sold her computer to me.
- 你的貨可以賣很好的價錢。
  You can sell your merchandise for a good price.

饅頭 mántou ㄇㄢˊ ˙ㄊㄡ

N steamed bun (Chinese style)

- 早餐我們吃饅頭喝粥。
  We have congee and steamed buns for breakfast.

★ 滿意 mǎnyì ㄇㄢˇ ㄧˋ

Vst to satisfy

- 我太太不滿意我。
  My wife isn't satisfied with me.
- Kate十分滿意自己的生活。
  Kate's fully satisfied with her life.
- 我做什麼都不能讓她滿意。
  Nothing I did would ever satisfy her.

★ 滿 mǎn ㄇㄢˇ

Vs. /Adj full

- 油箱差不多滿了。
  The petrol tank is almost full.
- 這兩個抽屜都滿了。
  Both drawers are full.
- 我應該把這瓶子裝到多滿？
  How full should I fill this bottle?

★ 慢 màn ㄇㄢˋ

Vs. /Adj slow

- 我的錶慢三分鐘。
  My watch is three minutes slow.
- 老人的動作很慢，很慢。
  The old man's movements were very, very slow.
- 我的舊電腦速度太慢了。
  My old computer is really slow.

慢性 mànxìng ㄇㄢˋ ㄒㄧㄥˋ

Vs-attr chronic

- 這種病通常是慢性病。
  This disease is often a chronic one.

★忙 máng ㄇㄤˊ

Vst busy

- 你忙什麼？
  What are you busy with?
- John正忙著準備考試。
  John's busy studying for his exams.
- 那時我很忙，現在不了。
  In those days I was very busy, but not now.

貓 māo ㄇㄠ

N cat

- 我喜歡貓。
  I love cats.

★毛[1a] máo ㄇㄠˊ

N hair

- 沙發上到處都是貓毛。
  There's cat hair all over the sofa.

毛[1b] máo ㄇㄠˊ

N wool

- 她買了那件綠色毛大衣。
  She bought that green wool coat.

★毛[2] máo ㄇㄠˊ

M ten cents

- 那是五毛的硬幣。
  That's a coin of 50 cents.

毛病 máobìng ㄇㄠˊ ㄅㄧㄥˋ

N defect

- 遲到是他的老毛病。
  Being always late was his old defect.

貿易 màoyì ㄇㄠˋ ㄧˋ

N trade

- 他們希望增加對臺灣的貿易。
  They're hoping to increase their trade in Taiwan.

★沒 méi ㄇㄟˊ

Adv not

- 你買了嗎？
  ―沒買。

Did you buy it? --- I didn't.

- 他穿著雨衣了嗎？
  —沒穿。
  Is he wearing a raincoat? --- He's not.

★沒有 méiyǒu ㄇㄟˊ ㄧㄡˇ

Adv to have not

- 我沒有錢。
  I don't have the money.
- 他們沒有孩子。
  They don't have any children.
- 他沒有音樂會的票。
  He doesn't have a ticket for the concert.

★每[a] měi ㄇㄟˇ

Det each

- 每張桌子坐八個人。
  Each table can seat eight people.
- 每一個水果她都洗了。
  She washed each piece of fruit.
- 你們每個人都填一份表格。
  Each of you should fill out an application.

每[b] měi ㄇㄟˇ

Det every

- 每八小時吃一顆藥。
  Take one pill every eight hours.
- 雨天除外，他每天步行上班。
  He walks to work every day except when it rains.
- 她每次看見我都向我打招呼。
  Every time she sees me, she says hello to me.

★美 měi ㄇㄟˇ

Vs. /Adj beautiful

- 這裡的風景真美。
  The scenery here is truly beautiful.
- Lisa是個美麗的女人。
  Lisa is a beautiful woman.

美金 měijīn ㄇㄟˇ ㄐㄧㄣ

N US dollar

- 這件大衣要一百美金。
  The coat costs 100 dollars.

美術館 měishùguǎn ㄇㄟˇ ㄕㄨˋ ㄍㄨㄢˇ

N art gallery

- 臺北有不少博物館和美術館。
  There're lots of museums and art galleries in Taipei.

★ 美洲 Měizhōu ㄇㄟˇ ㄓㄡ

N America

- 在美洲可能會遇到各種天氣。
All kinds of climates can be found in America.

梅子 méizi ㄇㄟˊ ˙ㄗ

N plum

- 這種梅子很酸。
This kind of plum is very sour.

★ 妹妹 mèimei ㄇㄟˋ ˙ㄇㄟ

N younger sister

- 我有兩個妹妹。
I have two sisters, who are both younger than I am.

悶 mēn ㄇㄣ

Vs. /Adj stuffy

- 窗戶都關著，房間裡很悶。
The windows were closed and the room was stuffy.

★ 門[1] mén ㄇㄣˊ

N door

- 門關上了嗎？
Is the door shut?
- 請你幫我開門。
Could you open the door for me?
- 離開時一定要鎖好後門。
Be sure to lock the back door when you leave.

門[2] mén ㄇㄣˊ

M measure word for course (in school)

- 我有三門必修課。
I have three compulsory courses.

★ 門口 ménkǒu ㄇㄣˊ ㄎㄡˇ

N doorway

- 車子停在門口。
The car is parked in the doorway.
- 我看見Bill站在門口。
I saw Bill standing in the doorway.

門鈴 ménlíng ㄇㄣˊ ㄌㄧㄥˊ

N doorbell

- 門鈴響了，看看是誰來了。
The doorbell is ringing. Go and see who's there.

米 mǐ ㄇㄧˇ

N rice

• 把米煮上二十分鐘。
Leave the rice to cook for 20 minutes.

米粉 mǐfěn ㄇㄧˇ ㄈㄣˇ

N rice noodles

• 我要一份炒米粉。
I want a helping of fried rice noodles.

密碼 mìmǎ ㄇㄧˋ ㄇㄚˇ

N password

• 不知道密碼，誰也用不了電腦。
Nobody can use the computer without knowing its password.

秘書 mìshū ㄇㄧˋ ㄕㄨ

N secretary

• 我的秘書會很快跟你聯繫。
My secretary will contact you soon.

免費 miǎnfèi ㄇㄧㄢˇ ㄈㄟˋ

V-sep free of charge

• 今天這家餐廳的甜點免費。
Today this restaurant offers desserts free of charge.

免疫 miǎnyì ㄇㄧㄢˇ ㄧˋ

Vp-sep to immune

• 我對這次的流感免疫了。
For this time, I'm immune to the flu.

面[a] miàn ㄇㄧㄢˋ

N face

• 她面朝下躺在床上。
She was lying face down on the bed.

面[b] miàn ㄇㄧㄢˋ

N side

• 寫在紙的這一面。
Write on this side of the paper.

• 牛排兩面各煎一分鐘。
Fry the steaks for one minute on each side.

• 他把奶油塗在烤麵包的一面。
He put butter on one side of the toast.

面試 miànshì ㄇㄧㄢˋ ㄕˋ

V interview

- 她正在參加那份工作的面試。
  She's being interviewed for the job.

麵 miàn ㄇㄧㄢˋ

N noodles

- 我在小吃店吃了一碗麵。
  I got a bowl of noodles at a snack bar.

麵包 miànbāo ㄇㄧㄢˋ ㄅㄠ

N bread

- 你喝湯時要吃點麵包嗎？
  Would you like some bread with your soup?

麵粉 miànfěn ㄇㄧㄢˋ ㄈㄣˇ

N flour

- Mary稱好麵粉，放進碗裡。
  Mary measured out the flour into the bowl.

麵線 miànxiàn ㄇㄧㄢˋ ㄒㄧㄢˋ

N thin noodles, Chinese style

- 那家店的麵線很好吃。
  The thin noodles that restaurant serves is really delicious.

廟 miào ㄇㄧㄠˋ

N temple

- 臺南地區有不少古廟。
  There's lots of ancient temples in the Tainan region.

★ **秒** miǎo ㄇㄧㄠˇ

M second (time)

- 我一百米跑十二秒，你呢？
  It takes me 12 seconds to run 100 metres. How about you?

民族 mínzú ㄇㄧㄣˊ ㄗㄨˊ

N ethnic group

- 漢人是中國最大的民族。
  The Hans are the biggest ethnic group in China.

名產 míngchǎn ㄇㄧㄥˊ ㄔㄢˇ

N famous product

- 這裡的名產是什麼？
  What are the famous products in this region?

A B C D E F G H J K L M N O P Q R S T W X Y Z X-

名單 míngdān ㄇㄧㄥˊ ㄉㄢ

N list

- 我們有一份參加者的名單。
  We have a list of participants.

名片 míngpiàn ㄇㄧㄥˊ ㄆㄧㄢˋ

N name card

- 可以給我一張你的名片嗎？
  May I have your name card?

名勝 míngshèng ㄇㄧㄥˊ ㄕㄥˋ

N sight

SG 名勝地

- 他們參觀了臺中的主要名勝。
  They had a tour of the main sights in Taichung.

★名字 míngzi ㄇㄧㄥˊ ˙ㄗ

N name

- 我想不起他的名字。
  I can't think of his name.
- 她沒有說出自己名字。
  She didn't say her name.
- 我聽見有人叫我的名字。
  I heard someone call my name.

★明年 míngnián ㄇㄧㄥˊ ㄋㄧㄢˊ

N next year

- 我女兒明年上小學。
  My daughter will go to primary school next year.
- 明年這裡有許多重要會議。
  Many important conferences will be held here next year.

明信片 míngxìnpiàn ㄇㄧㄥˊ ㄒㄧㄣˋ ㄆㄧㄢˋ

N postcard

- 明信片的正面是我們的旅館。
  The front of the postcard shows a picture of our hotel.

★明天 míngtiān ㄇㄧㄥˊ ㄊㄧㄢ

N tomorrow

- 她明天就二十歲了。
  She will be 20 tomorrow.
- 可能明天會出太陽。
  Perhaps it will be sunny tomorrow.

抹布 mǒbù ㄇㄛˇ ㄅㄨˋ

N rag

CN mābù

- 拿塊抹布把這髒東西抹掉。
  Get a rag to mop up this mess.

★ 某 a mǒu ㄇㄡˇ

Det certain

- Mike住在樓上某個房間裡。
  Mike lives in a certain room upstairs.

某 b mǒu ㄇㄡˇ

Det some

- 她在英國某大學學習。
  She's studying in some college in England.

目的地 mùdìdì ㄇㄨˋ ㄉㄧˋ ㄉㄧˋ

N destination

- 我們到達目的地時又累又餓。
  We arrived at our destination tired and hungry.

★ 母親 mǔqīn ㄇㄨˇ ㄑㄧㄣ

N mother

CN mǔqin

- 下星期天是母親節。
  Next Sunday will be Mother's Day.

拇指 mǔzhǐ ㄇㄨˇ ㄓˇ

N thumb

- 他的拇指受傷了。
  He had an injury to the thumb.

木瓜 mùguā ㄇㄨˋ ㄍㄨㄚ

N papaya

- 你要來一片木瓜嗎？
  Would you like a slice of papaya?

N

★ **拿** [a] ná
ㄋㄚˊ

V to take

- 她給我錢，我沒拿。
  She tried to give the money, but I didn't take it.
- 他沒問就把錢拿走了。
  He took the money without asking.
- 打牌的人每人拿三張牌。
  Each player takes three cards.

★ **拿** [b] ná
ㄋㄚˊ

V to hold

- 能幫我拿著包嗎？
  Could you hold my bag for me?
- 他的手受傷了，無法拿東西。
  He hurt his hands and can't hold anything.
- 把圖片拿高一點，我看不見。
  Can you hold the picture up? I can't see it.

★ **哪** nǎ
ㄋㄚˇ

Det which

- 哪幾件行李是你的？
  Which pieces of luggage are yours?
- 指給我看你要哪個。
  Show me which one you want.
- 請告訴我到南門坐哪路公車？
  Please tell me which bus to take for the Gate South.

★ **哪裡** [a] nǎlǐ
ㄋㄚˇ ㄌㄧˇ

N where

- 你去哪裡？
  Where are you going?
- 我不知道她在哪裡。
  I don't know where she is.
- 我在哪裡可以換零錢？
  Where can I change coins?

哪裡 [b] nǎlǐ
ㄋㄚˇ ㄌㄧˇ

N which place

- 上海和北京，你比較喜歡哪裡？
  Shanghai and Beijing, which place do you prefer?

★ **哪兒** nǎr ㄋㄚˇ ㄦ

N where (spoken)

- 你住哪兒？
  Where do you live?

★ **那**[1] nà ㄋㄚˋ

Det that

- 那三雙鞋很貴。
  Those three pairs of shoes are all very expensive.
- 剛才來的那個人是誰？
  Who is that person who just came here?
- 這支筆是我的，那支是他的。
  This pen is mine. That one is his.

★ **那**[2a] nà ㄋㄚˋ

Conj then

- 那怎麼辦？
  Then what can be done?
- 你想買，那就買吧！
  If you want to buy it, then buy it.
- 我真的該走了。
  —好，那就再見吧！
  I really have to go. --- OK, Bye, then.

那[2b] nà ㄋㄚˋ

Conj in that case

- 你都懂了，那我就不重複了。
  You've got it. In that case, I won't repeat it.

那邊[a] nàbiān ㄋㄚˋ ㄅㄧㄢ

N over there

- 我也要去那邊嗎？
  Shall I go over there as well?
- 他們正在那邊照相。
  They are taking photos over there.
- 你願意坐在靠窗那邊嗎？
  Would you like to sit over there by the window?

那邊[b] nàbiān ㄋㄚˋ ㄅㄧㄢ

N that side

- 山的那邊有一所學校。
  There's a school over that side of the mountain.

那裡[a] nàlǐ ㄋㄚˋ ㄌㄧˇ

N there

- 你在那裡嗎？
  Are you in there?

- 我馬上就會到那裡。
  I'll be right there.
- 你究竟去不去那裡？
  Will you go there at all?

那裡[b] nàlǐ ㄋㄚˋ ㄌㄧˇ

N that place

- 你是怎麼找到那裡的？
  How did you find that place?

★ 那麼[a] nàme ㄋㄚˋ ˙ㄇㄜ

Conj then

- 如果你不說，那麼我說。
  If you won't speak up, then I will.
- 他不去，那麼我們得勸他去。
  He won't go. Then we should persuade him to go.
- 你不喜歡喝茶，那麼喝什麼呢？
  You don't like tea. Then what do you like to drink?

那麼[b] nàme ㄋㄚˋ ˙ㄇㄜ

Conj in that case

- 聽說她不在，那麼我們不去了。
  She is said to be not in. In that case, we shall not go.
- 機票賣完了。
  －那麼坐火車吧！
  The air tickets are all sold out.
  --- In that case, let's go by train.

★ 那樣 nàyàng ㄋㄚˋ ㄧㄤˋ

Adv that way

- 那樣做不行。
  It won't do to act the way you did.
- 你別那樣想。
  Don't think in that way.
- 這事不能那樣辦。
  It can't be done that way.

那兒 nàr ㄋㄚˋ ㄦ

N over there (spoken)

- 我把我的書包忘在那兒了。
  I left my satchel over there.

奶奶 nǎinai ㄋㄞˇ ˙ㄋㄞ

N grandma

SG MY 婆婆

- 奶奶總是在聖誕節送我禮物。
  Grandma always remembers me on Christmas Day.

耐心 nàixīn ㄋㄞˋ ㄒㄧㄣ

N patience

- 老師必須對孩子很有耐心。
  Teachers must have a lot of patience with children.

★南 nán ㄋㄢˊ

N south

- 哪邊是南？
  Which way is south?

★南部 nánbù ㄋㄢˊ ㄅㄨˋ

N southern part

- 這是臺灣南部最大的城市。
  This is the biggest city in the southern part of Taiwan.

★南方 nánfāng ㄋㄢˊ ㄈㄤ

N the South

- 明天他們將從南方回來。
  They will return from the South tomorrow.

★難[a] nán ㄋㄢˊ

Vs. /Adj difficult

- 這次測驗眞難。
  This test is really difficult.
- 第二個問題比第一個難。
  The second question is more difficult than the first one.
- 他發現要找份工作很難。
  He's finding it difficult to get a job.

難[b] nán ㄋㄢˊ

Vs. /Adj hard

- 華語難嗎？
  Is Chinese hard?
- 很難相信他們怎麼會輸。
  It is hard to believe how they can lose.
- 很難找到一家好的法國餐廳。
  It's hard to find a good French restaurant.

★難過[a] nánguò ㄋㄢˊ ㄍㄨㄛˋ

Vs. /Adj be heartbroken

- Tom的狗死了，他難過得吃不下飯。
  Tom was so heartbroken that he refused to eat, when his dog died.

難過[b] nánguò ㄋㄢˊ ㄍㄨㄛˋ

Vs. /Adj sad

- 聽說你要離開，我很難過。
  It makes me sad to hear you have to go away.
- 聽到這壞消息，我心裡很難過。
  I was sad to hear about the bad news.
- 看她那樣難過，我也十分難過。
  I was terribly sad as I found her so grieved.

★ 男 nán ㄋㄢˊ

Vs-attr male

- 這是男病房。
  This is a ward for male patients.

★ 男孩 nánhái ㄋㄢˊ ㄏㄞˊ

N boy

- Steve是個聰明的男孩。
  Steve is a clever boy.

★ 男人[a] nánrén ㄋㄢˊ ㄖㄣˊ

N man

- 那個戴眼鏡的男人是我的父親。
  The man wearing glasses is my father.

男人[b] nánrén ㄋㄢˊ ㄖㄣˊ

N men

- 男人能做的事，女人也能做。
  What men can do, women also can.

★ 呢 ne ˙ㄋㄜ

Ptc sentence final particle, used for requesting confirmation

- 我不要，你呢？
  I don't want it, how about you?
- 現在沒問題，以後呢？
  It's OK now, how about later?
- 你好嗎？
  －還不錯，你呢？
  How are you doing? --- Not bad, and you?

★ 內 nèi ㄋㄟˋ

N [bound form] inside

- 博物館內遊客不許照相。
  Tourists are not allowed to take photos inside the museum.

內褲 nèikù ㄋㄟˋ ㄎㄨˋ

N briefs

SG MY 底褲

- 她穿著白色的棉內褲。

She was wearing white cotton briefs.

內容 nèiróng
ㄋㄟˋ ㄖㄨㄥˊ

N content

- 這本書的內容很豐富。
  The book is rich in content.

內向 nèixiàng
ㄋㄟˋ ㄒㄧㄤˋ

Vs. /Adj introverted

- 那件事情使他變得很內向。
  That incident made him introverted.

內衣 nèiyī
ㄋㄟˋ ㄧ

N underwear

- 你要帶些暖和的內衣。
  You'll need to take some warm underwear.

嫩 nèn
ㄋㄣˋ

Vs. /Adj delicate

- 小孩皮膚很嫩。
  Young children have very delicate skin.

能[a] néng
ㄋㄥˊ

Vaux be able to

- 她完全能照顧自己。
  She's well able to take care of herself.
- 我今天不舒服，不能去上班。
  I'm unwell today and won't be able to go to work.

能[b] néng
ㄋㄥˊ

Vaux can

- 飛機降落的時候，不能打手機。
  You can not use your cell phone during the airplane's descent.
- 他很高，手能碰到天花板。
  He's so tall that he can touch the ceiling.
- 這裡能停車嗎？
  －這裡不能。
  Can we park here? --- No, parking is not allowed here.

★你 nǐ
ㄋㄧˇ

personal pronoun you

- 你需要每天練習。
  You need to practice every day.

★妳 nǐ
ㄋㄧˇ

personal pronoun you (female)

- 小姐，請問妳要點什麼？
  What would you like to order, young lady?

★ 你們 nǐmen
ㄋㄧˇ ˙ㄇㄣ

personal pronoun you (plural)

- 今天晚上你們有什麼計劃？
  Are you doing anything special for tonight?
- 信是寫給你們倆的。
  The letter is addressed to both of you.
- 你們大家都必須仔細聽著。
  You must all listen carefully.

★ 年 nián
ㄋㄧㄢˊ

N year

- 我認識她五年了。
  I've known her for five years.
- 我兩年前來到這裡。
  I arrived here two years ago.
- 他現在是第三年在臺灣生活。
  He's in his third year living in Taiwan.

黏 nián
ㄋㄧㄢˊ

Vs. /Adj be sticky

- 膠水不黏了。
  The glue isn't sticky anymore.

年級 niánjí
ㄋㄧㄢˊ ㄐㄧˊ

N grade

- 我女兒剛念一年級。
  My daughter is only a first grade pupil.

年紀 niánjì
ㄋㄧㄢˊ ㄐㄧˋ

N age

- 我在你的年紀時已經結婚了。
  When I was your age, I was already married.

年假 niánjià
ㄋㄧㄢˊ ㄐㄧㄚˋ

N annual leave

- 他的年假至少有三十天。
  His basic annual leave is 30 days.

年齡 niánlíng
ㄋㄧㄢˊ ㄌㄧㄥˊ

N age

- 保費多少錢跟年齡有關係。

The amount of insurance fee depends on your age.

年輕 niánqīng ㄋㄧㄢˊ ㄑㄧㄥ

Vs. /Adj young

- 他看起來很年輕。
  He looks very young.

年終 niánzhōng ㄋㄧㄢˊ ㄓㄨㄥ

N end of the year

- 今年他拿到了三個月的年終獎金。
  He got a bonus equal to three month's salary at the end of the year.

★ 念 niàn ㄋㄧㄢˋ

V to read aloud

- 請你把課文念一遍。
  Could you please read the text out?
- Mary在班上念出了自己寫的詩。
  Mary read out her poem in front of the class.

鳥 niǎo ㄋㄧㄠˇ

N bird

- 他帽子上有一隻鳥。
  A bird is on his hat.

尿[1] niào ㄋㄧㄠˋ

N urine

- 廁所地板上都是尿。
  There's urine all over the floor of the toilet.

尿[2] niào ㄋㄧㄠˋ

V to take a piss

- 小孩子很容易尿在褲子上。
  Kids wet their pants easily.

★ 您 nín ㄋㄧㄣˊ

personal pronoun you (honorific)

- 可以請問您一個問題嗎？
  May I ask you a question?

檸檬 níngméng ㄋㄧㄥˊ ㄇㄥˊ

N lemon

- 我的茶裡有一片檸檬。
  I have a slice of lemon in my tea.

牛 niú ㄋㄧㄡˊ

N cow

- 她養了一頭牛。

She keeps a cow.

牛奶 niúnǎi ㄋㄧㄡˊ ㄋㄞˇ

N milk

- 我喝咖啡時加很多牛奶。
  I drink my coffee with lots of milk.

牛排 niúpái ㄋㄧㄡˊ ㄆㄞˊ

N beef steak

- 我喜歡嫩一點的牛排。
  I like my steak underdone.

牛肉 niúròu ㄋㄧㄡˊ ㄖㄡˋ

N beef

- 他們在火上烤牛肉。
  They roasted beef on the fire.

★ **濃** [a] nóng ㄋㄨㄥˊ

Vs. /Adj heavy

- 玫瑰花香味很濃。
  The rose has a heavy fragrance.
- 他的華語，美國口音很濃。
  He speaks Chinese with a heavy American accent.

濃 [b] nóng ㄋㄨㄥˊ

Vs. /Adj thick

- 湯要又鮮又濃。
  The soup should be nice and thick.
- 她頭髮又黑又濃。
  Her hair is thick and black.
- 空氣中的香菸味眞濃。
  The air was thick with cigarette smoke.

農曆 nónglì ㄋㄨㄥˊ ㄌㄧˋ

N the lunar calendar

- 中國人習慣過農曆新年。
  Chinese people are accustomed to celebrate their Lunar New Year.

弄 [1] nòng ㄋㄨㄥˋ

N lane

- 地址是中山路三巷六弄九號。
  The address is: 9, Sub-lane 6, Lane 3, Chungshan Road.

弄 [2] nòng ㄋㄨㄥˋ

V to work on

- 每個週末他都在弄他的汽車。
  Every weekend he was working on his car.

暖和 nuǎnhuo
ㄋㄨㄢˇ ˙ㄏㄨㄛ

Vs. /Adj warm

- 天氣真好，暖和但不熱。
  The weather is nice and warm, but not hot.

暖氣 nuǎnqì
ㄋㄨㄢˇ ㄑㄧˋ

N heat

- 暖氣沒有開，房間裡很冷。
  The heat wasn't on and the room was freezing.

★ 女 nǚ
ㄋㄩˇ

N female

- 女計程車司機不常見。
  It is rare to find a female taxi driver.

女兒 nǚér
ㄋㄩˇ ㄦˊ

N daughter

- Anne有兩個女兒。
  Anne has two daughters.

★ 女孩 nǚhái
ㄋㄩˇ ㄏㄞˊ

N girl

- 她是鄰居家的女孩。
  She's the girl of my neighbours.

女人 [a] nǚrén
ㄋㄩˇ ㄖㄣˊ

N woman

- 那個女人很漂亮。
  That woman is beautiful.

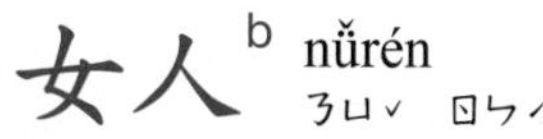

女人 [b] nǚrén
ㄋㄩˇ ㄖㄣˊ

N women

- John不了解女人。
  John doesn't understand women.

歐元 Ōuyuán ㄡ ㄩㄢˊ

N Euro

- 我來自法國，身上只有歐元。
  I came from France and I have only euros with me.

★ 歐洲 Ōuzhōu ㄡ ㄓㄡ

N Europe

- 坐飛機從歐洲到臺灣要多久？
  How long will it take to fly from Europe to Taiwan?
- 他們坐火車在歐洲各地旅遊。
  They traveled around Europe via train.

嘔吐 ǒutù ㄡˇ ㄊㄨˋ

V to vomit

- Mary病了，一直嘔吐。
  Mary is ill and keeps vomiting.

★ 哦 ó ㄛˊ

Ptc interjection

- 哦，她也來了。
  Oh, she's come too.
- 哦，他還會說德語？
  Well, he also speaks German?
- 哦，會有這樣的事？
  Really? How could there be such things?

★ 喔 ō ㄛ

Ptc sentence final particle, used as a reminder

- 不要忘記交作業喔！
  May I ask you not to forget to hand in your assignment!

P

爬[a] pá ㄆㄚˊ

V to climb

- 我不願意爬梯子。
  I'm not going to climb ladders.

爬[b] pá ㄆㄚˊ

V to crawl

- 大部分孩子走路以前得學會爬。
  Most of the children have to learn to crawl before walking on their own.

怕[a] pà ㄆㄚˋ

Vst be afraid of

- 我小時候怕黑。
  I was afraid of the dark when I was a child.
- 他怕被警察抓住。
  He was afraid of being caught by the police.
- 我沒有告訴她，怕她不高興。
  I didn't tell her because I was afraid of upsetting her.

怕[b] pà ㄆㄚˋ

Vst be scared of

- 我一直怕狗。
  I've always been scared of dogs.
- 小女孩怕坐飛機。
  The little girl is scared of flying.
- 他怕一個人睡。
  He's scared of sleeping alone.

排[1] pái ㄆㄞˊ

M line of

- 路旁有一排樹。
  There's a line of trees by the roadside.
- 這一排房子正對著馬路。
  The line of houses fronted straight onto the road.

排[2a] pái ㄆㄞˊ

V to line up

- 杯子在桌子上排好了。
  Glasses were lined up on the table.
- 很多人在電影院前排隊買票。

There are many people lined up in front of the theater buying tickets.

排[2b] pái
ㄆㄞˊ

V to arrange

- 把椅子排成三行。
  Arrange these chairs in three rows.
- 請你把花盆排起來。
  Would you please arrange the flowerpots?

排球 páiqiú
ㄆㄞˊ ㄑㄧㄡˊ

N volleyball

- 他們在打排球。
  They are playing volleyball.

牌 pái
ㄆㄞˊ

N cards

- 我一點也不會打牌。
  I'm no good at cards.

牌子 páizi
ㄆㄞˊ ˙ㄗ

N brand

- 我很喜歡那個牌子的咖啡。
  I really enjoy that brand of coffee.

派 pài
ㄆㄞˋ

V send

- 公司派我去跟Muller先生談話。
  The company sent me down to talk to Mr. Muller.

盤 pán
ㄆㄢˊ

M measure word for plate

- 我點了一盤義大利麵。
  I ordered a dish of spaghetti.
- 他切了一盤水果請大家吃。
  He prepared a plate of fruits for us.

盤子 pánzi
ㄆㄢˊ ˙ㄗ

N plate

- 把蔬菜放在盤子裡。
  Put the vegetables on a dish.

旁邊[a] pángbiān
ㄆㄤˊ ㄅㄧㄢ

N (in the) neighborhood

- 花店在鞋店旁邊。
  The florist's is in the neighborhood of the shoes shop.

旁邊[b] pángbiān
ㄆㄤˊ ㄅㄧㄢ

N nearby

- 旁邊有一棵樹。
  There's a tree nearby.

旁聽 pángtīng ㄆㄤˊ ㄊㄧㄥ

V to audit

- John旁聽師範大學的課。
  John audited classes at Normal University.

胖 pàng ㄆㄤˋ

Vs. /Adj fat

- 我才八十公斤，還不算胖。
  Weighting only 80 kilos, I should not be considered fat.

★跑 pǎo ㄆㄠˇ

Vi to run

- Kate從外面跑進來。
  Kate entered running from outside.
- 我身體不行，跑不了那麼快。
  I'm not fit enough to run so fast.
- 你看見Mary往哪個方向跑嗎？
  Did you see which direction Mary ran?

泡[a] pào ㄆㄠˋ

V to brew

- 我給媽媽泡了一杯茶。
  I brewed a cup of tea for my mother.

泡[b] pào ㄆㄠˋ

V to soak

- 冬天泡一個熱水澡，眞舒服。
  It's very comfortable to soak in a warm bath in wintertime.

★陪 péi ㄆㄟˊ

V to accompany

- Ida請我陪她去吃飯。
  Ida asked me to accompany her to the dinner.
- 他陪我們參觀博物館。
  He accompanied us visiting the museum.
- 她常常陪父母旅遊。
  She always accompanies her parents on travelling.

噴嚏 pēntì ㄆㄣ ㄊㄧˋ

V to sneeze (note that in Chinese, the support verb da/打 must cooccur in the context to form a compound verb)

- Ted開始咳嗽，打噴嚏。
  Ted started coughing and sneezing.

★ **朋友** péngyǒu ㄆㄥˊ ㄧㄡˇ

N friend

CN péngyou

- 她的朋友非常關心她。
  Her friends really care about her.
- 我們做朋友很多年了。
  We've been friends for many years.
- 他在臺灣交了不少朋友。
  He made quite a few friends in Taiwan.

便宜 piányí ㄆㄧㄢˊ ㄧˊ

Vs. /Adj cheap

- 才兩百塊？眞便宜。
  Only 200 dollars? That's really cheap.

★ **片** piàn ㄆㄧㄢˋ

M piece of

- 來一片西瓜吧！
  How about a piece of watermelon.
- 我午餐只吃了一片巧克力。
  I just had a piece of chocolate for my lunch.
- 他在一小片紙上寫了點東西。
  He wrote something on a small piece of paper.

騙 piàn ㄆㄧㄢˋ

V to cheat

- 他騙了我五百塊錢。
  He cheated me out of five hundred dollars.

★ **漂亮** piàoliàng ㄆㄧㄠˋ ㄌㄧㄤˋ

Vs. /Adj beautiful

CN piàoliang

- Janny長得漂亮。
  Janny is very beautiful.
- 那件衣服眞漂亮。
  That dress is really beautiful.
- 花園裡的花漂亮。
  The flowers in the garden were beautiful.

啤酒 píjiǔ ㄆㄧˊ ㄐㄧㄡˇ

N beer

- 我更喜歡德國啤酒。
  I prefer German beer.

疲倦 píjuàn
ㄆㄧˊ ㄐㄩㄢˋ

Vs. /Adj be tired

- 長途飛行後我們都十分疲倦。
  We were all really tired out after our long flight.

頻道 píndào
ㄆㄧㄣˊ ㄉㄠˋ

N channel

SG MY 播道

- 我們看五頻道的新聞，好嗎？
  Shall we watch the news on Channel 5?

品質 pǐnzhí
ㄆㄧㄣˇ ㄓˊ

N quality

CN pǐnzhì，「質量」zhìliàng

- 這種牌子的酒品質很差。
  This brand of wine is of poor quality.

坪 píng
ㄆㄧㄥˊ

M ping, unit for measuring surface, equal to 3.3 square meter, used specifically in Taiwan

CN 平方

- 這個房間有多少坪？
  How many ping are there in this room?

平安 píngān
ㄆㄧㄥˊ ㄢ

Vs. /Adj safe

- 我們祝他們旅行平安愉快。
  We wished them a safe, happy trip.

平常[1] píngcháng
ㄆㄧㄥˊ ㄔㄤˊ

Adv usually

- 我平常晚上十點睡覺。
  I usually go to bed at 10 p.m.

平常[2a] píngcháng
ㄆㄧㄥˊ ㄔㄤˊ

Vs. /Adj common

- 跑步是很平常的運動。
  Jogging is a very common exercise.

平常[2b] píngcháng
ㄆㄧㄥˊ ㄔㄤˊ

Vs. /Adj ordinary

- 現在離婚是很平常的事。
  Divorce is an ordinary thing nowadays.

蘋果 píngguǒ
ㄆㄧㄥˊ ㄍㄨㄛˇ

N apple

- 這個蘋果太酸，我不愛吃。

This apple is too sour. I don't like it.

平原 píngyuán
ㄆㄧㄥˊ ㄩㄢˊ

N plain

- 中國東北是一個大平原。
The northeast of China is a huge plain.

葡萄 pútáo
ㄆㄨˊ ㄊㄠˊ

N grape
CN pútao

- 我們買了一串葡萄。
We picked a bunch of grapes.

普洱茶 pǔěrchá
ㄆㄨˇ ㄦˇ ㄔㄚˊ

N Pu'er tea

- 她喜歡喝普洱茶。
She's fond of Pu'er tea.

普通[a] pǔtōng
ㄆㄨˇ ㄊㄨㄥ

Vs. /Adj common

- 這家餐廳的菜很普通。
The food served in this restaurant is very common.

普通[b] pǔtōng
ㄆㄨˇ ㄊㄨㄥ

Vs. /Adj ordinary

- 我只是個普通人。
I'm just an ordinary people.

Q

★ **七** qī ㄑㄧ

numeral seven

- 我們有七個人到。
  There were seven of us there.
- 早上七點就開始排隊了。
  Queues form by 7 a.m. already.

★ **騎** qí ㄑㄧˊ

V to ride

- 他騎馬穿過草地。
  He rode a horse across the meadow.
- 我騎腳踏車上班。
  I ride my bicycle to work.
- 她一直沒有學會騎摩托車。
  She had never learned to ride a motorcycle.

★ **其他** qítā ㄑㄧˊ ㄊㄚ

Det other

- 還有其他問題沒有？
  Are there any other questions?
- 她比班上其他兒童聰明。
  She is smarter than all the other children in her class.
- 我還想邀請一些其他的朋友。
  I've got some other friends I'd like to invite.

期末 qímò ㄑㄧˊ ㄇㄛˋ

N end of the term

CN qī mò SG 年終

- 期末有許多測驗。
  There are many quizzes at the end of the term.

期末考 qímòkǎo ㄑㄧˊ ㄇㄛˋ ㄎㄠˇ

N final exam

CN qī mò kǎo SG 年終考

- 你得通過期末考。
  You ought to pass the final exam.

期中 qízhōng ㄑㄧˊ ㄓㄨㄥ

N middle of the term

CN qī zhōng SG 年中

- 期中休假一個星期。
  There'll be a week's break in the middle of the term.

期中考 qízhōngkǎo
ㄑㄧˊ ㄓㄨㄥ ㄎㄠˇ

N mid-term test

CN qī zhōng kǎo SG 年中考試

- 期中考是什麼時候？
  When will be the mid-term tests?

奇異果 qíyìguǒ
ㄑㄧˊ ㄧˋ ㄍㄨㄛˇ

N kiwi fruit

CN 獼猴桃

- 我要了一個奇異果沙拉。
  I ordered a kiwi fruit salad.

★起 qǐ
ㄑㄧˇ

V to raise

- 早起是我的習慣。
  It is my custom to raise early.

起飛 qǐfēi
ㄑㄧˇ ㄈㄟ

Vi to take off

- 飛機晚了一個小時起飛。
  The plane took off an hour late.

起來 1 qǐlái
ㄑㄧˇ ㄌㄞˊ

Vi to get up

CN qǐ lai

- 我們到九點鐘才起來。
  We didn't get up until nine.

起來 2 qǐlái
ㄑㄧˇ ㄌㄞˊ

Vi to start to do something

- 小孩子哭起來了。
  The child started crying.

起薪 qǐxīn
ㄑㄧˇ ㄒㄧㄣ

N starting salary

- 她起薪五萬，外加佣金。
  She gets a starting salary of fifty thousand plus commission.

汽車 qìchē
ㄑㄧˋ ㄔㄜ

V car

- 路的兩旁都停著汽車。
  Cars were parked on both sides of the road.

氣候 qìhòu
ㄑㄧˋ ㄏㄡˋ

N climate

- 你會很快習慣這裡的氣候的。
  You'll soon get used to the climate here.

氣流 qìliú
ㄑㄧˋ ㄌㄧㄡˊ

N air current

- 因爲氣流太強，飛機不能降落。

The air current was too strong, the plane can't operate landing.

氣溫 qìwēn
ㄑㄧˋ ㄨㄣ

N temperature

- 現在外面氣溫是攝氏八度。
  The outside temperature is now 8°C.

企業 qìyè
ㄑㄧˋ ㄧㄝˋ

N enterprise

CN qǐyè

- 需要給小企業更多的幫助。
  More help should be given to small enterprises.

契約 qìyuē
ㄑㄧˋ ㄩㄝ

N lease

CN 合同hétong

- 租房子以前，要看清楚契約。
  Read carefully les terms of the lease before renting a house.

★前[a] qián
ㄑㄧㄢˊ

N front

- Mary在前排。
  Mary is in the front row.
- 請從前門進去。
  Please enter from the front door.
- 我的腳踏車前燈不亮了。
  My front bike light isn't working.

★前[b] qián
ㄑㄧㄢˊ

N prior to, used after a verb in Chinese

- 你出發前，最好安排好一切。
  All the arrangements should be completed prior to your departure.

★錢 qián
ㄑㄧㄢˊ

N money

- 你能借我點錢嗎？
  Could you lend me some money?
- 他存的錢不是很多。
  He doesn't save very much money.
- 我們花了些錢吃晚飯。
  We spent some of the money on dinner.

★淺 qiǎn
ㄑㄧㄢˇ

Vs. /Adj shallow

- 這個湖很淺。
  This lake is quite shallow.
- 游泳池這一頭比較淺。
  The water is shallower at this end of the pool.
- 把魚放在一個淺盤裡。
  Place the fish in a shallow dish.

★ **千** qiān ㄑㄧㄢ

N thousand

- 這劇院能坐三千人。
  The theater seats three thousand.
- 買下來大約要五千元。
  It cost somewhere around five thousand dollars.
- 一千多人參加了會議。
  There were over 1000 people at the meeting.

簽 qiān ㄑㄧㄢ

V to sign

- 老闆簽了支票。
  The boss signed the check.

簽名 qiānmíng ㄑㄧㄢ ㄇㄧㄥˊ

V-sep sign one's name

- 請在這裡簽名。
  Please sign your name here.

簽約 qiānyuē ㄑㄧㄢ ㄩㄝ

V-sep sign a contract

- 我跟房東簽了約。
  I've signed a contract with the landlord.

簽證 qiānzhèng ㄑㄧㄢ ㄓㄥˋ

N visa

- 她的簽證還沒有辦下來。
  Her visa hasn't been issued yet.

★ **前面** qiánmiàn ㄑㄧㄢˊ ㄇㄧㄢˋ

N front side

CN qiánmian

- John在我前面。
  John is in front of me.
- Janny坐在鏡子前面看起書來。
  Jane sat down in front of the mirror and started reading.
- 這張桌子的前面比後面大。
  The front part of this table is larger than the back part.

★ **前年** qiánnián ㄑㄧㄢˊ ㄋㄧㄢˊ

N year before last

- 我是前年開始學華語的。

I began to learn Chinese the year before last.

- 她的孩子是前年出生的。
  Her child was born the year before last.

★強 qiáng ㄑㄧㄤˊ

Vs. /Adj strong

- 風力相當強。
  The wind is rather strong.
- 他的中文能力很強。
  He's strong in Chinese.

牆 qiáng ㄑㄧㄤˊ

N wall

- 那男孩想跳過一面牆。
  The boy tried to leap over a wall.

牆壁 qiángbì ㄑㄧㄤˊ ㄅㄧˋ

N wall

- 浴室的牆壁是藍色的。
  The bathroom walls were painted blue.

搶 qiǎng ㄑㄧㄤˇ

V to rob

- 他們搶了我所有的東西。
  They robbed me of all my possessions.

★敲 qiāo ㄑㄧㄠ

V to knock

- 進來前請敲門。
  Please knock at the door before entering.
- 我敲了敲計程車的車窗。
  I knocked on the taxi window.

橋 qiáo ㄑㄧㄠˊ

N bridge

- 從橋下走，然後往左轉。
  Go under the bridge and then turn left.

橋牌 qiáopái ㄑㄧㄠˊ ㄆㄞˊ

N bridge

- 他們四個人正在打橋牌。
  The four of them were having a game of bridge.

巧克力 qiǎokèlì ㄑㄧㄠˇ ㄎㄜˋ ㄌㄧˋ

N chocolate

- 我給她買了一盒巧克力。
  I bought her a box of chocolate.

切 qiē ㄑㄧㄝ

V to cut

- 請你把蘋果切成四塊。
  Can you cut the apple into four pieces?

親戚 qīnqī ㄑㄧㄣ ㄑㄧ

N relative

- 我在這裡沒有親戚。
  I have no relatives here.

★親自 [a] qīnzì ㄑㄧㄣ ㄗˋ

Adv in person

- 我必須親自見她。
  I must meet her in person.
- 你必須親自簽名。
  You have to sign for it in person.
- 他要親自來取票。
  He has to collect his tickets in person.

★親自 [b] qīnzì ㄑㄧㄣ ㄗˋ

Adv personally

- 這件事我會親自處理。
  I'll see to it personally.
- 她親自寫信向我表示感謝。
  She wrote personally to thank me.

寢室 qǐnshì ㄑㄧㄣˇ ㄕˋ

N dormitory

- 我們寢室有三個室友。
  We have three roommates in our dormitory.

★輕 qīng ㄑㄧㄥ

Vs. /Adj light

- 這袋子輕，很好拿。
  The bag is light to carry.
- 你可以拿這個箱子，它很輕。
  You can carry this box, it's fairly light.
- 下次，處罰就不會這樣輕了。
  Next time the punishment will not be so light.

青菜 qīngcài ㄑㄧㄥ ㄘㄞˋ

N vegetable

- 你可以在超級市場裡買到很多不同的青菜。
  You can buy many different vegetables in the supermarket.

★輕鬆 qīngsōng ㄑㄧㄥ ㄙㄨㄥ

Vs. /Adj relaxed

- 這音樂很輕鬆。
  This music is very relaxing.
- 一回到家，我就感到特別輕鬆。
  Once at home, I feel really relaxed.

★ **清楚** qīngchǔ ㄑㄧㄥ ㄔㄨˇ

Vs. /Adj clear

CN qīngchu

- 那錄音不很清楚。
  That recording isn't very clear.
- 我剛剛說的清楚了嗎？
  Is what I just said clear?
- 你的意思很清楚，我明白。
  Your meaning is clear. I understand it.

情況 [a] qíngkuàng ㄑㄧㄥˊ ㄎㄨㄤˋ

N condition

- 其中一個病人，情況很嚴重。
  One of the patients was in a critical condition.

情況 [b] qíngkuàng ㄑㄧㄥˊ ㄎㄨㄤˋ

N situation

- 我跟她說了一下現在的情況。
  I explained to her the current situation.

情緒 qíngxù ㄑㄧㄥˊ ㄒㄩˋ

N mood

- 她今天的情緒不好。
  She had a bad mood.

晴天 qíngtiān ㄑㄧㄥˊ ㄊㄧㄢ

N be sunny

- 天氣預報說明天會是晴天。
  The weather report says it will be sunny tomorrow.

★ **請** [1] qǐng ㄑㄧㄥˇ

V may I ask you

- 我想請你幫忙。
  May I ask you a favour.

★ **請** [2a] qǐng ㄑㄧㄥˇ

V to request

- 主席請大家安靜。
  The chairman requested silence.
- 能不能請你不要再講了？
  May I request you to stop talking?

- 請你不要在飯館裡吸菸。
  You are requested not to smoke in the restaurant.

★ **請**[2b] qǐng ㄑㄧㄥˇ

V to invite

- 在會上他們請我發言。
  At the meeting they invited me to speak.
- 我們該請誰來參加聚會？
  Who should we invite to the party?
- 你爲什麼不請她跟你一起去？
  Why don't you invite her along?

請假 qǐngjià ㄑㄧㄥˇ ㄐㄧㄚˋ

V-sep to ask for leave

- 他請假一個星期去渡假。
  He asked for a week's holiday leave.

請客 qǐngkè ㄑㄧㄥˇ ㄎㄜˋ

V-sep to treat

- 這次我請客。
  It's my treat this time.

慶生 qìngshēng ㄑㄧㄥˋ ㄕㄥ

V-sep to celebrate one's birthday

- 我們出去吃飯給爸爸慶生。
  We're going out for a meal to celebrate Dad's birthday.

慶生會 qìngshēnghuì ㄑㄧㄥˋ ㄕㄥ ㄏㄨㄟˋ

N birthday party

HK 生日會

- 今晚你去參加Janny的慶生會嗎？
  Are you going to Jane's birthday party tonight?

慶祝 qìngzhù ㄑㄧㄥˋ ㄓㄨˋ

V to celebrate

- 你們國家的人怎樣慶祝新年？
  How do people celebrate New Year in your country?

秋季 qiūjì ㄑㄧㄡ ㄐㄧˋ

N autumn

- 我要參加學校的秋季運動會。
  I'd like to participate in the autumn games of the school.

★ **秋天** qiūtiān ㄑㄧㄡ ㄊㄧㄢ

N autumn

• 今年秋天一直很暖和。
It's been a very mild autumn this year.

球 qiú ㄑㄧㄡˊ

N ball

• 我的球呢？
Where's my ball?

球隊 qiúduì ㄑㄧㄡˊ ㄉㄨㄟˋ

N team

• 他今年會在這個球隊打球嗎？
Is he going to be in the team this year?

球賽 qiúsài ㄑㄧㄡˊ ㄙㄞˋ

N ball game

• 我喜歡看球賽。
I like to watch the ball game.

球員 qiúyuán ㄑㄧㄡˊ ㄩㄢˊ

N player

• 這個隊有不少有名的球員。
The team has many famous players.

區 qū ㄑㄩ

N district

• 臺北你喜歡哪一區？
Which is your favourite district of Taipei?

★ 去 qù ㄑㄩˋ

Vp to go

• 如果你要去的話，請快點。
Hurry up please, if you're going.

★ 去年 qùnián ㄑㄩˋ ㄋㄧㄢˊ

N last year

• John是去年的今天去臺灣的。
John went to Taiwan today last year.

去世 qùshì ㄑㄩˋ ㄕˋ

Vp to die

• 他還在上學時父母就去世了。
His parents died while he was still at school.

全部[1] quánbù ㄑㄩㄢˊ ㄅㄨˋ

Vs-attr whole

• 全部工作都是她一個人做

A B C D E F G H J K L M N O P Q R S T W X Y Z X-

的。
She did the whole job herself.

全部[2a] quánbù ㄑㄩㄢˊ ㄅㄨˋ

Adv whole

- 昨天的新聞全部都是棒球。
  The baseball covers the whole news yesterday.

全部[2b] quánbù ㄑㄩㄢˊ ㄅㄨˋ

Adv entirely

- 這些事全部由他們處理。
  All this is to be handled entirely by them.

全票 quánpiào ㄑㄩㄢˊ ㄆㄧㄠˋ

N full-fare ticket

- 他十二歲了，得買全票。
  He's already twelve years old and has to pay a full-fare ticket.

全天 quántiān ㄑㄩㄢˊ ㄊㄧㄢ

N all day

- 這個博物館全天都有人服務。
  Services are available all day in this museum.

★ 卻 què ㄑㄩㄝˋ

Adv unexpectedly

- 這家餐廳的菜很貴，卻不好吃。
  This restaurant is quite expensive, and unexpectedly the food is awful.

確定[a] quèdìng ㄑㄩㄝˋ ㄉㄧㄥˋ

Vst to ascertain

- 你能不能確定這件事的原因呢？
  Could you ascertain the cause of what had happened?

確定[b] quèdìng ㄑㄩㄝˋ ㄉㄧㄥˋ

Vst to confirm

- 我不能確定會有多少人來。
  I cannot confirm the number of comers.

裙子 qúnzi ㄑㄩㄣˊ ˙ㄗ

N skirt

- Mary穿紅裙子。
  Mary is in a red skirt.

R

★ **然後** ránhòu ㄖㄢˊ ㄏㄡˋ

Adv afterwards

- 我們先看戲，然後吃飯。
  Let's go to the theatre first and eat afterwards.
- 先開會討論然後再投票。
  We'll have a meeting for discussion, and afterwards there will be vote.
- 他們喝了茶，然後開車回家。
  They had tea and afterwards drove home.

讓 [a] ràng ㄖㄤˋ

V to allow

- 我不讓貓進入臥室。
  I don't allow the cat in the bedroom.
- 警察讓我們的車子通過。
  The police allowed our car to pass through.
- 你認爲你爸爸會讓你去嗎？
  Do you think dad will allow you to go?

讓 [b] ràng ㄖㄤˋ

V to let

- 讓他出去。
  Let him go out.
- 打開窗子，讓新鮮空氣進來。
  Open the window to let the fresh air in.

★ **熱** rè ㄖㄜˋ

Vs. /Adj hot

- 水有多熱？
  How hot is the water?
- 這裡太熱了，我開開窗好嗎？
  It's so hot here. Can I open the window?
- 那碗麵，你趁熱吃了吧。
  That bowl of noodles, eat it while it's hot.

熱門 [1] rèmén ㄖㄜˋ ㄇㄣˊ

N popular

- 學華語是個熱門。
  Learning Chinese is a popular

discipline.

熱門 [2a] rèmén
ㄖㄜˋ ㄇㄣˊ

Vs. /Adj popular

- 足球在臺灣不是熱門運動。
  Football is not very popular in Taiwan.

熱門 [2b] rèmén
ㄖㄜˋ ㄇㄣˊ

Vs. /Adj be popular

- 這種小說最近非常熱門。
  The kind of fiction is rather popular lately.

熱水 rèshuǐ
ㄖㄜˋ ㄕㄨㄟˇ

N hot water

- 我們家裡整天有熱水。
  We have constant hot water in the house.

熱水器 rèshuǐqì
ㄖㄜˋ ㄕㄨㄟˇ ㄑㄧˋ

N heater

- 你關掉熱水器了嗎？
  Did you turn the heater off?

人 [a] rén
ㄖㄣˊ

N human being

- 人都需要愛。
  All human beings need love.

人 [b] rén
ㄖㄣˊ

N people

- Mary對人很客氣。
  Mary is polite in her dealing with people.
- 有兩百人參加會議。
  There were 200 people present at the meeting.
- 向人要東西不是他的習慣。
  It was not his habit to ask people for things.

人 [c] rén

ㄖㄣˊ

N person

- 他就是這樣的人。
  He's just such a person.

人口 rénkǒu
ㄖㄣˊ ㄎㄡˇ

N population

- 這個城市有近三百萬人口。
  The city has a population of nearly three million.

人民 rénmín
ㄖㄣˊ ㄇㄧㄣˊ

N people

- 總統得到人民的支持。
  The president has the support of the people.

人民幣 rénmí bì ㄖㄣˊ ㄇㄧㄣˊ ㄅㄧˋ

N Renminbi (RMB) standard currency of Mainland China

- 人民幣對美金的匯率上升了。
  The RMB has risen against the US dollar.

人員 rényuán ㄖㄣˊ ㄩㄢˊ

N staff member

- 辦公室大約有二十個工作人員。
  There're about 20 staff members in the office.

韌帶 rèndài ㄖㄣˋ ㄉㄞˋ

N ligament

- 他拉傷了右膝的韌帶。
  He tore a ligament in his right knee.

★任何 rènhé ㄖㄣˋ ㄏㄜˊ

Det any

- 她對哲學沒有任何興趣。
  She hasn't shown any interest at all in philosophy.

★認識 rènshì ㄖㄣˋ ㄕˋ

Vst to be acquainted

CN rènshi

- 你認識那個人嗎？
  Are you acquainted with that man?
- 他們是在工作中互相認識的。
  They got acquainted with each other at work.

★認爲 rènwéi ㄖㄣˋ ㄨㄟˊ

Vs. /Adj to believe

- 我認爲你是對的。
  I believe that you are correct.
- 專家認爲今年冬天會非常冷。
  Experts believe that we'll have a terrible winter.

日場 rìchǎng ㄖˋ ㄔㄤˇ

N matinee

- 日場五點開始。
  The matinee starts at five.

★日期 rìqí ㄖˋ ㄑㄧˊ

N date

CN rìqī

- 日期全亂了。
  There has been a mix-up over the dates.
- 你訂好婚禮的日期了嗎？
  Have you set a date for the wedding?
- 信上的日期是2013年8月30日。
  The date on the letter was 30th August 2013.

日圓 rìyuán ㄖˋ ㄩㄢˊ

N Japanese yen, standard currency of Japan

- 這本書要五千日圓。
  The book costs 5000 Japanese yen.

溶化 rónghuà ㄖㄨㄥˊ ㄏㄨㄚˋ

Vpt to melt

- 冰塊在熱水裡溶化了。
  The hot water melted the ice cubes.

容易[a] róngyì ㄖㄨㄥˊ ㄧˋ

Vs. /Adj easy

- 學寫漢字不容易。
  It's not so easy to learn to write Chinese characters.

容易[b] róngyì ㄖㄨㄥˊ ㄧˋ

Vs. /Adj simple

- 那工作看起來很容易。
  The job looked quite simple.

肉 ròu ㄖㄡˋ

N meat

- 這塊肉很好切。
  This piece of meat cuts well.

★如果 rúguǒ ㄖㄨˊ ㄍㄨㄛˇ

Conj if

- 如果你要他來，他就來。
  He will come if you need him.
- 如果你喝咖啡，我也喝。
  If you would like to have coffee, I too will have.
- 如果天氣好轉，她明天會到。
  She will arrive tomorrow if the weather improves.

乳房 rǔfáng ㄖㄨˇ ㄈㄤˊ

N breast

- Lisa到醫院去做乳房檢查。
  Lisa went to the hospital to have a checkup on breasts.

入口 rùkǒu

ㄖㄨˋ ㄎㄡˇ

N entrance

- 博物館的入口在哪裡？
  Where is the entrance to the museum?

★ 軟 ruǎn

ㄖㄨㄢˇ

Vs. /Adj soft

- 這張床太軟。
  This bed is too soft.
- 把洋蔥煮軟。
  Cook the onions until they go soft.
- 那毛衣又軟又暖和。
  That sweater is both soft and warm.

軟體 ruǎntǐ

ㄖㄨㄢˇ ㄊㄧˇ

N software

CN 軟件

- 硬體沒問題，但軟體有問題。
  The hardware is fine, but the software has a problem.

S

★ 三 sān ㄙㄢ

numeral three

• 這部電影她看了三次。
She watched the film three times.

三餐 sāncān ㄙㄢ ㄘㄢ

N three meals of the day, e.g. breakfast, lunch and dinner

• 一天三餐包括在費用中。
The charge includes three meals a day.

散步 sànbù ㄙㄢˋ ㄅㄨˋ

V-sep to stroll

• 晚飯後他們在公園裡散步。
They strolled in the park after dinner.

喪假 sāngjià ㄙㄤ ㄐㄧㄚˋ

N compassionate leave

• 她已經申請了三天喪假。
She has applied for three days' compassionate leave.

森林 sēnlín ㄙㄣ ㄌㄧㄣˊ

N forest

• 河邊有森林。
There's a forest by the riverside.

殺 shā ㄕㄚ

V to kill

• 他殺了那個人。
He killed the man.

紗布 shābù ㄕㄚ ㄅㄨˋ

N gauze bandage

• 他在流血，需要一些紗布。
He's bleeding, and needs some gauze bandages.

沙發 shāfā ㄕㄚ ㄈㄚ

N sofa

• 她躺在沙發上看電視。
She was lying on the sofa watching TV.

沙漠 shāmò ㄕㄚ ㄇㄛˋ

N desert

- 沙漠中非常熱。
  The heat in the desert was extreme.

曬 shài ㄕㄞˋ

V to bask in the sun

- 貓趴在地上曬太陽。
  The cat is lying on the ground under the sunlight.

★山 shān ㄕㄢ

N mountain

- 這座山眞高啊！
  How high this mountain is!
- 上山容易，下山難。
  It is easier to climb a mountain than to walk down a mountain.

商店 shāngdiàn ㄕㄤ ㄉㄧㄢˋ

N store

- 你們商店賣玩具嗎？
  Does the store sell toys?

商務 shāngwù ㄕㄤ ㄨˋ

N business affairs

- 我不打算跟你談公司的商務。
  I'm not prepared to discuss my company's business affairs with you.

商學院 shāngxuéyuàn ㄕㄤ ㄒㄩㄝˊ ㄩㄢˋ

N business school

- 她在臺北商學院修一門課程。
  She's doing a course at Taipei business school.

上[1] shàng ㄕㄤˋ

complement upward

- 電梯正在往上。
  The elevator is going upward.

上[2] shàng ㄕㄤˋ

N [bound form] bound word used with zai/在 (to be) to form a locative pattern which can be rendered in English by the preposition 'on'

- 我的鑰匙在桌子上。
  My keys are on the table.

上班 shàngbān ㄕㄤˋ ㄅㄢ

V-sep go to the office

- 我早上九點上班。
  I go to the office at nine.

★上次 shàngcì ㄕㄤˋ ㄘˋ

Adv last time

- 上次我不在這裡。
  I wasn't here last time.
- 上次你去過哪些地方？
  Where did you to last time?
- 我們倆上次見面時剛到臺北。
  The last time we met both of us had just arrived in Taipei.

上課 shàngkè ㄕㄤˋ ㄎㄜˋ

V-sep to attend class

- 我上課時總愛打瞌睡。
  I always felt sleepy when I attended classes.

上面 shàngmiàn ㄕㄤˋ ㄇㄧㄢˋ

position marker, which can be rendered in English by the preposition 'above' above

CN shàngmian

- 門上面有一個鐘。
  There's a clock above the door.

上鋪 shàngpù ㄕㄤˋ ㄆㄨˋ

N upper berth

- 她睡上鋪，我睡下鋪。
  She's in the upper berth and I, in the lower berth.

上司 shàngsi ㄕㄤˋ ㄙ

N superior

CN 領導

- 他和他的上司工作關係很好。
  He had a good working relationship with his superior.

上網 shàngwǎng ㄕㄤˋ ㄨㄤˇ

V-sep to get on the Internet

- 我每天都上網看新聞。
  I get on the Internet every day to read news.

★ 上午 shàngwǔ ㄕㄤˋ ㄨˇ

N morning

- 我花了一個上午找資料。
  I spent the morning searching for data.

★ 上旬 shàngxún ㄕㄤˋ ㄒㄩㄣˊ

N first ten day of a month

- 我下月上旬會回來。
  I'll be back within the first ten days of next month.

上演 shàngyǎn ㄕㄤˋ ㄧㄢˇ

V to perform

• 周末將上演幾個新戲。
Several new plays will be performed on the weekend.

燒[a] shāo
ㄕㄠ

V to burn

• 我把她的舊信全燒了。
I burnt all her old letters.

• 你不能在這裡燒垃圾。
You're not allowed to burn your trash here.

燒[b] shāo
ㄕㄠ

V to cook

• 今天我給你燒一條魚。
Today I'll cook you a fish.

燒餅 shāobǐng
ㄕㄠ ㄅㄧㄥˇ

N baked cake

CN shāo bing

• 她早飯吃了一塊燒餅。
She ate a piece of baked cake for breakfast.

★ 少[a] shǎo
ㄕㄠˇ

Vs. /Adj a few

• 這種情況很少。
There are only a very few occurrences of this kind.

• 參加會議的人很少。
Few people attended the meeting.

★ 少[b] shǎo
ㄕㄠˇ

Vs. /Adj less

• 我的錢比你的少。
I have less money than you do.

• 今年下的雪比去年少。
There was less snow this year than last year.

★ 少數 shǎoshù
ㄕㄠˇ ㄕㄨˋ

N minority

• 我們是少數。
We're in the minority.

• 在我們辦公室裡，男人是少數。
Men are in the minority in our office.

蛇 shé
ㄕㄜˊ

N snake

• 那座山上有不少蛇。
There are lots of snakes in that mountain.

舌頭 shétou
ㄕㄜˊ ˙ㄊㄡ

N tongue

- 哦，我咬到了我的舌頭。
Ow, I just bit my tongue.

設備 shèbèi ㄕㄜˋ ㄅㄟˋ

N equipment

- 使用這台設備很容易。
The equipment is quite simple to use.

社會學 shèhuìxué ㄕㄜˋ ㄏㄨㄟˋ ㄒㄩㄝˊ

N sociology

- 她在臺師大主修社會學。
She's majoring in Sociology in Taiwan Normal University.

社團 shètuán ㄕㄜˋ ㄊㄨㄢˊ

N community

- 他在當地社團非常出名。
He's well-known in the local community.

攝氏 shèshì ㄕㄜˋ ㄕˋ

N degree centigrade

- 溫度仍然是攝氏十五度。
The temperature was still 15 degrees centigrade.

攝影 shèyǐng ㄕㄜˋ ㄧㄥˇ

N photography

- 他們都對攝影很有興趣。
They are all interested in photography.

★誰 shéi ㄕㄟˊ

pronoun who

CN shuí

- 你找誰？
Who are you looking for?
- 你到底是誰？
Who might you be?
- 坐在那邊的人是誰？
Who's that person sitting over there?

設計[1] shèjì ㄕㄜˋ ㄐㄧˋ

V to design

- Mike設計了一個非常成功的軟體。
Mike has designed a very successful software.

設計[2] shèjì ㄕㄜˋ ㄐㄧˋ

N design

- 有一些設計比其他的好。
Some designs are better than others.

伸 shēn ㄕㄣ

V to stretch out

- Joe伸手去拿雨傘。
  Joe stretched out his hand to take the umbrella.

★ **深** shēn ㄕㄣ

Vs. /Adj deep

- 雪下了一公尺深。
  It snowed one meter deep.
- 這裡的河水很深。
  The river is quite deep here.
- 這個湖有二十公尺深。
  The lake has a depth of 20 meters.

★ **申請** shēnqǐng ㄕㄣ ㄑㄧㄥˇ

V to apply for

- 他申請了獎學金。
  He applied for a scholarship.
- 她打算申請新的工作。
  She tried to apply for a new job.

身體 shēntǐ ㄕㄣ ㄊㄧˇ

N health

- 她身體健康。
  She enjoys good health.

★ **什麼** shénme ㄕㄜˊ ˙ㄇㄜ

pronoun what

- 這是什麼？
  What's this?
- 你在做什麼？
  What are you doing?
- 我不記得Steve說過什麼。
  I don't recollect what Steve said.

生 [1] shēng ㄕㄥ

N [bound form] bound word for pupil, student

- 那時他還是一個高中生。
  He was still a high school student at that time.

生 [2a] shēng ㄕㄥ

V to give birth to

- Mary生了一個女孩。
  Mary gave birth to a baby girl.

生 [2b] shēng ㄕㄥ

V be born

- John是十二月生的。
  John was born in December.

身高 shēngāo ㄕㄣ ㄍㄠ

V to be, followed by an expression of height

- Matt身高一百八十公分。
  Matt is one meter eighty.

生病 shēngbìng ㄕㄥ ㄅㄧㄥˋ

V-sep to get sick

- Mary生病了。
  Mary has got sick.

生產 [1] shēngchǎn ㄕㄥ ㄔㄢˇ

V to produce

- 這個地區生產牛奶。
  This area produces milk.

生產 [2] shēngchǎn ㄕㄥ ㄔㄢˇ

N to give birth to

- 大部分的母親在醫院生產。
  Most of the mothers give birth to their baby in the hospital.

生詞 shēngcí ㄕㄥ ㄘˊ

N new words

- 我記不住這麼多生詞。
  I can't remember so many new words.

★ 生活 shēnghuó ㄕㄥ ㄏㄨㄛˊ

N life

- 他們過著非常簡單的生活。
  They lead a very simple life.

生日 shēngrì ㄕㄥ ㄖˋ

N birthday

- 我的生日離聖誕節很近。
  My birthday is very near Christmas.

省 [1a] shěng ㄕㄥˇ

Vst save money

- 我喜歡這種省錢的主意。
  I love this kind of money-saving ideas.
- 我走路上班，可以省車錢。
  I save on fares by walking to work.
- 週末前買票可以省三百臺幣。
  You can save 300 Taiwan dollars if you buy your tickets before weekend.

省 [1b] shěng ㄕㄥˇ

Vst save time

- 新方法省錢又省時間。
  The new method saves both time and money.

A B C D E F G H J K L M N O P Q R S T W X Y Z X-

- 如果你坐火車就可以省時間。
You'll save time if you take the train.

★ 省 ² shěng
ㄕㄥˇ

N province

- 中國有多少個省？
How many provinces are there in China?

升 shēng
ㄕㄥ

V to promote

- 他升教授了。
He was promoted to the rank of professor.

剩 shèng
ㄕㄥˋ

V be left

- 什麼也沒剩。
There's nothing left.

剩下 shèngxià
ㄕㄥˋ ㄒㄧㄚˋ

V to leave
CN shèng xia

- 我沒剩下多少錢。
I haven't got any money left.
- 我還剩下很多功課沒做。
I still have plenty of homework left.

★ 濕 shī
ㄕ

Vs. /Adj wet

- 別弄濕了鞋子。
Don't get your shoes wet.
- 小心走路，地板很濕。
Walk with caution. The floor is wet.

失火 shīhuǒ
ㄕ ㄏㄨㄛˇ

Vp-sep be on fire

- 房子失火了。
The house is on fire.

★ 十 shí
ㄕˊ

numeral ten

- 公車上有十個人。
There were ten people on the bus.
- 我們大約十點鐘出發。
We're leaving round about ten.
- 雪已經下了十天了。
Snow had been falling for ten days.

食譜 shípǔ
ㄕˊ ㄆㄨˇ

N recipe

- 照著這個食譜就可以炒飯吃。
Just follow this recipe for fried rice.

食物 shíwù ㄕˊ ㄨˋ

N food

- 剩下這麼多食物，眞可惜。
It seems a pity to have all this food left over.

食指 shízhǐ ㄕˊ ㄓˇ

N index finger

- 我的食指流血了。
My index finger is bleeding.

時差 shíchā ㄕˊ ㄔㄚ

N jet lag

- 因爲時差的關係，我睡不著。
Because of jet lag, I can't fall asleep.

時代[a] shídài ㄕˊ ㄉㄞˋ

N era

- 我們生活在電腦時代。
We live in a computer era.

時代[b] shídài ㄕˊ ㄉㄞˋ

N time

- 時代變了，我也變了。
Times have changed and so have I.

時候 shíhòu ㄕˊ ㄏㄡˋ

N when

CN shíhou

- 客人來的時候，他還在睡覺。
His visitors came when he was still in bed.
- 你記得他們離開的時候嗎？
Do you remember the time when they left?

★時間 shíjiān ㄕˊ ㄐㄧㄢ

N time

- 還有多少時間？
What's the time left?
- 請再給我一些時間。
Can I have more time?
- 現在的時間是十點鐘。
The time is now ten o'clock.

石頭 shítou ㄕˊ ˙ㄊㄡ

N stone

- 前面有一堆石頭。
  There's a pile of stones ahead.

實在 [1a] shízài ㄕˊ ㄗㄞˋ

Adv indeed

- 我遲到了，實在抱歉。
  I'm late, and I'm very sorry indeed.

實在 [1b] shízài ㄕˊ ㄗㄞˋ

Adv really

- 我實在不了解你的意思。
  I really can't understand what you mean.

★實在 [2a] shízài ㄕˊ ㄗㄞˋ

Vs. /Adj practical

- 實在一點，先算算要多少錢。
  Let's be practical and work out the cost first.

實在 [2b] shízài ㄕˊ ㄗㄞˋ

Vs. /Adj real

- 實在一點，他不會借給你錢。
  Get real! He's never going to lend you money.

★使 shǐ ㄕˇ

V to make, with a causative meaning

- 那裙子使你看起來瘦一點。
  That skirt makes you look thinner.

使用 [a] shǐyòng ㄕˇ ㄩㄥˋ

V to use

- 這個工具使用起來很方便。
  The tool is very easy to use.

使用 [b] shǐyòng ㄕˇ ㄩㄥˋ

V to utilize

- 大學生都會使用電腦。
  All the students know how to utilize computer.

市 shì ㄕˋ

N [bound form] bound word for a city name

- 臺北市在臺灣北部。
  The city of Taipei is located at the north Taiwan.

市場 shìchǎng ㄕˋ ㄔㄤˇ

N market

SG 巴剎

- Mary在市場擺攤子。
  Mary runs a stand in the market.

市區 shìqū ㄕˋ ㄑㄩ

N urban district

- 他家在市區。
  He lives in the urban district.

市中心 shìzhōngxīn ㄕˋ ㄓㄨㄥ ㄒㄧㄣ

N city center

- 市中心不能停車。
  It's impossible to park in the city center.

★是 shì ㄕˋ

Vst to be

- 誰是第一個？
  Who is first, please?
- 她是我們公司的人。
  She is one of the staff of our company.
- 他們四個不是中國人。
  The four of them are not Chinese.

式 shì ㄕˋ

N [bound form] bound word for style

- 她喜歡吃西式早餐。
  She enjoys breakfast Western-style.

事[a] shì ㄕˋ

N matter

- 發生了什麼事？
  What's the matter?

事[b] shì ㄕˋ

N thing

- 那是她的事。
  That's her thing.

事假 shìjià ㄕˋ ㄐㄧㄚˋ

N casual leave

- 她經常請病假或事假。
  She takes the sick or casual leave very often.

事情[a] shìqíng ㄕˋ ㄑㄧㄥˊ

N matter

CN shìqing

- 這事情很嚴重。
  That is the serious matter.

事情[b] shìqíng ㄕˋ ㄑㄧㄥˊ

N thing

- 事情變了。
  Things have changed.

事務 shìwù
ㄕˋ ㄨˋ

N affairs

- 他住院時由我處理他的事務。
  I'm looking after his affairs while he's in hospital.

室 shì
ㄕˋ

N [bound form] bound word for room

- 我在716室。
  I'm in room 716.

室友 shìyǒu
ㄕˋ ㄧㄡˇ

N roommate
CN 同屋

- Gary是我大學裡的一個室友。
  Gary's one of my college roommates.

★試 shì
ㄕˋ

V to try

- 我想再試一次。
  I'd like to try that again.
- 今年春天我想試著打網球。
  I want to try playing tennis this spring.
- 我們休息一下，然後再試。
  Let's have a rest and then we'll try again.

試用 shìyòng
ㄕˋ ㄩㄥˋ

V to try out

- 我在試用一台新電腦。
  I'm trying out a new computer.
- John得試用所有新軟體。
  John got to try out all the new software.

世界 shìjiè
ㄕˋ ㄐㄧㄝˋ

N world

- 科技改變了世界。
  Technology has changed the world.

視聽 shìtīng
ㄕˋ ㄊㄧㄥ

Vs. /Adj audiovisual

- 課堂上使用視聽教材很成功。
  The use of audiovisual material in the classroom was very successful.

★ **收**[a] shōu
ㄕㄡ

V to receive

- 你還的錢，我們收到了。
  We've received your payment.
- 我們還沒有收到你的來信。
  We have not received your letter.
- 他們每人都會收到一份禮物。
  All of them will receive a gift.

★ **收**[b] shōu
ㄕㄡ

V to collect

- 他正向房客收房租。
  He's collecting rent from tenants.

★ **收**[c] shōu
ㄕㄡ

V to gather

- 我們把東西收了就離開了。
  We gathered our things together and left.

收費 shōufèi
ㄕㄡ ㄈㄟˋ

V-sep to charge

- 打電話要不要收費？
  Do they charge for the use of the telephone?

收銀台 shōuyíntái
ㄕㄡ ㄧㄣˊ ㄊㄞˊ

N cash desk

- 食品部的收銀台在哪裡？
  Where's the cash desk of the Food Department?

★ **熟**[a] shóu
ㄕㄡˊ

Vs. /Adj cooked

- 雞肉還沒熟。
  The chicken isn't cooked yet.

★ **熟**[b] shóu
ㄕㄡˊ

Vs. /Adj ripe

- 蘋果還沒有熟，很酸。
  The apples are not yet ripe. They're sour.

★ **熟**[c] shóu
ㄕㄡˊ

Vs. /Adj familiar

- 她的名字我很熟。
  Her name is familiar to me.
- 我個人跟他並不熟。
  I'm not personally familiar with him.
- 電話裡的聲音聽上去很熟。

The voice on the phone sounded familiar.

★ 手 shǒu ㄕㄡˇ

N hand

• 去洗手。
Go wash your hands.

• 這張椅子很重，得用兩隻手搬。
The chair is so heavy that you have to carry it with both hands.

手背 shǒubèi ㄕㄡˇ ㄅㄟˋ

N back of the hand

• 她的手背流血了。
Her back of the hand is bleeding.

手臂 shǒubì ㄕㄡˇ ㄅㄧˋ

N arm

• 我搬東西搬到手臂都痠了。
My arms are sore from all the lifting.

手錶 shǒubiǎo ㄕㄡˇ ㄅㄧㄠˇ

N watch

• 你的手錶幾點了？
What time does your watch say?

手工 shǒugōng ㄕㄡˇ ㄍㄨㄥ

Vs. /Adj handmade

• 我們的餃子都是手工做的。
All of our dumplings are entirely handmade.

手機 shǒujī ㄕㄡˇ ㄐㄧ

N mobile phone

• 我打他手機，沒打通。
I called him on his mobile, but I couldn't get through.

手術 shǒushù ㄕㄡˇ ㄕㄨˋ

N operation

• 這次手術可使她多活兩三年。
The operation could prolong her life by two or three years.

手套 shǒutào ㄕㄡˇ ㄊㄠˋ

N gloves

• 我需要一副新手套。
I need a new pair of gloves.

手腕 shǒuwàn ㄕㄡˇ ㄨㄢˋ

N wrist

- Ted抓著我的手腕。
  Ted seized me by the wrist.

手心 shǒuxīn ㄕㄡˇ ㄒㄧㄣ

N center of the palm

- Mary把花輕輕地放在手心。
  Mary put the flower gently in the palm of her hand.

手續 shǒuxù ㄕㄡˇ ㄒㄩˋ

N formality
CN shǒuxu

- 我們正在辦理畢業手續。
  We are now proceeding with the graduation formalities.

手掌 shǒuzhǎng ㄕㄡˇ ㄓㄤˇ

N palm

- 他的手掌比我的大。
  His palm is larger than mine.

手指 shǒuzhǐ ㄕㄡˇ ㄓˇ

N fingers

- 她的手指又瘦又長。
  She had long scrawny fingers.

手肘 shǒuzhǒu ㄕㄡˇ ㄓㄡˇ

N elbow

- 別用手肘碰我！
  Stop jabbing me with your elbow!

首先[a] shǒuxiān ㄕㄡˇ ㄒㄧㄢ

Adv first

- 我首先去臺北，然後去臺南。
  I first went to Taipei and then Tainan.

首先[b] shǒuxiān ㄕㄡˇ ㄒㄧㄢ

Adv first of all

- 首先，請讓我介紹一下新朋友。
  First of all, allow me to introduce our new friends.
- 首先，我要感謝各位的幫忙。
  First of all, I'd like to thank everyone for helping.

瘦 shòu ㄕㄡˋ

Vs. /Adj thin

- 她的男朋友又高又瘦。
  Her boyfriend is tall and thin.

★ 受傷 shòushāng ㄕㄡˋ ㄕㄤ

V-sep be wounded

- 我的腿受傷了。
  I was wounded in the leg.

輸 shū ㄕㄨ

Vp to lost

- Bob玩牌輸了一大筆錢。
  Bob lost a fortune at cards.

★ 書 shū ㄕㄨ

N book

- 我喜歡這類的書。
  I love this type of book.
- 有時間應該多看幾本書。
  Do read more books when you have the time.

書店 shūdiàn ㄕㄨ ㄉㄧㄢˋ

N bookshop

- 我打電話給書店訂一本書。
  I called the bookshop to order a book.

書法 shūfǎ ㄕㄨ ㄈㄚˇ

N calligraphy

- 我非常欣賞中國的書法。
  I admire the Chinese calligraphy.

書房 shūfáng ㄕㄨ ㄈㄤˊ

N study

- Neil經常在書房裡工作到很晚。
  Neil always stays up late in his study.

書櫃 shūguì ㄕㄨ ㄍㄨㄟˋ

N bookcase

SG MY 書櫥

- 請把書放回書櫃裡。
  Please put the book back to the bookcase.

書桌 shūzhuō ㄕㄨ ㄓㄨㄛ

N desk

- Mary正坐在書桌前。
  Mary was sitting at her desk.

蔬菜 shūcài ㄕㄨ ㄘㄞˋ

N vegetables

- 再吃點蔬菜吧。
  Have some more vegetables.

★ 舒服 shūfú ㄕㄨ ㄈㄨˊ

Vs. /Adj comfortable
CN shūfu

- 這床不太舒服。
  The bed wasn't particularly comfortable.
- 你在這裡睡舒服嗎？
  Were you comfortable sleeping here?
- 這件衣服穿起來很舒服。
  The dress is very comfortable to wear.

叔叔 shúshu ㄕㄨˊ ˙ㄕㄨ

N uncle

- 叔叔打算來我們家住幾天。
  My uncle wishes to stay with us for a few days.

鼠 shǔ ㄕㄨˇ

N [bound form] mouse

- 她是鼠年生的。
  She was born in the Year of Mouse.

★數 shǔ ㄕㄨˇ

V to count

- 別忘了數找回來的錢。
  Don't forget to count the change.
- 我來數一下這裡有多少人。
  Let me count to see how many people there are here.

★屬 shǔ ㄕㄨˇ

V be born under one of the twelve signs of the Chinese zodiac, represented by twelve animals

- 你屬什麼？－屬鼠。
  Which sign of the Chinese zodiac were you born under? --- Mouse.

★樹 shù ㄕㄨˋ

N tree

- 校園裡有很多樹。
  There're lots of trees in our campus.

刷卡 shuākǎ ㄕㄨㄚ ㄎㄚˇ

V to swipe card

- 你得刷卡才能進入大樓。
  You need to swipe your card to get in the building.

涮 shuàn ㄕㄨㄢˋ

V to dip-boil

- 我來教你怎麼涮羊肉。
  I'll show you how to dip-boil

thin slices of mutton.

★ **雙** shuāng ㄕㄨㄤ

M pair of

- 她有一雙大眼睛。
  She has a huge pair of eyes.
- 他有五雙運動鞋。
  He has five pairs of sneakers.
- 這雙襪子的另一支在哪裡？
  Where is the pair of this sock?

雙人 shuāngrén ㄕㄨㄤ ㄖㄣˊ

Vs-attr double

- 他們需要一張雙人床。
  They need a double bed.

★ **水** shuǐ ㄕㄨㄟˇ

N water

- 我很渴，要喝水。
  I'm thirsty. I want to drink some water.
- 天花板漏水了。
  The water leaked from the ceiling.

水費 shuǐfèi ㄕㄨㄟˇ ㄈㄟˋ

N water bill

- 水費有一千台幣。
  The water bill came to 1000 Taiwan dollars.

水溝 shuǐgōu ㄕㄨㄟˇ ㄍㄡ

N ditch

SG 龍溝

- 他掉進水溝裡。
  He fell into a ditch.

水管 shuǐguǎn ㄕㄨㄟˇ ㄍㄨㄢˇ

N pipe

- 廚房的水管斷了。
  A pipe was broken in the kitchen.

水果 shuǐguǒ ㄕㄨㄟˇ ㄍㄨㄛˇ

N fruit

- 給他們買點新鮮水果吧。
  Let's get some fresh fruit for them.

水餃 shuǐjiǎo ㄕㄨㄟˇ ㄐㄧㄠˇ

N dumpling

- 我最喜歡羊肉水餃。
  I like boiled lamb dumplings best.

水泡 shuǐpào ㄕㄨㄟˇ ㄆㄠˋ

N blister

- 爬了一天的山，我的腳起水泡了。
  My feet were blistered from climbing mountain all day.

水災 shuǐzāi
ㄕㄨㄟˇ ㄗㄞ

N floods

- 大雨使這個地區發生水災。
  The heavy rain has caused floods in this region.

水準 shuǐzhǔn
ㄕㄨㄟˇ ㄓㄨㄣˇ

N level

CN 水平

- 這個班的水準很高。
  The level of the class is high.

稅 shuì
ㄕㄨㄟˋ

N tax

- 我三分之一的薪水都交了稅。
  One third of my salary goes in tax.

★睡 shuì
ㄕㄨㄟˋ

Vi to sleep

- 你睡得好嗎？
  Did you have a good sleep?
- John一直睡到中午。
  Rod slept straight through until noon.
- 我以為你已經睡了。
  I thought you would be sleeping now.

★睡覺 shuìjiào
ㄕㄨㄟˋ ㄐㄧㄠˋ

V-sep to sleep

- 我昨天晚上十點鐘睡覺。
  I went to sleep at ten o'clock last night.

順便[a] shùnbiàn
ㄕㄨㄣˋ ㄅㄧㄢˋ

Adv by the way

- 順便一提，明天要考試。
  By the way, there is a test tomorrow.

順便[b] shùnbiàn
ㄕㄨㄣˋ ㄅㄧㄢˋ

Adv on someone's way

- 我出去時順便幫你倒垃圾。
  I can throw the trash for you on my way out.

★說[a] shuō
ㄕㄨㄛ

V to say

A B C D E F G H J K L M N O P Q R S T W X Y Z X-

- 你說過你認識他。
  You said you knew him.
- 只說對不起是不夠的。
  Just saying you're sorry isn't good enough.
- 他有沒有說發生了什麼事？
  Did he say what happened?

★ 說[b] shuō ㄕㄨㄛ

V to talk about

- 你在說什麼？我是最早到的。
  What are you talking about? I arrived first.

★ 說話 shuōhuà ㄕㄨㄛ ㄏㄨㄚˋ

V-sep to speak

- 你在跟誰說話？
  To whom are you speaking?
- 她停了好一會兒才又說話。
  There was a long pause before she spoke again.
- 我認識她，但沒跟她說過話。
  I know her, but not to speak to.

碩士 shuòshì ㄕㄨㄛˋ ㄕˋ

N master degree (holder)

- Ted是文科碩士。
  Ted is a Master of Arts.

司機 sījī ㄙ ㄐㄧ

N driver

- 司機從車上下來。
  The driver got out of his car.

私人 sīrén ㄙ ㄖㄣˊ

Vs-attr private

- 那些都是我父親的私人信件。
  Those are my father's private letters.

思想 sīxiǎng ㄙ ㄒㄧㄤˇ

N ideas

- 留學生帶回了新思想。
  Foreign students brought back new ideas.

★ 死 sǐ ㄙˇ

Vp to die

- Bill死了三年了。
  Bill died three years ago.
- 她生病死了。
  She died of an illness.

★ **四** sì ㄙˋ

numeral four

- 他已經結婚，有四個孩子。
  He's married with four children.

四季 sìjì ㄙˋ ㄐㄧˋ

N seasons of the year

- 人的情緒可能受到四季影響。
  Our mood is possibly affected by the seasons of the year.

四聲 sìshēng ㄙˋ ㄕㄥ

N the four tones of Mandarin Chinese

- 學好華語四聲很費時間。
  Mastering the four tones takes time.

★ **送** sòng ㄙㄨㄥˋ

V to send

- 我們一定得送他們點禮物。
  We must send them some sort of gift.
- 我們在母親節送花給媽媽。
  We sent Mom flowers for Mother's Day.

素 sù ㄙㄨˋ

Vs. /Adj vegetarian

- 她午飯吃了一個素比薩餅。
  She ate a vegetarian pizza for lunch.

素食 sùshí ㄙㄨˋ ㄕˊ

N vegetarian meal

- 我們都點了素食。
  We all ordered the vegetarian meal.

★ **速度** sùdù ㄙㄨˋ ㄉㄨˋ

N speed

- 現在你要放慢速度。
  Lower your speed now.
- 我的腳踏車有五種速度。
  My bicycle has five speeds.
- 開車速度是每小時一百公里。
  The car is going at the speed of 100 km an hour.

速食 sùshí ㄙㄨˋ ㄕˊ

N fast food

HK 快餐

- 我不喜歡吃速食。

I hate fast food.

塑膠 sùjiāo ㄙㄨˋ ㄐㄧㄠ

Vs-attr plastic

CN 塑料

- 我喜歡可愛的塑膠湯匙。
  I like cute plastic spoons.

宿舍 sùshè ㄙㄨˋ ㄕㄜˋ

N dormitory

- 學校有很多宿舍。
  There are quite a lot of dormitories in the campus.

痠 suān ㄙㄨㄢ

Vs. /Adj sore

- 運動後，我全身好痠。
  My whole body is sore after work out.

酸 suān ㄙㄨㄢ

Vs. /Adj sour

- 這蘋果還不熟，酸的。
  The apple wasn't ripe yet. It was sour.

算[a] suàn ㄙㄨㄢˋ

V to calculate

- 收費按小時算。
  Rates are calculated on an hourly basis.
- 我想算一下我們需要多少錢。
  I'm trying to calculate how much money we need.

算[b] suàn ㄙㄨㄢˋ

V to count

- 老師說，遲到十分鐘就算缺席。
  Our teacher said that being late for ten minutes will count as absence.

蒜 suàn ㄙㄨㄢˋ

N garlic

- 別放那麼多蒜。
  Don't go so heavy on the garlic.

★雖然 suīrán ㄙㄨㄟ ㄖㄢˊ

Conj although

- 廚房雖然小，但設計得很好。
  Although small, the kitchen is well designed.
- 雖然身體不好，他仍然工作。
  Although in poor health, he

continued to work.

- 雖然不冷，她還是穿著外套。
  She kept her coat on, although it wasn't cold.

隨便[1] suíbiàn ㄙㄨㄟˊ ㄅㄧㄢˋ

Vs. /Adj casual

- 她的生活態度很隨便。
  She had a casual attitude to life.

隨便[2] suíbiàn ㄙㄨㄟˊ ㄅㄧㄢˋ

Adv casually

- 我們在電話裡隨便聊聊。
  We chatted casually on the phone.

★歲 suì ㄙㄨㄟˋ

N [bound form] age

- 你女兒幾歲？
  What's your daughter's age?

★碎 suì ㄙㄨㄟˋ

complement to crumble

- Mary把餅乾都弄碎了。
  Mary crumbled all the cookies.

★所 suǒ ㄙㄨㄛˇ

M measure word for places

- 當地政府蓋了一所新醫院。
  The local government has built a new hospital.
- 我想送孩子到一所好的學校。
  I want to send my children to a good school.
- 他們終於有錢買一所房子了。
  At last they were able to afford a house.

★所以[a] suǒyǐ ㄙㄨㄛˇ ㄧˇ

Conj so

- 我牙痛，所以去看了醫生。
  I had a toothache so I went to see a dentist.
- 我找不到你，所以就走了。
  I couldn't find you so I left.
- 我餓了，所以吃了個三明治。
  I was feeling hungry so I ate a sandwich.

★所以[b] suǒyǐ ㄙㄨㄛˇ ㄧˇ

Conj therefore

- 他累得很，所以睡得很熟。
  He was very tired, and therefore he fell sound asleep.
- 經理現在忙，所以不能來。
  The manager is busy now, and therefore he cannot come.
- 這張床比較大，所以更舒服。
  The bed was bigger and therefore more comfortable.

★所有 suǒyǒu ㄙㄨㄛˇ ㄧㄡˇ

Vs-attr all

- 他們所有人都要來考試。
  They all need to take the exam.

所長 suǒzhǎng ㄙㄨㄛˇ ㄓㄤˇ

N chairperson

- 他是我們的研究所所長。
  He is the chairperson of our institution.

鎖[1] suǒ ㄙㄨㄛˇ

N lock

- 請用這把鑰匙開那把鎖。
  Please open that lock with this key.

鎖[2] suǒ ㄙㄨㄛˇ

V to lock

- 她離開時忘記鎖門。
  She forgot to lock the door when she left.

鎖匠 suǒjiàng ㄙㄨㄛˇ ㄐㄧㄤˋ

N locksmith

- 哪裡可以找到鎖匠？
  Where can we find a locksmith?

T

★ **他** tā ㄊㄚ

pronoun he

- 是他，還是她？
  He, or she?

★ **她** tā ㄊㄚ

pronoun she

- 你告訴她時，她怎麼說？
  What did she say when you told her?

★ **他們** tāmen ㄊㄚ ˙ㄇㄣ

pronoun they

- 我看他們長得完全一樣。
  They look precisely the same to me.

★ **牠** tā ㄊㄚ

pronoun it/animate, nonhuman

- 牠是我的小狗。
  It's my puppy.

★ **它** tā ㄊㄚ

neuter pronoun it/inanimate

- 報紙我看了，你把它拿走吧。
  I've finished with the newspaper. You can take it away.

台 [a] tái ㄊㄞˊ

M measure word for machine

- 辦公室有一台影印機。
  There is a copy machine in the office.

台 [b] tái ㄊㄞˊ

M measure word for TV set

- 我們買了一台電視機。
  We bought a TV set.

★ **太** tài ㄊㄞˋ

Adv too

- 我的褲子太緊了。
  My trousers are too tight.
- 你覺得音樂太大聲了嗎？
  Do you think the music is too loud?
- 你在湯裡放了太多的鹽。
  You've put too much salt in the soup.

太太[1] tàitai
ㄊㄞˋ ˙ㄊㄞ

N wife

- 你見過我的太太嗎？
  Have you met my wife?

太太[2] tàitai
ㄊㄞˋ ˙ㄊㄞ

Form of address Mrs

- 我認識李先生和李太太。
  I know Mr. and Mrs. Lee.

台幣 táibì
ㄊㄞˊ ㄅㄧˋ

N Taiwan dollar

- 我想要換新台幣。
  I would like to exchange for the New Taiwan dollars.

颱風 táifēng
ㄊㄞˊ ㄈㄥ

N typhoon

- 颱風快來了。
  The typhoon is coming.

★ 態度 tàidù
ㄊㄞˋ ㄉㄨˋ

N attitude

CN tàidu

- 她的態度突然變了。
  Her whole attitude suddenly changed.
- 你最好改變你的態度。
  You'd better change your attitude.
- John對生活態度積極。
  John has a positive attitude to life.

★ 太陽 tàiyáng
ㄊㄞˋ ㄧㄤˊ

N the sun

- 太陽出來了。
  The sun appeared.

彈 tán
ㄊㄢˊ

V to play (musical instruments, e.g. guitar, piano)

- 你彈吉他比我好多了。
  You play the guitar much better than I do.

★ 談[a] tán
ㄊㄢˊ

V to discuss

- 你應該跟醫生談這個問題。
  You should discuss this problem with your doctor.

★ 談[b] tán
ㄊㄢˊ

V to talk about

- 你要跟我談什麼事？
  What do you want to talk to

me about?

- 今天我們只談這個問題。
  Today we are going to talk about this question only.
- 他們一直在談結婚的事。
  They've been talking about getting married.

★ **談話** tánhuà ㄊㄢˊ ㄏㄨㄚˋ

V-sep to talk

- 我聽到他們在隔壁房間談話。
  I could hear them talking in the next room.

毯子 tǎnzi ㄊㄢˇ ˙ㄗ

N blanket

- 她給孩子蓋上毯子。
  She put a blanket over the child.

湯 tāng ㄊㄤ

N soup

- 我給你加點湯吧？
  Shall I help you to some more soup?

湯匙 tāngchí ㄊㄤ ㄔˊ

N spoon

- 請你給我一支乾淨的湯匙。
  Could I have a clean spoon, please?

堂 táng ㄊㄤˊ

M measure word for period (class)

- 我每天有四堂華語課。
  I have four periods of Chinese everyday.

★ **躺** tǎng ㄊㄤˇ

Vi to lie

- Jane躺在床上看電視。
  Jane was lying on the bed watching television.
- 不要在沙發上躺太長時間。
  Don't lie on the couch for too long.
- 這隻貓就喜歡躺在沙發上。
  The cat just loves to lie on the sofa.

糖 táng ㄊㄤˊ

N sugar

- 你喝咖啡加糖嗎？
  Do you take sugar in your coffee?

糖醋 tángcù
ㄊㄤˊ ㄘㄨˋ

N sweet and sour

- 做糖醋排骨要用鳳梨。
  We need pineapple to make the sweet and sour ribs.

糖尿病 tángniàobìng
ㄊㄤˊ ㄋㄧㄠˋ ㄅㄧㄥˋ

N diabetes

- Lisa得了糖尿病。
  Lisa is suffering from the diabetes.

堂弟 tángdì
ㄊㄤˊ ㄉㄧˋ

N younger boy cousin from mother side

- 我堂弟喜歡看棒球。
  My boy cousin likes to watch baseball.

堂哥 tánggē
ㄊㄤˊ ㄍㄜ

N older boy cousin from mother side

- 我堂哥新年才會回來。
  My boy cousin will return on New Year.

堂姐 tángjiě
ㄊㄤˊ ㄐㄧㄝˇ

N older girl cousin from mother side

- 我堂姐今年到日本讀書。
  My girl cousin is studying abroad in Japan this year.

堂妹 tángmèi
ㄊㄤˊ ㄇㄟˋ

N younger girl cousin from mother side

- 我堂妹現在在讀國中。
  My little girl cousin is in middle school.

燙 tàng
ㄊㄤˋ

Vst to burn

- 熱茶燙了我的喉嚨。
  The hot tea burnt my throat.

討論[1] tǎolùn
ㄊㄠˇ ㄌㄨㄣˋ

V to discuss

- 我們討論了應不應該去。
  We discussed whether we should go or not.

討論[2] tǎolùn
ㄊㄠˇ ㄌㄨㄣˋ

N discussion

- 這次討論對我們很有用。
  This discussion is useful to us.

★ 套[a] tào
ㄊㄠˋ

M suit of (clothes)

- 她穿著一套新衣服。
  She's wearing a new suit of

clothes.

★ 套[b] tào ㄊㄠˋ

M set of (furniture)

- 我們訂了一套家具。
  We've ordered a set of furniture.

套餐 tàocān ㄊㄠˋ ㄘㄢ

N table d'hôte

- 這小飯館只有套餐。
  This small restaurant offers table d'hôte only.

套房 tàofáng ㄊㄠˋ ㄈㄤˊ

N suite

- 學校附近有租給學生的套房。
  One can find suites for rent to the students near the campus.

套裝 tàozhuāng ㄊㄠˋ ㄓㄨㄤ

N suit

- Mary穿了一身藍色套裝。
  Mary's wearing a blue suit.

特別[a] tèbié ㄊㄜˋ ㄅㄧㄝˊ

Vs. /Adj special

- 她笑的樣子有點特別。
  She has a special way of smiling.

特別[b] tèbié ㄊㄜˋ ㄅㄧㄝˊ

Vs. /Adj unique

- 他的個性很特別。
  He has a very unique personality.

特價 tèjià ㄊㄜˋ ㄐㄧㄚˋ

V on sale

- 這些書正在特價。
  These books are on sale.

★ 踢 tī ㄊㄧ

V to kick

- 別踢我的車子。
  Please don't kick my car.
- 他踢了我的腿。
  He kicked me in the leg.
- Ian把球踢到牆的另一邊去了。
  Ian kicked the ball over the wall.

T恤 tīxù ㄊㄧ ㄒㄩˋ

N T-shirt

- 她的T恤很貴。
  Her T-shirt is very expensive.

提 tí
ㄊㄧˊ

V to lift

- 這箱子太重了，我提不動。
I can't lift the box, it's too heavy.

提款卡 tíkuǎnkǎ
ㄊㄧˊ ㄎㄨㄢˇ ㄎㄚˇ

N cash card

- 幸虧我帶了提款卡。
Fortunately I had my cash card with me.

提款機 tíkuǎnjī
ㄊㄧˊ ㄎㄨㄢˇ ㄐㄧ

N cash machine

- 附近有提款機嗎？
Is there a cash machine around here?

題目 tímù
ㄊㄧˊ ㄇㄨˋ

N topic

- 討論的題目是「工作與家庭」。
The topic of the discussion is 'Work and Family'.

體檢[1] tǐjiǎn
ㄊㄧˇ ㄐㄧㄢˇ

N checkup

- 他去醫院做體檢。
He saw the doctor for a check-up.

體檢[2] tǐjiǎn
ㄊㄧˇ ㄐㄧㄢˇ

V to have checkup

- 體檢很重要。
It's important to have regular checkups.

體育 tǐyù
ㄊㄧˇ ㄩˋ

N sport

- 我對體育不是特別感興趣。
I'm not especially interested in sport.

體育館 tǐyùguǎn
ㄊㄧˇ ㄩˋ ㄍㄨㄢˇ

N gym

- 他們在體育館打排球。
They played volleyball in the gym.

替[1] tì
ㄊㄧˋ

Prep for (beneficiary)

- 沒人會替你工作。
Nobody will do your work for you.
- 替我買一瓶牛奶，好嗎？
Would you buy a bottle of

milk for me, please?

- 請你替我把這個包裹包好。
Will you do up this parcel for me?

替 [2a] tì
ㄊㄧˋ

V to replace

- 現在沒有人能替她。
Right now there's no one who can replace her.

替 [2b] tì
ㄊㄧˋ

V to take one's place

- 今天他病了，我替他。
He's ill today. I'll take his place.

★ 天 [a] tiān
ㄊㄧㄢ

N day

- 我這些天很忙。
I'm very busy these days.
- 前幾天我見過Joe。
I saw Joe the other day.
- 這次旅行五天左右。
The trip will take around five days.

★ 天 [b] tiān
ㄊㄧㄢ

N sky

- 九月，天特別藍。
The sky is especially blue in September.
- 天突然暗了下來。
The sky suddenly went dark.

天花板 tiānhuābǎn
ㄊㄧㄢ ㄏㄨㄚ ㄅㄢˇ

N ceiling

- 大廳的天花板又高又好看。
The hall has nice, high ceilings.

天氣 tiānqì
ㄊㄧㄢ ㄑㄧˋ

N weather

- 明天天氣會怎麼樣？
What will the weather be like tomorrow?

天然氣 tiānránqì
ㄊㄧㄢ ㄖㄢˊ ㄑㄧˋ

N gas

- 這個地區有大量的天然氣。
The region has large gas reserves.

天線 tiānxiàn
ㄊㄧㄢ ㄒㄧㄢˋ

N antenna

- 電視機的天線在陽台上。
The antenna is on the terrace.

天主教 tiānzhǔjiào ㄊㄧㄢ ㄓㄨˇ ㄐㄧㄠˋ

N Catholicism

- 宗教班用了三天討論天主教。
  The religion class spent three days discussing Catholicism.

★ 填 tián ㄊㄧㄢˊ

V to fill in (form)

- 我不會填這張表。
  I don't know how to fill in this form.
- 請填上你的電話號碼。
  Please fill in your phone number.

甜 tián ㄊㄧㄢˊ

Vs. /Adj sweet

- 這飲料太甜了。
  The drink is too sweet.

舔 tiǎn ㄊㄧㄢˇ

V to lick

- 小孩把湯匙舔乾淨了。
  The child licked the spoon clean.

★ 條 1a tiáo ㄊㄧㄠˊ

M measure word for fish

- 我們要一條大一點的魚。
  We want a bigger fish.

★ 條 1b tiáo ㄊㄧㄠˊ

M measure word for road

- 我們決定走另一條路。
  We decided to take another road.

★ 條 2 tiáo ㄊㄧㄠˊ

unit word piece of (news, information)

- 我有一條消息告訴你。
  I have a piece of news to tell you.

調 tiáo ㄊㄧㄠˊ

V to mix

- 怎麼調出綠色？
  What colors would I mix to green?

調味料 tiáowèiliào ㄊㄧㄠˊ ㄨㄟˋ ㄌㄧㄠˋ

N seasoning

CN MY 調味品 / 調料

- 湯太淡，再加點調味料吧。
  The soup is bland. Do add some more seasoning.

A B C D E F G H J K L M N O P Q R S T W X Y Z X-

★ 跳 tiào ㄊㄧㄠˋ

V to jump

- 小孩用一隻腳跳。
  The child jumped on one foot.
- 讓我們一起往前跳。
  Let's jump forward together.
- 小偷跳上了一輛汽車逃跑了。
  The thief jumped into a car and made his escape.

★ 貼 tiē ㄊㄧㄝ

V to stick

- 這封信還沒貼郵票。
  There's no stamp stuck on this envelope.

★ 聽 tīng ㄊㄧㄥ

V to listen (to)

- 好好聽我說。
  Listen to me carefully.
- 我們坐著聽音樂。
  We sat down listening to music.
- 你今天早上聽新聞了嗎？
  Did you listen to the news this morning?

廳 tīng ㄊㄧㄥ

N room

- 他們在哪一廳表演？
  Which room are they performing?

停車場 tíngchēchǎng ㄊㄧㄥˊ ㄔㄜ ㄔㄤˇ

N car park

- 這個停車場沒有停車位了。
  There aren't any parking spaces left in the car park.

★ 通 tōng ㄊㄨㄥ

V to lead

- 這條路通到海邊。
  The path led down to the seaside.

通風 tōngfēng ㄊㄨㄥ ㄈㄥ

Vs-sep to air

- 房間要經常通風。
  Do air the room regularly.

通知[1] tōngzhī ㄊㄨㄥ ㄓ

N notice

- 我收到通知了。
  I've received the notice.

通知[2] tōngzhī ㄊㄨㄥ ㄓ

V to notify

- 這項決定已經通知了每個人。
  The decision has been notified to everyone.

同事 tóngshì ㄊㄨㄥˊ ㄕˋ

N colleague

- 我跟幾位同事討論過這件事。
  I discussed the issue with some of my colleagues.

★ 同意 tóngyì ㄊㄨㄥˊ ㄧˋ

Vst to agree

- 我完全同意。
  I couldn't agree more.
- Mike同意不去了。
  Mike agreed not to go.
- 她同意我這麼做。
  She agreed with what I've done.

★ 痛 tòng ㄊㄨㄥˋ

Vs. /Adj painful

- 傷口非常痛。
  The wound is extremely painful.
- 你的手臂很痛嗎？
  Is your arm very painful?
- 她發現呼吸的時候會痛。
  She was finding it painful to breathe.

偷 tōu ㄊㄡ

V to steal

- 那男孩偷了父母的錢。
  The boy stole money from his parents.

★ 頭[1] tóu ㄊㄡˊ

N head

- 我的頭有點痛。
  I've got a pain in my head.
- 球打到我的頭。
  A ball hit me on the head.
- 戴上帽子，頭會暖和一點。
  Put the head on to keep your head warm.

★ 頭[2] tóu ㄊㄡˊ

M head of (cattle, sheep)

- 他們有一百頭牛。
  They own 100 head of cattle.

頭等 tóuděng ㄊㄡˊ ㄉㄥˇ

Vs-attr first class

- 我想要成爲頭等會員。
I would like to become the first class member.

頭痛 tóutòng ㄊㄡˊ ㄊㄨㄥˋ

Vs. /Adj to have a headache

- 他頭痛。
He has a headache.

頭暈 tóuyūn ㄊㄡˊ ㄩㄣ

Vs. /Adj to feel dizzy

- 我頭有點暈。
I feel a little dizzy.

投[a] tóu ㄊㄡˊ

V to cast (a vote)

- 總統選舉，我一定會去投票。
I definitely will cast a vote for the presidential election.

投[b] tóu ㄊㄡˊ

V to throw

- 她把垃圾投進垃圾桶裡。
She throws the trash in the trash can.

投保 tóubǎo ㄊㄡˊ ㄅㄠˇ

V-sep to insure

- 你給家裡的財產投保了嗎？
Have you insured the contents of your home?

投影機 tóuyǐngjī ㄊㄡˊ ㄧㄥˇ ㄐㄧ

N projector

CN 投影儀

- 投影機突然壞了。
Suddenly the projector was broken.

★突然 túrán ㄊㄨˊ ㄖㄢˊ

Adv suddenly

- 突然有人敲門。
Suddenly there was a knock on the door.
- 突然開始下雨了。
Suddenly it started to rain.
- 就在這時候，她突然走了出去。
Meanwhile she went out suddenly.

圖書館 túshūguǎn ㄊㄨˊ ㄕㄨ ㄍㄨㄢˇ

N library

- 我在圖書館借了五本書。
I borrowed five books from the library.

A B C D E F G H J K L M N O P Q R S T W X Y Z X-

★ **吐[1]** tù ㄊㄨˋ

V to spit

- 小孩把食物吐回盤子裡。
  The child spat the food back onto his plate.
- 我把變酸了的牛奶吐了出來。
  I spat out the sour milk.

吐[2] tù ㄊㄨˋ

V to throw up

- 他酒喝得太多，吐了。
  He threw up after drinking too much.

退 tuì ㄊㄨㄟˋ

V to return (goods)

- 我們把電暖器退回商店。
  We returned the heater to the store.

推薦信
tuījiànxìn
ㄊㄨㄟ ㄐㄧㄢˋ ㄒㄧㄣˋ

N letter of recommendation

- 公司給她寫了一封推薦信。
  The company wrote her a letter of recommendation.

腿 tuǐ ㄊㄨㄟˇ

N leg

- 他腿長，跑得快。
  He's got long legs and runs fast.

退休 tuìxiū ㄊㄨㄟˋ ㄒㄧㄡ

V to retire

- 我打算在六十歲時退休。
  I'm planning to retire at 60.

吞 tūn ㄊㄨㄣ

V to swallow

- 他吞下了一整顆葡萄。
  He swallowed a whole grape.

臀部 túnbù ㄊㄨㄣˊ ㄅㄨˋ

N rear

- Ted摔傷了臀部。
  Ted hurt his rear when he fell.

★ **脫** tuō ㄊㄨㄛ

V to take off

- 天氣太熱，他脫了外套。
  It's really hot, and he took off his jacket.

拖[a] tuō ㄊㄨㄛ

V to drag

- 我把桌子拖進廚房裡。
  I managed to drag the table into the kitchen.

拖[b] tuō ㄊㄨㄛ

V to tow

- 警察把車拖走了。
  The police towed the car away.

拖把 tuōbǎ ㄊㄨㄛ ㄅㄚˇ

N mop

CN 拖布tuōbù

- 我們需要拖把。
  We need a mop and bucket.

托運 tuōyùn ㄊㄨㄛ ㄩㄣˋ

V to consign

- 這些行李你必須托運。
  You have to consign all these items.

W

瓦斯 wǎsī
ㄨㄚˇ ㄙ

N gas

CN SG 煤氣

- Mary把瓦斯關小了。
  Mary turned down the gas.

襪子 wàzi
ㄨㄚˋ ˙ㄗ

N sock

- 這些襪子該洗了。
  These socks need to be washed.

★ 哇 wa
˙ㄨㄚ

interjection wow

- 哇！這棵樹眞高！
  Wow! The tree is really tall!

★ 外 wài
ㄨㄞˋ

Vs-attr outside

- 這棟房子的外牆是白色的。
  The outside of the house was painted white.

外幣 wàibì
ㄨㄞˋ ㄅㄧˋ

N foreign currency

- 我只有外幣，沒有台幣。
  I have only some foreign currencies, but no Taiwan dollars.

外帶 wàidài
ㄨㄞˋ ㄉㄞˋ

Vi take-out

- 我要外帶兩杯咖啡。
  I want two take-out coffees.

外公 wàigōng
ㄨㄞˋ ㄍㄨㄥ

N grandpa (mother side)

CN 姥爺

- 我外公已經九十歲了。
  My grandpa is already 90 years old.

★ 外國 wàiguó
ㄨㄞˋ ㄍㄨㄛˊ

N foreign country

- 你在外國住了幾年？
  How long have you been in foreign countries?

外籍 wàijí
ㄨㄞˋ ㄐㄧˊ

Vs-attr foreign

- 我們公司有不少外籍人員。
We have a lot of foreign staff in our company.

★ **外面** wàimiàn ㄨㄞˋ ㄇㄧㄢˋ

N outside

CN wàimian

- 教室外面有兩個學生。
There are two students outside the classroom.

外婆 wàipó ㄨㄞˋ ㄆㄛˊ

N grandma (mother side)

CN 姥姥

- 下星期我們全家要一起去外婆家。
Our family's going to visit grandma next week.

外套 wàitào ㄨㄞˋ ㄊㄠˋ

N jacket

SG MY 冷衣、寒衣

- 穿上外套，天氣很冷。
Put your jacket on. It's quite cold.

★ **外頭** wàitou ㄨㄞˋ ˙ㄊㄡ

N outside

- 你從外頭開不了門。
You can't open the door from the outside.
- 我的衣服外頭不髒，裡頭髒。
The outside of my clothes is clean, but the inside is dirty.

外向 wàixiàng ㄨㄞˋ ㄒㄧㄤˋ

Vs. /Adj outgoing

- Kate個性外向。
Kate has an outgoing personality.

外語 wàiyǔ ㄨㄞˋ ㄩˇ

N foreign language

- 會一門外語很有用。
Knowing a foreign language is useful.

★ **完** wán ㄨㄢˊ

Vp to finish

- 電影還沒完呢。
The film isn't finished yet.
- 工作進行得怎麼樣？
—快完了。
How's the work going? --- We've nearly finished.

★ **完全**[1] wánquán ㄨㄢˊ ㄑㄩㄢˊ

Vs. /Adj complete

• 你給我的資料不完全。
The information you gave me was not complete.

★ 完全[2] wánquán ㄨㄢˊ ㄑㄩㄢˊ

Adv completely

• 我完全同意你的意見。
I agree with you completely.

• 我完全忘了今天是她的生日。
I completely forgot that it's her birthday today.

• 她完全變了，我認不出來了。
She'd completely changed. I didn't recognize her.

★ 玩[a] wán ㄨㄢˊ

V to enjoy oneself

• 你到臺灣旅行玩得愉快嗎？
Did you enjoy yourself on your trip to Taiwan?

★ 玩[b] wán ㄨㄢˊ

V to play

• 街上不能玩球。
You can't play ball on the street.

• 橋牌要四個人玩。
It takes four persons to play bridge.

• Bill繼續玩他的電腦。
Bill just carried on playing on his computer.

★ 晚 wǎn ㄨㄢˇ

Vs. /Adj be late

• 你來晚了。
You're late.

• 時間太晚了，我得走了。
It's very late. I've got to go.

• 天哪！我不知道這麼晚了。
Goodness! I'd no idea it was so late.

晚會 wǎnhuì ㄨㄢˇ ㄏㄨㄟˋ

N evening party

• 我們星期六有個晚會。
We're having an evening party on Saturday.

★ 晚上[1] wǎnshàng ㄨㄢˇ ㄕㄤˋ

N evening

CN wǎnshang

• 我父母今天晚上不在。
My parents are away this evening.

- 明天晚上你打算做什麼？
What are you doing tomorrow evening?

★ **晚上** [2] wǎnshàng
ㄨㄢˇ ㄕㄤˋ

Adv evening

- 我大部分的功課晚上做。
I do most of my studying in the evening.

碗 wǎn
ㄨㄢˇ

N bowl

- 用小碗吃麵，大碗吃飯。
Eat your noodles in a small bowl, and eat your rice in a big one.

★ **萬** wàn
ㄨㄢˋ

N ten thousand

- 他大概賺一萬塊錢。
He earns somewhere in the region of ten thousand.
- 有三萬人看了那場足球比賽。
Thirty thousand spectators watched that football match.

★ **往** [a] wǎng
ㄨㄤˇ

Prep to (direction)

- 他叫我往左轉。
He told me to turn to the left.

★ **往** [b] wǎng
ㄨㄤˇ

Prep toward

- 他很快地往市中心開去。
He's speeding towards the city center.

網咖 wǎngkā
ㄨㄤˇ ㄎㄚ

N internet cafe

CN MY HK 網吧

- 這家網咖吸引許多年輕人。
This Internet cafe attracts many young people.

★ **網路** wǎnglù
ㄨㄤˇ ㄌㄨˋ

N internet

CN MY HK 網絡

- 我在網路上找資料。
I searched the Internet for information.

網球 wǎngqiú
ㄨㄤˇ ㄑㄧㄡˊ

N tennis ball

- 這個網球不大好，換一個吧。
This tennis ball is not good. Change a new one.

網頁 wǎngyè ㄨㄤˇ ㄧㄝˋ

N web page

- 去年他開始給公司設計網頁。
  He began designing Web pages for our company last year.

網站 wǎngzhàn ㄨㄤˇ ㄓㄢˋ

N website

- 他管理公司的網站。
  He supervises the Website of the company.

★ 忘 wàng ㄨㄤˋ

Vst to forget

- 別忘了我的話。
  Don't forget what I said.
- 那件事我怎麼也忘不掉。
  I can't forget that incident, no matter how hard I try.
- 哎呀，我忘了你總是對的。
  Oops! I forgot you're always right.

★ 忘記 wàngjì ㄨㄤˋ ㄐㄧˋ

Vst to forget

- 我們忘記帶照相機了。
  We forgot to bring our cameras with us.
- 她把過去的事情都忘記了。
  She forgot all about the past.
- 我常常忘記別人的電話號碼。
  I'm always forgetting people's phone numbers.

危險[1] wéixiǎn ㄨㄟˊ ㄒㄧㄢˇ

N danger

CN wēixiǎn

- 他在路上碰到不少危險。
  He passed through lots of dangers on his way.

危險[2] wéixiǎn ㄨㄟˊ ㄒㄧㄢˇ

Vs. /Adj dangerous

- 你晚上一個人走路很危險。
  It's dangerous for you to walk alone at night.

★ 位 wèi ㄨㄟˋ

M measure word, used as a polite form addressed to someone deserving respect

- 學校來了一位新老師。
  We have a new teacher in our

school.

位置 wèizhì
ㄨㄟˋ ㄓˋ

N location

CN wèizhi

• 新路的位置對我們很方便。
The location of the new road is convenient for us.

位子 wèizi
ㄨㄟˋ ˙ㄗ

N seat

• 那邊還有一個空位子。
There's still a vacant seat over there.

胃 wèi
ㄨㄟˋ

N stomach

• 我的胃不太好。
I have a weak stomach.

胃口 wèikǒu
ㄨㄟˋ ㄎㄡˇ

N appetite

• 我的胃口很好。
I have a good appetite.

★喂 wèi
ㄨㄟˋ

interjection a shout, used to get someone's attention

• 喂，快來呀！
Hey, quickly come over here!

• 喂，你找誰？
Hey, who are you looking for?

味道 wèidào
ㄨㄟˋ ㄉㄠˋ

N flavour

CN wèidao

• 這湯沒什麼味道。
This soup doesn't have much flavour.

味精 wèijīng
ㄨㄟˋ ㄐㄧㄥ

N MSG

CN 味素

• 這些食品沒加味精。
These foodstuffs are MSG-free.

★爲了[a] wèile
ㄨㄟˋ ˙ㄌㄜ

Prep for the sake of

• 爲了孩子的健康，她不抽菸了。
She gave up smoking for the sake of her child's health.

• 我只是爲了方便才這樣做的。
I did this solely for the sake of convenience.

★ 爲了[b] wèile ㄨㄟˋ ˙ㄌㄜ

Prep in order to

- 爲了有個好位子，我早來了。
  I arrived early in order to get a good seat.
- 爲了趕上火車，她起得很早。
  She got up very early in order to catch the train.

★ 爲什麼 wèishénme ㄨㄟˋ ㄕㄣˊ ˙ㄇㄜ

Adv why

- 爲什麼不試一試？
  Why not have a try?
- 爲什麼沒人這麼說？
  Why didn't anyone just say so?
- 你爲什麼喜歡這個電視節目？
  Why do you like this TV show?

衛浴 wèiyù ㄨㄟˋ ㄩˋ

N sanitary-ware

- 衛浴部在商店的另一邊。
  The sanitary-ware department is at the other end of the shop.

★ 溫 wēn ㄨㄣ

Vs. /Adj warm

- 水還是溫的。
  The water is still warm.
- 這啤酒是溫的。
  This beer's warm.

★ 溫度 wēndù ㄨㄣ ㄉㄨˋ

N temperature

- 溫度升高了三度。
  The temperature has risen by three degrees.
- 要用合適的溫度來烤蛋糕。
  Make sure that you bake your cake at the correct temperature.

溫暖 wēnnuǎn ㄨㄣ ㄋㄨㄢˇ

Vs. /Adj warm

- 房間裡很溫暖。
  It is very warm in the room.

文 wén ㄨㄣˊ

N language

- 你看出來了嗎？這是什麼文？
  Have you made it out? What language is it?

★ 文化 wénhuà ㄨㄣˊ ㄏㄨㄚˋ

N culture

- 雖然住了很久，他還是不了解那裡的文化。
  He doesn't understand the culture of that place despite a long stay.

文學 wénxué ㄨㄣˊ ㄒㄩㄝˊ

N literature

- 我很喜歡英國文學。
  I'm quite fond of English literature.

文章 wénzhāng ㄨㄣˊ ㄓㄤ

N papers

- 她的文章很好懂。
  Her papers are easy to read.

蚊子 wénzi ㄨㄣˊ ˙ㄗ

N mosquito

- 那裡蚊子太多了。
  There were too many mosquitoes there.

★問 wèn ㄨㄣˋ

V to ask

- Gary問我去不去。
  Gary asked me whether I would be there.
- 你要是不懂就問好了。
  If you don't know, just ask.
- 她問我對文章的看法。
  She asked my opinion of the paper.

★問題[a] wèntí ㄨㄣˋ ㄊㄧˊ

N problem

- 問題就在這裡。
  That's exactly the problem.
- 老師不夠是個大問題。
  The shortage of teachers poses a major problem.
- 那樣還是沒有解決我的問題。
  That still doesn't solve my problem.

★問題[b] wèntí ㄨㄣˋ ㄊㄧˊ

N question

- 有誰有問題嗎？
  Does anyone have any questions?
- 我們想問你一個問題。
  We wanted to ask you a question.
- 我無法回答那個問題。
  I'm afraid I can't answer that question.

★ **我** wǒ ㄨㄛˇ

pronoun I

- 我來自臺北。
  I'm from Taipei.

★ **我們** wǒmen ㄨㄛˇ ˙ㄇㄣ

pronoun we

- 你知道我們在哪裡嗎？
  Do you have any idea where we are?

臥房 wòfáng ㄨㄛˋ ㄈㄤˊ

N bedroom, related to dormitory

MY 睡房

- 他們課本忘在臥房裡沒帶出來。
  They didn't bring their course books with them, leaving them in their bedroom.

臥室 wòshì ㄨㄛˋ ㄕˋ

N bedroom, related to residence

MY 睡房

- 我家的臥室不大，但是很舒服。
  The bedroom in our house is not big, but it's very comfortable.

烏龍茶 wūlóngchá ㄨ ㄌㄨㄥˊ ㄔㄚˊ

N Oolong Tea

- 他泡烏龍茶請大家喝。
  He's brewing us some Oolong Tea.

無聊[a] wúliáo ㄨˊ ㄌㄧㄠˊ

Vs. /Adj boring

- 他真無聊。
  He's really boring.

無聊[b] wúliáo ㄨˊ ㄌㄧㄠˊ

Vs. /Adj bored

- 你要是覺得無聊，可以看書。
  You can read while you get bored.

無名指 wúmíngzhǐ ㄨˊ ㄇㄧㄥˊ ㄓˇ

N third finger

- 他運動時不小心傷到了無名指。
  He hurt his third finger by accident while playing sports.

無線 wúxiàn ㄨˊ ㄒㄧㄢˋ

Vs-attr wireless

- 我買了一個無線電話。
  I bought a wireless phone.

★ 五 wǔ ㄨˇ

numeral five

- 我女兒五歲了。
  My daughter is five years of age.
- 五公里外有一個加油站。
  There is a petrol station five kilometers away.
- 我們結婚五年，非常幸福。
  We've been happily married for five years.

舞會 wǔhuì ㄨˇ ㄏㄨㄟˋ

N dance

- 晚飯後會有一個舞會。
  Following the dinner, there will be a dance.

誤點 wùdiǎn ㄨˋ ㄉㄧㄢˇ

V-sep to delay

- 飛機要誤點幾個小時。
  The flight would be delayed several hours.

物理 wùlǐ ㄨˋ ㄌㄧˇ

N physics

- 他物理學得好，化學普通。
  He's good at physics and fair at chemistry.

吸 xī ㄒㄧ

V to sip

- 我們用吸管吸杯子裡的果汁。
  We sipped the juice from the glass through a straw.

稀飯 xīfàn ㄒㄧ ㄈㄢˋ

N congee

- 早餐我一般吃稀飯。
  Usually I have congee for breakfast.

★ 西方 xīfāng ㄒㄧ ㄈㄤ

Vs-attr western

- 你了解西方文化嗎？
  Are you acquainted with western culture?

西瓜 xīguā ㄒㄧ ㄍㄨㄚ

N watermelon

- 這些西瓜還沒有熟。
  These watermelons aren't ripe yet.

★ 西部 xībù ㄒㄧ ㄅㄨˋ

N western part

- 那個城市在西部。
  The city is located in the western part.

★ 西亞 Xīyǎ ㄒㄧ ㄧㄚˇ

N West Asia

- 他明年想去西亞國家旅遊。
  It is his intention to visit the West Asian countries next year.

西裝 xīzhuāng ㄒㄧ ㄓㄨㄤ

N suit

- 他在西裝外面加了一件大衣。
  He wore an overcoat over his suit.

膝蓋 xīgài ㄒㄧ ㄍㄞˋ

N knee

- John的膝蓋受傷了。
  John hurt his knee.

A B C D E F G H J K L M N O P Q R S T W X Y Z X-

吸管 xīguǎn ㄒㄧ ㄍㄨㄢˇ

N straw

SG MY 吸水草、水草

- Mary用吸管來喝她的可樂。
  Mary drank her Coke through a straw.

★希望[1] xīwàng ㄒㄧ ㄨㄤˋ

N hope

- 孩子是父母的希望。
  Children are their parent's hope.
- 她病得很重，但還有希望。
  She's very ill, but there's still hope.
- 醫生認爲他的病沒有希望了。
  The doctor said that his recovery is beyond hope.

★希望[2] xīwàng ㄒㄧ ㄨㄤˋ

Vst to hope

- 我希望他能早一點回來。
  I hope he shall return a bit earlier.
- 希望有人找到她的護照。
  Let's just hope someone finds her passport.
- 我們大家希望有個好天氣。
  We all hope the weather will be nice.

★習慣[1a] xíguàn ㄒㄧˊ ㄍㄨㄢˋ

N custom

- 早起是我的習慣。
  It is my custom to rise early.

★習慣[1b] xíguàn ㄒㄧˊ ㄍㄨㄢˋ

N habit

- 這個習慣很難改。
  This habit is very difficult to change.
- 別咬指甲，那是個壞習慣。
  Stop biting your nails. It's a bad habit.

★習慣[2] xíguàn ㄒㄧˊ ㄍㄨㄢˋ

Vs. /Adj to get used to

- 她還不習慣說華語。
  She was not used to speaking Chinese.
- 我不習慣這麼早就上床。
  I'm not used to going to bed so early.
- 很快你就會習慣城市生活了。

You'll soon get used to living in the city.

★ **洗** xǐ ㄒㄧˇ

V to wash

- 用肥皂洗洗手。
  Wash your hands with soap.
- 襪子沒洗乾淨。
  The socks haven't been washed clean.
- 我爸在外面洗車。
  My Dad is washing our car outside.

洗手間 xǐshǒujiān ㄒㄧˇ ㄕㄡˇ ㄐㄧㄢ

N toilet

- 有人在用洗手間。
  Someone is using the toilet.

洗衣機 xǐyījī ㄒㄧˇ ㄧ ㄐㄧ

N washing machine

- 洗衣機又壞了。
  The washing machine's broken again.

洗澡 xǐzǎo ㄒㄧˇ ㄗㄠˇ

V-sep to take a bath

- 她每天晚上都洗澡。
  She takes a bath every night.

★ **喜歡** xǐhuān ㄒㄧˇ ㄏㄨㄢ

Vst to like

CN xǐhuan

- 我喜歡你這件夾克。
  I like your jacket.
- 我喜歡喝很濃的咖啡。
  I like my coffee quite strong.
- 有人喜歡海，有人喜歡山。
  Some people like the sea, others prefer the mountains.

系 xì ㄒㄧˋ

N department

- 我們大學有二十多個系。
  There are more than 20 departments in our university.

★ **細**[a] xì ㄒㄧˋ

Vs. /Adj slender

- Mary的腰很細。
  Mary has a slender waist.

★ **細**[b] xì ㄒㄧˋ

Vs. /Adj fine

- 我的頭髮很細。
  I've got very fine hair.

蝦 xiā ㄒㄧㄚ

N shrimp

• 我點了一盤蝦。
I ordered a shrimp dish.

★ 下[1] xià ㄒㄧㄚˋ

N [bound form] down

• 他們往下看。
They looked downward.

★ 下[2] xià ㄒㄧㄚˋ

V to go down

• 誰先下？
Who's going down first?

• 經理下樓去了。
The manager went down the stairs.

下巴 xiàbā ㄒㄧㄚˋ ㄅㄚ

N chin

• 他的下巴很短。
He has a very short chin.

下班 xiàbān ㄒㄧㄚˋ ㄅㄢ

V-sep to come off duty

• 你什麼時候下班？
When do you come off duty?

★ 下次 xiàcì ㄒㄧㄚˋ ㄘˋ

N next time

• 下次我再告訴你。
I'll tell you next time.

• 下次見到她時，我就告訴她。
The next time I see her, I'll tell her.

下課 xiàkè ㄒㄧㄚˋ ㄎㄜˋ

V-sep to dismiss (class)

• 現在下課。
The class is dismissed.

★ 下面[a] xiàmiàn ㄒㄧㄚˋ ㄇㄧㄢˋ

N bottom

CN xiàmian

• 你鞋子的下面是什麼東西？
What's that on the bottom of your shoe?

★ 下面[b] xiàmiàn ㄒㄧㄚˋ ㄇㄧㄢˋ

N underneath

• 椅子下面有一隻貓。
There's a cat underneath the chair.

★ **下鋪** xiàpù ㄒㄧㄚˋ ㄆㄨˋ

N bottom bunk

- 你睡下鋪還是上鋪？
  What do you want, bottom or top bunk?

★ **下午** [1] xiàwǔ ㄒㄧㄚˋ ㄨˇ

N afternoon

- 你明天下午要做什麼？
  What would you like to do tomorrow afternoon?

★ **下午** [2] xiàwǔ ㄒㄧㄚˋ ㄨˇ

Adv afternoon

- 我們下午見面了。
  We met each other in the afternoon.

夏季 xiàjì ㄒㄧㄚˋ ㄐㄧˋ

N summertime

- 夏季我們這裡旅遊的人不少。
  We got quite a few tourists here in summertime.

★ **夏天** [1] xiàtiān ㄒㄧㄚˋ ㄊㄧㄢ

N summer

- 夏天臺北熱嗎？
  Is summer in Taipei hot?

★ **夏天** [2] xiàtiān ㄒㄧㄚˋ ㄊㄧㄢ

Adv (in the) summer

- 我們夏天常常到海邊去游泳。
  We often go swimming by the seaside in summer.
- 夏天我們要外出。
  We're going away in the summer.

★ **先** xiān ㄒㄧㄢ

Adv first

- Mike先說，我後說。
  Mike will speak first and I'm after him.

鹹 xián ㄒㄧㄢˊ

Vs. /Adj salty

- 這個菜有點太鹹了。
  The dish is a bit too salty.

線 xiàn ㄒㄧㄢˋ

N line

- 從A點到B點畫一條線。
  Draw a line from point A to point B.

★ **箱子** xiāngzi ㄒㄧㄤ ˙ㄗ

N box

- 箱子裡放了他們的照片。
  Their photos are in the box.

鄉下 xiāngxià ㄒㄧㄤ ㄒㄧㄚˋ

N country

- 去年我離開臺北到鄉下去住。
  I quit Taipei last year and went to live in the country.

★ **香** xiāng ㄒㄧㄤ

Vs. /Adj fragrant

- 這果醬很香，而且有點甜。
  The jam is fragrant and slightly sweet.

香草 xiāngcǎo ㄒㄧㄤ ㄘㄠˇ

N vanilla

- 我要香草口味的冰淇淋。
  I would like vanilla-flavoured ice cream.

香蕉 xiāngjiāo ㄒㄧㄤ ㄐㄧㄠ

N banana

- 請給我一根香蕉，行嗎？
  Can I have a banana, please?

香料 xiāngliào ㄒㄧㄤ ㄌㄧㄠˋ

N spice

- Mary在湯裡加了些香料。
  Mary added some spices to the soup.

香片 xiāngpiàn ㄒㄧㄤ ㄆㄧㄢˋ

N scented tea

- 奶奶習慣下午喝杯香片。
  Grandma's used to have a cup of Scented Tea in the afternoon.

香味 xiāngwèi ㄒㄧㄤ ㄨㄟˋ

N fragrance

- 這香味太濃了。
  How strong the fragrance is!

★ **相信** xiāngxìn ㄒㄧㄤ ㄒㄧㄣˋ

Vst to believe

- 我相信他說的話。
  I believe what he said.
- 我相信她明天會到。
  She's arriving tomorrow, I believe.
- 我不相信她只有二十歲。
  I don't believe she's only 20.

★想[a] xiǎng
ㄒㄧㄤˇ

Vst to think

- 我也是這麼想的。
  I think so too.
- 我想你這樣做不公平。
  I think that you're being unfair.
- 我在想下一步該怎麼辦。
  I'm thinking about what my next move should be.

★想[b] xiǎng
ㄒㄧㄤˇ

Vst to want

- 我很想喝一杯。
  I really want a drink.
- 她一直想去臺灣。
  She'd always wanted to go to Taiwan.
- 先生，有人想見你。
  Someone wants to see you, sir.

享受 xiǎngshòu
ㄒㄧㄤˇ ㄕㄡˋ

V to enjoy

- 她關心別人，享受生活。
  She cares about people and enjoys life.

★向 xiàng
ㄒㄧㄤˋ

Prep toward

- Bill向我走來。
  Bill is walking towards me.
- 他們的車向車站開去。
  They were driving towards the station.
- 我看見他向Joe跑過去。
  I saw him running towards Joe.

巷 xiàng
ㄒㄧㄤˋ

N lane

- 他的房子在39巷。
  His house is in Lane 39.

★項 xiàng
ㄒㄧㄤˋ

M measure word for item

- 我報名了幾項活動。
  I've signed up for several activities.

★像 xiàng
ㄒㄧㄤˋ

V to look like

- 週末過後，公園像個垃圾場。
  After the weekend, the park looked like a refuse dump.

巷子 xiàngzi
ㄒㄧㄤˋ ˙ㄗ

N alley

- 我們住在同一條巷子裡。
  We live in the same alley.

★ 先生[a] xiānshēng
ㄒㄧㄢ ㄕㄥ

N mister

- 我想Muller先生正在吃午飯。
  I think Mr. Muller is at lunch.

★ 先生[b] xiānshēng
ㄒㄧㄢ ㄕㄥ

N sir

- 先生，你的鑰匙掉了。
  Sir! You dropped your keys.

現金 xiànjīn
ㄒㄧㄢˋ ㄐㄧㄣ

N cash

- 我沒有帶多少現金。
  I didn't bring enough cash.

線上 xiànshàng
ㄒㄧㄢˋ ㄕㄤˋ

N on line
CN xiànshang

- 我每個星期三在線上學華語。
  I learn Chinese on line every Wednesday.

★ 現在 xiànzài
ㄒㄧㄢˋ ㄗㄞˋ

N at present

- 現在我有空。
  I'm free at present.

消防 xiāofáng
ㄒㄧㄠ ㄈㄤˊ

N fire-protection

- 大樓裡的消防安全要做好。
  Fire-protection must be secured in the building.

消化 xiāohuà
ㄒㄧㄠ ㄏㄨㄚˋ

V to digest

- 這種食物不容易消化。
  This kind of food is not easy to digest.

消炎 xiāoyán
ㄒㄧㄠ ㄧㄢˊ

Vp-sep to reduce inflammation

- 護士在給我的傷口消炎。
  The nurse was reducing the inflammation of my wound.

★ 小[a] xiǎo
ㄒㄧㄠˇ

Vs. /Adj small

- 這是個小問題。
  It's just a small problem.

★ 小[b] xiǎo
ㄒㄧㄠˇ

Vs. /Adj young

• 他比我小三歲。
He's three years younger than I.

小便[1] xiǎobiàn
ㄒㄧㄠˇ ㄅㄧㄢˋ

N urine

• 你需要檢查小便。
You have to have your urine tested.

小便[2] xiǎobiàn
ㄒㄧㄠˇ ㄅㄧㄢˋ

Vi to urinate

• 狗在屋裡小便。
The dog urinated in the house.

小菜 xiǎocài
ㄒㄧㄠˇ ㄘㄞˋ

N side dish

• 我很餓，先點些小菜吧！
I'm starved. Let's order some side dishes first.

小費 xiǎofèi
ㄒㄧㄠˇ ㄈㄟˋ

N tip

• 你留小費了嗎？
Did you leave a tip?

★ 小孩[a] xiǎohái
ㄒㄧㄠˇ ㄏㄞˊ

N kid

• 她已經結婚，有兩個小孩。
She's married with two kids.

★ 小孩[b] xiǎohái
ㄒㄧㄠˇ ㄏㄞˊ

N youngster

• 現在的小孩幾乎每天都上網。
Youngsters nowadays get on the Internet almost every day.

小號 xiǎohào
ㄒㄧㄠˇ ㄏㄠˋ

N small size

• 這件襯衫你有小號的嗎？
Do you have this shirt in small size?

★ 小姐 xiǎojiě
ㄒㄧㄠˇ ㄐㄧㄝˇ

N miss

• 再見，Brown小姐。
Goodbye, Miss Brown.

• 我想約見Woods小姐。
I'd like to make an appointment with Miss Woods.

小聲 xiǎoshēng
ㄒㄧㄠˇ ㄕㄥ

Vs. /Adj to lower (voice)

- 請你小聲一點。
  Could you lower your voice a bit?

★ 小時 xiǎoshí ㄒㄧㄠˇ ㄕˊ

N hour

- 我每晚學習兩個小時。
  I study for two hours every night.
- 他們一個多小時前就睡了。
  They went to bed over an hour ago.
- 我們在電話裡談了一個小時。
  We talked on the phone for an hour.

小說 xiǎoshuō ㄒㄧㄠˇ ㄕㄨㄛ

N fiction

- 我喜歡看小說。
  I like to read fiction.

小偷 xiǎotōu ㄒㄧㄠˇ ㄊㄡ

N thief

- 抓小偷！
  Stop thief!

小腿 xiǎotuǐ ㄒㄧㄠˇ ㄊㄨㄟˇ

N shank

- 他很擔心自己受傷的小腿。
  He was very worried about his injured shank.

★ 小心[a] xiǎoxīn ㄒㄧㄠˇ ㄒㄧㄣ

Vs. /Adj attentive

- 他對這些問題很小心。
  He is very attentive to these problems.

★ 小心[b] xiǎoxīn ㄒㄧㄠˇ ㄒㄧㄣ

Vs. /Adj careful

- 小心！地板很滑。
  Be careful! The floor's slippery.

小學 xiǎoxué ㄒㄧㄠˇ ㄒㄩㄝˊ

N junior school

- 你兒子上的是哪所小學？
  Which junior school did your son go to?

小學生 xiǎoxuéshēng ㄒㄧㄠˇ ㄒㄩㄝˊ ㄕㄥ

N pupil

- 她教三十個小學生。
  She's in charge of 30 pupils.

A B C D E F G H J K L M N O P Q R S T W X Y Z X-

小指 xiǎozhǐ
ㄒㄧㄠˇ ㄓˇ

N little finger

MY 尾指

- 我發現他的小指受傷了。
  I noticed his little finger was injured.

★笑[a] xiào
ㄒㄧㄠˋ

V to laugh

- 聽到這件事，我笑了。
  I laughed at that story.

★笑[b] xiào
ㄒㄧㄠˋ

V to smile

- 她對我笑了。
  She smiled at me.

校園 xiàoyuán
ㄒㄧㄠˋ ㄩㄢˊ

N campus

- 他們住在校園裡。
  They live on campus.

★些 xiē
ㄒㄧㄝ

Det some

- 請給我些糖。
  Give me some sugar, please.
- 她出去買些東西。
  She went out for some shopping.
- 我們在找有些經驗的人。
  We're looking for someone with some experience.

★鞋 xié
ㄒㄧㄝˊ

N shoe

- Tim穿四十號的鞋。
  Tim wears size 40 shoes.
- 我打算給自己買雙新鞋。
  I'm going to treat myself to a new pair of shoes.

鞋櫃 xiéguì
ㄒㄧㄝˊ ㄍㄨㄟˋ

N shoe cabinet

MY 鞋架、鞋櫥

- 鞋櫃就在門口。
  The shoe cabinet is just in the doorway.

★寫 xiě
ㄒㄧㄝˇ

V to write

- 這個字怎麼寫？
  How do you write this character?
- 你可以在紙的兩面寫。
  You can write on both sides of the paper.

- 這篇文章寫得非常好。
  The article is very well written.

★ 血 xiě ㄒㄧㄝˇ

N blood

CN SG xuè

- Ted受傷了，流了很多血。
  Injured, Ted lost a lot of blood.

血管 xiěguǎn ㄒㄧㄝˇ ㄍㄨㄢˇ

N blood vessel

CN SG xuèguǎn

- 她血管太細，不好找。
  Her blood vessels are too thin to find easily.

血型 xiěxíng ㄒㄧㄝˇ ㄒㄧㄥˊ

N blood group

CN SG xuèxíng

- 你的血型是什麼？
  What is your blood group?

血壓 xiěyā ㄒㄧㄝˇ ㄧㄚ

N blood pressure

CN SG xuèyā

- 我的血壓正常。
  My blood pressure is normal.

★ 謝謝 xièxie ㄒㄧㄝˋ ˙ㄒㄧㄝ

Vst to thank

- 請替我謝謝他。
  Thank him for me.
- 謝謝你的幫忙。
  Thank you for your help.

心裡 xīnlǐ ㄒㄧㄣ ㄌㄧˇ

N mind

- 她總是心裡有什麼就說什麼。
  She always says what's on her mind.

★ 心情 xīnqíng ㄒㄧㄣ ㄑㄧㄥˊ

N mood

- 他今天心情怎麼樣？
  What kind of mood is he in today?
- Jill今天的心情不好。
  Jill's in a bad mood today.
- 你今天早上心情不錯啊！
  You're in a good mood this morning!

心臟 xīnzàng ㄒㄧㄣ ㄗㄤˋ

N heart

- 經常運動對心臟有好處。

Regular exercise is good for the heart.

★新 xīn
ㄒㄧㄣ

Vs. /Adj new

- 這相機是新的嗎？
Is this camera new?
- 你的錶看上去是新的。
Your watch looks new.

新聞 xīnwén
ㄒㄧㄣ ㄨㄣˊ

N news

- 有什麼新聞？
What's the news?

新鮮 xīnxiān
ㄒㄧㄣ ㄒㄧㄢ

Vs. /Adj fresh
CN xīnxian

- 這條魚還新鮮。
This fish is still fresh.

欣賞 xīnshǎng
ㄒㄧㄣ ㄕㄤˇ

V admire

- 我很欣賞她的雙腿。
I admire her legs.

薪水 xīnshuǐ
ㄒㄧㄣ ㄕㄨㄟˇ

N salary
CN 工資

- 他的薪水相當高。
He draws a substantial salary.

★信[1] xìn
ㄒㄧㄣˋ

N letter

- 我打算給她寫一封信。
I intended to write her a letter.

★信[2] xìn
ㄒㄧㄣˋ

Vst to believe

- 這些事我早就不信了。
I stopped believing in all that long ago.

信封 xìnfēng
ㄒㄧㄣˋ ㄈㄥ

N envelope

- 我需要一個信封寄這封信。
I need an envelope for this letter.

信件 xìnjiàn
ㄒㄧㄣˋ ㄐㄧㄢˋ

N correspondence

- 請把信件寄到這個地址。
Please send correspondence to this address.

信箱 xìnxiāng
ㄒㄧㄣˋ ㄒㄧㄤ

N mailbox

- 我的信箱全是帳單。
  My mailbox is full of bills.

信仰[1] xìnyǎng
ㄒㄧㄣˋ ㄧㄤˇ

N belief

- 他有他的信仰。
  He has a belief of his own.

信仰[2] xìnyǎng
ㄒㄧㄣˋ ㄧㄤˇ

V to believe

- 我信仰基督教。
  I believe in Christianity.

信用卡 xìnyòngkǎ
ㄒㄧㄣˋ ㄩㄥˋ ㄎㄚˇ

N credit card

- 你們這可以用信用卡嗎？
  Do you take credit cards?

信紙 xìnzhǐ
ㄒㄧㄣˋ ㄓˇ

N letter paper

- 他向我要了幾張信紙。
  He asked me for some letter paper.

★星期 xīngqí
ㄒㄧㄥ ㄑㄧˊ

N week

CN xīngqi

- 醫生說他必須住院一個星期。
  The doctor said he must be hospitalized for a week.

- 下一個星期我會很忙。
  I'm going to be very busy for the next week.

★星期天 xīngqítiān
ㄒㄧㄥ ㄑㄧˊ ㄊㄧㄢ

N sunday

CN xīngqiiān

- Max通常星期天來這裡。
  Max generally comes here on Sunday.

- 下星期天是我生日。
  It's my birthday a week on Sunday.

型 xíng
ㄒㄧㄥˊ

N type

- 你喜歡哪一型的手機？
  Which type of cell phone do you like?

行李 xínglǐ
ㄒㄧㄥˊ ㄌㄧˇ

N luggage

- 他帶著三件行李去旅行。
  He's traveling with three pieces of luggage.

行李箱 xínglǐxiāng ㄒㄧㄥˊ ㄌㄧˇ ㄒㄧㄤ

N suitcase

- 晚上我收拾了我的行李箱。
  I packed my suitcase in the evening.

★姓[1] xìng ㄒㄧㄥˋ

N surname

- 李是我的姓。
  My surname is Lee.

★姓[2] xìng ㄒㄧㄥˋ

V to have... as surname

- 我姓李，不姓林。
  I have Lee as surname, not Lin.

★姓名 xìngmíng ㄒㄧㄥˋ ㄇㄧㄥˊ

N name

- 他沒有說出自己的姓名。
  He didn't say his name.
- 在中國，姓名相同的人很多。
  There are many people sharing the same full name in China.

★幸虧 xìngkuī ㄒㄧㄥˋ ㄎㄨㄟ

Adv fortunately

- 幸虧他帶了雨傘。
  Fortunately, he brought his umbrella.

★興趣 xìngqù ㄒㄧㄥˋ ㄑㄩˋ

N interest

- 音樂是我最大的興趣。
  Music is my main interest.
- 我對他的事情沒有興趣。
  I take no interest in his business.

胸 xiōng ㄒㄩㄥ

N chest

- 我的胸痛得厲害。
  I have a sharp pain in my chest.

胸部 xiōngbù ㄒㄩㄥ ㄅㄨˋ

N chest

- 球剛好打中他的胸部。
  The ball hit him right in the chest.

修[a] xiū ㄒㄧㄡ

V to repair

- 這輛車太舊，別再修了。
  The car is too old. Just stop repairing it.

修[b] xiū
ㄒㄧㄡ

V take course

- John打算修一門電腦課。
John is planning to take a computer course.

修理 xiūlǐ
ㄒㄧㄡ ㄌㄧˇ

V to fix

- 我不懂怎麼修理電腦。
I don't know how to fix computers.

休假 xiūjià
ㄒㄧㄡ ㄐㄧㄚˋ

V-sep take leave

- 你爲什麼不休幾天假？
Why don't you take a few day's leave?

休息 xiūxí
ㄒㄧㄡ ㄒㄧˊ

Vs. /Adj to take a rest
CN xiūxi

- 累了，就休息一下。
Take a rest if you're tired.

★選[a] xuǎn
ㄒㄩㄢˇ

V to choose

- 我們選Phil當我們的代表。
We chose Phil to be our representative.

選[b] xuǎn
ㄒㄩㄢˇ

V to select

- 你只能從四個中選一個。
You can only select one out of the four.

★需要[1] xūyào
ㄒㄩ ㄧㄠˋ

N need

- 你有什麼需要，請跟我說。
Just tell me whatever needs you may encounter.

★需要[2] xūyào
ㄒㄩ ㄧㄠˋ

V to need

- 我們需要大家的幫忙。
We need help from you all.

★許多[a] xǔduō
ㄒㄩˇ ㄉㄨㄛ

Det many

- Mike在台北住了許多年。
Mike has lived in Taipei for many years.

★許多[b] xǔduō
ㄒㄩˇ ㄉㄨㄛ

Det much

• 你並沒有喝許多酒。
You haven't drunk much of the wine.

靴子 xuēzi ㄒㄩㄝ ˙ㄗ

N boot

• 她只買了一雙靴子。
She bought nothing but a pair of boots.

★ 學[a] xué ㄒㄩㄝˊ

V to learn

• Lisa在學跳舞。
Lisa's learning to dance.

• Ron在學騎摩托車。
Ron is learning how to ride a motorcycle.

★ 學[b] xué ㄒㄩㄝˊ

V to study

• 你學的是哪一個課程？
What subject are you studying?

學費 xuéfèi ㄒㄩㄝˊ ㄈㄟˋ

N school fees

• 我無法相信學費這麼貴。
I can't believe school fees are so high.

學分 xuéfēn ㄒㄩㄝˊ ㄈㄣ

N credit

• 華語是一門六個學分的課程。
Chinese is a course for six credits.

學期 xuéqí ㄒㄩㄝˊ ㄑㄧˊ

N semester

CN xuéqī

• 這個學期李先生教我們華語。
We have Mr. Lee for Chinese this semester.

★ 學生 xuéshēng ㄒㄩㄝˊ ㄕㄥ

N student

CN xuésheng

• 這些學生學得很快。
These students are quick at learning.

• 學生買電腦可以打折。
Students are entitled to a discount in buying computers.

學士 xuéshì ㄒㄩㄝˊ ㄕˋ

N bachelor

• 他是我們大學的文學士。
He's a Bachelor of Arts from

our university.

★ **學習** [a] xuéxí
ㄒㄩㄝˊ ㄒㄧˊ

V to learn

- 學習語言很有意思。
  It's very interesting to learn a language.

學習 [b] xuéxí
ㄒㄩㄝˊ ㄒㄧˊ

V to study

- 我要用暑假的時間來學習法語。
  I'm going to study French during the summer vacation.

學校 xuéxiào
ㄒㄩㄝˊ ㄒㄧㄠˋ

N school

- 我和他上同一所學校。
  He and I went to the same school.

學院 xuéyuàn
ㄒㄩㄝˊ ㄩㄢˋ

N college

- 華語系是我們學院的一部分。
  The Chinese department is part of our college.

學者 xuézhě
ㄒㄩㄝˊ ㄓㄜˇ

N scholar

- 學者在這問題上意見不同。
  Scholars differ on this issue.

雪 xuě
ㄒㄩㄝˇ

N snow

- 外面還有很多雪。
  There are still lots of snow outside.

訓練 [1] xùnliàn
ㄒㄩㄣˋ ㄌㄧㄢˋ

V to train

- 她的工作是訓練護士。
  Her job is to train nurses.

訓練 [2] xùnliàn
ㄒㄩㄣˋ ㄌㄧㄢˋ

N training

- 他的訓練不夠。
  He lacks training.

鴨 yā ㄧㄚ

N duck (meat)

- 我喜歡吃鴨，不喜歡吃雞。
  I prefer duck to chicken.

★壓[a] yā ㄧㄚ

V to press

- 你得把行李箱裡的衣服壓壓。
  You have to compress your clothes in the suitcase.

★壓[b] yā ㄧㄚ

V to crush

- 別壓我的帽子。
  Don't crush my hat.
- 這個紙盒不能壓。
  This paper box mustn't be crushed.

★壓力 yālì ㄧㄚ ㄌㄧˋ

N pressure

- 水的壓力很可怕。
  The pressure of the water is horrible.
- 這件事給他帶來很大的壓力。
  This matter put a lot of pressure on him.

押金 yājīn ㄧㄚ ㄐㄧㄣ

N deposit

MY 抵押金、頭期

- 訂房間就得先付押金。
  You must pay a deposit if you want to reserve a room.

牙齒 yáchǐ ㄧㄚˊ ㄔˇ

N tooth

- 我的牙齒對酸的食物非常敏感。
  My teeth are highly sensitive to foods that taste sour.

牙膏 yágāo ㄧㄚˊ ㄍㄠ

N toothpaste

- 你用什麼牙膏？
  What kind of toothpaste do you use?

牙刷 yáshuā
ㄧㄚˊ ㄕㄨㄚ

N toothbrush

- 哪一把牙刷是你的？
  Which toothbrush is yours?

雅房 yǎfáng
ㄧㄚˇ ㄈㄤˊ

N studio apartment

- Anne在學校附近租了一間雅房。
  Anne rented a studio apartment close to the campus.

亞軍 yǎjūn
ㄧㄚˇ ㄐㄩㄣ

N runner-up

- John是冠軍，Carl是亞軍。
  The winner is John, and the runner-up, Carl.

★亞洲 Yǎzhōu
ㄧㄚˇ ㄓㄡ

N Asia

CN SG Yàzhōu

- 我們來自亞洲。
  We are from Asia.
- 中國在亞洲的東部。
  China is in the east of Asia.

★呀 ya
˙ㄧㄚ

Ptc sentence final particle, esp. used to soften the tone of a statement

- 恭喜呀！
  Well, congratulations!
- 哪裡買的魚呀？
  Say, where did you buy the fish?
- 你要問問大家呀。
  You should take advice of everyone, I mean.

醃 yān
ㄧㄢ

V to preserve

- 這些肉是用鹽和香料來醃的。
  These meats were preserved in salt and spices.

鹽 yán
ㄧㄢˊ

N salt

- 請不要在菜裡放太多鹽。
  Please don't put too much salt in the dish.

研究[1] yánjiù
ㄧㄢˊ ㄐㄧㄡˋ

V to research

CN SG yánjiū

- 他們正在研究一種新藥。
  They are researching a new medicine.

研究[2] yánjiù
ㄧㄢˊ ㄐㄧㄡˋ

N research

CN SG yánjiū

- 我還在爲我的論文進行研究。
  I'm still doing research for my thesis.

研究生 yánjiùshēng
ㄧㄢˊ ㄐㄧㄡˋ ㄕㄥ

N graduate student

CN SG yánjiū shēng

- 今年我們系有七名研究生。
  There are seven graduate students in our department this year.

研究所 yánjiùsuǒ
ㄧㄢˊ ㄐㄧㄡˋ ㄙㄨㄛˇ

N research institute

CN SG yánjiū suǒ

- 她在研究所得到一份工作。
  She got a job in a research institute.

研討會 yántǎohuì
ㄧㄢˊ ㄊㄠˇ ㄏㄨㄟˋ

N seminar

- 七十人參加了這次研討會。
  70 people attended the seminar.

★ 顏色[a] yánsè
ㄧㄢˊ ㄙㄜˋ

N color

- 我想要淺一點的顏色。
  I'd prefer a lighter color, please.

★ 顏色[b] yánsè
ㄧㄢˊ ㄙㄜˋ

N hue

- 她買了各種顏色的花。
  She bought flowers of various hues.

嚴重 yánzhòng
ㄧㄢˊ ㄓㄨㄥˋ

Vs. /Adj serious

- 他的病很嚴重。
  He got a serious illness.
- 幸虧這次水災不算嚴重。
  Luckily, the flood was not serious.

演 yǎn
ㄧㄢˇ

V to act (role)

- John在這電影裡演一個老人。
  John acts as an old man in the film.

演唱會 yǎnchànghuì
ㄧㄢˇ ㄔㄤˋ ㄏㄨㄟˋ

N vocal recital

- 他在演唱會上唱了幾首老歌。
  He sang some of the old songs at the vocal recital.

演講 yǎnjiǎng
ㄧㄢˇ ㄐㄧㄤˇ

V to speak

- Mary在晚會上演講。
  Mary spoke at the evening party.

眼睛 yǎnjīng
ㄧㄢˇ ㄐㄧㄥ

N eye

CN yǎnjing

- 我的眼睛不舒服。
  I have trouble with my eyes.

驗 yàn
ㄧㄢˋ

V to examine

- 海關正在驗我們的護照。
  The customs officers are examining our passports.

羊 yáng
ㄧㄤˊ

N sheep

- 我們養了五百隻羊。
  We tend 500 sheep.

羊肉 yángròu
ㄧㄤˊ ㄖㄡˋ

N mutton

- 我愛吃紅燒羊肉。
  I like stewed mutton.

陽台 yángtái
ㄧㄤˊ ㄊㄞˊ

N terrace

- Brown一家在陽台吃午飯。
  The Brown's had lunch on the terrace.

楊桃 yángtáo
ㄧㄤˊ ㄊㄠˊ

N star fruit

- 把楊桃切成片，加到沙拉裡去。
  Slice up the star fruits and add them to the salad.

洋裝 yángzhuāng
ㄧㄤˊ ㄓㄨㄤ

N suit

SG MY 連身裙

- 爲什麼不穿那套灰色洋裝？
  Why not put on the grey suit?

養 yǎng
ㄧㄤˇ

V to raise

- 他有三個小孩要養。
  He has three children to rise.

A B C D E F G H J K L M N O P Q R S T W X Y Z X-

癢 yǎng
ㄧㄤˇ

Vs. /Adj tickle

- 我的背很癢。
  My back tickles.

★ 樣 yàng
ㄧㄤˋ

M type of

- Mary帶了三樣水果。
  Mary brought three types of fruit.

腰 yāo
ㄧㄠ

N waist

- 他胖得沒有腰。
  He's so fat that he has no waist.

搖 yáo
ㄧㄠˊ

V to rock

- 別搖了，小孩已經睡著了。
  Stop rocking, the baby has already gone to sleep.

★ 咬 yǎo
ㄧㄠˇ

V to bite

- 他被狗咬了。
  She was bitten by a dog.

★ 要[1a] yào
ㄧㄠˋ

V must

- 你要小心。
  You must be careful.

★ 要[1b] yào
ㄧㄠˋ

V need

- 我看書要戴眼鏡。
  I need glasses for reading.

★ 要[2] yào
ㄧㄠˋ

Vaux to want

- 你要買什麼？
  What do you want to buy?
- 你要我到機場接你嗎？
  Do you want me to pick you up at the airport?

★ 要不然[a] yàobùrán
ㄧㄠˋ ㄅㄨˋ ㄖㄢˊ

Adv if not

- 我會九點到，要不然十點到。
  I'll be there in nine. If not in ten.
- 你去我就去，要不然我不去。
  I'll go if you're going. If not I won't go.

★ **要不然**[b] yàobùrán ㄧㄠˋ ㄅㄨˋ ㄖㄢˊ

Adv otherwise

- 快，要不然就趕不上車了。
  Hurry up. Otherwise, we'll miss the bus.
- 穿上大衣，要不然你會感冒的。
  Put your coat on, otherwise you'll get cold.

★ **要是** yàoshì ㄧㄠˋ ㄕˋ

Conj if

- 我要是你呀，我馬上去。
  If I were in your place, I'd go immediately.
- 你要是嫌麻煩，那就算了。
  If you don't want to take the trouble, then forget it.
- 你要是碰見她，替我問個好。
  If you meet her, say hello from me.

藥 yào ㄧㄠˋ

N medicine

- 他喉嚨痛，吃了點兒藥。
  He took some medicine for his sore throat.

藥房 yàofáng ㄧㄠˋ ㄈㄤˊ

N pharmacy

- 附近有一家藥房。
  There's a pharmacy in the neighborhood.

藥方 yàofāng ㄧㄠˋ ㄈㄤ

N prescription

- 帶著這張藥方到藥房去。
  Take this prescription to the chemist's.

藥劑師 yàojìshī ㄧㄠˋ ㄐㄧˋ ㄕ

N pharmacist

- 他是醫院裡的藥劑師。
  He works as pharmacist in the hospital.

藥局 yàojú ㄧㄠˋ ㄐㄩˊ

N pharmacy, esp. used in Taiwan

- 這種藥在藥局買得到。
  One can find this medicine at the pharmacy.

鑰匙 yàoshi ㄧㄠˋ ˙ㄕ

N key

SG MY 鎖匙

• 你有這把鎖的鑰匙嗎？
Have you got the key to this lock?

爺爺 yéye
ㄧㄝˊ ˙ㄧㄝ

N granddad
SG MY 公公

• 爺爺現在很老了。
Granddad is very old now.

★也 yě
ㄧㄝˇ

Adv also

• 我的男朋友也叫Mike。
My boyfriend was also called Mike.

• 她是同事，也是好朋友。
She's a colleague, and also a great friend.

• 我喜歡音樂，也喜歡畫畫。
I like music, but also I like paintings.

★也許[a] yěxǔ
ㄧㄝˇ ㄒㄩˇ

Adv maybe

• 也許這只是一個誤會。
Maybe it's all just a misunderstanding.

• 也許他是對的，但也許不是。
Maybe he's right, but maybe not.

• 小孩看上去八歲，也許九歲。
The child looked like he was eight, maybe nine.

★也許[b] yěxǔ
ㄧㄝˇ ㄒㄩˇ

Adv perhaps

• 她也許在隔壁。
Perhaps she's next door.

• 明天也許會下雨。
Perhaps it will rain tomorrow.

• 我想也許我們可以外出吃飯。
I thought perhaps we'd dine out.

★夜 yè
ㄧㄝˋ

N night

• 你能讓我在這裡過一夜嗎？
Could you put me up for the night here?

★頁 yè
ㄧㄝˋ

M page

• 答案在下一頁。
The answers are over the page.

• 他在報告裡新加了一頁。

He added a new page to his report.

★ 夜裡 yèlǐ ㄧㄝˋ ㄌㄧˇ

N night

- 他常常在夜裡給我打電話。
He often called me at night.

夜市 yèshì ㄧㄝˋ ㄕˋ

N night market
MY 夜市場

- 這裡有好幾個夜市。
There are quite a few night markets here.

業務 yèwù ㄧㄝˋ ㄨˋ

N business

- 全國各地都有我們的業務。
Our business operates all over the country.

★ 一 yī ㄧ

N one

- 一次拿一個。
Take one at a time.

★ 衣服 [a] yīfú ㄧ ㄈㄨˊ

N clothes

- 我洗澡以後，穿上乾淨衣服。
After taking a bath, I put on clean clothes.

★ 衣服 [b] yīfú/fu ㄧ ㄈㄨˊ

N clothing

- Mary買了一套新衣服。
Mary bought a new set of clothing.

衣架 yījià ㄧ ㄐㄧㄚˋ

N hanger

- 把你的夾克掛在衣架上。
Put your jacket on a hanger.

醫生 yīshēng ㄧ ㄕㄥ

N doctor

- 你找醫生看過病沒有？
Have you consulted your doctor about your illness?

醫師 yīshī ㄧ ㄕ

N medical practitioner

- 他是老人診所的醫師。
He works as medical practitioner in a clinic for the elderly.

醫學院 yīxuéyuàn ㄧ ㄒㄩㄝˊ ㄩㄢˋ

N medical school

- 我小女兒在醫學院唸書。
  My little daughter is in medical school.

醫院 yīyuàn ㄧ ㄩㄢˋ

N hospital

- 馬上送她到醫院！
  Take her to the hospital right now!

★ 咦 [a] yí ㄧˊ

interjection why, showing surprise

- 咦，你怎麼又來了？
  Why, you are here again!

★ 咦 [b] yí ㄧˊ

interjection hey, showing annoyance

- 咦，這是怎麼回事？
  Hey, what's all this about?

★ 咦 [c] yí ㄧˊ

interjection well, emphasizing something you are saying

- 咦，還要我來教你怎麼做？
  Well, do you really want me to teach you how to do it?

★ 移 yí ㄧˊ

V to move

- 把桌子往邊上移。
  Move the table to the side.
- 請大家把椅子往前移。
  Please move your chair forwards.

★ 以後 yǐhòu ㄧˇ ㄏㄡˋ

Adv afterwards

- John不久以後就走了。
  Soon afterwards John left.
- 不久以後她回到臺灣。
  She returned to Taiwan not long afterwards.
- 三天以後，有人在校園見到他。
  Three days afterwards he was seen in the campus.

★ 以內 [a] yǐnèi ㄧˇ ㄋㄟˋ

N less than

- 這件衣服在兩千塊以內我就買。
  I'll buy it if the dress is less than 2000 dollars.

★ 以內[b] yǐnèi ㄧˇ ㄋㄟˋ

N within

- 這附近一公里以內沒有商店。
  Within a kilometer from here there's no shop at all.

★ 以前[1a] yǐqián ㄧˇ ㄑㄧㄢˊ

N ahead of, used with zai/在to form an adverbial pattern

- 在我以前有四個人到了餐廳。
  There were four people ahead of me at the restaurant.

★ 以前[1b] yǐqián ㄧˇ ㄑㄧㄢˊ

N prior to, used with zai/在to form an adverbial pattern

- 會議在他到達以前開始了。
  The meeting started prior to his arrival.

★ 以前[2] yǐqián ㄧˇ ㄑㄧㄢˊ

Adv previously

- 我以前是老師。
  Previously, I was a teacher.
- 這棟房子以前是旅館。
  The building has previously been used as a hotel.

★ 以上 yǐshàng ㄧˇ ㄕㄤˋ

N more than

- 我們需要三個以上的華語老師。
  We need more than three teachers of Chinese.

★ 以外[a] yǐwài ㄧˇ ㄨㄞˋ

N in addition to, used after a noun to form a nominal pattern

- 中文以外他還想學別的語言。
  In addition to Chinese, he wants to learn other language.

★ 以外[b] yǐwài ㄧˇ ㄨㄞˋ

N other than, used after a noun to form a nominal pattern

- 衣服以外你還想買什麼嗎？
  Other than clothes, what else do you want to buy?

★ 以下 yǐxià ㄧˇ ㄒㄧㄚˋ

N less than

- 今天的溫度在15度以下。
  The temperature today is less than 15 degrees.

★ **已經** yǐjīng ㄧˇ ㄐㄧㄥ

Adv already

- 已經是夏天了。
  It's summer already.
- 她已經回家了嗎？
  Has she already gone back home?
- 我到的時候，會議已經開始。
  The meeting had already started when I arrived.

★ **椅子** yǐzi ㄧˇ ˙ㄗ

N chair

- 房間裡有一把椅子。
  There's a chair in the room.

★ **一半** yíbàn ㄧˊ ㄅㄢˋ

N half

- 九點的時候只來了一半學生。
  Only half the students had arrived at nine o'clock.

★ **一定** yídìng ㄧˊ ㄉㄧㄥˋ

Adv definitely

- 你一定要去加拿大嗎？
  Will you definitely go to Canada?
- 我一定在中午以前回到家裡。
  I'll definitely be home before noon.

★ **一共** yígòng ㄧˊ ㄍㄨㄥˋ

Adv altogether

- 一共有七個人。
  There were seven people altogether.
- 一共是五千台幣。
  That'll be 5000 Taiwan dollars altogether.

★ **一下** yíxià ㄧˊ ㄒㄧㄚˋ

complement a little while

- 我想休息一下。
  I want to take a break.

★ **一樣** yíyàng ㄧˊ ㄧㄤˋ

Vs. /Adj same

- 這兩幅畫我看都一樣。
  The two pictures look the same to me.
- Ted不在，情況就不一樣了。
  Things just won't be the same without Ted.

- 我們兩人想法一樣：太貴了。
  We both think the same - it's too expensive.

★ **億** yì 一ˋ

N billion

- 這個國家大概有三億人口。
  The population of this country amounts to about three billion people.

★ **一點兒** yìdiǎr 一 ㄉㄧㄢˇ ㄦ

Adv a little bit

- 這件事有一點兒怪。
  This affair is a little bit odd.

★ **一會兒** yìhuǐr 一ˋ ㄏㄨㄟˇ ㄦ

N a little while

CN yíhuìr

- 我們再等一會兒就出發。
  Let's wait again a little while before we go.

★ **一起** yìqǐ 一ˋ ㄑㄧˇ

Adv together

- 你要一起吃晚飯嗎？
  Would you like to get together for dinner?
- 他們一起工作。
  They work together.

★ **一些** yìxiē 一ˋ ㄒㄧㄝ

Quantifier some

- 有一些問題還沒有弄清楚。
  Some problems still remain to be cleared up.
- 去年我去過亞洲一些國家。
  I've been in some Asian countries last year.

★ **一直**[a] yìzhí 一 ㄓˊ

Adv always

- 我一直住在臺北。
  I've always been living in Taipei.

★ **一直**[b] yìzhí 一 ㄓˊ

Adv straight

- 請從這裡一直往東走。
  Keep straight on from here towards the east.

藝術 yìshù 一ˋ ㄕㄨˋ

N art

- 我不大懂現代藝術。

I don't quite understand modern art.

★ **意思**[a] yìsī
ㄧˋ ㄙ

N implication

• 這句話包含好幾層意思。
This statement has several implications.

★ **意思**[b] yìsī
ㄧˋ ㄙ

N meaning

• 這個詞的意思是什麼？
What's the meaning of this word?

印 yìn
ㄧㄣˋ

V to print

• 這本書他們印了一萬本。
They printed 10 000 copies of the book.

音量 yīnliàng
ㄧㄣ ㄌㄧㄤˋ

N volume

• 你可以調低電視機的音量嗎？
Could you turn the volume down on the TV?

音樂 yīnyuè
ㄧㄣ ㄩㄝˋ

N music

• 現在很難找到好的音樂。
It's hard to find good music nowadays.

音樂會 yīnyuèhuì
ㄧㄣ ㄩㄝˋ ㄏㄨㄟˋ

N concert

• 我們今晚去聽一場音樂會。
We are going to a concert tonight.

銀行 yínháng
ㄧㄣˊ ㄏㄤˊ

N bank

• 馬路對面有一家銀行。
There's a bank on the other side of the street.

銀幕 yínmù
ㄧㄣˊ ㄇㄨˋ

N screen

• Lisa十年前第一次上銀幕。
Lisa first appeared on the screen ten years ago.

英文 yīngwén
ㄧㄥ ㄨㄣˊ

N English (language)

• 你用英文說吧，大家都懂。
You can say it in English. Ev-

erybody here understands it.

★ 因爲 yīnwèi ㄧㄣ ㄨㄟˋ

Conj because

- 他沒來上課，因爲感冒了。
  He missed the class because of the cold.

飲料 yǐnliào ㄧㄣˇ ㄌㄧㄠˋ

N drink

MY 飲品

- 你要喝點兒飲料嗎？
  Would you like a drink?

★ 應該 yīnggāi ㄧㄥ ㄍㄞ

Vaux should

- 你不應該說這樣的話。
  You should not talk like this.

贏 yíng ㄧㄥˊ

Vpt to win

- 誰贏了這場辯論？
  Who won the debate?

螢幕 yíngmù ㄧㄥˊ ㄇㄨˋ

N screen

CN 螢幕 / 螢屏

- 電視的螢幕突然壞了。
  The TV screen suddenly doesn't work.

影片 yǐngpiàn ㄧㄥˇ ㄆㄧㄢˋ

N film

- 這是一部愛情故事影片。
  The film is a love story.

★ 影響 1 yǐngxiǎng ㄧㄥˇ ㄒㄧㄤˇ

N influence

- 這件事對他們有什麼影響？
  What's the influence of this affair on them?

★ 影響 2a yǐngxiǎng ㄧㄥˇ ㄒㄧㄤˇ

V to affect

- 這個決定會影響我們的生活。
  This decision will affect our lives.

★ 影響 2b yǐngxiǎng ㄧㄥˇ ㄒㄧㄤˇ

V to influence

- 我不會影響你的決定。
  I won't influence your decision.

影印 yǐngyìn ㄧㄥˇ ㄧㄣˋ

V to photocopy
MY 複印

• 請給我影印這兩頁。
Could you photocopy these two pages for me?

★ 硬[a] yìng
ㄧㄥˋ

Vs. /Adj firm

• 這張沙發太硬。
This sofa is too firm.

★ 硬[b] yìng
ㄧㄥˋ

Vs. /Adj hard

• 幾個月沒下雨了，土地很硬。
After months without rain, the ground was very hard.

★ 硬[c] yìng
ㄧㄥˋ

Vs. /Adj stiff

• 被子太硬，能換一下嗎？
The covers are too stiff. Could you change them?

應徵 yìngzhēng
ㄧㄥˋ ㄓㄥ

V to answer a call for (job)
CN 應聘

• 我應徵了一家網路公司的工作。
I answered the call for a job in an Internet company.

★ 由[a] yóu
ㄧㄡˊ

Prep by, used as agentive marker

• 這件事由他決定。
The matter was decided by him.

★ 由[b] yóu
ㄧㄡˊ

Prep from, used as source marker

• 水災是由颱風引起的。
Flood resulted from the typhoon.

油[1] yóu
ㄧㄡˊ

N oil

• 在鍋裡放一點兒油。
Put a little oil in the pan.

油[2] yóu
ㄧㄡˊ

Vs. /Adj greasy

• 我得洗頭，我的頭髮太油了。
I have to wash my hair because it's really greasy.

油膩 yóunì
ㄧㄡˊ ㄋㄧˋ

Vs. /Adj oily

• 這種食品太油膩，最好少

A B C D E F G H J K L M N O P Q R S T W X Y Z X-

吃。
This kind of food is too oily, the less you eat the better.

油條 yóutiáo
ㄧㄡˊ ㄊㄧㄠˊ

N fried sticks (snack usually eaten at breakfast)

- 早餐吃油條配豆漿吧！
  Let's have fried sticks and soybean milk for breakfast.

游 yóu
ㄧㄡˊ

V to swim

- Tom游過了河。
  Tom swan across the river.

游泳 yóuyǒng
ㄧㄡˊ ㄩㄥˇ

V to swim

- 你不太會游泳，對吧？
  You can't swim very well, can you?

遊戲 yóuxì
ㄧㄡˊ ㄒㄧˋ

N game

- 這是他們最喜歡玩的遊戲。
  It's a favorite game of theirs.

郵差 yóuchāi
ㄧㄡˊ ㄔㄞ

N postman
CN 郵遞員

- 郵差一般中午左右到這裡來。
  The postman usually comes here around noon.

郵遞區號
yóudìqūhào
ㄧㄡˊ ㄉㄧˋ ㄑㄩ ㄏㄠˋ

N postcode
CN 郵政編碼。MY 郵區編號

- 別忘記寫郵遞區號。
  Don't forget to write down the postcode.

郵費 yóufèi
ㄧㄡˊ ㄈㄟˋ

N postage

- 這封信郵費是多少？
  What's the postage on this letter?

郵票 yóupiào
ㄧㄡˊ ㄆㄧㄠˋ

N stamp

- 她把一張郵票貼到信封上。
  She stuck a stamp on the envelope.

郵筒 yóutǒng
ㄧㄡˊ ㄊㄨㄥˇ

N postbox

SG 郵箱

- 附近有郵筒嗎？
  Is there a postbox around here?

★ 尤其 yóuqí ㄧㄡˊ ㄑㄧˊ

Adv especially

- 這裡很潮濕，尤其在三月。
  It's really humid here, especially in March.
- 我喜歡鄉村，尤其在春天。
  I love the country, especially in spring.

★ 又 yòu ㄧㄡˋ

Adv again

- John又遲到了。
  John's late again.
- 她今天又來了。
  She came again today.
- 他又弄丟了雨傘。
  He lost his umbrella again.

★ 有[a] yǒu ㄧㄡˇ

V to have

- 他在那邊有一棟房子。
  He has a house over there.
- 當老師必須有耐心。
  You need to have patience to be a teacher.

★ 有[b] yǒu ㄧㄡˇ

V to possess

- 你有護照嗎？
  Do you possess a passport?
- 不同的工人有不同的技術。
  Different workers possess different skills.

★ 有的 yǒude ㄧㄡˇ ˙ㄉㄜ

Det some

- 有的人同意，有的人不同意。
  Some people agree and some are not.
- 這次考試，有的題目太難了。
  Some questions on this exam were too difficult.

★ 有點兒 yǒudiǎr ㄧㄡˇ ㄉㄧㄢˇ ㄦ

Adv a little bit

- 看樣子他有點兒醉了。
  I'm afraid he's a little bit drunk.
- 我今天有點兒累，明天再

去吧。
I'm a little bit tired today. Let's go tomorrow.

有空 yǒukòng ㄧㄡˇ ㄎㄨㄥˋ

Vs. /Adj be free

- 星期五晚上你有空嗎？
  Are you free on Friday night?

★ 有名 yǒumíng ㄧㄡˇ ㄇㄧㄥˊ

Vs. /Adj famous

- 臺南是最有名的城市之一。
  Tainan is one of the most famous cities.

有趣 yǒuqù ㄧㄡˇ ㄑㄩˋ

Vs. /Adj interesting

- 這個故事很有趣。
  The story is quite interesting.

★ 有時候 yǒushíhòu ㄧㄡˇ ㄕˊ ㄏㄡˋ

Adv sometimes

CN yǒushíhou

- 我有時候得工作到很晚。
  I sometimes have to work late.

有線 yǒuxiàn ㄧㄡˇ ㄒㄧㄢˋ

Vs-attr cable

- 這家旅館有有線電視。
  One can watch cable TV in this hotel.

★ 有用[a] yǒuyòng ㄧㄡˇ ㄩㄥˋ

Vs. /Adj helpful

- 考試帶著計算機十分有用。
  It's helpful to have a calculator for the exam.

★ 有用[b] yǒuyòng ㄧㄡˇ ㄩㄥˋ

Vs. /Adj useful

- 這件衣服爬山時會有用。
  This dress would be useful for mountain-climbing.

友情 yǒuqíng ㄧㄡˇ ㄑㄧㄥˊ

N friendly sentiments

- 我們兩個人的友情是不會變的。
  The friendly sentiments between two of us will remain unchanged.

友善 yǒushàn ㄧㄡˇ ㄕㄢˋ

Vs. /Adj friendly

- 旅館的服務人員很友善。

The staff of the hotel is very friendly.

友誼 yǒuyí
ㄧㄡˇ ㄧˊ

N friendship

- 他們之間的友誼加深了。
  The friendship between them deepened.

★右邊 yòubiān
ㄧㄡˋ ㄅㄧㄢ

N right side

- 請站右邊。
  Please stand on the right side.

幼稚園 yòuzhìyuán
ㄧㄡˋ ㄓˋ ㄩㄢˊ

N kindergarten
CN 幼兒園

- 附近有兩所幼稚園可以選擇。
  There are two kindergartens in the area to choose from.

佣金 yòngjīn
ㄩㄥˋ ㄐㄧㄣ

N commission

- 以上價格不包括佣金。
  The above price excludes any commission.

★永遠 yǒngyuǎn
ㄩㄥˇ ㄩㄢˇ

Adv forever

- 我們永遠是朋友。
  We shall be friends forever.
- 我將永遠愛你。
  I'll love you forever.

★用[1] yòng
ㄩㄥˋ

V to use

- 這個詞用在這裡不好。
  This is not the proper word to use here.

★用[2] yòng
ㄩㄥˋ

Prep by, used as instrument marker

- 我能用支票付款嗎？
  May I pay by check?

魚 yú
ㄩˊ

N fish

- 這一條魚做得眞好。
  The fish was cooked to perfection.

★愉快[a] yúkuài
ㄩˊ ㄎㄨㄞˋ

Vs. /Adj happy

- 我們在這裡非常愉快。
  We've been very happy here.

A B C D E F G H J K L M N O P Q R S T W X Y Z X-

★ **愉快**[b] yúkuài ㄩˊ ㄎㄨㄞˋ

Vs. /Adj pleasant

- 跟你一起工作很愉快。
  It's pleasant to work with you.

語法 yǔfǎ ㄩˇ ㄈㄚˇ

N grammar

- 我不喜歡語法。
  I hate grammar.

語言 yǔyán ㄩˇ ㄧㄢˊ

N language

- 想要學好語言就要常練習。
  Regular practice is required if you want to master a language.

雨季 yǔjì ㄩˇ ㄐㄧˋ

N rainy period

- 這裡的雨季是五月到八月。
  The rainy period here is from May to August.

雨天 yǔtiān ㄩˇ ㄊㄧㄢ

N rainy weather

- 我討厭雨天。
  I hate rainy weather.

浴室 yùshì ㄩˋ ㄕˋ

N bathroom

SG MY 沖涼房

- 樓上有浴室和廁所。
  There's a bathroom and a lavatory upstairs.

預約 yùyuē ㄩˋ ㄩㄝ

V to make an appointment

- 去之前最好先預約。
  It's worth making an appointment before you go.

★ **元** yuán ㄩㄢˊ

N dollar

- 他每個月賺五萬元。
  He makes 50,000 dollar a month.

員 yuán ㄩㄢˊ

N bound word for member

- 這隻狗也是我們家的一員。
  This dog too is a member in our family.

★ **圓**[1] yuán ㄩㄢˊ

Vs. /Adj round

- 這種水果小而圓。
  The fruit are small and round.
- 她的臉很圓。
  She has a round face.

★ 圓 2 yuán ㄩㄢˊ

Vs. /Adj orthographic variant for 【元】。

★ 原來 a yuánlái ㄩㄢˊ ㄌㄞˊ

Adv originally

- 我原來不知道他的名字。
  Originally I didn't know his name.

★ 原來 b yuánlái ㄩㄢˊ ㄌㄞˊ

Adv unexpectedly

- 原來John是Mary的兒子。
  Unexpectedly John is Mary's son.

原味 yuánwèi ㄩㄢˊ ㄨㄟˋ

N natural flavor

- 這些麵線沒加調味料，是原味的。
  The vermicelli has no ingredients added and contains only natural flavors.

★ 原因 yuányīn ㄩㄢˊ ㄧㄣ

N reason

- 我不知道她辭職的原因。
  I don't know the reason why she quit her job.
- 我們不能這麼做有幾個原因。
  There are several reasons why we can't do that.
- 由於某種原因，他今天來不了。
  For some reason or other, he couldn't come today.

原子筆 yuánzǐbǐ ㄩㄢˊ ㄗˇ ㄅㄧˇ

N ballpoint pen

CN 圓珠筆

- 我喜歡用原子筆而不用鉛筆。
  I prefer using ballpoint pen to pencil.

★ 遠 yuǎn ㄩㄢˇ

Vs. /Adj far

- 那裡不太遠。
  It's not very far.
- 車站有多遠？
  How far is it to the station?
- 我家離公司不遠。

My home is not far from office.

★ **願意** yuànyì ㄩㄢˋ ㄧˋ

Vaux willing to

- 你願意去就去。
  If you're willing to go, you can go.
- 我非常願意幫忙。
  I'm perfectly willing to help.
- 他們願意付多少錢？
  How much are they willing to pay?

★ **約** yuē ㄩㄝ

V to date

- 我們約個日子一起吃午飯吧。
  Let's date to have lunch together.

★ **越・越** yuè yuè ㄩㄝˋ ㄩㄝˋ

paired adverbials the more... the more

- 越多越好。
  The more the better.
- 你越說，我越不懂。
  The more you explain, the more perplexed I become.

★ **月** yuè ㄩㄝˋ

N month

- 到這個月她就九歲了。
  She'll be nine this month.
- 申請時間只有三個月。
  The application period will last for three months only.
- John下個月要回家來看看。
  John is coming home for a visit next month.

★ **月亮** yuèliàng ㄩㄝˋ ㄌㄧㄤˋ

N moon

CN yuèliang

- 今晚的月亮真好！
  What a fine moon it is tonight!
- 今晚看不見月亮。
  There's no moon tonight.

月台 yuètái ㄩㄝˋ ㄊㄞˊ

N platform

CN 站臺

- 他在月台上跟我說再見。
  He said goodbye to me on the platform.

閱讀 yuèdú ㄩㄝˋ ㄉㄨˊ

V to read

- 我的興趣是閱讀和聽音樂。

My interests include reading and music.

約會 yuēhuì
ㄩㄝ ㄏㄨㄟˋ

N appointment

- 我們的約會訂在十點半。
  Our appointment was fixed at 10:30.

樂器 yuèqì
ㄩㄝˋ ㄑㄧˋ

N instrument

- John會五種不同的樂器。
  John can play five different instruments.

運動[1] yùndòng
ㄩㄣˋ ㄉㄨㄥˋ

Vi to exercise

- 你運動不夠。
  You don't exercise enough.

運動[2] yùndòng
ㄩㄣˋ ㄉㄨㄥˋ

N sport

- 運動讓你保持健康。
  Sport keeps you fit.

運費 yùnfèi
ㄩㄣˋ ㄈㄟˋ

N carriage

SG 運輸費

- 一共三千台幣，包括運費。
  That'll be 3000 dollars, including carriage.

Z

★ 再 zài ㄗㄞˋ

Adv again

- 明天你不要再遲到了。
  Please don't be late again tomorrow.
- Chris再也沒有提起過她。
  Chris never referred to her again.
- 我沒聽清楚，請你再說一遍。
  I didn't hear it clearly. Please say it again.

★ 在[1] zài ㄗㄞˋ

Prep at (location)

- 這輛公車在臺大停嗎？
  Does this bus stop at National U of Taiwan?
- 我們將在Muller家會面。
  We'll meet at Muller's.
- 我在靠角落的桌子旁等著。
  I was waiting at a corner table.

★ 在[2] zài ㄗㄞˋ

Vi to be located at

- 我們公司在市中心。
  Our company is located in the city center.

贊成 zànchéng ㄗㄢˋ ㄔㄥˊ

Vst be in favor of

- 我們都贊成他的辦法。
  We were all in favor of his way of doing.

★ 咱們 zánmen ㄗㄢˊ ˙ㄇㄣ

pronoun we (inclusive)

- 咱們喝杯咖啡，好嗎？
  Shall we have a coffee?

★ 髒[a] zāng ㄗㄤ

Vs. /Adj dirty

- 別把身上弄得太髒。
  Try not to get too dirty!
- 你的襯衫怎麼弄得這麼髒？
  How did your shirt get so dirty?
- 我覺得身上很髒，又餓又冷。
  I felt dirty, hungry, and cold.

★ **髒** [b] zāng ㄗㄤ

Vs. /Adj filthy

- 這裡面髒得很。
  It's filthy in here.

★ **糟糕** [a] zāogāo ㄗㄠ ㄍㄠ

Vs. /Adj chaotic

- 這裡的交通很糟糕。
  The traffic here is chaotic.

★ **糟糕** [b] zāogāo ㄗㄠ ㄍㄠ

Vs. /Adj messy

- 他的房間看起來很糟糕。
  His room looked so messy.

★ **早** zǎo ㄗㄠˇ

Vs. /Adj early

- 你來得眞早！
  You're early!
- 那年春季來得特別早。
  Spring was unusually early that year.
- 現在給他們打電話太早了嗎？
  Is it too early to phone them?

★ **早上** zǎoshàng ㄗㄠˇ ㄕㄤˋ

N early morning

CN zǎoshang

- 我習慣早上去跑步半小時。
  I'm used to do jogging for half an hour in the early morning.

★ **早晚** zǎowǎn ㄗㄠˇ ㄨㄢˇ

Adv sooner or later

- 你早晚得做決定。
  Sooner or later you will have to make a decision.
- 這件事早晚會發生。
  It was bound to happen sooner or later.

★ **怎麼** zěnme ㄗㄣˇ ˙ㄇㄜ

Adv how come

- 怎麼人家沒邀請你呀？
  How come you've not been invited?
- 你怎麼沒打電話給我？
  How come you didn't call me?
- 我怎麼當時沒想到這點？
  How come I didn't think of it?

★ **怎樣** [a] zěnyàng ㄗㄣˇ ㄧㄤˋ

Adv how

- 我在想怎樣去那兒。

I'm trying to think how to get there.

- 這種情況怎樣處理？
How is this to be dealt with?
- 她現在怎樣？感覺好點兒了嗎？
How is she now? Is she feeling better?

★ **怎樣** [b] zěnyàng
ㄗㄣˇ ㄧㄤˋ

Adv in what way

- 她是怎樣看著你的？
In what way does she look at you?

炸 zhá
ㄓㄚˊ

V to fry
SG zhá

- 炸魚的時候，油的溫度要高。
Keep the oil hot when you fry the fish.

展覽 zhǎnlǎn
ㄓㄢˇ ㄌㄢˇ

N exhibition

- 美術館正舉辦照片展覽。
The Museum of Art is staging an exhibition of photographs.

★ **站** [1] zhàn
ㄓㄢˋ

Vi to stand

- Lisa站在門口等我。
Lisa stood by the door and waited for me.
- 他三分鐘前站在那邊。
He was standing over there three minutes ago.
- 沒有座位了，我們只好站。
There are no seats left. We'll have to stand.

站 [2] zhàn
ㄓㄢˋ

N stop

- 我們是這一站下嗎？
Is this our stop?

蘸 zhàn
ㄓㄢˋ

V to dip

- 他把刷子在油漆裡蘸了蘸。
He dipped his brush in the paint.

★ **張** [a] zhāng
ㄓㄤ

M measure word for sheet of paper

- 你寫在一張紙上吧。
Write it down on a piece of paper.

A B C D E F G H J K L M N O P Q R S T W X Y Z X-

- 她給我一張白紙。
  She handed me a piece of blank paper.

★ 張[b] zhāng
ㄓㄤ

M measure word for tickets

- 你能給我弄一張票嗎？
  Will you get me a ticket?
- 我想訂兩張去臺北的票。
  I'd like to book two tickets to Taipei.

★ 長 zhǎng
ㄓㄤˇ

V to grow

- 蔬菜長得很好。
  The vegetables are growing well.
- 小孩開始長頭髮了。
  The child began to grow hair.

漲 zhǎng
ㄓㄤˇ

V to raise

- 最近學費漲了不少。
  Recently the tuition fee has raised a lot.

漲價 zhǎngjià
ㄓㄤˇ ㄐㄧㄚˋ

V-sep to go up (price)

- 火車票又漲價了。
  Train fares are going up again.

脹 zhàng
ㄓㄤˋ

Vs. /Adj be bloated

- 吃完飯我覺得肚子好脹。
  I felt bloated after the meal.

帳單 zhàngdān
ㄓㄤˋ ㄉㄢ

N bill

- 帳單包括服務費在內。
  The bill is inclusive of the service charge.

帳號 zhànghào
ㄓㄤˋ ㄏㄠˋ

N account number

- 請輸入你的帳號。
  Please enter your account number.

帳户 zhànghù
ㄓㄤˋ ㄏㄨˋ

N account

- 你在我們銀行開帳戶了嗎？
  Have you opened an account in our bank?

蟑螂 zhāngláng
ㄓㄤ ㄌㄤˊ

N cockroach

- 她在廚房發現一隻大蟑螂。
  She found a big cockroach in the kitchen.

招待[1] zhāodài ㄓㄠ ㄉㄞˋ

V to treat

- 今天晚餐由我來招待。
  This dinner is on me.

招待[2] zhāodài ㄓㄠ ㄉㄞˋ

N reception

- 我們受到他們熱情的招待。
  We received a warm reception from them.

★ 找[a] zhǎo ㄓㄠˇ

V to look for

- Anne一直在找你。
  Anne has been looking for you all the time.

★ 找[b] zhǎo ㄓㄠˇ

V to search for

- 我在找我的眼鏡。
  I'm searching for my glasses.

★ 找錢 zhǎoqián ㄓㄠˇ ㄑㄧㄢˊ

V to give change

- 收銀員找我三百塊錢。
  The cashier gave me 300 dollars change.

★ 兆 zhào ㄓㄠˋ

M million billion

- 他們花了一兆元買下那家大公司。
  They bought the big company for one million billion dollars.

★ 照[a] zhào ㄓㄠˋ

V to face (mirror)

- Anne在照鏡子。
  Anne looked at herself in the mirror.

★ 照[b] zhào ㄓㄠˋ

V to illuminate

- 大門被一排燈照著。
  The main entrance was illuminated by a row of lamps.

★ 照[c] zhào ㄓㄠˋ

V to photograph

- 我照相總是照不好。
  I always photograph badly.

A B C D E F G H J K L M N O P Q R S T W X Y Z X-

照片 zhàopiàn ㄓㄠˋ ㄆㄧㄢˋ

N photo

- 申請簽證，你得交三張照片。
  To apply for visa, you need to submit three photos.

照相 zhàoxiàng ㄓㄠˋ ㄒㄧㄤˋ

V-sep take picture

- 我們在旅館前照了相。
  We had our picture taken in front of the hotel.

摺 zhé ㄓㄜˊ

V to fold

- 她把信摺起來放進信封裡。
  She folded the letter and put it in an envelope.

哲學 zhéxué ㄓㄜˊ ㄒㄩㄝˊ

N philosophy

- Ian在大學學的是哲學。
  Ian studies philosophy at university.

★ 這 zhè ㄓㄜˋ

Det this

- 這藥很有用。
  This medicine is very effective.
- 聽聽這個笑話吧。
  Wait till you hear this joke.
- 這件衣服比那件便宜。
  This dress is cheaper than that one.

★ 這邊[a] zhèbiān ㄓㄜˋ ㄅㄧㄢ

N here

- 「我在這邊！」我大聲叫著。
  “I’m over here!” I shouted out.

★ 這邊[b] zhèbiān ㄓㄜˋ ㄅㄧㄢ

N this side

- 站到我這邊來吧。
  Stand on this side of me.

★ 這裡[a] zhèlǐ ㄓㄜˋ ㄌㄧˇ

N here

- 這裡誰說英文？
  Who speaks English here?
- 你在這裡幹什麼？
  What are you doing here?
- 我們在這裡吃，好嗎？
  Shall we eat here?

★ 這裡[b] zhèlǐ
ㄓㄜˋ ㄌㄧˇ

N this place

- 我不喜歡這裡。
  I don't like this place.
- 咱們離開這裡吧！
  Let's get out of this place.

★ 這麼 zhème
ㄓㄜˋ ˙ㄇㄜ

Adv so

- 她是這麼說的。
  She did say so.
- 她這麼說是有原因的。
  She has her own reasons for saying so.

★ 這兒 zhèr
ㄓㄜˋ ㄦ

N here (spoken)

- 那地方大概在這兒的西北方。
  That place lies roughly northwest of here.

★ 這樣 zhèyàng
ㄓㄜˋ ㄧㄤˋ

Adv this way

- 這樣做有什麼不對呢？
  What's wrong with doing it this way?
- 不能這樣比較兩個國家。
  We can't compare two countries in this way.
- 我就喜歡這樣，你別管我了。
  Just leave me alone. I like to go this way.

★ 著 zhe
˙ㄓㄜ

Ptc progressive marker

- 外面下著雪。
  It's snowing outside.
- 我正聽著收音機。
  I'm listening to the radio now.
- 大門口站著兩個司機。
  Two drivers were standing at the gate.

★ 眞[1] zhēn
ㄓㄣ

Adv really

- 她走路眞慢。
  She walks really slowly.
- 昨天晚上眞冷。
  It was really cold last night.
- 她只是說說，不會眞做的。
  She's all talk, she won't really do it.

★ 眞[2] zhēn
ㄓㄣ

Vs. /Adj real

- 那本書裡的故事是眞的。
  The story of that book was real.

★ **眞是**[a] zhēnshì ㄓㄣ ㄕˋ

Adv indeed

- 她眞是漂亮。
  She is pretty, indeed.

★ **眞是**[b] zhēnshì ㄓㄣ ㄕˋ

Adv truly

- 我眞是抱歉。
  I am truly sorry.

疹 zhěn ㄓㄣˇ

N rash

- Mary喝酒就會起疹子。
  Mary comes out in a rash if she drinks.

★ **陣** zhèn ㄓㄣˋ

M measure word for wind

- 一陣大風把門吹關上了。
  A strong wind blew the door shut.

徵 zhēng ㄓㄥ

V to recruit

- 這所學校在徵英文老師。
  The school is recruiting teachers of English.

蒸 zhēng ㄓㄥ

V to steam

- 這魚應該蒸十五分鐘。
  The fish should be steamed for 15 minutes.

蒸餃 zhēngjiǎo ㄓㄥ ㄐㄧㄠˇ

N steamed dumpling

- 你要什麼，水餃還是蒸餃？
  What do you want? Boiled or steamed dumplings?

★ **整個** zhěngge ㄓㄥˇ ˙ㄍㄜ

V-attr whole

- 整個假期我都浪費掉了。
  I wasted the whole holiday.
- 整個房間的人都回過頭看他。
  The whole room turned and looked at him.

★ **正** zhèng ㄓㄥˋ

Adv coincidentally

- 你要去臺北嗎？我也正要

去。
Are you going to Taipei? What a coincidence! I'm going up there too.

正常 zhèngcháng ㄓㄥˋ ㄔㄤˊ

Vs. /Adj normal

- 考試前覺得緊張是正常的。
  It's normal to feel nervous before an exam.

正式 zhèngshì ㄓㄥˋ ㄕˋ

Vs. /Adj formal

- 明天的晚會請穿得正式點。
  Put on your formal dress for tomorrow's party.

★正在 zhèngzài ㄓㄥˋ ㄗㄞˋ

Adv currently

- 她目前正在設計新的軟體。
  She is currently working on new software.

證 zhèng ㄓㄥˋ

N bound word for card

- 我還沒有拿到學生證。
  I haven't got my student card yet.

證件 zhèngjiàn ㄓㄥˋ ㄐㄧㄢˋ

N papers

- 請讓我看一下你的證件。
  Let me see your papers.

證明 zhèngmíng ㄓㄥˋ ㄇㄧㄥˊ

N proof

- 你身上帶有什麼證明嗎？
  Have you got any proof on you?

政治 zhèngzhì ㄓㄥˋ ㄓˋ

N politics

- 她一直對政治感興趣。
  Politics have always interested her.

症狀 zhèngzhuàng ㄓㄥˋ ㄓㄨㄤˋ

N symptom

- 這種病最初的症狀是發燒。
  The first symptom of the disease is a fever.

汁 zhī ㄓ

N juice

• 只剩下一盒蘋果汁。
There's only one carton of apple juice left.

★ 枝 zhī ㄓ

M measure word for stalk (plant)

• John送給她一枝紅玫瑰。
John sent her a single red rose.

★ 隻 a zhī ㄓ

M measure word for bird

• 一隻鳥在我們旁邊飛過。
A bird flew right by us.

★ 隻 b zhī ㄓ

M measure word for boat

• 要是我們有一隻小船就好了。
If only we had a boat!

★ 隻 c zhī ㄓ

M measure word for small animal

• 鄰居家養了三隻貓。
The neighbour keeps three cats.

★ 隻 d zhī ㄓ

M measure word for hand (part of body)

• 他把一隻手搭在我的肩上。
He placed a hand on my shoulder.

★ 知道 zhīdào ㄓ ㄉㄠˋ

Vst to know

CN zhī dao

• 我知道那地方，但從沒去過。
I know of that place but I've never been there.

• 每個人都知道這首歌的歌詞。
Everyone knows the words to this song.

脂肪 zhīfáng ㄓ ㄈㄤˊ

N fat

• 這種產品不含動物脂肪。
This product contains no animal fat.

★ 之後 zhīhòu ㄓ ㄏㄡˋ

Conj afterward

• 我們喝了茶，之後去買東西。
We had tea, and afterwards went shopping.

• 先看電影，之後可以去吃

飯。
Let's go and see a film first, and afterwards we could go for a meal.

★ 直接 zhíjiē ㄓˊ ㄐㄧㄝ

Adv directly

- 他們可以直接用華語交談。
They can directly communicate to each other in Chinese.
- 新規則不會直接影響我們。
The new rules won't directly affect us.

職業 zhíyè ㄓˊ ㄧㄝˋ

N occupation

- 這兒填上你的姓名、職業等。
Put down your name, occupation, etc. here.

★ 只[a] zhǐ ㄓˇ

Adv just

- 我只要一塊蛋糕。
I'll just have one piece of cake.

★ 只[b] zhǐ ㄓˇ

Adv only

- 我只買好的葡萄酒。
I only buy good wine.

★ 只好[a] zhǐhǎo ㄓˇ ㄏㄠˇ

Adv have to

- 她不在，我只好回家。
Since she's not in, I have to go home.

★ 只好[b] zhǐhǎo ㄓˇ ㄏㄠˇ

Adv no alternative but

- 他的車壞了，只好走回家。
As his car was broken down, he had no alternative but to walk home.

★ 只要 zhǐyào ㄓˇ ㄧㄠˋ

Adv as long as

- 只要你來，什麼時候都可以。
It doesn't matter when you come, just as long as you come.
- 只要身體好，就能享受生活。
As long as you are in good health, you can enjoy life.

A B C D E F G H J K L M N O P Q R S T W X Y Z X-

★ **只有[a]** zhǐyǒu ㄓˇ ㄧㄡˇ

Adv except for

- 他一身黑，只有領帶是紅色。
  He was dressed all in black except for a red necktie.

★ **只有[b]** zhǐyǒu ㄓˇ ㄧㄡˇ

Adv only

- 只有她答應幫助我。
  Only she promised to help me.
- 我身上只有一百塊錢。
  I have only one hundred dollar with me.
- 這棟房子只有一個出口。
  The house has only one exit.

指導 zhǐdǎo ㄓˇ ㄉㄠˇ

V to guide

- 學生需要老師來指導他們。
  Students need teachers to guide them.

指甲 zhǐjiǎ ㄓˇ ㄐㄧㄚˇ

N nail

- Mary把指甲塗成鮮紅色。
  Mary painted her nails a bright red.

指教 zhǐjiào ㄓˇ ㄐㄧㄠˋ

Vs. /Adj to give advice

- 請多多指教。
  Please give us your advice.

★ **至少** zhìshǎo ㄓˋ ㄕㄠˇ

Adv at least

- 至少讓我付自己的票吧。
  At least let me pay for my own ticket.
- 這看來至少花了你三千元。
  This must have cost you at least 3000 dollars.
- 到那裡至少要花二十分鐘。
  It will take you at least 20 minutes to get there.

治 zhì ㄓˋ

V to cure

- 我要點治頭痛的藥。
  I want some medicine to cure headache.

治療 zhìliáo ㄓˋ ㄌㄧㄠˊ

V to treat

- 他在醫院治療，不能來上

課了。
Under medical treatment in hospital, he was able to attend his classes.

★ 中[a] zhōng
ㄓㄨㄥ

N [bound form] center, used with zai/在 to form a prepositional pattern, e.g. in the center (of)

- 我的學校在城中。
  My school is located in the center of the city.

★ 中[b] zhōng
ㄓㄨㄥ

N [bound form] middle, used with zai/在to form a prepositional pattern, e.g. in the middle (of)

- 他在會議中睡著了。
  He felt asleep in the middle of the meeting.

★ 中部 zhōngbù
ㄓㄨㄥ ㄅㄨˋ

N central part

- 我還沒去過美國中部。
  I haven't been in the central part of the States yet.

中等 zhōngděng
ㄓㄨㄥ ㄉㄥˇ

Vs-attr middle

- 她丈夫是中等身高。
  Her husband is of middle height.

中號 zhōnghào
ㄓㄨㄥ ㄏㄠˋ

N size medium

- John穿中號襯衫。
  John wears a size medium shirt.

中級 zhōngjí
ㄓㄨㄥ ㄐㄧˊ

Vs-attr intermediate

- 我正在上中級華語課。
  I'm attending an intermediate Chinese class.

★ 中間 zhōngjiān
ㄓㄨㄥ ㄐㄧㄢ

N in the middle

- 中間那位是Mike。
  Mike is the one in the middle.
- 別站在馬路中間。
  Don't stand in the middle of the street.
- Kate把盒子放在桌子中間。
  Kate put the box in the middle of the table.

★ 中文 Zhōngwén
ㄓㄨㄥ ㄨㄣˊ

N Chinese (language)

- 我的中文不好，可以請你說慢一點嗎？

A B C D E F G H J K L M N O P Q R S T W X Y Z X-

My Chinese isn't very good. May I ask you to speak a bit slower?

★ 中午 zhōngwǔ ㄓㄨㄥ ㄨˇ

N noon

- Jane通常睡到中午。
  Jane usually sleeps until noon.
- 他們在中午離開了。
  They left at noon.
- 我們中午十二點見了面。
  We met at 12 noon.

★ 中心[a] zhōngxīn ㄓㄨㄥ ㄒㄧㄣ

N center

- 旅館在城市的中心。
  The hotel is in the center of the city.

★ 中心[b] zhōngxīn ㄓㄨㄥ ㄒㄧㄣ

N heart

- 自由廣場在臺北市的中心。
  The Square of Freedom is in the heart of Taipei.

中學 zhōng xué ㄓㄨㄥ ㄒㄩㄝˊ

N junior high school

- 我弟弟在念中學。
  My younger brother is attending junior high school.

中學生 zhōngxuéshēng ㄓㄨㄥ ㄒㄩㄝˊ ㄕㄥ

N high school student

- 我妹妹還是個中學生。
  My younger sister is still a high school student.

中藥 zhōngyào ㄓㄨㄥ ㄧㄠˋ

N traditional Chinese medicine (substance used for treating illness)

- 她對中藥相當了解。
  She knows quite a lot about traditional Chinese medicine.

中醫 zhōngyī ㄓㄨㄥ ㄧ

N traditional Chinese medicine (treatment and study of illness)

- 越來越多的西方人接受中醫。
  Traditional Chinese medicine is now being accepted by more and more Westerners.

中指 zhōngzhǐ ㄓㄨㄥ ㄓˇ

N middle finger

- 在有些國家比中指是很不禮貌的。
  Raise your middle finger is

very impolite in some countries.

鐘 zhōng ㄓㄨㄥ

N clock

- 我一看鐘就知道我遲到了。
  The sight of the clock reminded me that I was late.

★ **鐘頭** zhōngtóu ㄓㄨㄥ ㄊㄡˊ

N hour

- 我每天有三個鐘頭的課。
  I have classes for three hours every day.

腫 zhǒng ㄓㄨㄥˇ

Vs. /Adj to swell

- 我的右腳踝腫了。
  My right ankle has swollen.

★ **種**[1] zhǒng ㄓㄨㄥˇ

M kind

- 你要哪種飲料？
  What kind of drink do you want?
- 這種行爲是不禮貌的！
  This kind of behavior is unrestrained.

★ **種**[2] zhǒng ㄓㄨㄥˇ

N type

- 我們賣三種茶，你要哪一種？
  We sell three types of tea. Which type do you want?

★ **種**[3] zhòng ㄓㄨㄥˋ

V to plant

- 我在花園裡種了一棵蘋果樹。
  I've planted an apple tree in the garden.

★ **重** zhòng ㄓㄨㄥˋ

Vs. /Adj heavy

- 小心！那袋子很重。
  Careful! That bag is pretty heavy.
- 這箱子太重，沒法拿。
  The box is too heavy to carry.

★ **重要** zhòngyào ㄓㄨㄥˋ ㄧㄠˋ

Vs. /Adj important

- 父母的關心對小孩很重要。
  Cares from the parents are very important to their child.

粥 zhōu ㄓㄡ

N porridge

- 冬天時我只想喝熱粥。
  I want nothing but hot porridge in the winter time.

★ **週** zhōu ㄓㄡ

N week

- Mike已經來這裡一週了。
  Mike has been here for a week.

★ **週末** zhōumò ㄓㄡ ㄇㄛˋ

N weekend

- 她外出過週末了。
  She has gone away for the weekend.

豬 zhū ㄓㄨ

N pig

- 他們一年養五百頭豬。
  They raise 500 pigs a year.

豬肉 zhūròu ㄓㄨ ㄖㄡˋ

N pork

- 中國人一般吃豬肉。
  The Chinese normally eat pork.

煮 zhǔ ㄓㄨˇ

V to boil

- 我煮了點兒麵當晚飯。
  I boiled some noodles for dinner.

主管 zhǔguǎn ㄓㄨˇ ㄍㄨㄢˇ

N person in charge

- 這裡誰是主管？
  Who's the person in charge here?

主任 zhǔrèn ㄓㄨˇ ㄖㄣˋ

N director

- 他得馬上到主任辦公室去。
  He's wanted immediately in the director's office.

主修[1] zhǔxiū ㄓㄨˇ ㄒㄧㄡ

N main subject

- 華語是他在大學的主修。
  His main subject at university is the Chinese language.

主修[2] zhǔxiū ㄓㄨˇ ㄒㄧㄡ

V to major

- Anne主修亞洲音樂史。

Anne majors in the history of Asian music.

★ **住[a]** zhù ㄓㄨˋ

Vi to live

- 我不想住在那裡。
  I don't want to live there.
- 我一個人住很開心。
  I'm quite happy living alone.
- 她在那裡住了一段時間了。
  She's been living there for some time now.

★ **住[b]** zhù ㄓㄨˋ

Vi to stay

- Matt在這裡會住到五月。
  Matt will stay here till May.

註冊 zhùcè ㄓㄨˋ ㄘㄜˋ

V-sep to enroll

- 新生明天開始註冊。
  The new students will begin enrolling tomorrow.

祝福[1] zhùfú ㄓㄨˋ ㄈㄨˊ

N blessing

- 我們向那對新婚夫婦祝福。
  We bestowed our blessing on the newlyweds.

祝福[2] zhùfú ㄓㄨˋ ㄈㄨˊ

V to bless

- 祝福你們身體健康。
  Bless you all, and may you enjoy a good health.

助教 zhùjiào ㄓㄨˋ ㄐㄧㄠˋ

N assistant (university)

- 我們大學的助教對學生很友善。
  The assistants in our college are very friendly towards us.

注射 zhùshè ㄓㄨˋ ㄕㄜˋ

V to inject

- 護士幫她注射了降血壓的藥。
  A nurse injected her with hypertensive.

★ **注意** zhùyì ㄓㄨˋ ㄧˋ

Vst to pay attention to

- 我注意聽她說話。
  I paid attention to what she was saying.

住院 zhùyuàn ㄓㄨˋ ㄩㄢˋ

V-sep to hospitalize

- 他去身體檢查住院三天。
  He was hospitalized for a checkup for three days.

住址 zhùzhǐ ㄓㄨˋ ㄓˇ

N home address

- 請寫下你的住址。
  Please write down your home address.

專輯 zhuānjí ㄓㄨㄢ ㄐㄧˊ

N special edition

- 她的文章刊登在專輯裡。
  Her paper appeared in the special edition.

專線 zhuānxiàn ㄓㄨㄢ ㄒㄧㄢˋ

N special line (telephone service)

- 專線的開放時間到午夜。
  The special line is open till midnight.

專業[1] zhuānyè ㄓㄨㄢ ㄧㄝˋ

Vs. /Adj professional

- 這個計畫看上去相當專業。
  This plan looks quite professional.

專業[2] zhuānyè ㄓㄨㄢ ㄧㄝˋ

N specialty

- 他的專業是電腦科學。
  His specialty is computer science.

★轉[a] zhuǎn ㄓㄨㄢˇ

V to change

- 風已經轉向了。
  The wind has changed direction.
- 我們在臺北轉機。
  We changed planes in Taipei.
- 請你不要再轉頻道了。
  I wish you'd stop changing the channel.

★轉[b] zhuǎn ㄓㄨㄢˇ

V to turn around

- 小孩轉身向他母親跑去。
  The child turned around and ran to his mother.

轉帳 zhuǎnzhàng ㄓㄨㄢˇ ㄓㄤˋ

N transfer

- 轉帳請到七號窗口。
  Please go to the window 7 for

transfer.

★ **裝** zhuāng ㄓㄨㄤ

V to pack

- 我正在把書裝進箱子裡。
  I'm packing my books into boxes.
- 她往包裡裝了幾件衣物。
  She packed a few things into a bag.

壯 zhuàng ㄓㄨㄤˋ

Vs. /Adj robust

- 他祖父身體還是很壯。
  His Grandpa was still very robust.

★ **準備** zhǔnbèi ㄓㄨㄣˇ ㄅㄟˋ

V to prepare

- 他們在廚房準備晚飯。
  They are preparing dinner in the kitchen.
- 我得給他們準備一間房間。
  I have to prepare a room for them.
- 我父母正忙著準備去渡假。
  My parents were busy preparing to go on holiday.

★ **桌子** [a] zhuōzi ㄓㄨㄛ ˙ㄗ

N desk

- 把桌子上所有的書拿走。
  Clear all those books off the desk.

★ **桌子** [b] zhuōzi ㄓㄨㄛ ˙ㄗ

N table

- 請把菜放在那張桌子上。
  Please place the dishes on that table.

★ **資料** [a] zīliào ㄗ ㄌㄧㄠˋ

N data

- John負責收集資料。
  John is in charge of data collection.

★ **資料** [b] zīliào ㄗ ㄌㄧㄠˋ

N material

- 你可以在網路上找課程資料。
  You can search for the course material on the Internet.

資訊 zīxùn ㄗ ㄒㄩㄣˋ

N information

CN 信息

• 你這資訊是從哪裡聽來的？
Where did you get this information?

★ 字 zì ㄗˋ

N character

• 你這個字寫錯了。
You wrote this character wrong.

• 漢字「樹」怎麼寫？
How to write the Chinese character for 'tree'?

字幕 zìmù ㄗˋ ㄇㄨˋ

N caption

• 我看不見銀幕上的字幕。
I can't see the caption on the screen.

★ 自動 zìdòng ㄗˋ ㄉㄨㄥˋ

Vs. /Adj automatic

• 這門是自動的。
The door is automatic.

★ 自己 zìjǐ ㄗˋ ㄐㄧˇ

N self

• 我給自己做早餐。
I'm cooking myself the breakfast.

• 我們自己沒辦法搬動沙發。
We couldn't move the sofa by ourselves.

自行車 zìxíngchē ㄗˋ ㄒㄧㄥˊ ㄔㄜ

N bicycle (term used in Mainland China)

CN SG 腳車

• 學生騎自行車上學。
Students go to school by bicycles.

★ 自由 zìyóu ㄗˋ ㄧㄡˊ

Vs. /Adj free

• 一年以後我就自由了。
I'll be free in a year.

• 他覺得跟父母住不自由。
Living with his parents, he doesn't feel free.

★ 總是[a] zǒngshì ㄗㄨㄥˇ ㄕˋ

Adv all the time

• 他總是在擔心我。
He worries about me all the time.

★ 總是[b] zǒngshì ㄗㄨㄥˇ ㄕˋ

Adv always

- 我總是坐地鐵。
I always travel by underground.

★ **總是** [c] zǒngshì ㄗㄨㄥˇ ㄕˋ

Adv constantly

- 流行的衣服總是在變。
Fashion is constantly changing.

綜合 zònghé ㄗㄨㄥˋ ㄏㄜˊ

Vs-attr comprehensive
CN zōnghé

- 這不是綜合辭典，是學習辭典。
This is not a comprehensive dictionary, but a learner's dictionary.

★ **走** [a] zǒu ㄗㄡˇ

Vi to leave

- 公車剛走。
The bus has just left.

★ **走** [b] zǒu ㄗㄡˇ

Vi to walk

- 我們一邊走，一邊聊天。
As we walked along, we had a chat.

走道 zǒudào ㄗㄡˇ ㄉㄠˋ

N passage
CN 過道

- 請留一個走道讓別人過。
Please clear a passage to let people through.

★ **走路** zǒulù ㄗㄡˇ ㄌㄨˋ

V-sep to walk

- 今天我們走了約十公里的路。
We've walked about 10 kilometers today.

租 zū ㄗㄨ

V to rent

- 我們要租車去旅行。
We want to rent a car for a trip.

租金 zūjīn ㄗㄨ ㄐㄧㄣ

N rent

- 這些套房租金高。
These apartments command high rents.

祖父 zǔfù ㄗㄨˇ ㄈㄨˋ

N grandfather
MY 公公

- 我們在看祖父的照片。
We're looking at grandfather's

photos.

祖母 zǔmǔ ㄗㄨˇ ㄇㄨˇ

N grandmother

MY 婆婆

- 我們去看了生病的祖母。
  We went to visit our sick grandmother.

祖先 zǔxiān ㄗㄨˇ ㄒㄧㄢ

N ancestor

- 他們的祖先是中國人。
  Their ancestors were Chinese.

足球 zúqiú ㄗㄨˊ ㄑㄧㄡˊ

N football

- 我不會踢足球。
  I'm no good at playing football.

嘴 zuǐ ㄗㄨㄟˇ

N mouth

- 把你的嘴再張開點。
  Open your mouth a little wider.

嘴巴 zuǐbā ㄗㄨㄟˇ ㄅㄚ

N mouth

- 她嘴巴長得很好看。
  She has a pretty mouth.

嘴脣 zuǐchún ㄗㄨㄟˇ ㄔㄨㄣˊ

N lips

- 她嘴脣上塗了口紅。
  Her lips were lips ticked.

醉 zuì ㄗㄨㄟˋ

Vs. /Adj be drunk

- 我沒醉，我還能喝。
  I'm not drunk, I can drink more.

★最 a zuì ㄗㄨㄟˋ

Adv most

- 這是中國飯館裡最常吃的菜。
  It is the kind of food most often served in Chinese restaurant.

★最 b zuì ㄗㄨㄟˋ

Adv best

- 你最喜歡哪種顏色？
  Which colour do you like best?
- 哪天晚上你最方便來？
  Which evening would suit you best to come?

★最好 zuìhǎo ㄗㄨㄟˋ ㄏㄠˇ

Adv had better

- 你最好先問問他。
  You'd better ask him first.
- 你最好想別的辦法。
  You'd better think of some other way.
- 你最好現在就去見她。
  You'd better go to see her now.

★ 最後[1] zuìhòu ㄗㄨㄟˋ ㄏㄡˋ

N last

- 小孩把最後一點麵包吃了。
  The child ate the last of the bread.

★ 最後[2a] zuìhòu ㄗㄨㄟˋ ㄏㄡˋ

Adv eventually

- 最後她找到了工作。
  Eventually she got a job.

★ 最後[2b] zuìhòu ㄗㄨㄟˋ ㄏㄡˋ

Adv finally

- 最後，他決定辭職。
  Finally, he decided to resign.
- 最後他接受了我們的觀點。
  Finally, he accepted our views.
- 父親最後同意讓我去旅行。
  My father finally agreed to let me go on the trip.

★ 最近[a] zuìjìn ㄗㄨㄟˋ ㄐㄧㄣˋ

N latest

- 你了解他們最近的計劃嗎？
  Do you know their latest plan?

★ 最近[b] zuìjìn ㄗㄨㄟˋ ㄐㄧㄣˋ

N the most recent

- 最近一次會議是在上星期三。
  The most recent meeting has been taken place on last Wednesday.

★ 昨天 zuótiān ㄗㄨㄛˊ ㄊㄧㄢ

N yesterday

- 昨天是星期三。
  Yesterday was Wednesday.
- 我昨天下午見到了她。
  I saw her yesterday afternoon.
- 我們昨天才從臺灣回國。
  We only got home from Taiwan yesterday.

★ 左 zuǒ ㄗㄨㄛˇ

N left

- 在下一個路口往左轉。
Take the next road on the left.

★ **左邊** zuǒbiān ㄗㄨㄛˇ ㄅㄧㄢ

N left side

- 照片裡Joe在Anne的左邊。
Joe is at the left side of Anne in the photo.

★ **左右** zuǒyòu ㄗㄨㄛˇ ㄧㄡˋ

N left and right

- 她左右兩邊站著學生。
Students stood to her left and right.

★ **坐** zuò ㄗㄨㄛˋ

Vi to sit

- 我坐在岸邊看海。
I sat on the shore and looked at the sea.
- 我可以坐在這兒嗎？
May I sit here?
- 她坐在鋼琴邊的椅子上。
She was sitting in a chair by the piano.

★ **座** [a] zuò ㄗㄨㄛˋ

M measure word for bridge

- 我們開車經過那座橋。
We drove across the bridge.

★ **座** [b] zuò ㄗㄨㄛˋ

M measure word for clock

- 房間的一角有一座大擺鐘。
There's a grandfather clocking the corner of the room.

★ **座** [c] zuò ㄗㄨㄛˋ

M measure word for mountain

- 那座山冬天會下雪。
We have snow in that mountain in winter.

★ **做** [a] zuò ㄗㄨㄛˋ

V to do

- 這樣做不太好。
It's not so good to do it this way.

★ **做** [b] zuò ㄗㄨㄛˋ

V to make

- 我用箱子幫貓做了一張床。
I made a bed for the kitten with a box.

做法 zuòfǎ ㄗㄨㄛˋ ㄈㄚˇ

N practice

- 我們希望這些做法立即停止。
  We expect these practices to cease forthwith.

作品 zuòpǐn ㄗㄨㄛˋ ㄆㄧㄣˇ

N work

- 這些畫都是我自己的作品。
  These paintings are all my own work.

座談會

zuòtánhuì
ㄗㄨㄛˋ ㄊㄢˊ ㄏㄨㄟˋ

N forum

- 他們就教材舉行一次座談會。
  They are holding a forum on teaching material.

座位 zuòwèi ㄗㄨㄛˋ ㄨㄟˋ

N seat

- 我的座位在第九排。
  My seat is in the ninth row.

作業 zuòyè ㄗㄨㄛˋ ㄧㄝˋ

N homework

- 你做完作業了嗎？
  Have you done your homework yet?

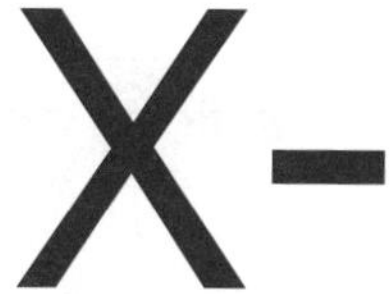

X光 X guāng
X ˙ㄍㄨㄤ

N X-ray

- 我們得給你的腿照一張X-光。
  We have to take an X-ray of your leg.

一、Mandarin Speaking Regions and Communities：

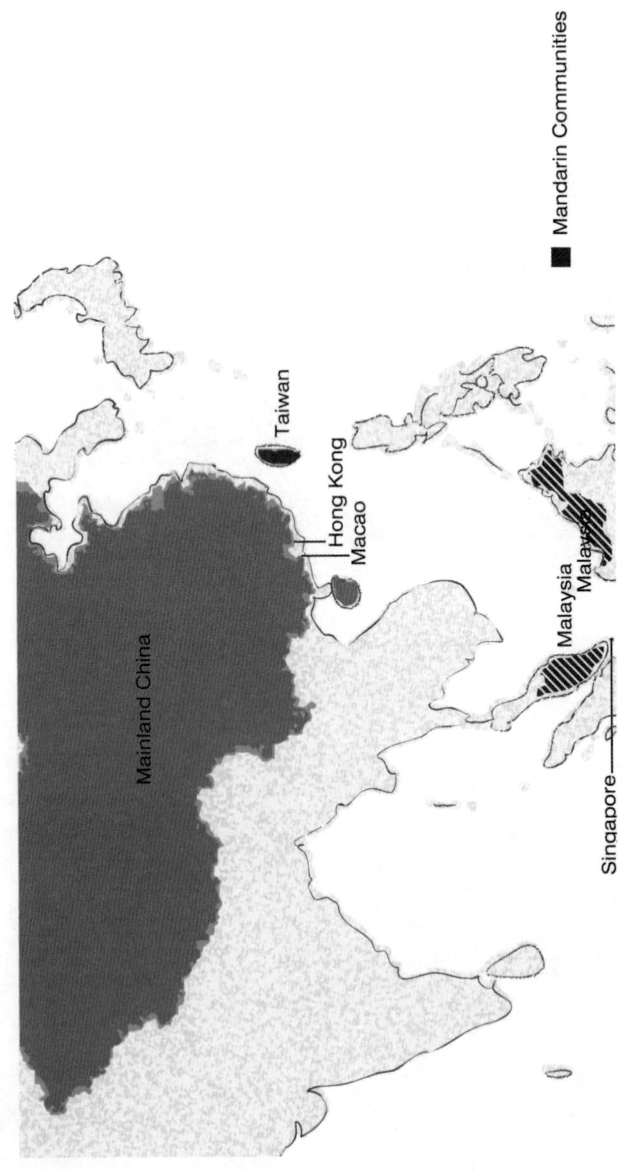

二、Taiwan traffic map

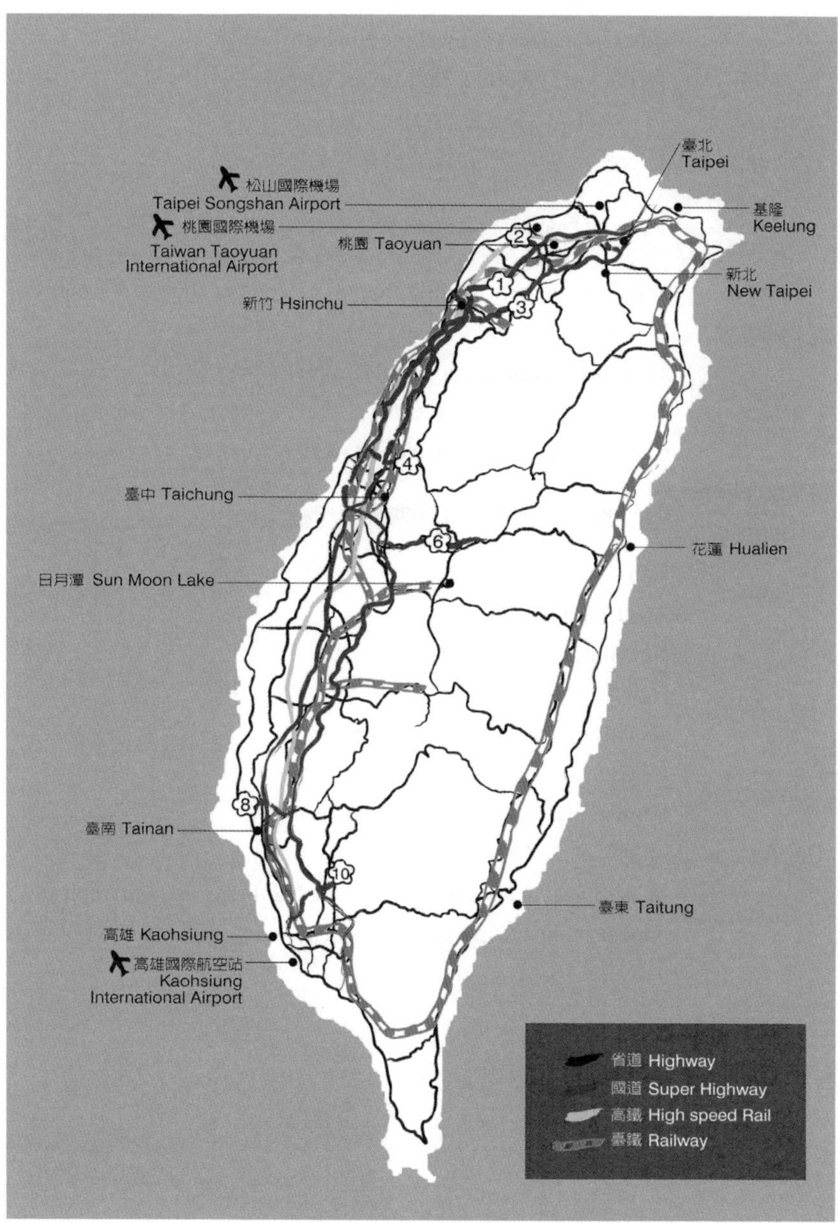

三、Introduction of Taiwan

Language	Official language – Mandarin Other languages – Taiwanese Hokkien, Hakka
Area	36,193 km2 (World's 38th largest island)
Population	23,354,061 (August, 2013)
Capital	Taipei
Highest point	Yushan (Jade Mountain) (3,952 meters)
Tallest building	Taipei 101 (World's tallest from 31 December 2004 to 4 January 2010)
International airports	Taiwan Taoyuan International Airport (TPE) Taipei Songshan Airport (TSA) Kaohsiung International Airport (KHH)
Population density	645/km^2 (World's 10th highest)
Ethnic groups	Han (98%) Austronesian (Aborigines) New immigrants
Currency	New Taiwan dollar (TWD) Usually written as NT$ or NTD
Time zone	UTC+8 Summer daylight saving time not observed
Calling code	+886
Climate	Sub-tropical monsoon climate in the Northern part, and tropical monsoon climate in the Southern part.

四、Flight time from Taipei to the world's major cities：

Country	City	The actual flying hours
亞洲 Asia		
韓國 Korea	首爾 Seoul	2 hrs 15 mins
日本 Japan	東京 Tokyo	3 hrs
菲律賓 Philippines	馬尼拉 Manila	2 hrs
香港 Hong Kong	香港 Hong Kong	1 hr 40 mins
中國大陸 Mainland China	北京 Beijing	3 hrs 15 mins
	上海 Shanghai	2 hrs
	大連 Dalian	3 hrs 15 mins
	青島 Qingdao	1 hr 45 mins
	哈爾濱 Harbin	3 hrs 30 mins
	鄭州 Zhengzhou	6 hrs
	南京 Nanjing	2 hrs
	成都 Chengdu	3 hrs 15 mins
	西安 Xi'an	3 hrs
	昆明 Kunming	3 hrs 20 mins
	廣州 Canton	2 hrs
	廈門 Xiamen	1 hr 30 mins
	烏魯木齊 Urumqi	5 hrs 30 mins
印度 India	新德里 New Delhi	7 hrs 30 mins Transit in Hong Kong
尼泊爾 Nepal	加德滿都 Kathmandu	8 hrs 10 mins Transit in Hong Kong
新加坡 Singapore	新加坡 Singapore	4 hrs 40 mins
馬來西亞 Malaysia	吉隆坡 Kuala Lumpur	4 hrs 30 mins
印尼 Indonesia	雅加達 Jakarta	5 hrs 40 mins

Country	City	The actual flying hours
大洋洲 Oceania		
美國 United States	夏威夷 Hawaii	7 hrs 30 mins Transit in Tokyo
澳大利亞 Ausralia	雪梨 Sydney	8 hrs 10 mins
紐西蘭 New Zealand	奧克蘭 Oakland	11 hrs
Country	City	The actual flying hours
美洲 America		
美國 United States	紐約 New York	17 hrs 30 mins
	舊金山 San Francisco	11 hrs 30 mins
	洛杉磯 Los Angeles	11 hrs 20 mins
加拿大Canada	溫哥華 Vancouver	11 hrs 30 mins
	多倫多 Toronto	14 hrs
阿根廷 Argentina	布宜諾斯艾利斯 Buenos Aires	28 hrs Transit in Tokyo
巴西 Brazil	里約熱內盧 Rio de Janeiro	3 hrs Transit in Tokyo
Country	City	The actual flying hours
歐洲 Europe		
德國 Germany	法蘭克福 Frankfurt	17 hrs
法國 France	巴黎 Paris	13 hrs 40 mins
義大利 Italy	羅馬 Rome	16 hrs
西班牙 Spain	馬德里 Madrid	19 hrs 20 mins
瑞士 Switzerland	蘇黎士 Zurich	17 hrs 20 mins Transit in Hong Kong
奧地利 Austria	維也納 Vienna	17 hrs Transit in Bangkok
荷蘭 Netherlands	阿姆斯特丹 Amsterdam	12 hrs 45 mins
英國 Britain	倫敦 London	16 hrs
瑞典 Sweden	斯德哥爾摩 Stockholm	19 hrs Transit in Tokyo
俄羅斯 Russia	莫斯科 Moscow	21 hrs 30 mins Transit in Bangkok

Country	City	The actual flying hours
非洲 Africa		
埃及 Egypt	開羅 Cairo	16 hrs
南非 South Africa	約翰尼斯堡 Johannesburg	16 hrs 10 mins

五、Sockets in Chinese speaking area

district	voltage	Socket shape
Mainland China	220	
Hong Kong	200	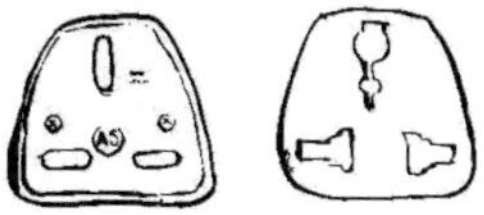
Taiwan	110	

六、Important festivals in the East and the West

Important Chinese festivals	Explanation
New Year's eve (29th or 30th day of the 12th or last lunar month)	Also called "dà nián yè", the last day before the start of the new lunar year.
Spring Festival/Chinese New Year (The first day of the 1st lunar month)	The festival that celebrates the 1st day of the 1st lunar month, which is the most important traditional festival for the Chinese. Commonly referred to as "guò nián" (literally means passing the year).
Lantern Festival (15th day of the 1st lunar month)	The first full moon after Spring Festival, which signifies the arrival of Spring. Also known as "xiǎo guò nián" (the lighter version of "guò nián").
Qingming Festival (Around April 5th)	Also known as Tomb Sweeping Day. This is the day when people honors their ancestors and tend to their graves.
Duanwu Festival or Dragon Boat Festival (5th day of the 5th lunar month)	People will race dragon boats and eat Zongzi (sticky rice dumplings) in order to commemorate the death of Qu Yuan, the poet and minister of the ancient state of Chu during the Warring States period.
Qixi (evening of the 7th day of the 7th lunar month)	The Chinese Valentine's Day.
The Ghost Festival (the 15th day of the 7th lunar month)	Offerings are made to the deceased in order to pray for "píng ān" (peacefulness).
Mid-Autumn Festival (the 15th day of the 8th lunar month)	The whole family gets together for a reunion and for admiring the full moon, eating moon cakes and pomelos.
Double 9th Festival (the 9th day of the 9th lunar month)	The homonym of "double 9th" in Chinese is "jiǔ jiǔ", which means "for a long time". Activities that honor the elderly or those that are related to climbing mountains are often held on this day.

Important Chinese festivals	Explanation
Buddha's birthday (the 8th day of the 4th lunar month)	This is the day to celebrate the birthday of Siddhartha Gautama, the founder of Buddhism. Worshippers will go to temples to join in the celebrations.
Teachers' Day (September 28th or September 10th)	The day when people expresses thanks to their teachers for the past year of teaching and guidance. Also the birthday of Confucius, the pioneer in education in ancient China.

Important festivals in the West	
Christmas day (December 25th)	聖誕節 Shèngdàn jié
Good Friday (the Friday preceding Easter Sunday)	耶穌受難日 Yēsū shòunàn rì
Easter (the first Sunday after the Spring Equinox)	復活節 Fùhuó jié
Halloween (October 31st)	萬聖節 Wànshèng jié
Valentine's Day (February 14th)	情人節 Qíngrén jié
Thanksgiving (the fourth Thursday of November)	感恩節 Gănēn jié

七、Measurement

長度 Linear measure									
公厘（millimeter）	1	10	1000	......	25.4	304.801	914.402	......	......
公分	0.1	1	100	100000	0.3	0.0328084	0.0109361	......	......
公尺（meter）	0.001	0.01	1	1000	0.0254	0.3048	0.9144	1609.35	1852
公里（kilometer）	......	0.00001	0.001	1	0.00003	0.00031	0.00091	1.60935	1.852
吋（inch）	0.03937	0.3937008	3937	39370	1	12	36	63360	72913.2
呎（feet）	0.00328	0.0328084	3.28074	3280.84	0.08333	1	3	5280	6076.1

長度 Linear measure									
碼（yard）	0.00109	0.0109361	1.09361	1903.61	0.02778	0.33333	1	1760	2025.37
哩（mile）	......	......	0.00062	0.62137	0.00002	0.00019	0.00057	1	1.15016
海浬（nautical mile）	......	......	0.00054	0.53996	0.00001	0300017	0.00049	0.86898	1

地積（面積）Square measure							
平方公尺（square meter）	1	100	1000	......	3.30579	4046.87	0,09
公畝（are）	0.01	1	100	1000	0.03306	4.04687	0.000929
公頃（hectare）	0.0001	0.01	1	100	0.00033	0.40469	......
平方公里（square kilometer）	......	0.0001	0.01	1	......	0.00405	......
平方呎（square feet）	10.76	1076,39	107639	10763910	35,58	43559,98	1
坪tsubo（píng）	0.3025	30.25	3025	302500	1	1224.18	9,37
美畝（acre）	0.00025	0.02471	2.47104	247.104	0.00082	1	0.000023

容量 Volume measure					
毫升（milliliter）	1	1000	89.5729	437.167	3784.33
公升（liter）	1.001	1	0.02957	0.47317	3.78533
盎司（ounce）	0.03382	33.8148	1	16	128
品脫（pint ）	0.00211	2.11342	0.0625	1	8
加侖（U.S. Gallon）	0.00026	0.26418	0.00781	0.125	1

重量 Weight measure					
公克（gram）	1	1000	......	600	453.592
公斤（kilogram）	0.001	1	1000	0.6	0.45359
公噸（tonne）	......	0.001	1	0.0006	0.00045
磅（pound）	0.00221	2.20462	2204.62	1.32277	1
台斤（catty）	0.03527	1.66667	1666.67	1	0.75599

八、Numbers

(一) Cardinal numbers

0	零 líng	10	十 shí	20	二十 èrshí	…	90	九十 jiǔshí
1	一 yī	11	十一 shíyī	21	二十一 èrshíyī	…	91	九十一 jiǔshíyī
2	二 èr	12	十二 shíèr	22	二十二 èrshíèr	…	92	九十二 jiǔshíèr
3	三 sān	13	十三 shísān	23	二十三 èrshísān	…	93	九十三 jiǔshísān
4	四 sì	14	十四 shísì	24	二十四 èrshísì	…	94	九十四 jiǔshísì
5	五 wǔ	15	十五 shíwǔ	25	二十五 èrshíwǔ	…	95	九十五 jiǔshíwǔ
6	六 liù	16	十六 shíliù	26	二十六 èrshíliù	…	96	九十六 jiǔshíliù
7	七 qī	17	十七 shíqī	27	二十七 èrshíqī	…	97	九十七 jiǔshíqī
8	八 bā	18	十八 shíbā	28	二十八 èrshíbā	…	98	九十八 jiǔshíbā
9	九 jiǔ	19	十九 shíjiǔ	29	二十九 èrshíjiǔ	…	99	九十九 jiǔshíjiǔ

100	一百 yìbǎi	100,000,000	一億 yíyì
1,000	一千 yìqiān	1,000,000,000	十億 shíyì
10,000	一萬 yíwàn	10,000,000,000	一百億 yìbǎi yì
100,000	十萬 shíwàn	100,000,000,000	一千億 yìqiān yì
1,000,000	一百萬 yìbǎi wàn	1,000,000,000,000	一兆 yízhào
10,000,000	一千萬 yìqiān wàn		

㈡ Ordinal numbers

For ordinal numbers, Chinese use「第」before the number.

1st	第一 dì-yī	5th	第五 dì-wǔ	9th	第九 dì-jiǔ
2nd	第二 dì-èr	6th	第六 dì-liù	10th	第十 dì-shí
3rd	第三 dì-sān	7th	第七 dì-qī		
4th	第四 dì-sì	8th	第八 dì-bā		

㈢ Counting Money

The basic monetary measure words in Chinese are 塊(kuài) "dollar", 毛(máo) "dime, ten cents," and 分(fēn) "cent." We add its noun錢(qián) "money" to the last measure word.

Examples:

	塊 kuài	毛 máo	分 fēn
$ 1.00	一塊（錢）yí kuài (qián)		
$ 2.00	兩塊（錢）liǎng kuài (qián)		
$ 0.60		六毛（錢） liù máo(qián)	
$ 0.09			九分（錢） jiǔ fēn (qián)
$ 3.20	三塊 sān kuài	兩毛（錢*） liǎng máo(qián)	
$ 0.55		五毛 wǔ máo	五分（錢*） wǔ fēn (qián)
$ 48.22	四十八塊 sìshíbā kuài	兩毛 liǎng máo	二分（錢*） èr fēn (qián)
$ 10.04	十塊 shí kuài		零四分（錢*） líng sì fēn (qián)
$ 10.40	十塊 shí kuài	零四毛（錢*） líng sì máo (qián)	
$ 100.05	一百塊 yìbǎi kuài		零五分（錢*） líng wǔ fēn (qián)
$ 100.50	一百塊 yìbǎi kuài	零五毛（錢*） líng wǔ máo (qián)	

The marked「錢」(qián)means optional for these expressions involving more than one unit.

九、Times

㈠ Dates

2000-02-02	西元（公元） xīyuán (gōngyuán)	兩千年二月二日 / 二零零零年二月二日 liǎng qiān nián Èryuè èr rì/ èr líng líng líng nián Èryuè èr rì
2013-09-27	西元（公元） xīyuán (gōngyuán)	二零一三年九月二十七日 èr líng yī sān nián Jiǔyuè èrshíqī rì
100 B.C.	西元（公元）前 xīyuán (gōngyuán)	一百年 qián yìbǎi nián

㈡ Week

Chinese name each day of the week by numbers, except Sunday.

Monday	星期一 Xīngqīyī	禮拜一 Lǐbàiyī
Tuesday	星期二 Xīngqīèr	禮拜二 Lǐbàièr
Wednesday	星期三 Xīngqīsān	禮拜三 Lǐbàisān
Thursday	星期四 Xīngqīsì	禮拜四 Lǐbàisì
Friday	星期五 Xīngqīwǔ	禮拜五 Lǐbàiwǔ
Saturday	星期六 Xīngqīliù	禮拜六 Lǐbàiliù
Sunday	星期日 / 星期天 Xīngqīrì/Xīngqītiān	禮拜日 / 禮拜天 Lǐbàirì/Lǐbàitiān

㈢ Clock

Basic time units and common expressions:

點（鐘） diǎn (zhōng)	o'clock
分 fēn	minute
刻 kè	15 minutes (a quarter of an hour)
半 bàn	30 minutes (a half-hour)
過 guò	plus, past, after (used before 30 minutes of the hour)
差 chā	minus, to, before (used after 30 minutes of the hour, counting toward the next hour)

Examples:

1:00	一點（鐘） yì diǎn (zhōng)		
1:01	一點 yì diǎn	零一分 líng yī fēn	一點過一分 yì diǎn guò yì fēn
2:00	兩點（鐘） liǎng diǎn (zhōng)		
2:02	兩點 liǎng diǎn	零二分/ líng èr fēn	兩點過兩分 liǎng diǎn guò liǎng fēn
3:15	三點 sān diǎn	十五分/ shíwǔ fēn/	三點一刻/ sān diǎn yí kè
4:30	四點 sì diǎn	三十分/ sānshí fēn/	四點半 sì diǎn bàn/
5:45	五點 wǔ diǎn	四十五分/ sìshíwǔ fēn/	五點三刻/ 差一刻六點 wǔ diǎn sān kè/ chā yí kè liù diǎn
6:58	六點 liù diǎn	五十八分/ wǔshíbā fēn/	差兩分七點 chā liǎng fēn qī diǎn
12:00	十二點（鐘） shíèr diǎn (zhōng)		

十、Measure words

Measure words with marks "*" below mean extra selected measure words to the items shown in this dictionary.

Measure word	Pinyin	Mandarin Phonetic Symbols	Meaning	Example	English Translation for Example
把	bǎ	ㄅㄚˇ	a handful of	她送給我一把臺灣茶葉。	She gave me a handful of Taiwan tea.
班	bān	ㄅㄢ	measure word for service in public transportation	我們只好坐下一班火車。 我坐上了最後一班公車。 飛高雄的飛機每天有五班。	We had to take the next train. I caught the last bus of the day. There are five flights to Kaohsiung every day.
包	bāo	ㄅㄠ	unit word for parcel	這包信件重兩公斤。	The parcel of mails weighs 2 kilo.
包	bāo	ㄅㄠ	unit word for packet	Ian每天抽一包香菸。	Ian consumes a packet of cigarettes every day.
包	bāo	ㄅㄠ	unit word for pack	她給了我一包口香糖。	She gave me a pack of gum.
杯	bēi	ㄅㄟ	unit word for cup	Amy給我倒了一杯咖啡。	Amy poured out a cup of coffee for me.

Measure word	Pinyin	Mandarin Phonetic Symbols	Meaning	Example	English Translation for Example
杯	bēi	ㄅㄟ	unit word for glass	你要一杯酒還是半杯？	Do you want a full glass of wine or half a glass?
*本	běn	ㄅㄣˇ	measure word for books, albums, etc.	桌上有三本書。	There are three books on the desk.
遍	biàn	ㄅㄧㄢˋ	time, used to express frequency.	請再說一遍。這封信我已經看了好幾遍了。	Please say it again. I've read over this letter several times.
部	bù	ㄅㄨˋ	measure word for novel books	這部小說已經翻譯成中文了。	The novel was translated into Chinese.
部	bù	ㄅㄨˋ	measure word for films	那是一部很棒的電影。	It's an excellent film.
部	bù	ㄅㄨˋ	measure word for machines	這部電視機壞了。	The television isn't working properly.
*頂	dǐng	ㄉㄧㄥˇ	measure word for hats	你戴這頂帽子很好看。	You look great with this hat.
*棟	dòng	ㄉㄨㄥˋ	measure word for buildings	哪棟樓是文學院?	Which building is the Faculty of Arts?
*朵	duǒ	ㄉㄨㄛˇ	measure word for flowers	這朵花送給你。	This flower is for you.

Measure word	Pinyin	Mandarin Phonetic Symbols	Meaning	Example	English Translation for Example
份	fèn	ㄈㄣˋ	measure word for documents	你訂哪一份報紙看？ 我已經給他們送去一份報告。	What newspaper do you subscribe to? I've sent out a report to them.
份	fèn	ㄈㄣˋ	measure word for jobs	我會得到那份工作的。 她幹這份工作有五年了。	I'm going to get that job. She's been in the job for five years.
分	fēn	ㄈㄣ	minute	現在是九點十分。	It's now ten minutes past nine.
*封	fēng	ㄈㄥ	measure word for letters	這封信是從臺灣寄來的。	This letter is (sent) from Taiwan.
幅	fú	ㄈㄨˊ	measure word for paintings	她送給我兩幅中國畫。	She gave me two Chinese paintings.
副	fù	ㄈㄨˋ	measure word for appearance of human beings	Mary那副模樣像她母親。	Mary has her mother's looks.
副	fù	ㄈㄨˋ	measure word for glasses	Jane戴了一副新眼鏡。	Jane wore a new pair of sunglasses.
個	ge	˙ㄍㄜ	general classifier	街上沒幾個人。 替我想一個辦	There are few people in the street. Think of an idea

Measure word	Pinyin	Mandarin Phonetic Symbols	Meaning	Example	English Translation for Example
				法。 離這裡只有兩個小時的車程。	for me. It's only two hours' drive from here.
*根	gēn	ㄍㄣ	measure word for long and thin objects	這根吸管太長了。	This straw is too long.
壺	hú	ㄏㄨˊ	pitcher of	她給我們泡了一壺茶。	She made a pitcher of tea for us.
架	jià	ㄐㄧㄚˋ	measure word for airplanes	一架飛機正在桃園機場降落。	An airplane is landing at TY airport.
架	jià	ㄐㄧㄚˋ	measure word for pianos	靠牆有一架鋼琴。	A piano stood against the wall.
家	jiā	ㄐㄧㄚ	measure word for restaurants	這家旅館接受信用卡。	This restaurant takes credit card.
家	jiā	ㄐㄧㄚ	measure word for shops	她曾經給一家公司當會計。	She worked as an accountant for a firm.
件	jiàn	ㄐㄧㄢˋ	measure word for clothes	她上星期買了三件衣服。	She bought three pieces of clothing last week.
件	jiàn	ㄐㄧㄢˋ	measure word for things	今天下午我有兩件事情要做。	I have two things to do this afternoon.
間	jiān	ㄐㄧㄢ	measure word for houses	他在台南有三間房子。	He owns three houses Tainan.

Measure word	Pinyin	Mandarin Phonetic Symbols	Meaning	Example	English Translation for Example
節	jié	ㄐㄧㄝˊ	measure word for a period (school)	Mary今天有三節中文課。	Mary has three periods of Chinese today.
棵	kē	ㄎㄜ	measure word for trees	我們種了三棵蘋果樹。	We planted three apple trees.
顆	kē	ㄎㄜ	measure word for teeth	牙醫拔掉了我兩顆牙。	The dentist pulled two of my teeth.
顆	kē	ㄎㄜ	measure word for grain	我左眼裡面有一顆沙子。	There's a grain of sand in my left eye.
顆	kē	ㄎㄜ	for head (vegetable)	我們用了整顆生菜做沙拉。	We used a whole head of lettuce for the salad.
口	kǒu	ㄎㄡˇ	measure word for people	他家有五口人。	There are five people in his family.
塊	kuài	ㄎㄨㄞˋ	measure word for small piece of objects	一塊巧克力夠了。 你要來一塊口香糖嗎？	Just a piece of chocolate. Would you like a piece of chewing gum?
塊	kuài	ㄎㄨㄞˋ	measure word for meat	你要來一塊烤雞肉嗎？	Would you like a piece of barbecued chicken?
塊	kuài	ㄎㄨㄞˋ	measure word for rocks	我們坐在那塊大石頭上吧。	Let's sit on that big rock.
*粒	lì	ㄌㄧˋ	measure word for grain-like things	他把飯吃得一粒米都不剩。	He ate up rice with no grain left (in the bowl).

Measure word	Pinyin	Mandarin Phonetic Symbols	Meaning	Example	English Translation for Example
輛	liàng	ㄌㄧㄤˋ	measure word for vehicles	他們在追那輛計程車。 他在存錢買一輛新的自行車。	They were running after the taxi. He's saving up for a new bicycle.
兩	liǎng	ㄌㄧㄤˇ	liang, a unit for measuring weight, equal to 31.25 grams. There are 16 liang in a jin.	我要送給他四兩茶葉當禮物。	I'll make him a present of four liang of tea.
*列	liè	ㄌㄧㄝˋ	measure word for things in a row	這列火車開往哪裡？	Where does this train go?
毛	máo	ㄇㄠˊ	ten cents	那是五毛的硬幣。	That's a coin of 50 cents.
門	mén	ㄇㄣˊ	measure word for courses (in school)	我有三門必修課。	I have three compulsory courses.
*面	miàn	ㄇㄧㄢˋ	measure word for flat and smooth objects	這面鏡子不大。	This mirror is not big.
秒	miǎo	ㄇㄧㄠˇ	second (time)	我一百米跑十二秒，你呢？	It takes me 12 seconds to run 100 metres. How about you?

Measure word	Pinyin	Mandarin Phonetic Symbols	Meaning	Example	English Translation for Example
盤	pán	ㄆㄢˊ	measure word for plates	我點了一盤義大利麵。 他切了一盤水果請大家吃。	I ordered a dish of spaghetti. He prepared a plate of fruits for us.
*匹	pī	ㄆㄧ	measure word for horses	這匹馬生病了。	This horse is sick.
片	piàn	ㄆㄧㄢˋ	piece of	來一片西瓜吧。	How about a piece of watermelon.
*篇	piān	ㄆㄧㄢ	piece of writing	這篇文章寫得很好。	This article is well written.
坪	píng	ㄆㄧㄥˊ	ping, unit for measuring surface, equal to 3.3 square meter, used specifically in Taiwan	這個房間有多少坪？	How many ping are there in this room?
*艘	sāo	ㄙㄠ	measure word for ships or boats	這艘輪船可以載三百人。	This cruise can carry 300 people.
*首	shǒu	ㄕㄡˇ	measure word for songs	這是一首中文兒歌。	This is a Chinese Children's song.
雙	shuāng	ㄕㄨㄤ	pair of	她有一雙大眼睛。	She has a huge pair of eyes.
所	suǒ	ㄙㄨㄛˇ	measure word for places	當地政府蓋了一所新醫院。	The local government has built a new hospital.

Measure word	Pinyin	Mandarin Phonetic Symbols	Meaning	Example	English Translation for Example
				我想送孩子到一所好的學校。 他們終於有錢買一所房子了。	I want to send my children to a good school. At last they were able to afford a house.
台	tái	ㄊㄞˊ	measure word for machines	辦公室有一台影印機。	There is a copy machine in the office.
台	tái	ㄊㄞˊ	measure word for TV sets	我們買了一台電視機。	We bought a TV set.
堂	táng	ㄊㄤˊ	measure word for a period (class)	我每天有四堂華語課。	I have four periods of Chinese everyday.
套	tào	ㄊㄠˋ	suit of (clothes)	她穿著一套新衣服。	She's wearing a new suit of clothes.
套	tào	ㄊㄠˋ	set of (furniture)	我們訂了一套家具。	We've ordered a set of furniture.
條	tiáo	ㄊㄧㄠˊ	measure word for fish	我們要一條大一點的魚。	We want a bigger fish.
條	tiáo	ㄊㄧㄠˊ	measure word for roads	我們決定走另一條路。	We decided to take another road.
頭	tóu	ㄊㄡˊ	head of (cattle, sheep)	他們有一百頭牛。	They own100 head of cattle.
位	wèi	ㄨㄟˋ	measure word, used as a polite form	學校來了一位新老師。	We have a new teacher in our school.

Measure word	Pinyin	Mandarin Phonetic Symbols	Meaning	Example	English Translation for Example
			addressed to someone deserving respect		
項	xiàng	ㄒㄧㄤˋ	measure word for items	我報名了幾項活動。	I've signed up for several activities.
樣	yàng	ㄧㄤˋ	type of	Mary帶了三樣水果。	Mary brought three types of fruit.
頁	yè	ㄧㄝˋ	page	答案在下一頁。 他在報告裡新加了一頁？	The answers are over the page. He added a new page to his report.
張	zhāng	ㄓㄤ	measure word for sheet of paper	你寫在一張紙上吧。 她給我一張白紙。	Write it down on a piece of paper. She handed me a piece of blank paper.
張	zhāng	ㄓㄤ	measure word for tickets	你能給我弄一張票嗎？ 我想訂兩張去台北的票。	Will you get me a ticket? I'd like to book two tickets to Taipei.
兆	zhào	ㄓㄠˋ	million billion	他們花了一兆元買下那家大公司。	They bought the big company for one million billion dollars.

Measure word	Pinyin	Mandarin Phonetic Symbols	Meaning	Example	English Translation for Example
陣	zhèn	ㄓㄣˋ	measure word for wind	一陣大風把門吹關上了。	A strong wind blew the door shut.
*支	zhī	ㄓ	measure word for armies or sport teams	這支棒球隊贏了很多場比賽。	This baseball team won a lot of games.
枝	zhī	ㄓ	measure word for stalk (plant)	John送給她一枝紅玫瑰。	John sent her a single red rose.
*枝	zhī	ㄓ	measure word for pens	我只有一枝筆。	I only have one pen.
隻	zhī	ㄓ	measure word for birds	一隻鳥在我們旁邊飛過。	A bird flew right by us.
隻	zhī	ㄓ	measure word for boats	要是我們有一隻小船就好了。	If only we had a boat!
隻	zhī	ㄓ	measure word for small animals	鄰居家養了三隻貓。	The neighbor keeps three cats.
隻	zhī	ㄓ	measure word for hands (part of body)	他把一隻手搭在我的肩上。	He placed a hand on my shoulder.
種	zhǒng	ㄓㄨㄥˇ	kind	你要哪種飲料？ 這種行為是不禮貌的！	What kind of drink do you want? This kind of behavior is unrestrained.
座	zuò	ㄗㄨㄛˋ	measure word for bridges	我們開車經過那座橋。	We drove across the bridge.

Measure word	Pinyin	Mandarin Phonetic Symbols	Meaning	Example	English Translation for Example
座	zuò	ㄗㄨㄛˋ	measure word for clocks	房間的一角有一座大擺鐘。	There's a grandfather clocking the corner of the room.
座	zuò	ㄗㄨㄛˋ	measure word for mountains	那座山冬天會下雪。	We have snow in that mountain in winter.

Index — Hanyu Pinyin

K

L

M

N

O

Index-English

A

C

D

E

F

G

N

O

P

Q

R

S

T

U

V

W

X

Y

Z

1X3U

Learner's Mandarin Chinese Dictionary--for Beginner Level

國際華語學習辭典

General Managing Editor（總策畫）：Shih-chang Hsin, Ph.D (信世昌)
(National Taiwan Normal University 國立臺灣師範大學)

Editor-in-Chief (主編)：Ting-au Cheng, Ph.D（鄭定歐）

Executive Editors (執行編輯)：Ming-yi Li (李明懿) Yu-chun Huang (黃郁純) Yu-li Luo (羅悠理)

Publisher（發行人）：Rong-chuan Yang（楊榮川）

Chief Editor（總編輯）：Xiu-Li Yang（楊秀麗）

Planning Editor（企劃主編）：Hui-juan Huang（黃惠娟）

Editor（責任編輯）：Hsiao-Wen Lu（魯曉玟）

Cover Design（封面設計）：Sheng-wen Huang（黃聖文）

Illustration（插畫）：Jing-yi Lyu（呂靜宜）

Publisher（出版者）：Wu Nan book publishing Co.（五南圖書出版股份有限公司）

Address（地址）：4th Floor, No. 339, Sec2. Hoping East Road, Da-an District, Taipei 106, Taiwan
（臺灣106 台北市大安區和平東路二段339號4樓）

Phone（電話）：(02)2705-5066　Fax（傳真）：(02)2706-6100

Website（網址）：https://www.wunan.com.tw

E-mail（電子郵件）：wunan@wunan.com.tw

Remittance Account（劃撥帳號）：01068953

Username（戶名）：Wu Nan book publishing Co.（五南圖書出版股份有限公司）

Legal adviser（法律顧問）：Linsheng An LLP Linsheng An attorney
（林勝安律師）

Date of Publication（出版日期）：2013年12月初版一刷
2023年11月二版一刷
2024年 9 月二版二刷

Pricing（定價）：NT$480元（新臺幣480元）

This research is partially supported by the "Aim for the Top University Project" of National Taiwan Normal University (NTNU), sponsored by the Ministry of Education, Taiwan, R.O.C. and the "International Research-Intensive Center of Excellence Program" of NTNU and National Science Council, Taiwan, R.O.C. under Grant no. NSC 103-2911-I-003-301.

國家圖書館出版品預行編目資料

國際華語學習辭典 = Learner's Mandarin Chinese dictionary : for biginner level/鄭定歐主編. --二版.--臺北市：五南圖書出版股份有限公司, 2023.11
面； 公分
ISBN 978-626-366-779-2（平裝）

1.漢語詞典

802.3 112019010

經典永恆·名著常在

五十週年的獻禮──經典名著文庫

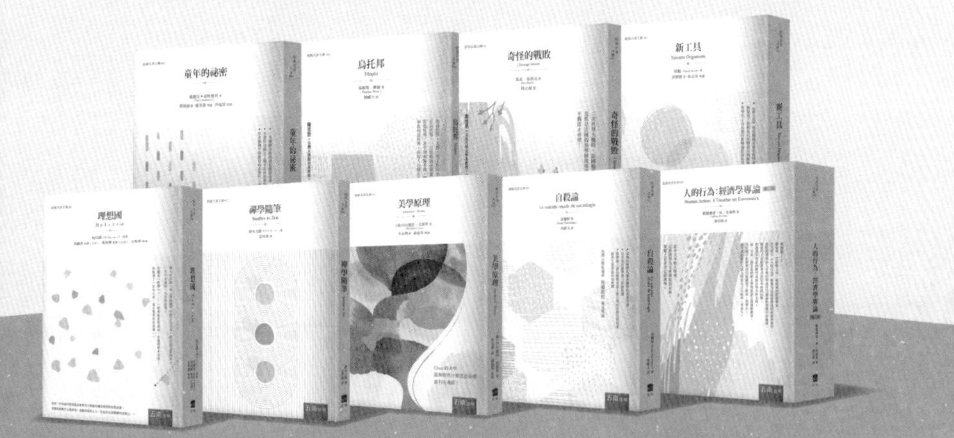

五南，五十年了，半個世紀，人生旅程的一大半，走過來了。
思索著，邁向百年的未來歷程，能為知識界、文化學術界作些什麼？
在速食文化的生態下，有什麼值得讓人雋永品味的？

歷代經典·當今名著，經過時間的洗禮，千錘百鍊，流傳至今，光芒耀人；
不僅使我們能領悟前人的智慧，同時也增深加廣我們思考的深度與視野。
我們決心投入巨資，有計畫的系統梳選，成立「經典名著文庫」，
希望收入古今中外思想性的、充滿睿智與獨見的經典、名著。
這是一項理想性的、永續性的巨大出版工程。
不在意讀者的眾寡，只考慮它的學術價值，力求完整展現先哲思想的軌跡；
為知識界開啟一片智慧之窗，營造一座百花綻放的世界文明公園，
任君遨遊、取菁吸蜜、嘉惠學子！